"Gong's first venture into adult fantasy, set in a claustrophobic, low-tech city where life is cheap and bodies are disposable, features wonderfully complex characters and a game to the death that is executed with aplomb."
—REBECCA ROANHORSE, *New York Times* bestselling author of the Between Earth and Sky trilogy

"Smart, imaginative, and brutal, *Immortal Longings* is a mind- and genre-bending epic that is as cutting and honest as it is unpredictable. Chloe Gong's assertive style is filled with razor's edge–prose, and her complex characters will hurt you, but in the most thrilling way. What a time to be alive for book lovers."
—WESLEY CHU, #1 *New York Times* bestselling author of The War Arts Saga

"Gripping [and] irresistible, Chloe Gong's *Immortal Longings* is a tour de force of Asian futurism, a provocative examination of self and destiny that melds the ruthless sensuality of *Crouching Tiger, Hidden Dragon* with the visceral urgency of *The Hunger Games*. This book left me breathless!"
—RYKA AOKI, author of *Light from Uncommon Stars*

"*Immortal Longings* is a grab-you-and-won't-let-go sort of book, as brutal and merciless as its characters. Everyone has secret plans, and everyone's life exists on the edge of betrayal. Each page is fierce and filled with yearning—I loved it."
—ANDREA STEWART, author of the Drowning Empire series

"If you find yourself hungry for a story that will cut you while you read and where betrayal lurks around every corner, you'll want to check this title out."
—NPR

"Chloe Gong has a particular flair for crafting elaborate and addictive stories."
—*HuffPost*

"The violent cities of San-Er and their complex politics come to life in this immersive, action-packed novel inhabited by characters impossible to let go of until the last page."
—*Good Housekeeping*

IMMORTAL LONGINGS

IMMORTAL LONGINGS

Flesh & False Gods

Book One

CHLOE GONG

SAGA PRESS

LONDON SYDNEY **NEW YORK** TORONTO NEW DELHI

SAGA PRESS

AN IMPRINT OF SIMON & SCHUSTER, LLC

1230 AVENUE OF THE AMERICAS, NEW YORK, NEW YORK 10020

First Saga Press trade paperback edition July 2024

SAGA PRESS and colophon are trademarks of Simon & Schuster, LLC

Simon & Schuster: Celebrating 100 Years of Publishing in 2024

For information about special discounts for bulk purchases, please contact Simon & Schuster Special Sales at 1-866-506-1949 or business@simonandschuster.com.

The Simon & Schuster Speakers Bureau can bring authors to your live event. For more information or to book an event, contact the Simon & Schuster Speakers Bureau at 1-866-248-3049 or visit our website at www.simonspeakers.com.

Interior design by Kathryn A. Kenney-Peterson

Manufactured in the United States of America

1 3 5 7 9 10 8 6 4 2

Library of Congress Cataloging-in-Publication Data is available.

ISBN 978-1-6680-0022-9
ISBN 978-1-6680-0023-6 (pbk)
ISBN 978-1-6680-0024-3 (ebook)

Age cannot wither her, nor custom stale
Her infinite variety. Other women cloy
The appetites they feed, but she makes hungry
Where most she satisfies. For vilest things
Become themselves in her, that the holy priests
Bless her when she is riggish.

—Shakespeare, *Antony and Cleopatra*

CHAPTER 1

A living thing, when faced with a break or injury, is compelled to heal itself. A cut will clot with blood, trapping in a person's qi. A bone will smooth over, knitting new threads at every split. And San-Er's buildings, when an inconvenience is identified, will rush to mend the sore, pinpointing every fracture and hurling remedies with vigor. From the top of the palace, all that can be seen are the stacked structures composing the twin cities, interlocked and dependent upon one another, some attached to a neighbor from the ground level and others connected only at the highest floors. Everyone in the kingdom of Talin wants to be in its capital—in these two cities masquerading as one—and so San-Er must grow denser and higher to accommodate, covering up its offenses and stenches with utter incoherence.

August Shenzhi tightens his grip on the balcony railing, tearing his gaze away from the horizon of rooftops. His attention should be with the marketplace below, which bustles at high volume inside the coliseum walls. Three generations ago, the Palace of Union was built beside San's massive coliseum—or perhaps it's more apt to say it was built *into* the coliseum, the north side of the elevated palace enmeshed with the coliseum's south wall, its turrets and balconies pulling apart stone and slotting itself right in to close the gap. Every window on the north side has a perfect view of the market, but none better than this balcony. Back when he still made public appearances, King Kasa stood here to make his speeches. The market would be cleared out, and his subjects would come to gather in the only plot of open space inside San-Er, cheering for their monarch.

There's nowhere quite like the coliseum. San-Er itself is only a small protrusion of land at the edge of the kingdom, its border with rural Talin marked by a towering wall, the rest of its perimeter hemmed in by sea. Yet despite its size, San-Er functions as a world of its own—half a million inhabitants crammed into each square mile, again and again. The needle-thin alleys between every building sag, the earthen ground always muddy because it is sweating with overexertion. Prostitutes and temple priests share the same doorway; drug addicts and schoolteachers nap under the same awning. It makes sense that the only space protected from builders and squatters is the coliseum, under the vigilant eye of royalty and untouched by the desperate expansion pressing in on its walls. They could raze the coliseum and build ten—perhaps twenty—new streets on the land cleared, squeeze in hundreds more apartment complexes, but the palace won't allow it, and what the palace says goes.

"Give me leave to strangle your uncle, August. I'm tired to death of him."

Galipei Weisanna strolls into the room, his voice echoing out onto the balcony. He speaks as he always does: clipped, terse, honest. Galipei is rarely willing to tell a lie, yet finds it of utmost priority to be running his mouth too, even when silence is a better option. August tips his head back to look at his bodyguard, and the crown in his hair shakes loose, hanging lopsidedly to the left. By the light of the palace, the red gems resemble fragments of blood encircling his bleached blond curls, its position so precarious that one wayward breeze would sweep the band of metal right off.

"Do be careful," August replies evenly. "High treason in the throne room tends to be frowned upon."

"So I suppose someone ought to be frowning at you as well."

Galipei comes to join him upon the balcony, then nudges August's crown back into place with a practiced familiarity. His presence is domineering, shoulders wide and posture tall, in contrast to August's lithe sharpness. Dressed in his usual dark work garb, Galipei looks a part of the night—if the night were decorated with buckles and straps holding various weapons that wouldn't otherwise keep against heavy leather. There's a melodic clanking when his body comes into contact with the gold-plated railing, his arms resting atop it to mimic August, but the sound is easily lost to the clamor of the market below.

"Who would dare?" August asks matter-of-factly. It's not a boast. It's the profoundly confident manner of someone who knows exactly how high his pedestal is because he hauled himself there.

Galipei makes a vague noise. He turns away from the walls of the coliseum, having searched for threats and finding nothing out of the ordinary. His attention shifts toward August's line of sight instead: a child, kicking a ball beside the closest row of market stalls.

"I heard that you took over preliminary organization for the games." The child draws nearer and nearer to the balcony. "What are you up to, August? Your uncle—"

August clears his throat. Though Galipei rolls his eyes, he takes the correction in stride.

"—your *father*, my apologies, is vexed enough with the whole palace these days. If you go pissing him off, he'll disown you in an instant."

A warm, southerly breeze blows up on the balcony, swallowing August's skeptical huff of breath. He pulls at his collar, fingers sliding against silk, the fabric thin enough to bring a chill to his skin. Let King Kasa push his adoption papers through a shredder. It won't matter soon. Maneuvering the last few years to get the paperwork to exist was only the first part of the plan. It is nowhere near the most important.

"Why are you here?" August asks in return, diverting the topic. "I thought Leida summoned your help for the night."

"She sent me back. San's border is fine."

August doesn't voice his immediate doubt, but he does frown. Other than the coliseum, the far edge of San right beside the wall is the only place within San-Er where civilians might have the space to gather and make a fuss, crowding around the mounds of trash and discarded tech. It never lasts long. The guards spread out and break them up, and then civilians can either spend an indeterminate amount of time in the palace cells or scatter back into the dense labyrinthine streets.

"Fascinating," August says. "I don't remember the last time there weren't riots the day before the games."

A few more steps, and the child will be directly underneath them. She pays no attention to her surroundings, weaving her ball in and out among the shoppers and sellers, her thin shoes clomping down on the uneven ground.

"This year's games should be quick work. There were hardly any applicants who volunteered for the draw."

By *hardly*, Galipei means that there were hundreds as opposed to thousands. The games used to be a far larger event, back when there were two kings funneling their coffers into the grand prize. Kasa's father had started them in his previous reign, and what began as a yearly one-on-one battle to the death eventually grew to a multicontestant affair, expanding past the coliseum and using all of San-Er as the playing field. Once, watching skilled fighters tear each other apart in the arena was mere entertainment, something that was distant to the ordinary civilian. Now, the games are a thrill that anyone can participate in, a solution to a kingdom simmering with complaints. *Don't worry if your babies drop dead because they have hollowed into starved husks*, King Kasa declares. *Don't worry that your*

4

elderly must sleep in cages because there is no more apartment space, nor that the neon light from the strip club across the alleyway keeps you awake night after night. Put your name in the lottery, slaughter only eighty-seven of your fellow citizens, and be awarded with riches beyond your wildest dreams.

"He drew his list, then?" August says. "All eighty-eight of our lucky participants?"

Eighty-eight, the number of luck and prosperity! the advertisement posters for the games declare. *You must register before the deadline for your chance to be among our esteemed competitors!*

"His Majesty is very proud of himself. He got through the names in record time."

August scoffs. It is not efficiency that had Kasa going so fast. Since August suggested an entrance fee two years ago, the random draw has shrunk significantly. One would think that the worsening conditions these days mean more are throwing in their lots for a chance to win, but the people of San-Er are only increasingly terrified that the games are a sham, that the victor will be cheated out of the grand prize just as the twin cities persistently cheat them out of rewards. They're not wrong. After all, August *did* fiddle with the draw this year to get one name in.

With a wince, he takes a step back from the balcony rail, releasing the tension in his neck. For only two distinct days of the year, the coliseum before him is cleared out and used as the arena it was originally built for. Today, it remains yet a marketplace. A compact, concentrated world of food hawkers splashed with oil and metalworkers clanging on blades and technicians fixing up unwieldy computers to resell. San-Er spends each moment functioning off the fumes of its last. There is no other way to survive.

"August." A touch on his elbow. August spares a glance to his side, meeting Galipei's steel-silver eyes. There's a warning in the way he flings his prince's name around, title and rank discarded. August does not take caution; he only smiles. That small quirk at his mouth, barely a change in his expression at all, and Galipei falters, taken aback by the rare expression.

August knows exactly what he's doing. Offer that brief distraction, and when Galipei's attention is turned elsewhere, he decides on his next move.

"Take my body inside."

Galipei's lips part in protest. He recovers quickly from his brief enthrallment. "Would you quit jumping like—"

But August has already left, fixing his sight onto the child and slamming right in, opening his new eyes with a quick snap. He has to adjust to the height change, off-balance for a second as the people nearby jolt in surprise. They know what has happened: the flash of light between jumps is unmistakable, marking the arc from old body to new. Though the palace has long made jumping illegal, it is still as common as a beggar swiping a rice cake from an unwatched stall. Civilians have learned to look away, especially when the light is flashing so closely to the palace.

They just don't expect their crown prince to be the one jumping.

August looks up at the palace. His body has dropped like a stone, collapsed in Galipei's arms to enter stasis. Without a person's qi, the body is only a vessel. But a vessel that belongs to the heir of the throne is an incredibly valuable possession, and when Galipei's gaze meets August's pitch-black eyes in the girl's body, he mouths what appears to be a threat to strangle him too.

August, however, is already walking in the other direction, giving Galipei no choice but to guard his birth body ferociously, lest someone come within ten feet and attempt to invade it. In any case, it wouldn't be hard for him to boot an intruder out. August's qi is strong—if his body were doubled, he could wrestle back control from the other person easily, either forcing them to find another host or subject them to being lost. When it comes to doubling other bodies, there is no vessel in the twin cities that he cannot invade as long they have come of age: twelve, maybe thirteen, when the gene for jumping manifests.

The problem isn't so much the matter of someone using his body for pleasure or power. It's troublemakers who might invade with the purpose of destroying his body out of protest, making one quick throw off the edge of a building before their prince can jump back.

August nearly collides with someone and flinches, ducking to find a less crowded path through the market. The sudden assault on his senses always takes some getting used to: the louder noises, the brighter colors. Perhaps he has dulled the senses of his birth body too much, and this is true normalcy. When a shoe-shiner barks at him from behind a stall and holds out a few coins, August simply reaches his small hands out and receives them, uncertain why. The child must be some sort of errand runner. All the better. Very few civilians are powerful enough to jump into children, which makes them the most trusted, darting between buildings and into every corner of San-Er without notice.

August makes quick time exiting the coliseum, emerging onto the one main street that acts as a thoroughfare from north to south of San. He is well-acquainted with the lefts and the rights of his byzantine city too, so he steps off the main street for the less populated routes, hurrying under drooping electric wires and barely wincing when the damp pipes overhead drip water down his neck. But the cold moisture irritates his skin after a while, and with a sigh, August enters a building, deciding to travel by staircase and wayward building passages instead. There isn't enough on this body to draw any conclusions about its identity, though that is an answer in and of itself. No markings or tattoos, so no allegiance to the Crescent Societies.

"Hey! Hey, stop there."

August—ever accommodating—stops. An elderly woman has called out to him, the picture of concern as she hovers in front of her apartment door, a water bucket clutched to her hip.

"Where are your parents?" she asks. "This area is no good. The Crescent Societies have their eye on it. You'll get yourself invaded."

"I have it handled." From the girl's body, his voice comes out high and soft and sweet. Only August's tone is too confident. Too regal. The woman can tell, and her expression shifts into suspicion, but August is already walking again. He follows the spray-painted directions on the walls, moving through another corridor to enter a neighboring building. Low moans filter through the thin plaster. Privately run hospitals are aplenty in this area, facilities filled with unhygienic practices and dirty tools, though they still receive a constant stream of patients because they charge far less than the proper places in Er. Half of these private facilities are surely body-trafficking schemes. Still . . . if a body goes missing here and there, no one cares enough to find out why. Certainly not the palace, no matter what August does.

He turns the corner. The atmosphere shifts immediately, cigarette smoke permeating the low ceilings in such thickness that the dim bulbs can hardly cut through. San is a city of darkness. It is nighttime now, but even when the sun rises, the buildings are so densely packed that the streets remain shrouded in shadow. He counts the doors as he passes: *One, two, three . . .*

He knocks on the third, his small fist easily fitting between the metal bars of the exterior door. When the second wooden door opens inward, there is a man who towers above him twice over, looking down his nose with a huff of air.

"We don't have scraps—"

August jumps again. It is instantaneous from the outside, he knows, as fast as that clap of light, but it always *feels* slow, like wading through a brick wall. The closer the jump, the thinner the wall; from the farthest away, at the absolute ten-foot limit, it always feels like forging through a mile of solid stone. Those who have gotten themselves lost between bodies are snagged here, condemned to wander about this incorporeal space forever.

When he opens his eyes, he's staring at the little girl again, her bright-orange eyes wide and confused. Not everyone in Talin can jump, and even among those with the gene for it, many have such weak abilities that they don't risk it, in case they attempt to invade a body and lose the fight for control. But at any point, gene or no gene, a body holding a single person's qi can be invaded, especially by someone like August. The girl figures out quickly what must have happened.

"Move along," August instructs, closing the inner door to the gambling den. The people inside saw the flash of light, aware that their bouncer is now occupied. Thankfully, August is expected.

"Your Highness!"

Though the den-keeper who runs up to him has a different face from the last time August was here, he knows it's the same person. Bodies can be switched, but the man's pale purple eyes remain the same.

"Have you found her?" August asks.

"Right in time, you're right in time," the man gushes, ignoring his question. "Come with me, please, Prince August."

August follows, careful with his steps. This body is large, muscular. He doesn't want to go too fast, or he might tip himself off-kilter and stumble. He closes his fists together and frowns, circling around the card dealings and mahjong tables with barely enough room to maneuver between them. His shoe crunches down on what could be a needle filled with heroin. A woman at one of the tables reaches out to touch his jacket, with no aim except to stroke its fine leather exterior.

"Right through here. The pictures should have finished developing by now."

The man holds open the door, and August walks through, looking around in the red light. Thin drying lines crisscross at his eye level, filled with dangling photographs in various shades. The man reaches up to unclip one. His fingers tremble as he lets the line spring back, cupping the photograph in his palms. Before he can extend the offering to August, however, he hesitates, eyes pinned on the picture.

"Something wrong?"

"No. No, nothing at all." The man shakes his head, erasing any appearance of doubt. "We scoured the records to their very roots. Not one database was left unturned. This is her, Your Highness. I promise. Your trust and sponsorship are appreciated."

August lifts an eyebrow. It is hard to do in this body. He gestures for the photograph instead, and the man hurries to pass it over. The entire darkroom seems to hold its breath. The vents stutter to a halt.

"Well," August says, "good job."

Though the light overhead runs only in one shade, coloring the photograph the wrong hue and washing out the subject's eyes, there is no doubt. The woman in the photograph is stepping off the stoop of a building—her nose and mouth covered with a mask, her hands gloved in leather, her body angled away in movement—but August would recognize her anywhere. She is not the sort to abandon her body, even under such circumstances. She would instead flaunt what she managed to keep, living in this city for five long years right under his nose.

"Oh, cousin," August says to the photograph. "You can hide no longer."

Princess Calla Tuoleimi, found at last.

CHAPTER 2

A droplet of water leaks from the ceiling. Then another. Calla Tuoleimi shoots a glare up, but it does nothing to stop the dripping on her neck. She can only shuffle an inch to the left, pressing closer to the dusty wall.

"What the fuck is taking so long?" Calla mutters under her breath.

She lingers at the bottom of her building's stairwell, guarding the entrance-way into the hall while her fingers weave three pieces of flax lily into a bracelet. Her apartment is at the other end of a long, winding corridor: a dingy ground-floor setup with cramped rooms and targets for crossbow practice plastered on the doors. Most days, she would hate to be outside of it, in these halls and stair-wells where orphan children and homeless squatters sit in the corners to beg or yell nonsense. There's no reason for anyone else to be hovering out here unless there is business to intercept at the entrance. Calla kicks her boot at a rock in the corner, dropping into a crouch.

Today, there is business to intercept. Everyone gets lost trying to find her apartment otherwise. And so she waits, weaving her bracelet to keep busy. Only a single light fixture mounted on the wall illuminates the muted afternoon, its flickering bulb set to go out at any moment. The electric grid is always past its capacity. Residents steal from the various lines and boxes, just as they steal water, attaching their homemade pipes wherever there is a pump belowground. San persistently smells of rot and theft—of muddy puddles stuffed with discarded trash bags, plastic water tubs discarded in the alleys for vagrants to leave their waste in. Lower floors will always feel the worst of it. Higher apartments that inch above the city skyline will, at the right time of the day, get a small fresh breeze floating in from the sea.

To suffer in San-Er is not a punishment, only a way of life. Any murmur from its inhabitants enmeshes immediately with the hum of its factories. The cities are perpetually covered with a blanket of noise, nothing in particular to be heard but nothing that can be drowned out.

Calla pauses her weaving, jerking her head up when she hears footsteps coming. There are plenty of other entrances into the building, either from the rooftop or from neighboring complexes that have bulldozed their exterior walls to share a more convenient corridor on certain floors. But the runners they send from the palace never know how to navigate these streets well: this cesspool of obscenities in the guise of a city, this living, breathing, heaving half of San-Er. They will walk the ground route, squinting at the faint markings outside the main doors of each apartment block before squeezing into the alleys and forging deeper. Eighty-eight packages are set to disperse across the twin cities today, carrying eighty-eight wristbands. One of them for Calla, even if that isn't what's on the official registry.

"What are you making?"

A kid pops his head out from underneath the stairs, and Calla glances over, her nose wrinkling. He's covered in muck, trousers flaking with brown clumps. As he toddles closer, the approaching footsteps finally come through the doorway. Calla squints in the hazy light. Too old. Too many grocery bundles trailing after them. Not a messenger. She leans aside and lets them pass to get to their apartment on the ground floor.

"Don't you know?" She peers at the kid again. "If you mind other people's business too much, a god will rush into your nose and take your body."

The kid frowns. "Who said?"

"You don't believe me?" Calla asks, finishing the bracelet. "Out in the provinces, they're so afraid of the gods that they won't even look at each other. Ask one question that's out of place, and it might be enough for a sneaky god to rush in and snuff out your qi."

She ties a nice little bow onto the end of her bracelet. Weaving flax lily—or even keeping a flax lily plant—is a habit of rural children out in the provinces too. Her bracelet-making stands starkly incongruous with the rest of her cultivated appearance: the blunt-cut bangs falling into her eyes, the black curtain of hair growing to her waist, the black mask strapped across the lower half of her face, muffling her voice.

Princess Calla Tuoleimi looks vastly different these days, but she's still wearing the same body, which is unexpected when she has wide pickings for an easy swap. She's thinner without the rich palace meals—her face sharper, almost gaunt. She lost her round cheeks after that first month in hiding, and scared herself each time she glanced into the mirror with how much meaner she appeared. Then she figured she might as well embrace her new fugitive appearance and grabbed a pair of scissors to shear straight bangs across her forehead, *just* slightly too long, to obscure her eyes. She never trims them now until it's an absolute menace to see. There's always the possibility that someone will recognize her. A low chance, given how little attention people pay to faces in a city where faces are always changing, but a chance nonetheless.

If the palace is to be believed, of course, Calla is dead. They caught her scaling the wall in an attempt to escape that night and dispensed justice, and San-Er can rest easy knowing no murderer princess hides in its streets. Certain members of the Crescent Societies have argued the contrary—they ask why a different dead body was brought back for Calla's funeral ceremony, why King Kasa is still so afraid to leave his palace. But the Crescent Societies have always questioned how the Palace of Union runs its kingdom, and they are but a small majority.

The kid harrumphs. "You're not very nice."

"Did I look nice to begin with?" Calla kicks her boot again, nudging another stone across the gritty floor. In the past hour, most of the building's residents have walked right past her without eye contact, catching a flash of her appearance in their periphery and deciding they would prefer not to get robbed. "Your parents ought to scold you for talking to strangers."

"My parents are dead."

His words are spoken dully. No fluctuation in tone, no twinge of emotion.

Calla sighs. She holds her arm out, offering the kid the bracelet she's just completed, along with a coin from her coat pocket. "Here. A gift. Maybe I *am* nice, after all."

The kid scampers forward and takes the bracelet and coin. As soon as his hand closes over the money, he turns and hurries out of the building door with a gleeful shriek, prepared to spend it at some shop stall or cybercafe. In his absence, there's another set of footsteps outside, approaching from the far end of the alley. These are softer, lighter.

By some instinct, Calla hurries forward, leaning through the doorway to look. Just as she sticks her head out, a boy appears before her, coming to a halt with a package clutched in his arms. He's tall, but no more than fifteen years old. The palace, hoping to prevent runners being jumped and their valuable devices stolen for the black market, will always send teenagers because they're difficult to invade before reaching full maturity. But sending youth is hardly a foolproof plan when any dedicated thief could simply pull a knife on them and call it a day. No one ever said the palace was smart.

"Hello," the runner says.

Calla grins. Her entire face shifts in that moment, her pencil-lined eyes crinkling into something predatory. She's long learned that the harder she smiles, the easier it is to prevent scrutiny of her identity. The expression doesn't have to carry any genuine warmth; it doesn't even have to look happy. So long as it swallows up the yellow of her eyes, aglow like an overcharged lightbulb. There are enough shades of yellow scattered throughout San-Er to make the sight commonplace on an offhanded glance, but there is only one other person with an utterly identical hue to hers, and it is the king. For three generations, royal yellow has been the defining hereditary mark of the Shenzhis in San and the Tuoleimis in Er, tinted dark by a ring of burnt umber unfurling from the center. But now Kasa has an adopted son, August, and there's no one left of Calla's bloodline—not since her parents perished and the throne of Er crumbled.

"You're a darling." Calla holds her hand out for the package. "Apartment 117, building 3, north side?"

The boy looks down, reading the small print written on the outside of the packaging.

"What do you know?" he says. "That's exactly right. Here you are."

He offers the package. His arms extend, not quite closing the distance between them. The alley is as gray as any other day, but when Calla reaches for the package, her attention settles on the boy's face, trying to pick out details in the gloom. It's strange that he wouldn't look directly at her. That he's staring at his shoes instead.

Calla's fingers skim right past the package and clamp onto his wrist.

The boy's gaze jerks up. Though the light is terrible, it's enough for his eyes to flash, for her to catch the silver of steel.

In San-Er, there's another term for such eyes. Next to royal yellow, the second-most infamous hue is Weisanna silver.

Calla slams the package from his hands at once. It splashes into a nearby puddle. Before the boy can think to react, she has already shoved him hard enough to topple to the ground, the flat of her boot stamped on his chest and pinning him down.

"Who the hell are you?" Calla spits. This is not a teenage boy. This is a member of the Weisanna family, the only bloodline in the city—perhaps the whole kingdom—with their birth bodies inaccessible to all intruders.

"Me?" the boy—the Weisanna—wheezes. "Princess Calla, perhaps you should worry about yourself."

Calla freezes. Her breath snags in her throat, turning her lungs as cold as ice. She's been caught. Someone knows.

"You better speak right now," she demands. "Before I—"

Her fist is already scrunched, fingers clenched so hard that her knuckles scream in pain against the rough fabric of her gloves. Then a woman appears at the end of the alley and startles at the scene before her, shifting her shopping basket from one arm to another.

"What is going on—"

"Don't!" Calla screams, holding her arm out.

It's too late. The woman has stepped just close enough, and a flash of light brightens the dark day, beaming from the boy to the woman. Before Calla can clear her vision, blinking hard to rid the imprint burned into her retinas, the woman is already darting into the building and up the stairs, her shopping basket abandoned. Of all times for a do-gooder to appear, it just *had* to be then.

"What happened?" the real runner asks from the floor. He blinks, his eyes magenta now.

Where other bodies are only impenetrable when they're already invaded, the Weisannas are born as if they are doubled, though they have but one set of qi. While they can occupy others with ease, others cannot occupy them back, even if a Weisanna abandons their birth body entirely and leaves their vessel in stasis on the ground. The Weisannas make up the entirety of the royal guard and a good portion of the palace guard; that sort of protection has kept the royal family of San on the throne with ease, scaring off security threats before they can emerge.

Calla mutters a curse, scooping up the fallen package. "Buy more protective charms. You just got invaded," she spits at the runner. Then she's hurtling up the stairs too, catching the briefest flash of the Weisanna before they've disappeared down the second-floor corridor into a neighboring building. San is almost entirely interconnected by links and passageways, by walls that were once outward-facing but are now mere dividers between building spaces. When Calla pauses at an intersection, she spots the Weisanna again through one of the pointless windows scattered about every floor. Those windows are the only hint that there was once space between the buildings of the city, before they started to meld with one another.

"Hey!" Calla roars.

The Weisanna keeps running, and Calla gives chase, storming into a different floor of the building with the heavy thump of her boots. There are crowds here. Too many people perusing the shops, gathered to inspect meats hanging from the butchers. Calla presses closer to the shop fronts, hoping to move along the edges, but then she walks right into a discarded pile of hair outside the barber's and nearly falls over. With tremendous disgust, Calla can only merge back into the center again, muttering a curse when she ducks to avoid being thwacked by a couple carrying a bulky personal computer for repair.

It would be so much faster if she jumps, but Calla does not—she will not. She merely keeps her steady pace, the damp package still clutched in her elbow, her eyes pinned on her target. It's almost as if the Weisanna is toying with her. Every time she thinks she has lost the trail, mixed in with one too many shoppers or pushed behind a group of construction workers hauling giant planks between them, she catches a flash again—just enough to follow up a set of stairs or along another passageway. Her surroundings flip between commercial and residential, the cool stone walls on either side of her growing wide to accommodate the stores or shrinking close to hold more space for apartments. Up and up and up, she climbs too, until suddenly the Weisanna is in sight, and Calla lunges for the absurdly vertical set of stairs, taking three at a time with each stride and smashing through the door at the end.

The natural sunlight almost blinds her. Its rays are weak, but they're a shock to adjust to nonetheless, and Calla throws a frantic hand over her face, fighting the wave of nausea before she spots her mark standing at the edge of the rooftop.

"You—"

She clamps a hand over their shoulder and spins them around, but it is no longer the Weisanna. The woman blinks, her eyes a faded red and muddled with confusion. *Damn*. The Weisanna jumped again without her notice. At some point in the pursuit, they set their sights on a new body and transferred over.

"What am I doing here?" the woman asks, her voice hitching.

"You shouldn't have interfered," Calla replies without sympathy. She points a finger to the door back into the building. "Go on."

For the briefest moment, the woman scans Calla up and down, trying to place the half of her face left uncovered. When that fails, she tears her gaze away and hurries off, not needing to be warned twice. The door to the rooftop slams shut, its echo loud.

Calla rips her mask from her face, heaving in a gulp of air.

Princess Calla, perhaps you should worry about yourself.

Calla emits a loud scream. The pigeons that were perched on a nearby television antenna fly away in fright. If King Kasa has found her, then she's dead. Forget the games. Forget justice. They'll have the Weisannas drag her into a room and put her neck under a blade.

One lone remaining pigeon coos, sounding disgruntled at Calla when she kicks the debris littered across the rooftop. It's filthy here, the premises used as a playground for children in the daylight hours and a hideout for drug addicts by nightfall. Discarded water kettles and half-broken ceramic toilet bowls decorate the middle like centerpieces; wooden construction slats and plastic chair legs scatter outward as the side arrangements. Calla drops into a crouch, but then her legs complain with exhaustion and she simply sits down, bothered more by her mood than whatever dirt will cling to her pants. Like half the city, she steals her water anyway: she'll turn the taps on later and soak her pants in the sink until they're clean, or until the pipelines in the hall shake a little too vigorously and the neighbors start to get suspicious.

For a long minute, she sits there fuming, her teeth gritted and her fists tight around the package. Then she curses under her breath and rips open a corner, shaking the plastic hard until a wristband falls out. The runner had been jumped by a Weisanna, but he really did come from the palace. So how many people know? Why give her access to the games?

The wristband snaps easily onto her arm, its magnetic buckle pulling the two straps into place. Calla extends her arm, bracing for the loud beep that comes as soon as the screen turns on. After a minute of gray on the screen display, the wristband buzzes, and the gray gives way to a blinking cursor against a blue light, the numbers 1 to 9 appearing at the bottom.

"How did we get here?" Calla mutters to herself. "Playing in the games like a starving street urchin."

It's almost unfair. Other players in the games have not come of age surrounded by palace tactics and weaponry drills. They have not trained relentlessly for five years hiding in a small apartment, all to make a perfect killing strike. Fighting them will be like snuffing out insects. Fighting them is beyond the point. It's the ultimate goal that her eyes are on: victory, and the person she will have access to when she is greeted as the winner of the games.

King Kasa, inside San's palace. In these last five years, he has not left its grounds once. And if he will not come out for Calla to make her kill, then she will be welcomed in by his own hand.

She runs her finger along the top of the wristband. There's an empty slot at the side for a chip, but those are distributed when the games begin. As soon as they're inserted, the chips cannot be removed, and as far as San-Er is concerned, their removal is the most boring way to face elimination. Pluck the chip out or fail to check in every twenty-four hours—at least it's a good method of withdrawal without losing your life.

Calla finds the buttons at last, though they are stubborn and difficult to trigger. The left one moves a yellow box around the numbers, and the one on the right makes a selection. Calla has watched enough of the games' reels and observed the televised surveillance footage across the city to know that it is asking for her identity number, unique to every citizen in San-Er. Instead of locks and keys, the doors in San-Er open to identity numbers; instead of passwords, banks in San-Er are accessed with those same identity numbers. In a place where bodies can be taken over in the blink of an eye, it is easy to look like someone else, yet impossible to live long under a falsity. Nothing can stop Calla from jamming herself into the body of a rich councilmember, but the second she tries to get into his home, she is caught. The second someone looks at her and sees a different eye color, the jig is up.

Besides, long-term occupation of a doubled body is risky. If the invader has weaker qi and isn't initially forced out by the vessel's original occupant fighting back, it's only a matter of time before things go wrong. Hallucinations, hearing voices, seeing ghosts. Memories melding together—two people merging into one. An ordinary civilian with the jumping gene would never hover long in someone else's body in case they're caught, but also because they don't know whether that body will be their very death. It takes a superbly confident person to believe they're too strong to be dragged down by anyone. And while Calla *is* devastatingly confident, she hardly wants to test the theory out.

The wristband chimes again, finally accepting her number. It's not her true number but, nonetheless, it is accepted. The screen flashes. Once. Twice. Three times.

12:00:02

12:00:01

12:00:00

Calla picks herself up, kicking the discarded package wrapping into the rest of the debris. She needs a shower. Might as well get clean before she walks right into a bloodbath.

◇◇◇◇◇

Elsewhere in San-Er, Anton Makusa finally gets his wristband. It's his own fault that he ended up chasing runners high and low through the twin cities, but he's unjustifiably disgruntled anyway. They had found their way to the residence registered under his identity number, but his apartment in San is small and cramped and loud with the bass of the music from the brothel three floors down, so he's rarely there. Those streets always reek with an unshakable stench, too close to the polluted Rubi Waterway that separates San and Er.

Anton kicks the door closed, releasing a breath and hitting the remote on the mantel at the same time. In the corner, the television flickers on and the walls start to hum. Safety at last, away from the palace runners, before they realize that this body is not his own. It's rather illegal to be hijacking young bankers and keeping them from their jobs for days on end. Sooner or later, someone at the bank will suspect a takeover situation and the palace guards will be knocking down the door of this luxury apartment in Er.

But by then, Anton will be gone.

"Please, please, hold your applause," he declares to the empty apartment. "I cannot handle so much adoration all at once."

His voice echoes. The living room before him is three times the size of his real residence, and even fitted with a balcony to the side. It's one of the largest living spaces in the entirety of the twin cities, which Anton knows because he's done his research—he scoured what was available of San-Er's architectural blueprints in the brief stint where he considered robbing the rich. That didn't last long; he doesn't have it in him to negotiate on the black market after he swipes valuables. Now he just mooches around, flitting across San-Er. When he wins the games, he can have something like this too. When he wins the games, there'll be no more lurking around corners and chasing after runners to get a measly little package.

Anton pushes the balcony doors open. The heat outside is palpable despite the rapidly falling dusk. It itches at his skin, dampening his desire for enjoyment. He wants to breathe in from the very top of San-Er, pretend that this is all his, but if it were that easy to fool himself, then Anton would be long dead from sheer stupidity.

"Bow before me," he calls out into the open. His voice tapers off, the charade losing amusement. It is hard to imagine an adoring crowd spread out before him when the view is only the neighboring building's dirty rooftop, littered with garbage. In Er, the streets run with less riffraff, and the buildings are given more breathing room. Here lie the financial districts, the banks, the schools, the businesses with employees who have some sway on the council or some ability to whisper into the king's ear. Five years ago, when the throne of Er fell and San-Er was merged into the one, the residents here complained the loudest about their streets growing rowdier with San's miscreants, but there was nothing they could do, not when their own royals had been slaughtered and San's king had the divine right to swallow up his brother's half. The Palace of Heavens was torn down after losing its rulers, replaced with residential complexes. Absent its matching half, the Palace of Earth was renamed the Palace of Union.

On the other rooftop, Anton's make-believe shouting has caught the attention of three men, squatting around a low plastic table with playing cards clutched in their hands and cigarettes dangling from their mouths. They stare at him for a second before brushing him off, two going back to their beer bottles while the third, who looks younger, spits out his cigarette and pulls a rude gesture.

The victors have never chosen to live like kings anyway. They take their immeasurable earnings and slink out into one of the Talinese provinces, away from prying eyes and desperate acquaintances, trying their best to forget everything they did in the games and get some fucking peace and quiet. While farmers move in the other direction— flee the provinces and flock toward San-Er to avoid starvation—a rich victor worries about nothing except the blood on their hands and the voices of the dead that haunt them late into the night.

"And now, for . . . report . . . tonight . . ."

Inside, the television has faded to static. Anton turns around, a frown already on his lips, but the static clears quickly, picking up a different signal and switching to a news broadcast. His confusion turns to rage in a single blink. King Kasa appears, adorned in jewels and seated at his throne. He smiles, his yellow eyes bright, but then Anton picks up a potted plant on the balcony and hurls it into the living room with all his strength, shattering the screen. King Kasa's oversaturated face blinks out of sight.

The apartment falls into silence. Night wraps fully around the balcony. With the television broken, his main light source and the background hum of noise disappears too.

Anton nudges his black hair out of his eyes. It will be a nuisance to get that fixed, but it's not his anyway. It was easy to get into this apartment: into this body and its assets. All he had to do was stand around the hallway and pretend to fix his shoe, once while the banker typed his identity number into the door and again the next day to catch any numbers he missed the first time. If Anton wanted, he could go dig into the banker's accounts right this moment, maybe call up a few of his friends and ask for loans. But that's too many layers to go through, too many people to talk to and risk exposing himself to the council's wrath. Better to laze around, eat up all the man's food, then bounce. He can find money a different way.

Anton looks at his wrist.

06:43:12

Six hours until the first event. Enough time to obtain another body before it starts. This one is on the frailer side, even if the face is pretty. Anton Makusa is picky when it comes to the bodies he occupies, and his narcissism takes first priority. He'll gravitate toward the masculine ones, same as the body he was born into, but he's not fussed if that isn't an option. What matters most is that they look good. Under the terms of his exile, his birth body was taken by the palace. The least he can do now is find worthy replacements.

A beep comes from his belt. He glances down, angling the screen of his pager up.

"For fuck's sake."

Patient bill overdue. Must pay in full by next week.

The message is from Northeast Hospital. It's also far from the first warning they have sent.

His arm is suddenly rock heavy as he unclips his pager, clutching it tight in his fist. A week. It should be enough for Anton to put something together for the person he's saving. In San-Er, whole lifetimes can pass in a week.

Still, he should drop by the hospital, find the attending doctor, and talk his way around pushing the bills off for just a bit longer. Hospitals in San-Er are known to act rashly, pull the plug and toss patients out the back door the moment their accounts stack up.

"Goddamn," he mutters. "Dammit, dammit, dammit—" He marches out to the balcony again, undoing the wristband on his arm too. As hard as he can, Anton hurls the wristband and pager onto the neighboring rooftop, stirring the attention of the three men from before.

"What gives?" one of them yells. The man stands. Drops his cigarette and strides to the edge of the rooftop to pick up the wristband. A breeze blows through the night, shaking the bulbs that hang from the electric wires and stirring the light that flashes across the stranger's face. His hair ruffles, thick crops of black falling into his eyes as soon as he straightens up.

Anton jumps. It is a risk: the roof edge is almost ten feet from him already, the distance stretched further by where the man stands. But Anton has always been a natural, has never stumbled where other people panic. To him, jumping feels like running, like sprinting through the air with his qi and halting to a stop wherever he pleases.

He opens his eyes. There's a grin on his lips—maybe it was already there when he arrived, maybe it's his own doing. The two others around the table call out, having seen the flash of light, and mutter complaints about invasion. Anton waves pleasantly before securing his wristband tightly around his new wrist and clipping the pager back on. His muscles feel strong, steady. When he breathes in and pushes through the rooftop door to take the stairs down, his lungs expand like he could keep inhaling and inhaling with no end.

"Spare some coins?"

At the end of the stairs, Anton reaches into his pockets without stopping in his stride. Beggars never hide out in the main buildings, not when palace guards patrol the markets and civilians report lurkers in the residential levels. The streets outside, meanwhile, are so narrow that no one would be able to walk by the moment someone sits down in a corner. So for those without anywhere else to go, stairwells and obscure corridors it is.

"Here." Anton scoops up every coin in his trouser pockets and tosses them down at the beggar's feet. "Take all of it."

He pushes through the main doors. The bustle of the shops invades his ears, the whine of dentist drills almost drowning out the "Thank you!" from the stairwell. Anton doesn't stop walking, his hands shoved into his now-empty pockets.

Finally, *finally*.

This is the first time he's been drawn in King Kasa's annual games. He has been tossing stolen identity numbers into the draw ever since he went into exile, chancing his life to save what—*who*—he lost. She remains on that hospital bed, still lying in sleep after seven years. The palace has the power to help, but August pretends he doesn't receive any of Anton's communications. King Kasa has the power to help, but he will not. He lets them suffer in their filth and misery instead, even those who once lived under his very roof.

Anton swipes an apple from a nearby stall, takes a bite, then throws it hard into a shop, hitting a wall calendar at the perfect angle to knock it off its hanging nail. The shop owner yells after him angrily, demanding to know what his problem is, but Anton is already moving away, searching for the next semblance of order to ruin. Prince August has tried his very best to squash Anton into the darkest depths of the city, make him slip away like another face in San-Er as if he did not once hold a piece of it.

But Anton is a Makusa. A family line of palace nobles that goes as far back as the Shenzhis have been royal.

He won't be tossed aside so easily. In fact, he'll destroy anyone who tries.

CHAPTER 3

The sun goes down. Night settles the muggy air, bringing the barest bite onto the streets. And in the darkness, a civilian wanders into a side alley, stumbling in his step. His name is Lusi, but no one calls him that. The foremen at the factory where he works bark at everyone all the same. His wife doesn't speak anymore. His daughter used to shout *Baba* across the apartment, only she is dead now—three weeks of a contagious plague, shooed off her hospital bed because they couldn't keep paying the fees. Her breathing stopped before they even returned home, her body bundled in those stolen white hospital linens, the last of her qi diminished.

"Come on!"

Lusi's sudden yell pierces into the empty alley. He's near-delirious. The pain at his side has reached an unbearable peak, but he won't go back to those wretched hospitals. His debt is already sky-high, bearing the cost of his daughter's last miserable days. Everything in this city makes his aches worse: the babies next door crying, the dampness in the hallways, the rent bills pouring in without end.

Lusi was not drawn for the games. It was his last hope, and still, the palace could not do this one thing for him.

"Take me! When did you care about the rules anyway?" He lurches forward, then stumbles, crashing onto his knees and sinking into the sludge of a puddle.

Lusi's next scream of frustration echoes even louder. Maybe it would be better if San-Er simply killed its people *faster*. Instead, it lets them rot. The elderly with nowhere else to go live stacked atop one another like animals inside enclosures. The children breathe asbestos in their schools and store poison in their lungs. Sometimes the sick and injured intentionally wander the streets during the games, hoping to be invaded. The games make jumping legal for the players, after all—they must answer for it by providing some sort of care. Collateral casualties who are gravely injured must be taken to the hospital free of cost; collateral casualties whose bodies are destroyed must be paid handsomely, and if their qi is killed alongside it, then their family members get the money. Plenty throw themselves in front of players on purpose, making a sacrifice so that their loved ones can eat. Each year, the smaller television networks interview the newly orphaned children who have been left with a small compensation and an empty apartment. It is hard to decide whether they should be envied or pitied.

"Do you hear me?" Lusi screams. "Do you—"

He freezes. Someone has appeared in his field of vision. The nearest alley bulb illuminates enough to present the newcomer's outline, coming closer and closer. Palace uniform. A masked face.

"Don't fret," they say evenly.

Lusi tries to get back onto his feet. Though he was calling for aid, his heart is suddenly beating fast, sensing terrible danger.

"Who are you?" he demands. "Stop right there—"

There's a flash of blinding light.

When Lusi stands, his movements are even and controlled. Lusi is not Lusi at all anymore, his consciousness stamped into the background, too weak to fight back. So his body turns on its heel and begins to walk.

◇◇◇◇◇

Calla pushes on the door of the Magnolia Diner, ducking under the turnstile at the door and watching her wristband tick down. It's late now, almost midnight. Almost time to report to the coliseum. Outside, San-Er is a series of loud clatters and clangs, pressing in through the open windows of the diner. The twin cities remain active at this hour, the restaurants filling orders and the brothels at their busiest, funneling people through the streets without pause.

Practically every street in San leads toward the coliseum grounds, because the Palace of Union is attached to the coliseum, and heavens forbid the palace be inconvenienced in any way. The marketplace that operates within the coliseum is the only outdoor market in San-Er, hawking the cheapest goods and unhealthiest foods, which Calla simply does not go near. She has spent a long time avoiding that part of the city. All these years, knowing that King Kasa stood nearby and she couldn't act . . . it has broiled a hot anger inside her, forcing her to steer clear of palace grounds until the day came that she could play her hand. She didn't think someone would recognize her outside of its vicinity. Perhaps she should have been more careful.

But she doubts that it was she who gave her own hand away.

"Yilas!" Calla tears her mask off, then calls out again without the muffle. *"Yilas."*

The diner patrons hardly pay her any heed. It's as crowded inside as it is on the main streets: old men in tank tops smoking their cigarettes, dripping with sweat to add to the filth that leaves the floor slick. Booths line the walls, crammed with schoolkids without parental supervision, yelling over their card games. Only Yilas glances up from the other side of the diner. She closes the logbook she was writing in and pushes away from the register with a roll of her pale-green eyes.

"You could have walked over like a normal person, you know." Yilas tightens the knot of her apron as she approaches, then nudges her dyed bangs away from her face. They're red today, which clashes with her eyes, but Yilas is the sort of person to purposely match a leather jacket with a silk dress. Half of Calla's wardrobe is borrowed from Yilas, so they look a matching pair with their dark-red coats, one size too large and draping down to their knees. "What are you in a fit about?"

Calla flashes a wide grin. "A fit? Me?" She twirls around to Yilas's side, throwing an arm over her shoulder. The grip looks casual, but Yilas's immediate wince speaks to the bone-crunching reality. "I've never thrown a fit in my life. Where's your darling girlfriend? I have some matters to discuss with you both."

Yilas looks up at Calla, chin tipped to accommodate their height difference. It's a shock that Calla manages to blend so well into the city when she's a head taller than average. Though Yilas scrunches her mouth a moment in thought, seeming to debate whether Calla has brought in a serious matter or only her dramatics, she does walk forward and take Calla with her, pushing through the kitchen door and then another into the diner's cramped office.

"Calla!" Chami greets, perking up at their appearance.

Calla lets go of Yilas and slams the office door closed behind them. Her grin drops at terrifying speed; the room seems to go cold, too, in concert.

"Sit down," Calla demands.

Chami's brows knit together with concern. Quietly, she drops back into her chair. Yilas makes a slower job of the task, strolling over to Chami and perching on the desk, giving the slightest shake of her head when Chami turns a questioning gaze to her. Before they left the palace in Er, Yilas and Chami had been Calla's attendants. And three years later, when Calla caused a bloodbath that soaked Er in red, she showed up on their front step asking for help. At the time of the massacre, Chami Xikai and Yilas Nuwa had long established themselves comfortably as civilians in San. Attendants used to come and go often—the Palace of Heavens was far less guarded than the Palace of Union is now. Hundreds passed through the walls in the three years between their departure and Calla's massacre, with a considerable fraction assigned as Calla's personal attendants. No one knew that Yilas and Chami had been her favorites, and so no one from King Kasa's forces has known to come sniffing around—yet. Calla has been living as Chami, staying under the radar but using her number when necessary. The real Chami uses Yilas's identity number, since the two are attached at the hip anyway. Take Chami away from Yilas for ten minutes, and she might spontaneously combust.

"Give me a list of everyone who has asked for your name recently," Calla says.

"What happened?" Chami's eyes grow unbelievably wide, the pink standing stark against her whites and even starker against the black ink she brushes over her bottom lashes. Even in the palace, Chami always looked pristine, as if she wrapped up her makeup at the end of each night and wore around her perfectly preserved efforts in the morning. "Did you take out a loan?"

Calla throws her mask at her, but Yilas's arm whips out, catching it before it can hit Chami. Yilas shoots her a glare.

"No," Calla hisses. "A Weisanna *found* me."

Yilas's expression shifts from annoyance to horror instantly, an exact mirror of the immediate dread that drops Chami's jaw.

"We haven't said anything," Chami hurries to supply before Calla can ask. "The diner has been operating per usual too. The same few Crescent Society members coming in at odd hours, the same few criminal patrons who come to swap change. Certainly no one has asked—"

Chami stops, cut to a halt when Calla raises her hand. Calla's gaze isn't even on her former attendant anymore. It's pinned on the table behind her.

"What is that?" She marches forward, eyes narrowing. "Is that a *computer?*"

A knock comes on the office door, interrupting Chami before she can answer. One of the diner waitresses pokes her head in, gesturing for Chami's attention frantically, and when Chami turns back to Calla with a pleading look, Calla waves her off with a sigh.

"I reiterate," she says when Chami hurries away. "Please don't tell me that's a computer."

"It was cheap," Yilas answers, pushing a button beneath the table with her shoe. The rectangular box starts to hum. When the screen of the bulky computer monitor flashes green, the box also starts to emit a sound, whining loud enough through the office space that Calla suspects the patrons outside must surely be able to hear it—

The noise stops. Calla drops the computer plug that she had pulled out of its socket, spitting a lock of long hair out of her mouth. Everyone in San-Er chases what is shiny. The poor mailmen have started complaining about electronic mailing, which Calla won't register for since she's a nameless criminal, but even if she could, *why* would she trust the ether to pass along her correspondences?

"Hey!" Yilas complains. "I was—"

"You were turning on a data feeder," Calla interrupts. She carries a pager, and that is the extent to which she'll allow the tech towers to follow her around. Prices have lowered across the twin cities for all the larger monitors; ordinary people have scrambled to purchase personal computers instead of dropping into the cybercafes that litter every street, but Calla didn't think Chami and Yilas were stupid enough to do so too.

"They'll know that Chami isn't registered! This whole thing is an identity—"

The door opens again, cutting her off. In that split second, Calla prepares to switch back to a grin, baring her teeth as wide as they will go, but it's only Chami again. Her face is pale. There isn't a single spot of blood in her cheeks.

"Calla," she whispers. "Come out here, please."

Fuck.

Calla swoops for the nearest sharpest thing she can find—a set of keys—and encloses it within her fist. In the Palace of Heavens, they trained her to use everything. Blades and arrows, explosives and projectiles, even the occasional firearm when they could scrounge up the gunpowder, despite its rarity in San-Er. They needed to prepare her, in case their kingdom went to war with its neighbor to the north, and Calla was to take a sector of Talin's army and march through the provinces.

Instead, she used everything she was taught against them. That was their own fault.

"Who is it?" Calla asks Chami, following her out. "Palace guard? Leida Miliu?"

Chami shakes her head helplessly. The captain of the guard is known to switch bodies often, but would Leida come for Calla personally?

"I could take a guess, but . . . you may as well see for yourself. He asked for you by name and told me not to play stupid when I denied it."

Calla stops right before the kitchen door. The keys cut into her palm. "Okay. Stay here. If I scream, drop to the floor immediately."

Before Chami can finish making her strangled noise, Calla has marched out, braced for battle. The diner appears as normal—smoke and movement and chaos, chopsticks clinking against ceramic bowls and teacups tapping against the glass table covers.

Then, Calla spots the anomaly. At one of the far booths, a man sits alone, his hair cropped close to his neck, a color unnatural to the people of Talin. It takes bleach and hours of chemical work for a blond so fair and gleaming. Within the borders of Talin, where jumping bodies is signaled by a change in eye color, dark hair is the one consistency against eyes running in every hue.

A palace brat, then, Calla decides immediately. No one outside the luxury of nobility would have the means otherwise. Yilas touches up her bangs with a cheap new color every few weeks; the elderly slather coarse dark dye onto their gray. But the frequency of fine treatment needed for glistening perfect *blond* is something only the palace can afford.

She strides closer, taking in the burgundy silk shirt, the myriad of jade rings encircling his fingers when he lifts his teacup to his mouth. Material observations rarely offer anything conclusive in a city where people can swap bodies at will. Here, though, there are enough details that Calla has gathered an unfortunate suspicion.

Not just any palace brat.

She approaches the booth. Slides into the opposite seat. When her companion's eyes flicker up, they are black, outlined with the barest blue that is only visible because Calla is looking for it.

"August," she says evenly. She puts the keys in her pocket. "It's been a while."

"Five years," Prince August replies, setting his cup down.

His voice is deeper than she remembers, his movements almost lethargic. Had she searched her memory, perhaps she would have recalled that this never-smiling face is August's birth body save for the new hair, but she wouldn't have expected him to approach her with such precious cargo. His personal bodyguard must be waiting outside. Or inside one of the bodies nearby, ready to spring to his defense at the smallest breach in safety.

"I trust you've been well?" he continues.

Calla leans back into the seat, resting her arm on the booth. Take her by surprise once, fine. A second time—that won't do at all. This is August Shenzhi, the golden boy with a one-track mind for climbing the palace ranks, no matter who he had to step on to get there. They didn't interact enough in their teenage years to become friends, but they've shared enough diplomatic visits that Calla has learned how the crown prince of San behaves—learned to ooze ease around him and let nothing be used against her.

"I've been better," she says. "It can't compare to life as heir to the throne, I'm sure. How's Galipei? Still in love with you?"

August's eyes narrow. His gaze darts to her wristband, dangling in full view of him.

"Bold of you to be saying such words when I could have you executed."

"Bold of you to threaten to execute me when I could gut you this very second."

"Ah," August sighs, reaching for the teapot. He pours Calla her cup, but she makes no move to touch it. "Here I was, thinking your bloodlust would fade with time."

Calla stares at him, saying nothing. If anything, she is only more unhinged now.

August taps his finger on the table. The order receipts and paper-thin menus tremble from the movement, trapped underneath the slab of glass.

"Did you think I wouldn't recognize Chami Xikai registering for the lottery? Or that I wouldn't remember she could barely bump into a wall without apologizing to it? You dug your own grave, cousin."

"I dug my own grave?" Calla leans onto the table, her elbows pressed to the glass. "I am *dead*, by the Palace of Union's own declaration. The funeral was a little lackluster, I must admit, but it was nice of King Kasa to broadcast it on every station. Even if you recognized Chami's name, why connect it to me? Perhaps my former attendant is interested in the games." She splays her hands. "No, my grave is perfectly untouched. Someone sent you to look for me."

The only signal of August's annoyance is the twitch of his sharp jaw. Before he speaks again, a waitress approaches with notepad in hand, rubbing flour off her nose.

"Can I—"

Calla shakes her head, and the waitress takes the gesture smoothly in stride. She lowers her orange-brown eyes and tucks the notepad into her apron, then leans in to check the teapot before whisking it away for refill.

"Believe it or not," August begins when the waitress is out of earshot, "I tracked you down of my own volition, not at the palace's instruction. King Kasa certainly wouldn't recognize Chami in the lottery list. His attention has never been for the small details." He lifts his teacup and takes a sip. "I alone have been looking for you, Calla. Ever since the Palace of Heavens went under."

It's a lot of effort to go through when he had no assurance that she was even alive. Calla kicks her feet up onto the table. August jolts with surprise, but he blinks it away as fast as it came, watching Calla fold her arms over her chest, her coat rustling as she adjusts her boots comfortably.

"You weren't afraid you were chasing ghosts?" she asks.

"I knew you were alive," August retorts immediately. "Otherwise, King Kasa wouldn't have locked himself up the moment you committed your little bloodbath. Otherwise, he wouldn't still be afraid to leave the palace's impenetrable security. He might have the rest of the twin cities fooled, but at least give me some credit."

The bitterness in his tone is clear. He makes no effort to hide it.

"So why haven't you told him?" Calla asks. "Go tattle and collect your points as heir."

"Because I'm seeking your help."

Calla can't help the snort that escapes. She unfolds her arms, then reaches over to poke a finger at August, mostly to see if he'll allow it. Her nail digs into the soft, vulnerable flesh of his arm. Maybe Galipei will reveal himself as one of the patrons nearby. Maybe he'll lunge over the booths and push her away before August can utter a word of complaint.

"What can I help you with?" she asks. Her tone turns teasing, condescending. "Patricide?"

Silence. August doesn't refute her. He only stares at her steadily, like it isn't a preposterous suggestion at all. Calla drops her feet from the table, quickly straightening up.

"Oh, shit. *Really?*"

"Are you so surprised?" he asks. His voice drops lower. "Don't tell me that wasn't why you enrolled in the games."

Of course it is. For five years, Calla Tuoleimi has been biding and biding her time, tending to the fury that burns beneath her ribs. There is but one task left in her vengeance: King Kasa's head plucked from his spine and flung across the coliseum. The image of it keeps her warm at night, propels her forward even when she feels listless and useless, another cog turning in these twin cities despite the power her title has . . . or had.

She's not a princess anymore.

She made sure of that when she killed both her parents and littered Er's throne room with the bodies of their guards. Her plan had been to destroy both thrones at once and wipe out the royal bloodline. The roots had been in place. Civilian grievances had reached their height. Protests erupted by the city wall every week. Given an opportunity, the people of San-Er could march into the palaces and raze them . . . she knew, she knew they could do it.

Calla forces herself out of her thoughts, pushing away the frustration that mounts whenever she thinks back to that night. She hadn't been fast enough. King Kasa had scrambled to protect himself as soon as the news of her massacre started to travel, knowing that he was next. Calla had no choice except to run, slipping into his city to wait while San's royal guard searched for Er's traitor princess. Now, so close to her second chance, she cannot sink into her anger, or she might never emerge. She has spent too long compartmentalizing every terrible impulse and smoothing them down to be palatable. When the time comes to confront the blistering shards that live inside her, it will have to be in one big swallow.

"Cousin," Calla simpers falsely, "if Kasa drops dead, can you count on installing yourself? You might be heir at the moment"—she reaches over the table, cupping her palm to his cheek—"but we have no true blood relation. The divine crown could reject you. Take the throne then, and the council will rebel against your rule before the people do."

August slaps her hand away, visible irritation strengthening in his expression. He is August Shenzhi now, but he was born August Avia, to a rubber-factory owner and his seamstress second wife. It wasn't until his father's sister married King Kasa that they were all brought into the palace when August was eight years old. Calla still remembers it. She was ten, attending that frightfully lavish wedding in an itchy dress with a collar that scratched her throat.

The Palace of Earth went through a year of tragedy when August was fourteen. First, his father died from illness. Then his half sister caught the yaisu sickness and his mother left the city, jumping to her death from the top of the wall. August started making his slow climb in the palace thereafter, a crowd favorite among the distant relatives—and most importantly, King Kasa's favorite. Shortly before eighteen-year-old Calla wrought havoc on her side of the city, August's aunt died as well, and the widowed king gave up on children of his own, naming August his heir instead.

"The crown has never rejected anyone before," August says. He keeps his words level, but there is a strain in his voice.

"Yes." Calla raises an eyebrow. "Because it has always been passed down the same bloodline, matched to the same familial qi. As it was made to."

There has always been one crown of Talin, even when the kingdom was split between two kings. It sits in the Palace of Union at present, never mind where, atop a satin pillow with guards stationed around it. Every coronation, it's brought out for a momentary fitting—if a ruler is righteous and suited to rule, it remains on; if a ruler is found inadequate, the crown will burst into sparks and revolt. Though they have been taught to believe it as a divine choosing,

Calla is mostly convinced that it's only science. As the story goes, there was one attempted usurper during the reign before Kasa's. A councilmember led a revolting force into the Palace of Earth, marching his province's armies in with weapons raised. But the moment the councilmember placed the crown on his own head, he was felled on the spot, keeling over with no discernible cause. His armies were dissolved, and his province was reassigned to another councilmember. The reign went on securely.

"Don't worry about it," August assures. "It will accept me."

Calla lifts her brow again, but her cousin keeps his gaze even. He's far too optimistic for someone trying to stick his foot into hundreds of years of hereditary succession.

Like every other physical object in the world, the royal crown holds a small amount of qi —nowhere near the amount that makes up a person's soul, but enough to provide a breath of life. Believers say it was made with a deciding power, guided by the old gods to seek out the royal who is most deserving to hold the throne of Talin.

Most likely, whatever ancient magic gave them the ability to jump between bodies also molded the crown, binding it to the Shenzhi and Tuoleimi bloodlines. Which means, of course, that everyone of that lineage should be found worthy.

"So what?" Calla asks, still contemptuous. "Kasa drops dead, then you take the crown? You can't wait it out, drop a little poison into his tea yourself?"

Her cousin shakes his head. "I cannot be suspected in the slightest," he says. "I want a public murder. One with a clear perpetrator, perhaps a wanted princess who plotted her way into the palace by winning the games. That way, no one can accuse me of being party to it—I can play the good, mournful son. Once you are hauled away, I'll install myself and pardon you out of the kindness of my new reign. Doesn't that sound wonderful?"

"No," Calla says plainly. "I don't want to see another reign. I want it gone. Besides, you're deluded if you think having the crown is enough for you to rule. Even if it accepts you, the council can still take it away"—she snaps her fingers—"like *that*."

It's not quite a smile that graces August's face, but something close enough. A quirk of a lip in fleeting amusement. As if he is tickled that such a thought would be proposed to him.

"Do you think we would be living like this if people didn't trust in the crown?" August asks. "You don't think our civilians would have risen up and demanded a new ruler by now? They believe in it, Calla. They need it for order. They may complain and bemoan the throne day after day, but an unshakable part of them decides that they aren't deserving of better as long as the crown says so."

The door to the Magnolia Diner chimes, and a group bustles in, each coming upon the turnstile slowly as their fingers scramble over the keypad. Almost pensively, August watches them pile into a booth.

"The council too. The crown's acceptance is a mandate of the land. Once it's on my head, no councilmember would dare yank it off. To deny it would be to deny Talin. If I have no right to be king even after the crown accepts me, then those on the council have no right to their plots of land either. They were installed by kings, were they not? Kings chosen by the crown."

Calla sits back, pursing her lips. The newcomers nearby are making themselves at home, the rise and fall of conversation in the diner adapting to their loud, excitable screeching. Yilas comes out from the back to take their orders and shoots a wary glance at Calla, but she does not intrude. She jots down several requests for spicy wontons, then returns to the kitchen.

"All right," Calla says. "Say that every other component falls into place. You could leave me in a cell once I carry this through. Why should I trust you?"

"Why shouldn't you?" August shoots back. He pushes his sleeves up, exposing his forearms to the blue-white light. Everyone else in this diner looks a little sickly under its cold glow, the usual malnourishment of the city rendered starker than ever. August could not look malnourished even if he tried. His features only stand out more, as does the small scar near his wrist.

On one diplomatic visit during their childhood, a servant had shattered a vase near August, the shards cutting his arm. King Kasa had whirled in, asking what happened, and instead of having the servant hauled away, August lied. He said that the vase fell by itself, that the blood dripping down his fingers was no matter. August, though cold and monotonous at times, is not hateful.

If given a throne, he would rule well. There are no good kings, but there are fair ones.

"What was your alternative, Calla?" August says quietly. "You must know that there is no other way to walk out of regicide alive. The palace guard would have you captive as soon as you strike him. You sign your own execution papers."

"If that's what it takes," Calla replies. "I would do it. My execution papers for Talin's freedom from his reign."

"Then listen to me. You don't need the execution papers at all. You have me. I will free you after you free the kingdom."

There's something about this that feels too convenient to be true. August has always seemed suspiciously well polished. Half of her is ready to accept her cousin's plan, while the other half knows she is too desperate for Talin's salvation, and desperation colors one's eyes from reason. It has been five long years—lonely years, working without the promise of success. The trap laid open for her here is so glaringly obvious, such a flashing red flag, that she has to wonder if August *is* being genuine, because how could someone trying to trick her possibly make a plan this transparent?

"You sit so comfortable as Kasa's prized heir." She needs to hear it in his own words. "Why would you want him gone?"

"You know the answer to that," August replies easily. "There were once two heirs of San-Er. Why did you kill your parents?"

Calla's knuckles whiten. Her palms sting with the memory of the maps she picked up that day five years ago, after she'd wandered into the war rooms without any aim and found pencil-drawn plans for the troops they were sending out into the provinces. That wasn't the only reason she snapped, but it was certainly the final push.

August nods. "That's why," he says to Calla's silence. "I know you, Calla. You don't really want the monarchy crumbled and burned to the ground—you want this version of it gone. You want Kasa off the throne. The Palace of Heavens had good tutors, I'm sure. Your formal education must have covered the kind of chaos that can arise out of a power vacuum."

Calla turns a frosty glare in his direction. "Maybe chaos is what we need."

"Come on." He fiddles with his sleeve again. "I know you're more mature now than the eighteen-year-old who tried to vanquish both palaces. You've had years to think about your mistakes. About what you could do differently this time. Say you *had* succeeded. What then? A capital of two hundred million people, descended into anarchy? A kingdom of three hundred million with no order? Don't tell me I've overestimated your intelligence."

This is what August does best. Clawing his fingers into someone's mind, deeper and deeper, until his own ideas have been planted there as the truest course of action.

"Listen to me," Prince August demands, giving her no time to think up a sarcastic response. "I am offering you a future where you walk out with your head intact and get what you want—what you *actually* want, not just the short-term imitation of it. The people fed. The city wall open. The kingdom flourishing. You were born a princess—you can even serve as an advisor to my throne, if you wish. But I must sit on the throne first. Are you in?"

The coliseum is near enough to the diner that they can hear an audible shift rumbling through San. The alley outside grows with noise, leading spectators en masse toward the palace for the Daqun, the opening of the games. These games are entertainment, whether on the television set at home or in the stands of the arena. Never mind eighty-seven of their fellow civilians being murdered by the end of it. Murder by sword or by the throne's refusal to save its most vulnerable from starvation . . . what's the difference? San-Er has so many fucking people that one life is as common as a cockroach, fit to be squashed and disregarded without remorse.

Calla turns away from her cousin, exhaling as she inspects her wristband. "Are you giving me a choice?"

"Of course." August tips his chin toward the diner windows. Though it is dark, though it is always dark down here, the movement of the crowds is visible, each head bobbing past the stained glass like shadow puppets controlled by strings from the skies. "The coliseum awaits. I won't pull you from the games, but you lose my help. You lose me keeping your wristband active even if you don't check in every twenty-four hours. You lose me wiping out your fellow contestants by invading their bodies and throwing them off buildings. Is that what you prefer: more blood on your hands by the end of this?"

She had forgotten how good August is at talking his way through anything. Calla can't help but let loose a small laugh. The games are starting. This is practically an offer of guaranteed victory. By that logic, maybe it's an easy decision after all.

"Very well," she agrees plainly. She can always back out later if she needs to. She can always kill August too, if he's only trying to use then discard her.

"Good." August reaches into his shirt pocket and brings out a small chip between his fingers. Without asking, he takes hold of Calla's arm clinically, then turns it so he can see the empty slot in her wristband. He puts the chip in, holding it until the screen emits a beep. The number 57 flashes bright.

"Here's my first gift to you," August says, releasing her arm. "Go get your weapons and run."

CHAPTER 4

Anton spends his last half hour of the countdown getting drunk.

It doesn't matter when it comes to his ability to play in the games. As soon as he leaves this body, he'll leave this pleasant haze too, and the original occupant will awaken to deal with the aftereffects.

Just as he is taking in the last of his glass, he feels fingers glide along his shoulder.

Anton freezes. He turns around in the darkness of the bar, squinting into the smudges of color and grayscale blurs.

"Buy me a drink?" the woman asks. She has a red mask strapped over her face, but that's more fabric than she's wearing anywhere else.

"Maybe another time." Anton sets down his glass, then points to the corner of the bar where a raucous group has been increasing in volume. "I think they might be interested."

Graciously, the woman inclines her head and backs away. The other prostitutes by the door watch the exchange and mark Anton off as a potential customer.

He has stayed long enough, gotten his degeneracy out of his system. For the next few weeks or months or however long the games go on, he'll have to be on guard at every moment. He's already pulling his jacket tight and undoing his wristband, eyes scouring the bodies he passes on his way out.

A drink spills on the floor in front of him. Anton skirts around the puddle smoothly, grimacing at the teetering man who spilled it. His moral compass is on the more delicate side compared to others with similar abilities in the twin cities, but that doesn't stop him from jumping around frivolously. In Talin, people are not attached to their bodies. Or rather, bodies are merely another asset to take ownership of—to rob, to borrow, to care for, like apartments and clothes.

Anton rams into one of the prostitutes at the door, pretending to stumble. As soon as the prostitute holds his arms out in aid, Anton pushes his wristband into his waiting hands, then jumps. Light flashes through the bar, drawing a few nearby cries, but Anton is already leaving through the front, closing his new fingers around his wristband and wiping a slight sheen off his forehead. When he steps into the night, he looks like any other man strolling the city before the games begin.

The palace has always declared jumping illegal. But having the gene is like being given a sense of taste: people couldn't be expected not to seek good food. Those who are caught jumping are fined and imprisoned, but that doesn't stop the thousands who do it every year. Those who commit crimes in other bodies—or claim that they had been taken over before a crime—end up in legal spirals that go on for so long the jury eventually gives up trying to pinpoint the true culprit and shoves every slightly guilty party into a cell for a year or two to answer for the technicality.

San-Er is defined by its mess, by its confusions and its blur of people meshing and tangling with one another. A birth body is not one's own. Bodies can be shed, removed from the self. Bodies belong to everyone but the one who was birthed into it, though if you're powerful, you might have a greater say on how long you can hold on to it.

Anton hasn't had contact with his birth body since his exile, but it matters little to him. Every miserable event, every bit of trauma that San-Er gifts him, comes through his memory, stays with him because of his memory. What good is attachment to one body?

As the alleyway narrows, Anton takes the next turn onto a wider route, heading in the direction of the coliseum. His head is clear now, thoughts flying at a thousand miles per hour. There's a pulsation underneath his feet, the *thump-thump-thump* of San's heartbeat thrumming just under the narrow, crumbling sidewalks and the muddy unpaved alleys. At the coliseum, the players will show up in various appearances because they know the body they enter with won't last long if they want to play to their best advantage. When he bites down on the inside of his cheeks, he doesn't realize how sharp his teeth are, and it almost cuts through before he tastes the first hint of blood and eases his jaw. He checks his wristband. The countdown is approaching five minutes.

The city's pulsating has grown louder. Accompanying the stomps of its spectators, who trickle through its sinuous routes and flood into its central blot, to the coliseum, standing tall beside the palace. Though there are no boundaries or ropes for spectators around the sides, they mingle a good distance away from the center, making it immediately clear who is a player and who is not.

Better for the audience to keep their distance than get accidentally impaled. This way, they can also pretend that everything is just a show, forgetting that the players entering the coliseum are readying to tear each other apart.

Anton's gaze shifts up once he makes his way to the center, observing one of the palace balconies at the south of the coliseum. The throne room. Prince August is up there somewhere, his eye on the games. Anton can feel it. It's hard to say whether his former best friend has discerned his participation, but once the players are drawn, there is no taking it back. He wouldn't put it past August to try nonetheless. In those years they had together in the palace, there was nothing Prince August was unwilling to do, so long as it would achieve his goals. He was at once Anton's best friend and biggest fear, the one he trusted most and could never let his guard down around. When he spent time with August, he never knew if he would get the sensible student who wanted some help with his history homework or the cold, calculating boy who once poured acid on Anton's hand because they needed to be near the infirmary while a councilmember was sick too.

"What's wrong with you?" Anton remembers hissing. His birth body would bear the scar for months afterward. "Why would you do that to me?"

"It's for a greater purpose," August replied plainly, with no room for argument. "I have to get into King Kasa's good graces. Or we can forget about our plan to leave."

"Hey! That's my spot!"

At the angry shout, Anton flinches back into the present, his unfamiliar body rippling with tension. He turns, then releases a quick breath, finding that the voice was directed not at him, but at another player standing in the distance. Sound carries well in the coliseum, placing the argument closer than it was. One of the arguing players shoves the other, and though they are far enough that Anton cannot make out their features under the coliseum's golden lights, their yelling echoes cleanly.

"Do you own the land now? Go stand elsewhere."

"I—"

The player raises his arm. The spectators near the entrance freeze, preparing to witness a premature fight, but then three other players nearby shout in warning, and the two separate from one another with vicious glares, finding their own spots in the arena to stand. When the Daqun starts, there is nothing that says the players need to hurt each other. But it's the opening event, the first moment when the killing can begin, and if there can be only one victor, who would lose the opportunity to take out their competitors at the earliest possible convenience?

Anton looks down. His wristband starts to flash the seconds of the final minute. He expected to feel more: to be nervous, delirious, frantic. Instead, a deadly calm settles over him, floods his fingertips and turns his lips cold. The purpose of the Daqun is to distribute chips for their wristbands, assigning a number to each of the eighty-eight. It's the easiest way to log who is killing who, to report on players in the reels without having to remember names and identities and histories. *Number Fourteen leads the charts today with expert axe-throwing*, the reels might croon, or *Number Thirty-Two is especially one to watch with their performance in the bloodbath*. The surveillance cameras see everything, and even if the footage quality is piss-poor, the tapes are available upon request for the television networks, so long as Leida Miliu has cleared them in the palace security room first. Every channel scrambles to air their report, working their producers to the bone while splicing together a unique tale out of the extensive raw footage they get from the palace every night. It's an annual show that the residents of San-Er will always watch, a show that the players will make grand by ensuring their kills are in view of a camera.

We are wretched, Anton thinks. But there is nothing to be done.

Another argument starts up to his left. This time, when Anton turns toward the noise, he finds too many standing in the general direction to even decipher where the voices are coming from, save that it's wafting into the darkness. He starts to count. Runs a quick perusal of the groups near and far. When there are three seconds left on his wristband, there's not enough time to do another count, but he doesn't think he was mistaken either.

Eighty-seven players, including himself.

Who would be stupid enough to skip out on the first event? Failing to secure a chip means immediate disqualification.

His wristband trembles. From the palace, the guards make their appearance on the throne room balcony. In unison, they toss down the bags in their arms, letting the eighty-eight identically colored beige sacks drop like deadweights on the coliseum ground.

And everything around him turns to mayhem.

The players rush for the bags. Reckless and uncaring and coming from every which direction, filling the spaces they can and shoving where they cannot. The only point of stillness is Anton.

He doesn't move. He watches.

One player is far larger than the rest, lumbering toward the biggest bag of the bunch and holding it to his chest. He has no difficulty bowling others out of his way; he takes a blade slash along the side of his arm and merely keeps going, running for one of the exits.

Anton rips his wristband off. Halfheartedly, they tell players not to invade each other. They've made it legal for the games—otherwise the players would do it anyway, and then the palace would get stuck either labeling every player a criminal or looking the other way for the sake of the people's entertainment. But still, they have to do their diligence to establish a standard for the viewers. They warn that jumping is dangerous, that players should avoid it for their own health, because the palace cares *so deeply* for their health. They warn that the yaisu sickness can happen to anyone: the result of exiting and entering the same body one too many times in rapid succession. If a player is weak and gets flung back into their own body after repeated failed invasions, it's a surefire way to burn up, their body taking sick and locking their qi in for certain death. The palace gets even more displeased if the nobility are invaded by the players. Prostitutes and gamblers can be thrown into the fray if their bodies are the ones doubled. If it is one of their own, however, the council gets involved, and the headache is so colossal that most players are wary about who they jump into for the sake of their own sanity.

Anton throws his wristband right into the player's path. He slams into the new body so hard and so fast that he's almost certain he has gone beyond notice, only then the outcries of protest start around him, and he figures his light flashed after all. A shame. Perhaps he should be grateful he didn't bounce out from the jump, which the palace warns is the norm, which was what almost killed Otta and left her comatose in the hospital. But he already knew he was stronger than everyone else in this arena, in these damned twin cities.

"Better luck next time," he shouts over his shoulder, scooping up the wristband in his path. He runs, wasting no time fighting or watching players tear into one another. When the spectators outside the arena dart back to avoid his path, Anton cuts a fast line through, hurrying into the nearest street, then taking another sharp turn.

He finds himself in a narrow alley lined with hair salons. The people here do not startle at his sudden appearance. After hours, they are either sweeping their floors or planted on tiny plastic chairs around a low table, blowing on their tea and watching their television screens in the corner. Any moment now, the live reports of the games will start, the news stations running whatever early surveillance footage they can get their hands on.

"Hey, catch."

The shopkeeper turns at Anton's call, frowning in puzzlement. On instinct he holds his arms out and catches the items that Anton tosses over. The young man's purple eyes widen, realizing what he is holding. By then, Anton is already in, blinking fast to focus the new body's poor vision, ducking quickly to escape the other player once he returns to consciousness.

Anton tears open the bag. His heart pounds hard, fingers rummaging through the coins in search of one stray chip. On the other side of the counter, the player starts to yell. Briefly, Anton pokes his head over the counter in concern, but it doesn't seem like the player is looking his way.

"Which one of you did it? Which one of you has the nerve?"

The beefy player kicks his foot at the ground, drawing a shriek from an elderly lady nearby and then a click of her tongue in reproach. With no memory of what his body was doing in the time he was occupied, he cannot gauge where the intruder's flash of light went unless someone else points it out. No one does.

The other shopkeepers stare and stay quiet, knowing the games started with the stroke of midnight. Anton remains hidden behind the counter, his hand still prodding through the bag. It's too late for the man to go back for a chip now. Any remaining bags will have been taken by those who stayed and fought. Even if they don't need more than one chip, they want the coins each bag comes with. This player has been eliminated. He should be happy; he could never have been the victor anyway, and so he has been spared his life.

By the roar he makes before storming off, clearly he does not agree.

Anton finally finds the chip and breathes out a sigh of relief. The alley has gone back to its low conversation. When he brings the chip out, its metallic lines catch the light above him, looking out of place alongside the rough coins and the sack's fraying burlap. He turns the wristband this way and that before realizing the slot runs vertical down the side. He presses the chip in.

The screen flashes white, before 86 appears in its place.

"All right," Anton mutters aloud. He gathers up the rest of the bag. "Let's play."

◇◇◇◇◇

The back door is stuck, sealed in by the mold and grit that has built up at the corners.

Calla plants a boot on the doorframe, then grips the knob tightly with both her hands. Her wristband passed the midnight countdown seconds ago. The other players will have started dispersing across San-Er. She tugs harder.

When the door finally opens, the motion is so vigorous that she stumbles a few steps, her coat rustling as she hits the wall.

"What's this, then?" An old man turns over his shoulder to examine who just broke his back door, a cleaning rag in one hand and a pipe in the other. "Am I being robbed?"

"No, you're being monopolized," Calla says breathlessly, flashing a smile and hurrying in. She tugs the cleaning rag away from the shopkeeper and slides a large monetary note into his palm instead. "Take this. I only ask that you close shop for five minutes."

Weapons are heavily regulated in San-Er. Which means there are only three shops in the twin cities selling them, intended exclusively for the palace guards—except in the twenty-four hours after the Daqun, when the shops will cater to the eighty-eight players of the games too, if they can show their wristband to make a single purchase. While the Daqun might be the first bloodbath, the three weapon shops across the cities will always be the next fight. Still, it's common knowledge that these shops are often in collaboration with the Crescent Societies, distributing items on the black market when profits are low. If players really lose their one weapon midway through the games and reappear with another, the newscasters will abstain from commenting on the switch for the sake of palace decorum.

The old man holds her legal tender up to the light and grunts, then pulls the security gate down over the front of his shop. Other players will soon be coming from the front of the building, weaving in and out of the numerous hallways and corridors.

"Quick, quick," Calla says, slapping her hand on the tabletop.

The shopkeeper narrows his faded-gray eyes, adjusting the cap on his head. "What's your number?"

"Fifty-Seven."

"Wristband?"

Calla shows him her wrist. The shopkeeper frowns.

"Hmm . . ."

"*Hmm?*" she mimics, an octave higher. "Come *on!*"

The shopkeeper finally reaches into the drawers around the table. He continues moving at leisurely speed as he brings out the rare stock, one after the other. The games do not suit a mere dagger or a standard sword. They require a flourish, a weapon that others will not know how to combat when taken by surprise.

"All my products guarantee good speed, deep cuts," he says. "What sounds good to you? A Yanyue dao?" He brings out a curved blade mounted on a wooden pole, with a red sash flowing off its end. "We've got a replica of the mythical"—he grunts, bringing out a heavy matching sword and saber—"Yitian jian and Tulong dao. If you can handle wielding them both at once, that is, because I won't have them parted. Or even . . ."

The table rattles as a giant mallet thumps beside the blades, its handle decorated with gold. Too lavish. Too gaudy.

Calla spares a glance at the digital clock on the shelves.

"How about a thin sword?"

"Thin?" The shopkeeper frowns, looking almost offended. "You want something thin?"

"Give me the skinniest, sharpest thing you have."

He mumbles something beneath his breath, hunching over carefully to look in a different drawer. After a few seconds, the shopkeeper brings out another sword, this one so narrow that it almost appears circular. When he turns it, letting the metal catch the light, Calla sees there is some flatness to the weapon after all—no more than an inch—tapering to create two bladed edges and allow for slashing.

Perfect. Calla holds out her hand, accepting it without further question.

"Are you sure? It's not very—"

The security gate shudders. In that single heartbeat, Calla's gaze whips over, and her arm strikes out of its own accord, drawing the sword from the shopkeeper's grip. The gate whips up; a figure lunges in. Before the player has scarcely taken three steps into the shop, Calla plunges forward and has her blade deep in his gut. She twists. Pulls it sideways until the sword exits.

The player drops. His wristband smacks against the linoleum ground with a discordant sound, followed by his body.

And Calla stumbles, losing her balance.

For the good of the kingdom. For the good of the kingdom.

She recovers quickly, her hand bracing against the wall before she can fall into the bloody puddle. The player stares up at her, eyes pale yellow and dull. If he had escaped fast enough, the body would merely be abandoned. It would sit empty, a bloodless vessel with a cut down its middle, ready to be reused and occupied by another once the cut slowly stitched itself together. Empty vessels know how to fix themselves, just as a plant can regrow its bud. But if the qi inside dies first, the body follows, rapidly gaining the odor of rot, skin sagging right off the bone.

The shopkeeper sighs. "This is not the first year the fight has been brought inside, but I do wish you would be more careful with the splatter."

Calla glances at her sword. The blood has dripped off, leaving the barest red stain upon the blade. She forces back the tightness in her throat, takes a deep breath until she has expelled the weight on her chest. The shopkeeper is waiting for her to respond, wearing the plainest expression on his face, and she clings onto the sight to convince herself that this is fair, that she's only doing what she is meant to do.

"Better hurry, then," the shopkeeper says, shooing her. "Out the back, go on."

Calla has never claimed to be good. She has never wanted to be good. But she seeks it in every corner of the twin cities: a sign that goodness is something Talin is capable of. Every day, she wakes up and she begs for what she has done to mean something, for the kingdom to tell her she is right to believe it could be honorable, that it's befitting to spill blood until there is nothing left of her, until all the pieces are gone, until she cannot feel this twinge of doubt each time her blade slips in and out. There is peace at the end of this. There must be.

Calla tightens her grip on her sword, takes its sheath, and whirls out the shop's back door. Each second in the open is a second exposed. Especially now, when the players are all congregating so close . . .

She pauses at the end of the alley, listening hard. The crackle of an electric wire. The whirring of an enormous factory exhaust fan. Someone is near, watching. The sleeves of Calla's red coat cut off shortly above her wrist; she doesn't bother hiding her wristband. If she is combatted, she'll fight as a player should.

The rustle finally comes again—from above. Calla darts back, grimacing when her boots splash into a dirty puddle, but she has narrowly avoided another player's sword. The woman whirls around, her face caught in a snarl, her hair scrunched in two symmetrical buns at the top of her head. Blue-white light darts along her blade, as if a live current of electricity is running through the metal. On the ground now, she gears up for another slash, her knees bent and braced.

Calla was trained like that too, to stand so that no one could tip her off-balance. To imagine herself as heavy as a mountain. For her first lesson, she was taught that she wasn't allowed to flinch, and they couldn't move on until she learned how to plant her feet down and hold her ground no matter how hard she was hit.

Don't you want to be strong? they had asked. *Don't you want to be infallible?*

Yes, Calla had answered. Twelve years old and honed to be a weapon. Fourteen years old and molded into an unquestioning arm of the throne.

Good. In her memory, every face in the training room blurs together—former generals and retired soldiers who held enough favor in the Palace of Heavens to be teaching the young princess. They didn't care to go easy on her. They all said the same things. *Take the cuts. Take the burns. You will heal, and you will be braver.*

Braver? I want to be stronger.

Strength is a conscious effort. First, you will be braver, and then you will be stronger.

They trained her for war. And she rose up to wage it on them.

The other player lunges. Calla's sword arm lifts without thought. Instinct determines how she holds herself, blocking the strikes and deflecting them away.

"Coward," the woman hisses. "Are this year's games made of the weakest that San-Er has to offer?"

"I hope you're not talking about me right now." Calla throws a glance over her shoulder. It would be a faster course of action to retreat. She only needs to find an opening . . .

The woman's next strike comes viciously, and Calla jolts, her lips thinning. There is hardly reason to be this intense so early in the games. To expend all this energy on the first fights.

"Disgusting," the woman sneers. "All of you putting yourself into the games when you do not care to play. Taking up the space and keeping us from our—"

Calla spins fast and cuts her sword across the woman's stomach. There comes a pause, a moment when the other player gasps and searches around, looking for a civilian body to jump into.

There is no one. It's always this moment when viewers find the most entertainment during the games. That gasp of shock, an overly assured player being proved wrong. No player would register unless they thought they had some chance of winning, and no player would think they had a chance of winning unless they were good at jumping. Being skilled at jumping creates a certain type of person that San-Er knows well: someone who cuts corners, someone who deserves to be taken down a notch. And in the games, it happens over and over again. The viewers lean close to their screens; their hearts leap to their throats.

"Disgusting," the woman says again, a whisper this time, and Calla grits her teeth. One more strike—it's so easy. A line of red appears across the woman's throat, and when Calla lowers her sword, the woman falls too, dead on the wet ground.

The alley is humming. The lightbulbs mounted to the walls flicker on and off, attracting small flying bugs that gather around the noise. Calla uses her boot to nudge the dead body, rolling its wrist over. 66 flashes on the screen, one more number to add to the first day's casualty count playing later tonight.

One of the alley bulbs shorts out. Calla peers into the water puddles and catches her own distorted reflection right then, hazed in red by the blood seeping from the woman's wounds. For a second, she wonders if there is another opponent looming over her, and she startles, whirling around.

Nothing. Just a camera installed on the wall. Just Calla—long hair tangled around her neck, face and clothes splattered with blood, her surroundings contorting around her as the surface of the puddle catches irregular light.

She doesn't look like herself. She's never really looked like herself.

Calla Tuoleimi, princess of Er. She could do nothing on a throne, but she can do everything with a sword in her hand.

CHAPTER 5

After midnight, when the twin cities drop into darkness proper, San-Er's facade glows with the light of its apartments. The wall at the north of San rises high, but not high enough to completely shield the buildings at the city's edge, each window emitting light and puffing with its attached air conditioner unit, abuzz, too, with the sound of running stoves and television sets glitching in the corner.

Despite the jumble, no building in the capital climbs higher than fourteen floors. Any more, and these meandering structures might pitch sideways from their own weight and fall over.

Calla's apartment is one of the few that sits relatively quiet. Already squashed and smothered below all the other floors, it is the final door at the end of a long, smoky hall filled with gambling parlors. The incessant clicking of mahjong tiles garners an echo different from other noises, creeping in under her door when she least expects it. Sometimes when she's nodding off on the couch, she'll wake with a start, convinced that the sound is someone coming to summon her for training, hard shoes gliding across the palace floor.

Her television is on mute. From the bedroom, Calla takes a drag on her cigarette, watching the smoke waft up and curl around the molding ceiling paint. Light streams in through her window, a kaleidoscope of neon that bleeds from different sources outside: red and gold through the brothel on the neighboring building's third floor, deep blue through the cybercafe on the sixth floor, flashes of everything pulsating off the restaurants dotting the nearby vicinity. How strange it is that San-Er glows brighter at night than during the day. Daytime here is dreary darkness, the streets repellant against sunlight. Nothing but the barest gray gloom, illuminating very little on its own.

Calla lifts onto her elbow. Now laughter drifts through her closed window, assailing the inside of her bedroom. By some instinct, she peers through the glass right while a group of teenagers meander past, drunk and happy, talking over one another and paying no heed to their volume.

She settles back onto her sheets, smoothing down a wrinkle. Calla has forgotten what it's like to laugh in a crowd, what it's like to talk to people at all, save for Chami and Yilas. These five years have been spent in as much solitude as she can bear, keeping her head down and her mask on. She takes the barest necessities from her former attendants to keep herself alive, but can risk no other work, no other participation in the twin cities. After all, she has a task far above the usual day-to-day business of a regular civilian in San-Er.

Sometimes, though, she feels the weight of loneliness shift and settle inside her rib cage. Like cold tendrils curling softly around her insides. Not enough to hurt, not enough to draw protest from her. But enough to serve as an ever-constant reminder: *Here I am, here I shall stay, you can never pull me away.*

Calla clambers up from her bed, tapping ash off her cigarette and drawing a meow of protest from her cat for the disruption. When she walks into the small living room, Mao Mao leaps off the edge of the mattress and pads after her with a growl. She doesn't bother with the overhead lights, so she navigates the living room by the glow of the television. Shadows draw long on every object nearby: the sword propped by the door, the oranges and bananas sitting upon the glass shelves built into a hollow in the wall. The moment Calla sits herself down in front of the bulky screen, the news program still on mute, Mao Mao curls around her ankles, preventing her from further movement.

Calla sighs, reaching down to scratch his furry head with her free hand. The longer the games go on, the less safe it'll be to come home. She's fine for the next few days while the players feel out a routine, but then the daily location pings will begin, and as they happen more and more often, it would be suicidal to be here when one goes off. Once another player knows where she lives, even if she escapes the first encounter, she can't come back to get some rest without risking an ambush.

The clock turns to three in the morning. The reels don't usually run through the night, but this is a special occasion. All the newscasters look enlivened as they switch cue cards, mouths moving much faster than their usual dull monotone. Calla leans forward again for the volume, turning it up just in time to hear *"and Fifty-Seven, our leading player thus far."*

"I beg your pardon?" Calla says, exhaling smoke. She stops scratching, and Mao Mao butts his head into her palm to protest. His face and ears are a sensible dark gray while the rest of his fur is an off-white, always molting clumps around the apartment because he enjoys following her to be petted. She picked him off the streets as a kitten when she first went into hiding, a companion while she spent hours upon hours throwing knives at the wall, and years later, as a consequence, her cat has attachment issues.

"Yes, indeed," the second newscaster says, as if he heard Calla's exclamation. *"With the opening event's conclusion and the players dispersed throughout the cities, the palace has reported our first numbers. It is absolutely thrilling to see twenty-three total hits, with ten attributed to Fifty-Seven."*

Calla chokes on her next inhale, cigarette smoke rushing out from her nostrils.

"For fuck's sake," she coughs. "Good job, August."

◇◇◇◇◇

"It is absolutely thrilling to see twenty-three total hits, with ten attributed to Fifty-Seven."

Though the night grows exceedingly late, there remains a flock of spectators outside a barbershop at the southern end of San, watching the outward-facing television screen. Anton no longer has access to the apartment with the fancy television—which, anyway, is shattered now, and would be even if he were still in that body—so he joins them, hovering at the periphery and smoothing his sleeve over his wristband.

The reels continue to play surveillance footage of the games. The palace guard tries its very best to regulate San-Er with these cameras, but they have one very fatal flaw: cameras can't pick up the light of body-jumping. When the Crescent Societies are responsible for most of San-Er's crime and their networks of people are the cities' most persistent jumpers, it's easy to understand why so many cases of trafficking and murder keep slipping under the palace's radar.

Why the palace has never bothered to address this loophole is beyond Anton's grasp. At the very least, the surveillance reels finally have their use during the games as a constant feed of the killing action. The television networks don't need to put film crews on the ground when there are already cameras installed at every corner. Proper film crews might even cause the Palace of Union to bristle, if networks were to share footage of the games that hadn't first crossed Leida's inspection. The people aren't ready for close-ups, in any case; they need those grainy high angles that render each player into a little avatar of themselves.

That way, San-Er doesn't have to see how far it has decayed. Slaughter as an accepted entertainment track. Slaughter as a shortcut to wealth.

Anton frowns, pushing closer to the barbershop screen. They're replaying Fifty-Seven's first kill inside the weapons shop. He dropped into the same one earlier, acquiring the crescent moon knives that now hide under his jacket. By the time he was there, the bloodstain he sees on screen was already long gone.

Fifty-Seven pulls her sword out. When she turns around, her long hair whips into her face, and though the footage is fuzzy, though the saturation is turned so low it is almost grayscale, her eyes are bright with their unidentifiable color.

The crowd around him starts murmuring about the player, stunned by how professional her strike looked, enthralled by how fast she was. As Anton stands there, however, staring at the screen even when the newsreel moves on, he realizes what it is that has caught *his* attention.

Number Fifty-Seven was not at the Daqun. He would remember someone like that. Even if she has swapped bodies since then, there was no one moving with her precision, because if there was, he would have marked her as a threat immediately.

"Interesting," he mutters, stepping away from the crowd. He pulls his collar up, ruffling the short hair at the base of his neck. No one gives him a second glance as he merges back onto the streets. "Very interesting."

San closes in around him. He picks his way through the wilting alleys, careful to watch his feet at the inclining steps on certain corners and paying even more attention at the declining ones in case he trips. If it weren't so dark, he might take the rooftops instead, hopping from building to building above the city instead of below, but at this hour, there will be Crescent Society members peddling drugs and littering needles, and Anton isn't eager to get into more fights than necessary, especially if they're not game related.

He hasn't been walking long when he comes across another gathering. Curiosity slows his stride. There's a clump of people inside a small shop—one of those little corner businesses among hundreds that line the street-sides, operating in close proximity to one another. While the shops next to it have shuttered, this one has its overhead lights thrown on, and the owner stands right in the middle upon a table, raving to his captive audience.

Instinctively, Anton eyes a body in the crowd and prepares to jump again, just to get the itch out of his system. Then his gaze catches on the shop owner delivering his spiel, and though he hears none of what the middle-aged man is saying, he does see the flashing wristband.

A better idea occurs to him. He doesn't mull on it a second time; once his mind is made, the course is set. Anton Makusa has always liked being the initial aggressor, and it has served him well for as long as he can remember . . . though, really, that isn't saying much. Anton remembers very little of his childhood, nothing but shades and impressions when he tries to think back. Maybe it's grief that has pushed it away. Maybe it's trauma, his mind protecting him from his past because it would hurt more to access it. He doesn't recall the palace before he was given a room alone. He doesn't recall the first eight years of his life except in vague feelings: when his father sat on the council and his mother, the daughter of a former councilmember, strolled through the corridors of the Palace of Earth like she owned the whole kingdom.

The Makusas were high palace nobles. And one day, when his father took the family out on vacation to their house in Kelitu, the province he oversaw in rural Talin, a group of country civilians charged into the house armed to the teeth. That's his earliest memory. It's the only memory that ever plays with vivid color in his mind's eye: his parents, diving in front of Anton and screaming for him to *Get back! Get back! Go hide!* and an intruder swinging steel and five-year-old Buira running and ten-month-old Hana upstairs crying as she woke up from the noise. That moment in time—that everlasting, terrifying moment—is the only reason he still remembers what his parents look like. When they were taking wound after wound, and all Anton could think was *If I could jump into the bad man, I could stop him. I could stop anyone who ever wanted to do bad things. If only I could jump.*

He knows now that it would have made no difference. There were too many of them. His parents might have tried, even if their skill was rusty given the palace's intolerance for jumping, but they were more worried about pushing him out of the way, and then it was too late. Anton had been only eight years old. He could do nothing except hide behind the cupboard and watch his parents die, watch the attackers snatch Buira and storm the house for Hana. He didn't know why they hadn't come searching for him. They had seen him when they entered the house, but he had been spared, maybe because the scene had been too chaotic and he slipped their mind, maybe because he was too old to be of any use. When the palace guard arrived from the distress call, they said his sisters were gone. Assumed dead, but likelier trafficked into rural Talin as farmhands where help was needed. Anton wants to believe they are dead. It seems like a better fate.

They never found out why his parents had been attacked or who was behind it. They simply appointed a new noble as Kelitu's councilmember and settled Anton back into the palace like nothing had ever happened. San-Er doesn't care. The throne doesn't care. Even councilmembers are replaceable if it lets King Kasa avoid acknowledging why his rural civilians hold such ire for his reign.

Anton would develop jumping when he was thirteen. The ability is hereditary, and so he had known he only needed to wait. He had passed those preadolescent years with a feverish energy, testing and testing until, one night, it finally happened.

Then he went overboard. With no parental figure to reprimand him or remind him that jumping was an act frowned upon in their elite society, he scared all his schoolmates with how often he did it—he even scared his best friend when they were reading together on a dull afternoon, jumping in and out of August Avia without permission, but August didn't tell him off. August only asked whether Anton had found anyone he *couldn't* jump into yet.

That was an easy question, the answers all obvious ones. Bodies that were too feverish and sick, which automatically repelled invading jumpers. Doubled bodies that had already reached a two-qi limit. The Weisannas, with their birth-right that somehow allowed an imitation of being doubled. Everyone else was fair game, so long as he concentrated hard enough.

The shop owner has reached the end of his spiel, if the interspersed laughter is any indication. Hovering outside the shop, Anton spots a hooked blade hang-ing off the man's belt, stained at the edges like he hadn't cleaned it properly after its last use. Given Anton's childhood, a natural assumption would be that he couldn't handle bloodshed. But blood is faultless. Blood is only a consequence. Better to draw blood before it can be drawn from you; better to exert power and hold control—to *seize* power and maintain control.

Anton leans his body up against the alley wall. He readies himself. After seven years in exile, he's learned that he'll always choose the easiest path. Not the most honorable, not the cleanest, not the messiest. If he's offered an oppor-tunity, he will take it.

Anton jumps, opening his eyes after the flash of light, standing in the middle of the crowd. They jerk back suddenly, blinking in bewilderment.

"My apologies," Anton says. His voice is scratchy, unaccustomed to such a low timbre. "You may wish to step back." Then he pulls the knife from the player's belt, holds it to his throat, and slashes. He feels the blood move fast, but before it can sap his own qi, Anton is jumping again, invading the body he left by the wall and letting the other player return to his own body, to the gaping wound made in the artery gushing at his neck. The crowd gasps—some in terror, some in delight.

Whatever their reaction, Anton is already hurrying away, looking for the nearest surveillance camera and tapping a finger to his wristband when he spots it. They need to know that it was his doing, in case the reels don't put two and two together without seeing the flash of light. He wants the hit logged to him.

He wants the palace to tremble.

◇◇◇◇◇

August follows the sound of the television broadcast into his study. He barely stops to shake the mud off his shoes first, even as he presses dirty prints onto the gleaming marble tiles. Palace servants apply a new layer of polish to the flooring every afternoon anyway. By tomorrow, all the mud will be gone.

The window in his study is open. When he enters, cheeks reddened from exertion, the cool easterly air from the distant seaside is a shock to his senses.

August reaches for a blindfold on his shelf.

"Dozing on the job?"

Galipei startles, jerking upright in his chair. Beside him sits August—or his birth body, blond head lolled downward and crown lopsided as if he's simply having a rest.

"I figured I'd hear intruders approaching," Galipei mutters, standing, "so long as it wasn't you and your ghost feet."

"Did you hear *me*?"

Galipei jolts again, his stance immediately shifting for combat, before the owner of the voice makes her appearance around the corner and Leida strides into the room. She pulls her breathing mask down to her chin so that they see her thin lips press into a line, immensely unimpressed.

"I'm starting to think you keep around one of the worst Weisannas," she says to August.

"I'm inclined to agree," August replies.

"*Excuse* me," Galipei protests.

They ignore him. August ties the blindfold over his forehead, fixing it just loose enough to fall into the body's eyes after he gets the last glimpse he needs to trigger the jump. When he opens his eyes from his own body, Galipei is already reaching for the one he vacated, a rapid grip around their neck to knock them out before they can grow fully conscious again. In a quick swoop, he throws the body over his shoulder, then takes the stranger from the study and out of the palace without being asked.

"Did something happen?" August asks when only Leida remains. He rises from the chair, working out the crooks and knots in his birth body. Now his shoes are clean, polished with wax and nary a speck of dust on them. His footsteps echo while he walks a slow circle of the room, trailing his finger over the desk and bookshelves. There is space—more space than necessary—up here, in the tallest turret of the palace.

"We picked up all the casualties." Leida puts her hands in her pockets, rustling her black nylon coat. She dresses in dark colors to blend in with San-Er, as does the rest of the guard, but contrary to the very purpose of dressing for concealment, Leida Miliu also wears dark-blue glitter around her dark-blue eyes regardless of which body she is in. When they were sixteen, August very narrowly escaped being her experiment because Leida had noticed his eyes carried that ring of blue in them and wanted to see whether glitter would bring out the color more.

Since her mother passed away last year and she was promoted, Leida no longer has time for the nonsense of tricking August into putting glitter on his eyes. Neither does August, really, but he has never had the time. Leida merely possesses the magnetic pull to demand anything she wants, even if her closest schoolmate was also the crown prince of San. She's only twenty-one years old, the same age as August, but given their peers used to joke that Leida Miliu came out of the womb giving orders, it's easy to see how the palace guards fell in line before her without the slightest muttering of dissent. Other units outside of San-Er are led by generals, slow-moving armies dispersed across Talin to maintain peace. San-Er's streets and buildings are not suited for large formations and order. They suit quick thinking and dirty tricks, and Leida has plenty of both. The palace guard runs entirely under her command, dispersed in little groups and reporting back to her a whole image of San-Er to piece together how the twin cities fare.

The cities are not thriving. But that's less Leida's fault and more the all-powerful incompetence that sits on the throne.

"Did you hear the report we gave out? Twenty-three hits since midnight."

August perches on the side of his desk, hands braced to either side of him. Galipei returns too, but instead of coming into the study again, he hovers at the circular doorway, picking at the whorls carved into the wood there.

"You phrased that as if we gave false information," August says plainly. "Did we?"

"No," Leida answers. "Twenty-three eliminations is correct." She pauses. "But if you paid attention to the count that the newscasters gave, only twenty-one were attributed to the players. You think anyone will notice the math?"

"Did they leave the games voluntarily?" Galipei asks from the doorway.

Leida reaches into her coat. She brings out a set of photographs, and though it was Galipei who made the suggestion, she doesn't spare him a glance, continuing to address only August.

"We can hope that the rest of San-Er assumes so, but we found the two other bodies. Both happened out of sight from any camera. Yaisu sickness."

August frowns. He gestures for the photographs. *The yaisu sickness.* Jumping, at the end of the day, is still a dangerous matter. Fail too many attempts to invade another body, and your own will start to burn from the inside out, unable to handle the barrage of exit and re-entry each time you're kicked back. He hasn't heard of a case in so long. Not since Otta. There have been other instances, surely, but no one is bringing them to the palace's attention when jumping is forbidden in the first place. They merely take the loss. If his palace-raised half sister couldn't be saved, there's little chance that anyone else in San-Er can survive the burning once it starts.

"Murder?" Galipei suggests, his voice booming from the door again. "The yaisu sickness can be brought on by another culprit."

If the murderer moves fast enough. In and out and in and out, using different bodies nearby to make landings but returning into the same victim. Then the body burns up, trapping the original occupant's qi and condemning them to death.

Leida finally turns to face Galipei, mouth pinched. "Murder, yes," she says. "But . . ."

"But why do the bodies look like this?" August says, finishing her thought. He crooks a single finger at his bodyguard, and Galipei bounds in quickly. When Galipei comes to his side to peer at the photographs too, his silver eyes widen, swallowing the light in the room.

"This is—"

"The Sican salute," Leida confirms. "Which is incomprehensible. How could Sicans have gotten into San-Er?"

Both elbows outward, fingers pressed together and thumbs cast straight to make a triangular shape. Flip open any textbook about Talin's war with Sica, and the Sican salute is the first image to be printed as an introduction: the proud gesture of a conquering, warmongering nation. Except here, it's awkward and stiff on both bodies, because their arms were certainly forced into the salute after death. The first photograph shows a burned corpse at the back of a shop. The walls stand sparse and bare, but the floors are littered with aluminum foil, blackened with the stains of heroin vapor. Depending on their priorities, some players will take their coins to these sorts of places first, pump themselves as high as the clouds before going to gather weaponry.

The second photograph is a similar scene. A burned corpse at . . . a factory, August guesses. There are machine pieces scattered near the body, misshapen springs and broken levers that were likely shoved into a back room as the quickest method of discarding unwanted objects.

"Even if they made it past the city wall," August muses, "how did they get an identity number?"

Leida stays silent. Galipei's frown deepens. Since their war with Sica, Talin's regulations have stayed the same. No identity number, no entry into San-Er.

The only reason why San-Er has a wall surrounding it in the first place is because it was the last stronghold before Talin finally won the war. The twin cities, located in the kingdom's southeast like a little tail, were the nation's last salvation at a time of need and their enemies' defeat, now the beating heart of Talin even while situated at its very, very corner. There used to be other cities inland, but they never recovered from being turned into battlegrounds, their deterioration exacerbated by heavy casualties and negligent bureaucrats. As time went on, it became easier for the countryside to migrate to the new capital rather than rebuild and tend to its problems, while San-Er advanced and built new factories, invented new technology and installed better signal towers, the rest of the provinces seemed to move backward, unable to put a plug in their drain of labor. Too many councilmembers have already complained about the ghost cities in their assigned provinces, a waste when those buildings could be torn down and the land used as farm plots more suited for the rural skill sets that remain prevalent past the wall of San-Er.

Despite the palace's preparedness for war, Sica has not posed a problem since its defeat. The border holds steady, cutting a line down the middle of the near-uninhabitable borderlands between the two nations. Talin minds its own, with most of its conquest energy on its rural provinces; Sica started expanding in the other direction, nursing its wounds after wasting so many resources failing to invade Talin.

If these deaths are truly a message from Sica, it is hard to imagine what could have prompted such a change in the air.

"Either way," Leida says suddenly, taking the photographs from August and gathering them up in her hands, "I'll keep an eye on the situation. Someone or other will report to the king once we've gauged the foreign threat—"

A series of drums play through the palace wing. August, Leida, and Galipei all freeze, running an immediate sweep of their eyes through the study, making the quickest catalog of what is currently out in the open. With that herald, a

71

commotion of activity follows before two royal guards push through into the study, yelling an all-clear.

King Kasa follows closely.

August breathes out. He levels his expression: pleasant, jovial, always at the ready to accommodate his king.

"August," King Kasa says. His golden-robed clothes are pristine, but his expression is haggard. He has been aging faster these past few years, looking wearier with every new day. Lines carve deeply into the sides of his eyes, the corners of his mouth. If August were a more patient person, he might wait for the natural tide to take his adopted father instead.

But he is not.

"You will come see me after the day's reels have finished."

The instruction has no room for argument. August inclines his head.

"Yes, of course," he replies smoothly. When his gaze darts to the side, Leida taps silently at the desk, where she has set down the photographs. August clears his throat, then adds, "If I may, there is some strange business that the palace guards have seen."

King Kasa puts his hand behind his back. His eyes narrow, and his wrinkles deepen tenfold. "How so?"

"There are yaisu deaths. We may have to investigate—"

But King Kasa is already walking out. "Deal with it," he calls back. "Report soon."

The guards trail behind him. The drums herald him into another part of the palace. And before long, the study is quiet again in the wake of the visit.

Unbelievable.

His Majesty hasn't left the perimeter of the palace in five years, and nothing will prompt him to do so now. No one can tell him otherwise. Er's councilmembers govern the sixteen provinces of Talin on the north side of the Jinzi River, while San's councilmembers govern the twelve provinces on the south side, which lie closer to the twin cities. The basin of the Jinzi River was the original site of Talin's civilization, in the days when the history books speak of old gods walking among mankind. Centuries passed, and the southward floods of the river turned the land plentiful for wet crops and produce, cultivating rice paddies for its farmers. The north stayed dry, which meant fields of grain and wheat and grazing animals, dependent only on the rainfall with the farther they migrated from the river. They used to keep Talin's palaces out there: the Palace of Heavens to the north, and the Palace of Earth to the south. Then the war with Sica came, and the nobles of the kingdom funneled into San-Er for protection. The Palace of Heavens was rebuilt in Er, the Palace of Earth in San, and once the war was over, there was no need to move again when they could assign council-members to overlook the territory they had once controlled directly, especially while San-Er flourished into Talin's core metropolis. The kings of Talin became the kings of San-Er, and the rest of the provinces became mere collateral re-sources that the twin cities could suckle at whenever was convenient.

Even a few years ago, when Calla's parents were still around, they used to meet with Kasa, sharing the reports their separate councils gave about each province, reviewing Talin's matters in tandem. Now, the councilmembers of Er report to King Kasa directly, the affairs of twenty-eight provinces and two cities directed to his solitary throne at the corner of the kingdom. The armies listen to their generals, the generals are loyal to their province councilmembers, and the whole council bows down to King Kasa. Such power is impossible to break without breaking the very nation. August is certain of this. The system has been instilled so deeply and for so long that the only possible path toward betterment is a smooth transference of the crown.

August pinches the bridge of his nose. He feels Leida's and Galipei's heavy observataion like a physical sensation. Instead of turning to meet either of them, he faces his window, searching for the line in the twin cities where the water cuts between San and Er. The palace turret is high up enough to sight it.

"Have you run through the names of the contestants?"

Leida's switch in topic takes him aback. He frowns. "Of course. I looked through all the entries before the lottery was drawn."

"Then you were slacking. Look at who was assigned to number Eighty-Six."

She pulls a screen from her pocket and passes the clunky device. August presses the left button, flipping through the names backward.

88 — Decre Talepo.

87 — Sai Liugu.

86 — Cedar Yanshu.

He senses Leida's observation grow even heavier. There is no minutia that she will miss while tending to palace tasks. She's waiting for his every reaction, watching to gauge if he is telling a white lie or genuinely in the dark. Leida doesn't know about his plan to recruit Calla as his weapon, so he's careful not to appear too flippant. Or else she might ask why he doesn't care, why he is so certain that every other player is going to die anyway.

"Cedar Yanshu," August reads aloud. He waits for something to register.

"Did you forget about those letters we got last year?" Leida asks.

August looks up from the screen immediately.

"No," he says, realization dawning. It is both an answer and a reaction. *No*, he did not forget. *No*, this is absolutely ridiculous.

"That's a stolen identity number," Leida says. Her voice leaves no room for doubt. "It's Anton Makusa."

The same identity he used last year to try to scam money from the palace. The moment he was caught, he disappeared again, returning to his exiled invisibility. Despite himself, August flicks his eyes to a spot on the wallpaper, a rectangular shape where a picture frame used to hang before it was torn right off. He couldn't get rid of its sun-faded imprint—because this part of the palace actually gets sunlight, unlike everywhere else in San—without tearing the wallpaper down and renovating the study anew, so even with the picture gone, its phantom remains. August, Anton, and Leida: the three of them a formidable trio with plans to transform Talin.

Before Anton walked away from them.

"Should we take him out?" Galipei asks.

August tosses the device onto his desk. He wipes his hands like the screen was slick with grime.

"It's fine," he says tightly. "He won't be trouble. He doesn't have the resources to be trouble. I don't want to draw more attention to this than necessary, and Anton is nothing if not an attention seeker."

He's also a powerful jumper. One who might put up a fight against Calla, who needs to win. But the mistake has been made, Anton Makusa has been drawn into the games, and now there's nothing to do except let him play and try not to wince when someone takes him down.

Before Leida can argue against the verdict, something tremendous shakes in the distance, creaking the floor beneath their feet. At once, August and Galipei hurry to the window, searching through the night. The disturbance is easy to see: an explosion engulfs a section of Er, the flames flickering high and tossing debris off the buildings it has swallowed.

Leida sighs. She strolls to the window too, albeit with an unhurried air.

"That's going to be tiresome to sort out," she says. "We'd better hope the nonplayer casualties are too poor to bring it to the council."

August says nothing. All else is forgotten in that moment, even Calla Tuoleimi and Anton Makusa, both entered as players in the king's games. There is much to tend to, starting with possible foreign intruders in his city wreaking havoc before he can take over.

He reaches out and slams his window closed.

CHAPTER 6

I f Calla hadn't grown up in the Palace of Heavens surrounded by maps and encyclopedias, she might have believed that a different kingdom beckons at the edge of San-Er, right where the land ends and gives way to sea.

She stands at the cliffs, looking out into the water. Each wave collides with harsh impact. Sprays salt up onto the city in droplets and splashes. There's nowhere else in San-Er that feels like this, like she could dive past the jagged rockface, slice into the water, and then just keep going and going. Ten paces to her left, she would merge back into the alleyway and the city of San would envelop her again. But so long as she stands here, she is the ruler of this new kingdom, the conqueror of a large, unknowable terrain.

Calla breathes in deep, folding her arms over her chest to fight off the chill. Along the rest of the coastline, the twin cities have built small bays to let fishermen push their boats out to sea, but the truth is, no one goes very far. South of San-Er, there is only nothingness. Venturing too great a distance risks complete disorientation, losing all chance of return. Some of Talin's bravest travelers say there are other island-nations out in the waters, but if they do exist, they are of no use to the kingdom. As far as Talin is concerned, their only foreign contact is in the north, past the rural provinces and bleeding up into Sica.

A shiver dances along her spine. Calla turns over her shoulder.

The palace claims that, before there was just San and Er in the southeast, ruled by one family and two kings, there used to be a third island city along the edges of Er, hundreds of years ago. A third king, who had also held some part of Talin, fleeing when Sica came. Then its ruler was struck down by divine intervention, deemed unfit to govern, and when he refused to relinquish his throne despite edicts from their gods, the entire city sank into the waters along with its civilians.

Calla has always had trouble believing that story. In the era before surveillance cameras and electronic records, the palace could change the truth whenever they wished, and their tale about a third city that once stood in the distance seems too convenient to be true. Unlike the rest of the kingdom, Calla doesn't even believe in divine will. If there are gods, then they are cruel for letting Talin carry on like this. Day after day, with no end in sight.

Calla finally steps away from the cliffs. She returns to the alley that will take her back into San, ducking into the tight passage with resolve tightening in her stomach. The time for lingering has passed. Her course of action today, which is not so different from these past few days since the Daqun, is to linger around the busiest parts of San, where she's most likely to find the other players. It's early morning, but the streets fall darker the moment she leaves the city periphery, moving farther inland. Grimacing, she pinches her nose to block out the acrid smells as she passes a row of factories. They rumble belowground, machines churning long bundles of noodles running side by side with those producing coat hangers and rubber plungers.

"Careful!"

Calla is ducking before the call even comes, swerving away from two men and the stepladder carried between them. They're covered in sweat, stripped down to the waist from the factory heat. Some cramped streets in San exist without fuss, where one can only hear the all-surround symphony of their dripping pipes. Others are their own revolving worlds, bursting with activity of every sort. When Calla finally reaches a quieter walkway, she releases her nose and takes a deep breath. The air still stinks. Water collects in every grimy nook, but wet rot is better than the stench of trash.

She looks at her wristband. No alarm. The day of the Daqun is always a whirl-wind, followed by silence thereafter. The palace does this on purpose, giving the games a false lull before they start sending their location pings. In such a dense environment, players could hide themselves away forever if they wanted to, and because there's nothing entertaining about that, each player is sent an alarm once a day to direct them toward their nearest competitor. Without these daily pings, they would be playing entirely based on luck, hoping to catch a flash of a wristband in the open. One round could last years. Even if Calla watches the newsreels and tries to remember her competitors' faces, most will change bodies at breakneck speed. Only Calla stays unchanging, opting to put a mask over her face instead.

She adjusts her mask cover, her face growing hot when it traps in her sigh. There is only one objective to playing in the games. Wipe the other players out as fast as possible, get her victory, kill the king. The quicker she does it, the quicker they are freed from this awful state of living. The quicker this collective suffering can ease and stop clanging through her ears every second.

As if the wristband heard her urges, it suddenly buzzes against her skin. Calla's heart begins to pound. *Finally.* She almost forgets her training, tempted to surge forward immediately in her eagerness. But her body knows how to re-gain control, its muscle memory running through the same series of commands: *Breathe in, calibrate, formulate action.* As she whips her arm up to tap the screen, she heaves a deep breath, letting the stench of the street still her nerves. They'll ping players in pairs or in small groups, which means it won't happen until they're within range of one another. The palace is always watching the wristbands move; they'll put in the alarm when the players aren't close enough to be ambushed, but aren't far enough to engage in a wild goose chase. Calla has time. She lets the rush of incoming battle temper her bones.

2 players nearby. Choose.

An arbitrary decision. She keys in the number 1 at the bottom of the screen, then looks around to take inventory of her surroundings. To her left, an impenetrable wall. To her right, another wall, but with a window that peers into a gambling den.

11 meters up.

Calla moves. She shoves her foot against a jutting brick and climbs in through the window, drawing cries of concern when she lands with a thump on the sticky den floor.

"Don't mind me," she says. She blows a kiss, which is rather difficult through the mask. "I'm only passing through."

Outside the gambling den, she skids into the main stairwell of the building, then sprints up the steps three at a time, boots clunking. Calla calculates the eleven meters, bursting through the first inner door she sees and emerging in a busy market area, shops on both sides and her wristband trembling incessantly. Her hair whips into her eyes as she peruses the scene, trying to catch an attack before it comes. Nothing seems out of the ordinary.

Nothing except Calla, standing in a leather coat with her sword sheathed at her side while shoppers in their plain cotton button-ups stare at her.

"Where are you?" Calla mutters under her breath, gauging the distance between floor and ceiling. About two meters, probably. Flat floor, flat ceiling. How many other levels has she climbed? Six? Which means . . .

Calla hurries through the market, searching for some other exit. She passes a candy store. A noodle shop. Finally, in front of a butcher whacking his cleaver down onto a pig's carcass, Calla spots a hatch inside his stall.

"Using this, thank you!" Calla calls, diving for the hatch and lifting it with a grunt. She jumps down before the butcher can respond, dropping into the passage running below the market. Vendors store their perishables here to keep them fresh, cold air running at a temperature that raises goose bumps on her arms immediately. She lands among a row of animal carcasses hanging by large hooks, her hands slapping onto the bloody floor to steady herself. Though she would have assumed the blood to be dried and old, when she lifts her hands and stands straight, her palms are marred with bright crimson. It's fresh.

She's already late to the party.

Calla's gaze whips up. Her eyes adjust to the back of the storage space, just in time to catch a player slash his knife across the throat of another, splattering more blood everywhere. The body drops, red pooling onto the floor. In seconds, it has flowed within distance of Calla's boots, the dimly lit passageway reeking of the metallic stink.

"Fuck."

She presses the first button on her wristband, stopping it from trembling. If the low sound didn't already signal her presence, her voice has certainly summoned the attention of the surviving player. He turns, tossing one of his knives into his other hand, wiping the blood from his face. There's a drop hanging just by his lip, and when his finger reaches it, he puts it right into his mouth, licking the blood clean off.

Absolutely depraved.

Calla draws her sword. There's not a moment to spare when she lifts it against his strike, one knife in each of his hands now, clanging down upon her. The crescent-curved blades stop inches from Calla's face, and she stifles a wince, eyes darting to take in her opponent. Her first instinct is to wonder if this is a Crescent Society member, but she sees no markings. A coincidence that he carries their usual weapons, then.

Suddenly, the player hooks his blades down hard, and Calla almost drops the sword. He's good. Too good. When he looks up, his eyes are black, and Calla blinks, certain for a moment that this is August. She lets go of her sword intentionally, taking the player by surprise when both their weapons clatter to the floor and her gloved hand whips toward him. She grabs his neck. Hooks her foot behind his knees.

There is one lightbulb in the passageway, hanging from the short ceiling. Going off her hunch, she seizes his jaw roughly as soon as they hit the floor, but when she turns his eyes toward the light, they come back flashing purple, not blue.

Not August. Someone else.

"Number Fifty-Seven," he says suddenly. He slams an elbow to her head, and when Calla spits a curse, he's quick to twist upright and press her into the bloody floor instead, his arm pinned upon her clavicle. In an instant, Calla turns her face away from the light, shaking her hair into her eyes. Where did his knives land? Nearby?

"How do you know who I am?" She reaches for her sword. The player stretches out to stop her. As soon as his attention snaps elsewhere, however, his hold on her eases a smidgeon, and she takes the opening to aim a hard kick to his middle and send him flying. Sword and knives alike lie scattered on the floor. The two of them pause, a standstill in the fight as they draw up their next moves.

The player smiles. The expression radiates into every line of his being, screaming with an appalling confidence, the kind that lights up a body no matter the vessel being occupied, no matter what sort of mouth is snarling its corners up.

The player lunges for his knives; Calla gets there first. By the narrowest margin, her fingers close around her sword grip, sending the blade up, which only makes the player smile harder when he swerves away. She's almost inclined to respect his terrifying boldness. This isn't what she expected out of the other combatants. A part of her likes it. It has gotten monotonous to be leagues above everyone else. Calla Tuoleimi is positioned to win every battle—that is not up for debate—but every once in a while, a challenge does enliven her spirit.

"Of course I know who you are," he replies, bringing his knives to his side. "It'd be very hard not to take notice."

Calla lands a strike, cutting his arm. He hisses and surges back, but Calla follows fast and slashes with her sword again. This time, he defends himself faster, and her blade only meets the carcass hanging to his right.

She yanks the sword out of the dead cow. "You're probably mistaken."

"I never make mistakes," the player replies. He hovers in his stance, watching her carefully. He's waiting to pick out a flaw in her fight patterns, waiting to sight a weakness he can exploit.

In a smooth arc, Calla transfers her sword from right hand to left and swings. "You must be some sort of god, then." He swerves, the blade missing his throat by the barest hairsbreadth. "What an honor it is"—she tries again, nicking his chest—"to kill a god."

The player wipes a smear of blood from his temple. He finally cannot back away any further, coming to the wall. Beside him, the player he already killed lies unblinking. The light is strong here, coming directly from that one bulb.

And somehow, his smile is back.

"You're beautiful."

Calla snorts behind her mask. "You can't see me."

"Who says I have to?"

"Do you flirt with every person you're trying to kill?"

"Only you, Fifty-Seven."

Finally, when she attacks again, he lifts his knives to meet her. They move in a blur, in a brutal and coordinated dance, making a mess of the storage room around them. It is difficult to decipher whether it's a piece of a carcass or a real limb until a beat after the strike, when congealed black blood bursts from the pig's ribs and splatters to the floor.

She can hear him breathing heavily. So long as they keep up this dance, she will outlast his maneuvers, and at his first stumble, she can strike—

The hatch into the storage room opens. A burst of sound drops in from the market above, and the other player looks up, giving Calla the chance to plunge her sword into his chest without hesitation.

Only as soon as the hilt of her sword strikes against chest bone, there's a blinding flash of light. Calla flinches, forcing herself not to look away. When the light clears, the body before her has murky-gray eyes, his mouth agape in surprise.

Calla tears out the sword, her teeth gritted in irritation. Without looking, she holds down the second button of her wristband, summoning emergency services. The body before her might survive if they stitch it up fast enough.

"Hey," Calla shouts. She grabs ahold of the ladder, hauling herself out of the storage passage. "I know you're still here!"

The people around the market stare at her in horror when she emerges. She stares right back, easing herself up from the hatch, sword still in her grip. He left his knives down there. More importantly, he left his wristband down there, and when players jump in the games, they need to move their wristband from body to body too, or else they face elimination at the twenty-four-hour mark when they haven't entered their identity number.

Calla stands, her knee twinging. She must have been hit at some point. She hardly noticed.

"Come out, come out," she sings, searching the faces before her for some signal of recognition. The lighting is too dim to find his black eyes. She turns on her heel . . .

Calla was expecting the player to return to the hatch so he could retrieve his belongings. Except at that moment, she catches a blur of movement farther down the market, and spots *another* open hatch in the floor.

Shit. There's more than one.

She breaks into a run. The crowd gets in her way immediately, as does a stack of chicken cages squawking one atop the other. When she finally circles around both roadblocks and skids to a stop beside the other hatch, it has slammed closed and won't lift when she tugs.

Not good. Too long has passed. Calla whips around, the hairs at the back of her neck standing ramrod straight, eyes pinned on the first hatch, now in the distance. The player would have to leave through that one, but has he come out already?

The people around the market shrink back as she lifts her sword in preparation. Where is the player, and how did he—

Calla feels a pressure on her left arm. Then a lack of weight when her wristband is plucked right off.

She whirls around.

"Goodbye!" the boy cries, his black eyes flashing under the market lights as he turns and runs.

Calla blinks. She is so taken aback that the player managed to occupy a *child* that she doesn't give chase until he is almost out of sight. By the time she sprints after him, he has already turned the corner. By the time she turns the corner too, the child is in the middle of climbing out through an unpaneled window.

They're six floors up from the ground. What does he think he's doing?

"Hey!"

He leaps. Calla rushes to the window, unable to believe her eyes. Once she glances down, however, she realizes the building has a net at its side, catching all the trash and debris to protect the temple below. The child bounces on the net, facedown, but the two wristbands slip through the gaps, dropping to the pavement around the temple. There's a flash of light.

The player has gotten away.

Calla touches her bare wrist. He has eliminated her from the games without killing her. She can count on one hand the number of times a player has made a non-lethal elimination over the years, not out of kindness but out of strategy. If someone absolutely cannot make a kill, they can force a withdrawal instead. Most players prefer the blood spilt. This one clearly recognized that he could not best Calla and chose to wait out the twenty-four hours until her wristband is deemed inactive.

"Well, that was fucking annoying," Calla mutters. She forces herself to take a deep breath. She's not a regular player; she has August to keep the wristband active. So it doesn't matter. She can get it back and stay in the games.

But she certainly underestimated whoever she just came in contact with.

◇◇◇◇◇

One room in the palace controls all the surveillance cameras across the cities, and so it is in a constant state of upheaval, each cubicle barely managing its responsibilities by the skin of its teeth. There used to be *half* the number of wires jutting out from the middle of the room and running across the floor like live snakes. Then the Palace of Union took in Er's control centers too, and now the electric companies break into a cold sweat every time they have to check the gauge for this part of San.

At the far cubicle, Pampi Magnes taps a series of commands on her bulky keyboard, eyes tracking the security cameras and conciliating them with the screen to her left. Her wrist itches, but she doesn't scratch. Even as a wisp of hair slides out of her ponytail and irritates the side of her cheek, she only resolves to tighten her ponytail tomorrow, maybe slick back her pin-straight black hair with gel.

She stays focused, her mouth puckered. Where the larger screen peruses footage of the twin cities, shuffling between different streets under her watch and showing movement from both outside and within the buildings, the small screen propped above her desk is a lay plan of the sector, showing only pinpoints that move when the players and their wristbands do.

Number Ten and Number Sixty-Four start to get nearer and nearer. She waits, observing whether Twenty-Three—lingering at the very border of her surveillance sector—will move in the same direction, but Twenty-Three walks away before long. Pampi hits the arrow keys until she can see Ten and Sixty-Four on the larger screen.

She presses more commands. The location pings go out.

14 meters to the left.

14 meters to the right.

The bright dots start to surge toward each other. The chaos on the larger screen is instant, food carts and trash bins overturned as the players break into a run and hurry to spot their opponent first. Pampi finally scratches her wrist, glancing over her shoulder. When she sees that the cubicles to either side of her are occupied with their own pings, she drags the clicker along her screen and sends a command over to the printer in the corner of the room.

Just as she is rising from her chair to go fetch the papers, the palace guards filter into the surveillance room.

"Pull up the border," Leida Miliu demands, and Pampi quickly slides her chair back into her desk again, hunching into her stall. She won't be seen. Not now, not yet.

Her colleagues who are unfortunate enough to be seated near the door scramble to their keyboards. One by one, their screens flicker to a different section of the wall around San. From what Pampi can see, peeking over her shoulder, the scene looks quiet. Leida Miliu, however, leans close to the screens, eyes narrowed like she's searching for something else.

The colleague next to Pampi peers over their cubicle divider, cigar dangling from his mouth.

"You have any clue what they're looking for?"

Pampi's eyes shoot to the printer. She swipes a hand across her clicker and clears her recent activity history.

"Aren't they always looking for something?" she asks.

"Yeah, *within* the city," the colleague replies. He puffs on the cigar, and Pampi wrinkles her nose, brushing a hand along her pressed collar, hoping the silk won't reek of the smell. "I hear the alarm is up for intruders trying to sneak into San-Er without citizenship."

He says it without conviction, merely repeating what others are whispering. It's a near impossibility, and most of San-Er is unconvinced. In all the years that the wall has been up, not once has anyone entered without permission, nor taken an illegal step in without being caught within seconds. Citizens of San-Er are either assigned an identity number at birth or granted one through immigration from the outside. Rural dwellers flock to the twin cities by the hundreds of thousands every year, especially right before the games. A handful will get citizenship; the remaining disperse to the nearest villages outside the wall, trying and trying each time the citizenship pool opens, usually to no avail.

Since Er's palace went down, it has become San's task to process the new immigration requests. They're still letting people in day after day. San-Er has long been full to the brim, one uneasy exhale away from collapsing in on itself. But even among such chaos, the twin cities are inhospitable to anyone without citizenship. Its streets are filled with thieves who snatch bodies like candy, and the rich will try their hardest to make it difficult for those playing imposter. Forget jobs and bank accounts being accessible only by identity number. Homes and offices open to identity numbers; public buildings have turnstile systems at their entryways requiring identity numbers for visitors passing through. Someone who sneaks in from the provinces could perhaps beg on the streets all their life, but even then, there's only so much time until a palace guard accosts them, demanding proof of their government-assigned identity.

"*I* hear," Pampi says, "that they're not merely intruders, but *Sicans*."

The man with the cigar grimaces and starts to ease away from the cubicle divider. There's too much unrest in the outermost areas of Talin right now to be speaking such nonsense. Pampi knows it, but she wants to test just how much she can get away with inside the palace.

"There cannot be Sicans in the kingdom," he says, though his surety of the claim wavers before he has even finished his sentence. San-Er is safe, but Talin is not. And if Talin is unguarded, then isn't it possible that foreign intruders might have arrived, that they might have found a way to enter the capital after time spent lurking in the provinces?

Pampi sneaks another look at the guards. When her colleague sits down at his desk and turns back to his computer, she allows herself the ghost of a smile. Under her sleeve, a blue crescent-moon tattoo is inked into the white of her skin.

Leida slaps her hand on the surveillance room door, startling those who are pretending not to watch her.

"Back to work," she shouts. "Keep the games in order, understand?"

She receives a series of affirmative responses. Everyone is too afraid of the captain of the guard to argue, lest they end up like the people she has hauled into a jail cell for no reason other than because they looked at her wrong.

Pampi hunches over her screens and waits for the palace guards to exit. Once the room returns to its usual activity, she goes to fetch the papers she's printed. Good. This will be useful.

In the handbag under her desk, her own wristband flashes the number 2, sitting idle in wait.

CHAPTER 7

The restaurants that operate near the coliseum are less a row of build-ings and more a collective operational body, second-floor kitchens with staircases that lead into the first-floor sitting area of another unit and third-floor seating areas that only get patrons from the dumpling shop on the fourth floor, directly above. Though San-Er is claustrophobic, at least everything one could want is always within reach.

Calla plucks a dish from a waitress's platter as she passes, leaving a coin in its place. The waitress doesn't even notice, too busy trying to fulfill the breakfast orders being shouted in her direction. With one finger twisting around the cord of the landline she's standing beside, Calla clamps down on the receiver with her shoulder, then uses her free hand to pinch the top of a dumpling and plop it into her mouth. She's barely listening to August on the other end.

"—you have to get it back. I'm not amused at all, Calla."

"When did I suggest this would be amusing?" she asks, words muffled around her mouthful of dumpling. She makes a round shape with her lips, sucking air in to cool the rich meat and salted cabbage on her tongue. It burns her throat as it goes down, but the fridge in her apartment has been bare since yesterday, so even the cheapest dumplings taste as good as gold on her empty stomach. She can imagine August pinching the bridge of his nose as he listens to her eating.

"None of this is going to work if you're eliminated."

"Hey," Calla says. She swallows her food and clears her throat to speak again. "Can you please get it together? I was already in these games before you got involved. I'm not getting eliminated that easily."

August gives an irritated huff. "Fine. I can keep your wristband functioning so that it doesn't expire today. Just get it back. Which player took it?"

Calla shrugs, then realizes that her cousin cannot see her. She was given his personal cellular number, but it's been so long since she used a telephone—not since she was in Er's palace—that she hardly remembers how they function. He's already furious that she didn't contact him immediately when the incident took place yesterday, but it isn't her fault that she needed to hunt down a public line first.

"I don't know," she replies. "I didn't think to ask while I was trying not to get stabbed. Male. Tall. Pale."

Another vexed noise from August. None of those physical descriptors mean anything when the body she's describing is at the hospital, returned to its original occupant. The newsreels had too much to cover last night with the first location pings starting across the twin cities, so Calla hadn't seen the fight at the market broadcast anywhere. Most of the battle had happened out of view from the cameras, in that storage space, so there was very little footage to offer. Today's reruns might insert coverage of Calla's wristband being stolen when they finish filtering through the bloodiest footage for the more boring encounters— Calla only needs to wait until one network is interested enough to announce her thieving opponent's number. After that, August can look at his lists and get her a name. She supposes that he could also go into the surveillance room right now and find the footage himself, but he's already meddling to keep her wristband active, and Leida Miliu might start asking questions if he attempts anything more.

"Start tracking him down," August demands, though surely he knows there isn't much Calla can do at present. "And keep an eye out—there's a possibility that the twin cities have been infiltrated by foreign agents from Sica. Their motive is unclear."

Calla frowns. She picks up another dumpling, but this time she only gnaws at the edges of its floury skin. "Are they planning to invade?"

"Again, hard to say."

"We're not even in contact with Sica anymore." At least, that was the case five years ago, the last time Calla got a glimpse into Talin's national affairs.

"Which is precisely why I'm puzzled," August says. "I can keep you updated. Just . . . find the idiot who took your wristband and eliminate him quickly."

Calla takes a proper bite of the dumpling. The hot juice inside dribbles down her chin, and she hurries to catch it. Heavens, if her old palace etiquette tutors could see her, they would have a heart attack. "Yes, Prince August. Your wish is my command."

August hangs up without a response. Meanwhile, when Calla sets the landline down, she chews thoughtfully on the rest of the dumpling, mulling over what August said. *Foreign agents from Sica.* The last maps she saw on her parents' tables had been pencil drawn, showing a completed conquest of the rural outskirts and almost broaching the mountains that separate their kingdom from Sica. Perhaps King Kasa has been inching even farther into the borderlands. Perhaps Sica is sending people to put a stop to it. And if that's the case, then she wishes they wouldn't, not for the same reasons as August, but because she's already fucking on it.

A flash of movement in her periphery breaks her train of thought. Calla swivels suddenly, just in time to see a kid duck behind a potted plant, like he didn't expect her to look his way. His hand closes around one of the large plant trunks, sleeve slipping up and revealing a wristband.

Calla draws her sword.

"Wait, please, don't!" the kid bellows. He emerges from behind the plant, arms above his head. His eyes are a dusty violet, the same as the flowers that grow by the Rubi Waterway. "You should at least wait until you get your wristband back."

"What?" Calla pulls a face. She doesn't have her mask on during meals, so it reaches the kid with full effect. "How much did you hear?"

The kid's gaze flickers over to the tables, and then, making an almost visible effort to lower his voice, he says, "Enough to hear you address the speaker on the other end as August."

Calla raises the sword higher, intent on making a strike and eliminating this potential leak. The kid throws his arms up again. Though his cheeks have a babyish roundness to them, his limbs are stick-thin with the mark of hunger.

"Wait, wait, wait! I know who took your wristband."

Oh? Calla lowers her arm. While she's hesitating, another waitress comes around the corner with a tray of food. The waitress pauses abruptly in her step when she sees Calla's sword, mouth opening and closing as if she's debating whether she ought to say something. A second later, she decides to charge right past and disappears down the stairs, the creak of each step echoing against the leaky walls. Calla makes up her mind.

"Come with me," she says, waving the kid closer. Once he is within distance, she clamps a hand to the back of his neck and steers him down the stairs, too, toward a smaller seating area. He looks nervous that her sword is still out, but he makes no remark. Obediently, he lets her push him into a booth, and perks up when she signals for a waiter by the counter to order more food.

"What's your name?" Calla asks, sliding her sword casually into the booth before she follows. At one of the other tables, there's a teenager craning his neck at her, likely trying to gauge whether she's a player of the games. She reaches for a napkin to wipe down the table, but the napkin itself is so dusty that she doubts it achieves much. When she tosses the wad away, she makes eye contact with the teenager and pretends to lurch in his direction. He stops craning and looks away quickly.

"I'm Eno," the kid replies.

"And how old are you, Eno?"

Eno scrunches his nose. "Fifteen. Not sure about this body, though. I gave away my birth one. Didn't like it much."

Calla folds her hands on the table. It's not uncommon for someone to abandon their birth body if there's another vessel they want to take over permanently. Sometimes they'll stumble onto one tossed on the streets. Sometimes two people decide to swap. Usually, though, long-term changes happen after purchasing a desirable vessel for a handsome price on the black market. On a much rarer occasion, there are those who feel so secure in their jumping abilities that they decide to permanently invade a body already occupied, staying doubled for so long that the weaker qi fades away, until only the invader's qi remains and they are once again a single occupant.

No matter the method, it's done persistently throughout San-Er for reasons great and small. If people don't like the way they look. If their birth body binds them to a gender presentation that isn't quite right. A person's qi lasts about a hundred natural years, give or take a decade on either side; that's a long while to spend in a miserable body. Those with the jumping gene can attempt to occupy new youthful bodies as they near the end of the line, but the gods haven't offered anyone true immortality yet. Once someone's qi reaches its end, it will fizzle away, just as someone with qi touched by illness won't grow healthier, no matter how many good bodies they tear through. Rotting qi will eat a body from the inside out until the qi is gone.

Calla can't guess Eno's reason for ditching his birth body, and she doesn't ask. The body that he wears looks younger than fifteen, though that could be Calla's poor gauge of these things too. She's twenty-three, and each year, everyone younger than her only looks more and more like a child. Out of habit, she scans the restaurant to see who is nearby and within view, not only to flag which patrons appear suspicious, but also to mark all of Eno's possible exit routes if he were to jump.

"Do you only invade masculine bodies your age?" she asks casually.

Eno nods. Two options, then. When he reaches over and prods her arm, she catches a flash of his wristband, the screen flashing 51. "This one's pretty. Your birth body?"

Calla smiles, though the expression is wholly a warning as she moves her arm away. ". . . Yes."

"Do you only invade feminine ones?" he asks in return.

"It doesn't matter to me." Calla gestures at the waiter again, catching his attention so he knows where to bring the food. "I don't leave this body, though."

Truth be told, she's never felt like she aligns one specific way, but she enjoys femininity and how it looks on her. Calla is a woman in the same way that the sky is blue. She understands that it's the easiest identifier to slap on and she doesn't mind it, but in actuality, the sky is an incomprehensible void, and Calla, too, feels closer to a nebulous, inexact entity. Before she is anything else, Calla is just . . . Calla.

Eno blinks. "You don't leave it, ever? Do you *have* the jumping gene?"

"Of course."

"But you don't jump? That's dangerous for the games."

It's not just dangerous; it's unheard of. No one would enroll with such a disadvantage—no one except Calla Tuoleimi, apparently.

"Yes, well"—Calla flicks her hair out of her face—"it is what it is."

This is her body. It belongs to her. It *is* her more than any collective identity.

"You didn't tell me your name," Eno says when the waiter sets down two bowls before them. Eno peers inside to find wonton noodles, then digs in immediately.

"Chami," Calla replies after a moment. She retrieves a pair of chopsticks from the dispenser and sticks it into her food. "So. How do you know who took my wristband?"

Eno's eyes light up. For the briefest second, there's hesitation in the posture of his shoulders, in the grip he has on his utensils. Though she says nothing, Calla makes note of it, tucking it away with the other tidbits in her mental inventory.

"I'm part of the Crescent Societies," he says. "Well . . . a new initiate. They let us keep a portion of the earnings if we run enough—"

"The point, please," Calla interrupts.

Eno clears his throat. "Right, right. The temples catch wind of which numbers are making which kills before the news broadcasts it. I heard through our network that Eighty-Six took Fifty-Seven's wristband." He looks Calla directly in the eye, as if to assure her he isn't lying. "I gather there aren't too many players who've lost their wristbands."

Calla leans forward, jabbing at the wontons. Eighty-Six graced the newsreels prominently right after the Daqun, his kills putting him among the group that are fighting for second place below Calla. It's not as if any of them can really upstage her when she's cheating, but it's still early days in the games.

"Who is Eighty-Six, then?" she asks.

"Oh, I know him. We're friendly. His name is Anton Makusa."

Calla's hand stops, frozen over the chopsticks. She has never met Anton Makusa, but she knows the name. She heard it often during her delegation visits to San. He was a palace brat, August's friend before Otta Avia caught the yaisu sickness. His parents were killed when he was young, but that wasn't what made his reputation in San-Er. It was his notorious jumping, flouting the rules and exemplifying the hypocrisy of palace elites by receiving only light punishments each time he was caught.

"He uses one fake identity or another most of the time, though, so you didn't hear it from me. I happened to snoop through his mail once. He lives near the Rubi Waterway, on San's side," Eno continues, not noticing Calla's reaction to the name. "Do you know Big Well Street? Three floors up from the brothel."

Calla leans back into the booth, mystified. She digs into her pocket for a cigarette. Strikes a match and lights it, taking one drag before tipping the ashes into her half-eaten bowl. Eno watches with explicit horror, aghast that she is wasting perfectly good food, but Calla's attention has drifted elsewhere.

How did *Anton Makusa* end up living above a brothel, playing in the games?

"Why are you helping me?" Calla asks suddenly. She blows smoke onto the table, and Eno flinches, coughing. "I hope you realize that you're allowing me to play again. One more contestant back in the ring."

"You were leading the scoreboard," he replies, "and you have some link to Prince August. I don't think you're out of the ring yet."

"Officially speaking, I am."

"But you're going to get yourself back in. And if I do this now, you'll help me later in the games, won't you?"

Calla makes a thoughtful noise from the back of her throat. It comes out rough, sprinkled with gravel. It's awfully bold of the kid to assume that she's the type willing to repay a favor. "You know there can only be one victor."

Eno sticks his nose into the air. "I still intend to give myself the best possible chance at winning. That victor could be me."

Calla snorts. Eno deflates a little. "Okay, well"—he lifts his wristband and taps at the spot where the chip is inserted—"at least I can opt out at any time."

At fifteen, some people haven't even finished developing their jumping yet, never mind honed it enough to compete with a bunch of killers. Calla doesn't like how casually he treats the matter, as if this is some playground adventure instead of a battle to the death.

"Why are you in the games anyway?" she asks. She douses her cigarette in her soup. "You may as well pull that chip now."

"No," Eno says immediately. He's almost at the last scraps of his bowl, still digging away. "My mother is in deep debt. Sooner or later, I'll be dead—if not by starvation, then by menial labor with no end. Might as well take the chance to make some cash."

Of course. These stories are as commonplace as rats in the alleys, and yet Calla still finds herself flinching every time she hears one.

"That's terrible."

Eno shrugs. "What else am I supposed to do? Even the Crescent Societies are no help so far. I'm bound to inherit her collectors one way or another."

She could try to imagine how a debt so large had piled up, but the possibilities are endless. Hospital bills, rent payments, bank loans for rash ideas that the people of San-Er chase to try to survive. Even if Eno hasn't done anything on his own, it's easy to be born into a dark hole of accounts and dues.

You shouldn't have to do anything, Calla wants to tell him. *No one should.*

But she remains quiet. When Eno finishes his bowl, he offers a salute and slides out from the booth, going his own way. Calla lets him leave without a farewell, one arm propped on the table and the other running her fingers over her hair, slicking her bangs out of her eyes and letting her hot forehead breathe. It isn't as though she expected San-Er to improve in the five years she spent hiding out. It isn't as though she was under some delusion that things were changing while she trained in that cramped little room, studying palace and city maps, balancing knives on her fingers and swords on her shoulders. Yet somehow, she thought there might be *some* shift. That the Palace of Heavens going down would rally the people to demand more, would make them realize that something once deemed the heavens *could* fall. She thought their own princess committing the slaughter would spark something in the cities—or at the very least, lead people to ask *why* anyone needed to starve if their rulers could prevent it.

But every year before the games, the riots still disperse within minutes of forming. The complaints go quiet before they can pick up an echo. The average civilian decides it is better to keep their mouths shut than lose their lives in a futile fight.

A shriek outside the restaurant jolts Calla from her reverie. She retrieves her sword, smooths her hair back into place, and halfheartedly throws more coins onto the table. When she peers out the window onto the narrow alley outside, it's so dark that she cannot discern anything, but the scream was high-pitched enough that she would bet it was a child's call. Eno.

There's a rusting metal ladder beside the window. Calla swings out and scrambles down a few rungs before jumping the rest of the way, landing hard. A rat scurries across her boot. She hurries forward, following the commotion and coming upon a brighter intersection.

Here, the buildings lean ever so slightly to the left, letting the sun's rays sneak onto the pavement. It's enough for Calla to clearly see the scene ahead, where another player is swinging an axe at Eno.

Eno ducks just in time, something clutched in his hands. When he brandishes his weapon of choice, it's revealed to be a whip, which might be the most useless weapon someone could have acquired after the Daqun. There's no space in these alleys to move a whip at maximum effect, to swing back and let the tail hit its victim with strength. Indeed, all he achieves is a pitiful hit, and then the axe is coming at him again, landing a fleshy strike on the side of his arm.

Calla's eyes dart to the alley walls. She doesn't see a surveillance camera nearby. This might be a blind spot.

"Ah!" Eno rolls and—to Calla's surprise—is fast enough to collide with the other player's leg, striking the back of the knee and taking her off-balance. The player lands flat on her back, but she remains within range of Eno, so Calla can already guess her next attack. Before the player can gear up, Calla starts to walk, hand braced against her hip. The walk turns to a stride, the stride to a dead sprint, and as the other player heaves her axe up from the ground, laser-focused on getting the blade into Eno's back, Calla has slid onto her knees and drawn her sword, slicing the blade across the player's neck and taking her head clean off.

The blood paints a half-moon in the alley. There's no light, no escape. If a body isn't too damaged, the qi can jump, but death tends to be immediate with decapitation. Jumping requires sight and intent. Eyes pinned to a target—never mind what the target is doing, so long as they are within view. It's rather difficult to achieve both factors if the brain isn't functioning anymore.

In the stillness of the alley, Eno rocks against the wall, barely keeping upright while he catches his bearings. He clasps a hand over his left arm, blood seeping through his fingers.

"Thanks," he breathes.

Calla wipes at her face, dotting at the moisture that's gathered by her temple. She doesn't know if it's sweat or blood.

"Don't worry about it." She straightens to her feet, shaking the crimson off the blade of her sword. When that doesn't work, she wipes the flat side on the cuff of her pants. "Think of this as a favor repaid."

Eno's mouth opens, but Calla is already flicking her hand at him in dismissal.

"Are you *shooing* me?" he asks.

"Go find another body," Calla snaps. "If you bleed out, then what was that all for?"

In response, Eno flashes a wide grin, as though Calla just gave him a friendly parting gift instead of saving his damn life. Someone will take it sooner or later anyway if he remains in the games. But she's glad it's not by gruesome axe bludgeoning, at the very least.

"See you around!" Eno calls, scampering off.

"I hope not," Calla mutters.

◇◇◇◇◇

If the program restarts one more time, Anton might burn down this whole cybercafe.

"Come on," he begs, smacking a hand to the machine's side. The bulky plastic casing shudders, as does the drink sitting beside the computer mouse. Sulian, who owns the café, gets on his case every time he comes in and doesn't buy food, even though the place's primary source of revenue is how many hours its customers spend seated in front of a computer. Anton's only compromise is a glass of whatever stale soft drink has been sitting in the refrigerator behind the counter.

"Hey."

Anton startles. He barely refrains from drawing his knives, recognizing Sulian's voice after a beat.

"Now, why would you creep up on me," he says cheerily, "knowing I could slit your throat?"

Sulian folds his arms. His lanky frame looks like it could blow away with the wind, which Anton supposes is why he's never seen the old man leave the café before. If he were ever to encounter Sulian at the markets one day, Anton would bowl over in shock.

"If you slit my throat, maybe I'll get an insurance payout. Even if that's only a fraction of the money you owe me," Sulian says.

He's practically yelling over the noise. This is *the* spot in San for a tech plug-in. Even those who can afford a personal computer come here to indulge in its ambience: the din of businessmen running their accounts and teenagers playing their multiplayer games. It's near-impossible to secure a seat at the café without calling Sulian ahead of time, and too many who come in end up sleeping around their monitors, not wanting to leave for the night. Most mornings consist of Sulian tossing customers out if they look like they can barely function, their screens off and no longer counting billed minutes.

The old man clears his throat. "Are you *ever* going to pay the tab you're racking up here?"

Anton takes a sip of his drink. That's right. He hasn't actually paid for his time in months.

"I will," he promises. It doesn't sound convincing even to his own ear. "Soon."

"Didn't you walk away from the Daqun with the most coins?" Sulian continues with a raised eyebrow. "I watch the reels, you know."

Anton grumbles under his breath. It's his own fault for letting Sulian glimpse the number on his wristband earlier, but of all the weird old men to trust in San-Er, Sulian is high on the list.

"Yes, but I don't have them anymore."

Sulian sighs, giving up. He returns to the kitchen, retrieving used plates and dirtied napkins from the three other customers along Anton's row. They barely notice, too enamored with their screens, which are actually moving instead of freezing on a blue panel as Anton's has.

The café is chaotic—and loud—enough for Anton to blend in unseen, but he also chose this computer on purpose. The three seated to his left would get in the way of an incoming pursuer, and the café's back exit is only two paces to his right, leading into a labyrinthine set of back corridors. It's too early for another location ping, since they tend to go off once every day, but he won't be taken unaware.

There's a sudden noise, and Anton swivels his gaze back to the computer. Nothing on the screen has changed. The noise is from his belt, where his pager hangs.

Your bill for the next month has been posted.

Anton unclips the pager and throws it at full force onto the table. The loud bang of plastic striking laminate doesn't bring him much satisfaction, though it stirs the laughter of teenagers behind him. He prefers Sulian's assumptions about his frivolous spending in casinos and brothels over this, the actual truth. That the hospital swallows every cent he manages to scrounge up, then spits its acid reflux back at him with more bills.

The screen finally unfreezes. Anton shuffles his chair closer, waiting for the modem under the table to stop whining. When he pulls up the browser, he keys in a stolen identity number to access the archived newsreels—good old Cedar Yanshu, the man living one floor above Anton's actual apartment who never checks his accounts and doesn't have the memory to refute Anton's activity under his identity—and navigates to the archives from the night of the Daqun.

Line by line, the page begins to load. Anton's eyes swivel to the side of the keyboard, where he has set the wristband out in the open. A few other café patrons have eyed the object curiously, trying to determine if it is indeed a wristband from the games or only a convincing replica. He'll bear the risk of attention to keep it within sight, needing to catch the moment it blinks out. *If* it blinks out.

He doesn't know why he didn't toss it as soon as he escaped Fifty-Seven. But he held on to it, and now he has far more questions than answers. He expected the wristband to shut off earlier today—even if Fifty-Seven typed in her identity number just before their fight at the market, twenty-four hours elapsed more than an hour ago.

Yet the wristband remains active, the **57** flashing each time he taps the screen. It even started whining when Anton's did to signal a nearby player, and he had to press a button quickly to shut it up before shoving the whole strap into his pocket. He could pull the chip out and deactivate it himself, but that feels like cheating. Especially when it's *supposed* to blink out on its own.

Who *is* this player? Skipping the Daqun, wristband active without its daily identity check. The requirement of a check-in is the main safeguard against random civilians stealing wristbands from dead players and cheating their way into the games. The palace would never allow for it.

So why is Fifty-Seven's still going? Is it a fluke? Is she a spy from within the palace? Perhaps King Kasa has no intention of paying a victor this year and put in a plant that he'll help to win.

Anton sifts through the digital archive, clicking recent files at random in search for the clip he saw. It takes a lot of loading and buffering, but eventually the server pulls up a video in a familiar weapons shop. The footage is as he remembers. Fifty-Seven, plunging her sword in, then yanking it out with an eerie smoothness. He doesn't know what exactly has captivated him so thoroughly. It's the same rapture he had when engaged in battle with her: she is never still enough for him to make out a clear detail, but the energy that bristles from her every move overwhelms him.

"Are you watching the Er massacre footage?"

For the second time that afternoon, Anton almost draws his knives on an innocent bystander.

"Felo," he says as he glances over his shoulder. Felo is too young to be jumping bodies, but even if he could, his pale-red eyes are so distinct that he would be recognized from any distance. It sometimes looks as though he has no irises, only permanently dried, irritated eye whites. "Hasn't anyone taught you not to sneak up on people?"

"I didn't think anyone could sneak up on you."

"Usually not," Anton grumbles. He's been so focused on watching the front for intruders that he forgot the people who know their way around can use the back entrance too. Felo is always hanging out at the café, coding games on the computers with his friends.

Felo shakes his head, as if chiding Anton in disappointment. Anton flicks the boy in the head.

"Why would I be watching the Er massacre?"

"That was my question to you," Felo retorts. "They have it everywhere if you just ask. Most video shops will throw it in free with a porn order. You don't need to waste money logging on to the internet."

Anton braces a hand against the back of his chair, turning fully now. "What the fuck are you doing watching porn? Aren't you thirteen?"

Felo crosses his arms. "Aren't you eighteen?"

"No! I'm twenty-five."

"Oh." Felo looks him up and down, unfolding his arms sheepishly. "You act younger."

Anton rubs his eye. "I'm going to try my very best not to take that as an insult. Go to *school*, Felo."

"I hate school." Felo leans closer to the screen now, squinting at the footage. It's zoomed in and heavily pixelated, cutting off most of the weapons shop and focused only on Fifty-Seven. "Never mind, it's not the massacre. That's my bad. I've watched the footage too many times. I thought it looked familiar."

He steps back, then somehow perfectly mimics Fifty-Seven's sword maneuver—right down to the brief snap of his elbow before ducking to avoid the brunt of the imaginary blood spray. Anton blinks, shocked, but Felo's attention has already been caught by something else, and he hurries off, skirting around the tables.

The Er massacre. At the time it happened, Anton had already washed his hands of San's royal family. Exiled onto the streets with his birth body confiscated by the palace, he had heard the news from the television, same as everyone else. He still remembers the body he'd been invading at the time, a musician living in Er, his whole apartment going into lockdown when the broadcasters spoke of Princess Calla Tuoleimi going rogue, taking a sword to her parents and strewing their guts across the throne room. The footage, he has heard, is a cult hit among the Crescent Societies and their criminals. Most of them admire the princess.

Anton runs a new search in the browser. He never met the other city's princess—always out of the palace by chance whenever there was a diplomatic visit from Er—though he knew August thought highly of her. He never sought out the footage after the incident either; the networks found it too inappropriate to show on the broadcasts. If they had played it—and only during the late-night segments when people were using their television screens for light against the heavy night—they would have censored it according to King Kasa's wishes.

King Kasa, however, cannot control underground or virtual distribution. When the first frame fills the screen, Anton knows that this must be the uncensored version.

Because it's *bad*.

Er's throne room had been decorated with lavish details and gold trimmings. Creatures of legend lined the two thrones, a jade statue set between the chairs and silk curtains hanging directly behind. The footage is from a security camera placed in the uppermost corner of the throne room, so when the princess marches in, the angle makes her look impossibly fast, arm raised immediately, blade in hand.

One of the guards that had been standing out of frame rushes in. The princess moves rapidly, cutting through him and turning to face the three others. Anton pauses here. He clicks into Fifty-Seven's footage again, rewinds and replays it, and Felo is absolutely right: the maneuver is near-identical. The way her arm arcs, the way her body moves.

Anton switches back to the Er massacre. As soon as the guards are down, the princess walks toward her parents. There are no more than two words exchanged. The king of Er holds his hands out, mouth open to say something. Calla isn't listening. She has already lopped off his head, her blade striking clean.

Anton is not squeamish by any means, but he blanches nonetheless. It's not the gore that he is bothered by. It's the ease with which she made the cut. He might sound like a hypocrite when he was killing only some few hours ago . . . except those were strangers. Mere hurdles in his way toward victory. The princess of Er swings at her own parents with the very same indifference. As the footage continues, her mother's head comes clean off too, landing by Calla's feet. There hadn't been any chance for the king and queen to consider jumping in a last-ditch effort to escape. Calla had been sure to slaughter all the others in the room first.

The video is nearing its final few seconds. On-screen, Calla simply stands there, covered in blood, surveying the bodies on the floor, the walls dashed with red. For months after the incident, there were mutterings that perhaps the princess had been jumped and occupied, that it was an intruder who had committed the crime. But Kasa's palace guard had chased Calla Tuoleimi out to the wall where she'd tried to flee, and the guard who'd fired the crossbow arrow that had landed between her eyes claimed that they'd undeniably been royal yellow. At the funeral—held separately from her parents'—Calla had been condemned as a treasonous renegade, not an innocent caught up in an invasion.

The footage cuts off. Slowly, Anton pulls up the other page, frozen on Fifty-Seven, putting it side by side with this still of Calla Tuoleimi. He zooms in on Fifty-Seven's eyes, that feline stare. The color doesn't show very well on grainy surveillance footage, but he remembers enough from their encounter to recall a flash of yellow.

If there was any doubt before, there is none now. Calla Tuoleimi is Number Fifty-Seven, and very much alive.

"Oh, Princess," he says. "We're about to make something very interesting of the games."

CHAPTER 8

There are reports of trouble in Eigi, the nearest province outside San's wall, and so August is sent out with ten palace guards to run reconnaissance. The councilmember who oversees this territory—who holds rank over the two or three generals commanding the battalion of soldiers in each province— has neither reported to the palace nor answered communication in twenty-four hours. Ever since the Makusa family was massacred by a guerrilla group in Kelitu Province years ago, any silence from councilmembers is to be taken seriously. And since King Kasa won't leave the palace, it's up to August to be his eyes and ears.

They already hit one bump in the road before they could leave San-Er. A film crew tried following them past the wall when the guards were raising the gates, sticking too close to the royal procession for comfort. The lesser television networks always grow desperate during the games. Without contacts in the palace, they can't get good surveillance footage fast enough; then without new and interesting observations about the reels, no one wants to watch their programming. They begin entertaining bizarre ideas like producing documentaries about rural Talin, thinking it'll somehow boost their viewership by showing something entirely outside the games. Leida was forced to shoo the crew away, warning that another infraction near the wall would be met with legal consequences. Casual travel in and out of San-Er is, after all, forbidden. Once someone becomes a citizen of the twin cities by birth or by lottery, there they remain, unless they are granted a formal departure permit. King Kasa is too afraid of what might happen if people are allowed free travel. Frequent movement on the border could allow rural occupants to slip into San-Er illegally, and San-Er cannot possibly strain its resources to care for illegal city residents.

Even though it was San-Er's throne that swallowed them and their lands into the kingdom's borders in the first place. Even though San-Er can put its citizen taxes on them just fine.

August breathes deep, taking in the fresh air as they travel through Eigi Province. His riding skills are terribly neglected, as are the city horses. They're seldom taken out for exercise, housed in small stables along the wall for the rare occasion that San-Er's forces need to leave the perimeter. When he is king, he will care for them. He will pave glorious roads throughout the provinces, funnel money outward to advance infrastructure. They will build transport, too, to get around—every type of advanced vehicle that the provinces currently use in prototypical form—and civilians inside the wall will come and go as they please, with the whole kingdom available to their every whim.

People will be happy. No one will say otherwise.

"Look at this." King Kasa was watching the reels this morning. Hands clasped behind his back, letting the servants tailor his collar while he stood before a screen that stretched to take up half the entertainment hall. There's something about the decoration in Kasa's wing of the palace that has always bothered August, and last year, he finally figured out why. Kasa persistently installs new technology without first getting rid of what lies underneath. Television screens hang side by side with wood carvings; speakers jut out from expensive bamboo screens that aren't produced anymore because their construction requires raw materials from Gaiyu Province. The other wings in the Palace of Union have modernized with the decades, have taken down most of their scroll paintings in favor of wires. Kasa's personal quarters have not.

"What am I looking at?" August replied politely. He had only entered the entertainment hall to receive his task. Even with time of the essence out in Eigi, King Kasa had not dismissed him immediately. He kept his adopted son waiting so he could point at the screen, showing a woman sinking to her knees as she screamed at someone out of the camera's view.

"What a pitiful sight," Kasa remarked. "She really ought to get up."

As if hearing his command, the woman on the screen hurried back onto her feet with renewed energy. Her wristband flashed on her arm. She disappeared from view just as another player entered the camera's frame, grinning like a maniac.

"They seem to be enjoying themselves," August said dryly.

King Kasa nodded in agreement. "Of course they are," he said. "I offer them more than they could dare imagine possessing. I am this kingdom's greatest benefactor."

Eigi stretches wide in front of August now, endless fields and open grounds sprawling until they hit the horizon. King Kasa tells the truth: he *is* the greatest benefactor of this kingdom. It is not the vast holdings in the royal vault that matter most, but the continued generation of such wealth, and who is the one holding this all together, clutching onto these provinces so that everything funnels in the direction of the palace? The games, at their core, are Kasa's way of telling his subjects to know their place. No matter what, everything in Talin flows back to him. There is nothing that can compete with his wealth, but stay in line, and he might just break off a piece and offer it generously. A gift; a consolation prize.

August tugs on his horse's reins, pulling their procession to a stop.

A stout building comes into view. They have arrived.

He waves at the guards to stop beating on the palace drums, eyeing the province's capital yamen. For people coming out of San-Er, the building is a sight that takes some getting used to. It serves as the administrative entrance into the village, rising one mere story with a wide roof that curls up at the edges to prevent rain from collecting. One entranceway opens into the courtyard, where all four sides are surrounded by the yamen, and beyond that, another exit at the back leads into the village. Some of the temples in San-Er still look like this, but they're buried in the shadows of the high-rises around them, washing out the rustic stone walls and intricate wooden detailing.

Keeping his distance, August climbs off his horse, then passes the reins to Galipei. Leida, meanwhile, maneuvers her horse from the back of the guard, approaching August's side.

"I told you that we would be fine today, didn't I?" He brushes off his jacket. "You didn't have to leave your post."

"I have a whole team of very capable stand-ins," Leida replies, swinging her leg off the saddle and hitting the ground hard. "San-Er won't fall without me for one day. You, however, are another matter."

Galipei makes a noise of protest on August's behalf. August pretends not to hear Leida. The yamen looks empty, its open structure void of activity. This is where the village's bureaucratic business is conducted, where the mayor should emerge for formalities as soon as the palace drums draw near.

August waits. He eyes the yamen walls.

And then, movement.

A man stumbles out from the yamen, his arm looped tightly around the neck of another. It takes August a moment to recognize the captive as the province's councilmember and another to realize that the unnatural quiet was the preparation for an ambush. Now a small group of rural civilians filters out from the yamen, wielding torches and branches.

It's the best they can do for weapons. The palace guards do not stir; they look upon the scene evenly. August exchanges a glance with Leida, and Leida nods.

"Stay where you are." The mayor—the man who is clutching the council-member—takes a deep breath. There's fabric tied around the lower half of his face, and August can't tell if this is a small attempt at concealing his identity or the makeshift methods of civilians bracing against plague when they don't have proper masks.

The mayor continues: "We have demands of the palace—"

But he doesn't have the chance to finish speaking. August jumps in easily, taking the briefest second to adjust. Galipei moves to catch his birth body; the palace guards surge forward at once without instruction.

"Go on," August says, releasing the councilmember from his arms.

The councilmember hurries forward. The palace guards swallow him up, then fan out. In seconds, the rural group forming the ambush from the yamen is disarmed and on their knees. It's almost too easy. Dissent is useless. August knows they hate the palace, but he's aggrieved about how stupid their plans are nonetheless. He can't blame them, because they don't know that he is already trying to depose the current king, but what's the point of taking more hours out of his day for these disorganized, futile attempts?

Leida holds out his cellular phone. August returns to his birth body and takes it, freeing her hands in time to grab the mayor when he blinks back into consciousness. She hauls the mayor off to the side before he can run, spitting a series of rote interrogative questions. The wind has picked up. The sensation is so unusual that it almost stings when a particularly strong gust blows against August's left.

He dials the palace.

"A poorly thought-out hostage situation," he reports when King Kasa answers. "We'll return within the day."

A beat of silence. Then it draws out, and August pauses, wondering what he's said wrong. Are they in trouble? His eyes raise in search of Galipei. Escape routes don't come easy in the provinces. Open space doesn't allow for disappearances, only full battles.

"This was in Eigi Province, yes?" King Kasa finally replies. "How is Mugo faring?"

"He's fine." August casts a look at the councilmember. Mugo hardly looks ruffled. "And yes. Our nearest province."

Another beat of silence. August has started to sweat.

"How big is its capital? About a thousand inhabitants in the village, from what I remember."

Small villages freckle each province, gathering rural populations together for commerce and trade. A provincial capital is usually no larger than the others, but the presence of its yamen designates it the base of administration within the province. Past the open archway, August can peer right through the courtyard and the back gate to see rough dirt streets and small shop fronts. The people idling on the other side of the yamen pay no heed to the scene unfolding outside the village walls.

"Yes," August replies. "I would be inclined to agree."

"Put me on speaker, please, August. I'd like to address the palace guard directly."

August does as he is told. Leida has moved off into the distance, and he wishes she would come back, just so she could have some sway on whatever King Kasa is about to instruct. But she is still interrogating the mayor, looming over him while he kneels, and the palace guards huddle closer, blocking her from August's view. All ten surround him: not large enough to create a unit, but enough to act as a functioning force for the palace. Enough to cause whispers through Talin tomorrow, when the rural dwellers wonder what brought the royal guard out to Eigi.

King Kasa's voice crackles through the phone.

"As sworn defenders of San-Er, there is no mercy for resistance. One wall is no longer enough. We need further protection."

August feels a stone sinking slowly into his stomach.

"Burn Eigi's capital down," King Kasa continues, and suddenly the stone turns leaden, plummeting to the very bottom at high speed. "Turn it to ash. If its people air their grievances with threats, then we shall simply take the breath from their lungs."

August turns off speakerphone and returns the device to his ear, but the palace guards have already heard every word. They cannot deny the command or pretend it was never heard.

"Your Majesty," August hisses. "This is San-Er's center for rice imports. It would be a loss—"

"We have plenty more in Yingu and Dacia. We can increase quotas in Cirea and start confiscations in Pashe. There is no excuse for insurgency."

The palace guards begin to move. They don't wait for August to look up and nod. August is here as a mere figurehead—they know that. The councilmembers won't care what he has to say, and the armies across Talin will not entertain him for a minute until Kasa's throne is his. No power can contradict the king's, no matter how shiny the crown prince title may be.

"Hey." Leida's call jolts August to attention. He feels the first flickers of heat on his face. The torches are being lit. "Hey!"

Leida halts before him. The flecks of blue glitter at her eyes shimmer in the daylight. The bright, bright daylight, unclogged by factory smoke and brothel glow, which somehow makes everything feel so much *worse*, revealing every facet of his fellow human, every flaw and distinction that the shadows of San-Er would hide.

"What?" August asks tiredly.

"What is this? Why are—"

The moment she starts forward, August snags her by the arm. He glances down to make sure the cellular phone has disconnected and finds that King Kasa hung up as soon as he finished speaking. He didn't even stick around to oversee how his command was being implemented.

"Instructions from the palace." August's voice is dull, emotionless. It has to be, because the guards are still listening. "We must punish insurrectionists against the throne, and when this village is razed, we will use the barren land to build a security base and oversee business regarding the wall."

Leida is quiet. She lets August keep his grip on her arm and says nothing, expression steeled for her guards, but her eyes are ablaze, reflecting the flames that will soon burn the village to ash. Within minutes, there is screaming. Store roofs cave in and street lanterns crumble to the ground. The sounds waft past the yamen and into their ears, burrow into their head and take root in the very deepest crevasses of their memory. August and Leida stare ahead, letting the palace guard fulfill its duty.

"Thank you," August says quietly.

"For?" Leida responds.

"Not making a fuss. That could have gone badly."

Leida's eyes shift to him. Her dark blue is vivid, edging into purple by the light of the inferno before them. It's almost too hot to remain where they stand.

"The mayor didn't say much," she says. "Only that they couldn't afford their taxes anymore."

"I suppose that is enough reason."

"Indeed. A reason that unfolds into myriads more." Leida turns around. As soon as she has her back to the flames, the heat suddenly feels unbearable to August, as if they had shared the burden before and now he is left to endure alone. "But that is nothing to the palace, so I suppose it is nothing to us."

Those inside the city walls are cockroaches, but those outside the city walls aren't even living creatures, merely parts of the landscape that the palace can mow over and reshape as it wishes. This is the kingdom of Talin, after all, and the king is the great hand chosen by the divine gods. The gods never choose wrong, and the gods place the crown on its wearer.

August finally turns around too, his fists clenched hard. He takes in the screams. All those who are trapped inside the burning buildings face imminent, painful death; all the rest who are displaced will starve to death in a few weeks or months. Those slaughtered today have it the easiest.

"Yes, it is nothing to us," August replies. "Long live King Kasa, may his reign go on for ten thousand years."

He walks back to his horse. It will be a long ride to return to San-Er before nightfall.

CHAPTER 9

Chami and Yilas have drawn Calla a rough map. Though she insisted she could memorize the route, it was too hard to explain with words how to get to Big Well Street as efficiently as possible, and her two former attendants brought out the pens instead, sketching the streets and running a thick red marker where she needed to go.

Big Well Street—unnecessarily long, perpetually busy, and crowded with establishments one atop the other—lies on San's side of the Rubi Waterway, but in these recent few years, access has been blocked off on either end by wooden slats and crisscrossed pipes meant to keep the palace guard out. Sometimes they still barge in for inspection, but it would be plain exhausting to keep at it when the people inside rebuild the barriers every time they're torn down. For regular folks trying to visit, the best course is to enter Er first, then take one of the bridges back into San, which drops smack-bang into the middle of Big Well Street.

Calla smooths out the map, glancing quickly at the markings before she chooses a bridge into Er. She *should* be more aware of how these city routes run, but it's hard to feel comfortable spending leisurely time out and about when she's a criminal who's supposed to be dead. Even when she was princess, she never spent long walking these alleys by herself. She knew the major buildings, the financial districts, and the meat market districts, could even label the places where most of the crime was and where the palace guard went the most often. But that was not the same. That didn't have the smell under her nose and the jolt in her boots as her feet strike against the muddy ground, coming off the bridge and into Er, where the shift between the two cities is tangible.

Calla pauses at the head of an alley. The shiver that dances down her neck is immediate. From where she stands, a thin shaft of sunlight from the day's last setting rays pierces her eyes directly. There is always less noise in Er. Which isn't to say it is a peaceful haven, only that the street hawkers are replaced with businessmen, the prostitutes at the corners with schoolteachers trying to grade essays while they walk. The alleys are paved, not quite wide enough to qualify for a road like those in the provinces, but enough that Er's residents will ride around on bicycles instead of skirting trash bags every moment as the people of San do.

Calla looks up, bringing a hand over her eyes. The sun disappears and drops Er into dusk. She's always been good at sensing aberrations. Now, her every nerve tells her that she is being watched. Her qi is stirring—better at hearing than her ears, better at feeling than any part of her skin. When one of the electric boxes on the wall bursts with a sudden spark, she draws her sword, dropping into a combative stance just before a blur of motion comes hurtling from the end of the alley.

An uncomfortable prickle strikes her chest, then a fit of nausea. Calla almost gasps. She hasn't felt this sensation in years. It fades as quickly as it came, but she has no doubt that someone just tried to invade her.

They have failed. They will always fail.

Calla is ready. That blur of motion comes closer, shoulder pitched down, not a single feature visible in the falling darkness. It doesn't matter: as soon as they are near enough, Calla kicks a foot onto the alley wall and somersaults, avoiding their hit and moving to land behind them. She doesn't crane her head to see; she only guesses. Her sword goes straight down her attacker's back—through the neck, then through the spine—before she has fully landed upon the ground yet.

Her boots thud heavily into the mud. She tugs her sword free. The attacker drops.

But . . . her blade comes out clean.

Calla blinks, uncomprehending. The prone figure on the floor is no longer moving. She waits, wary in the event of a fake-out. Almost a minute passes before Calla inches toward the body, daring to investigate. Her breath held, she grabs a fistful of clothing and turns the attacker over until their face is no longer pressed to the ground.

"What the fuck?"

Their eyes are blank: no irises, no color. This is an empty vessel.

Calla rests her hands on her knees. How is that possible? She didn't see any light. There was no one around for the attacker to jump into. August's warning about agents from Sica flashes in her head, but the thought is so preposterous she can't even begin entertaining it. Have Sicans developed a new way of *jumping*? Into bodies that aren't within sight? Without their qi flashing visibly?

Shakily, she can only bustle back a few steps to pick up the map she dropped and hurry away, leaving the bloodless vessel in the alley. Someone will find it and take it, she's sure. There is very little that can leave Calla stunned, but seeing an empty vessel—occupied with qi while they were lunging at her seconds ago but void of it when she was sticking a sword through their neck—is high on her list of unfathomable sights.

"Compartmentalize," Calla orders herself. She scans the walls, squinting to read the directional street markings. She can hear the Rubi Waterway getting fainter, so she's going the wrong way. She turns and follows the sound back to the bridges. "Focus on the matter at hand."

Really, she isn't sure what sort of matter entails a random attack from a possible Sican agent. There are far too many people in San-Er for it to be a co-incidence that they came after her. Were they hunting a player of the games at random? Or were they hunting Princess Calla Tuoleimi? She knows there are certain groups in San-Er that are convinced she's alive, but those rumors surely have not traveled past Talin's borders.

Calla makes it to the bridge, fingers tracing the dusty side barriers. She weaves in and out of the groups congregated on the thin stone structure, ignor-ing the dumpling stalls and the purse sellers with their wares laid out on a big red rug. As soon as she steps onto the main street, she knows she has arrived at the right place. A clump of middle-aged men squat outside one of the doors, so much cigarette smoke around them that it makes a visible gray cloud. While they shout at one another in conversation, she circles around them and ducks into Snowfall, Big Well Street's primary brothel.

Snowfall. Named for the blinding white that blankets the provinces when the seasons turn cold. San-Er has not seen snow in centuries, which makes the concept all the more exotic.

It's pandemonium inside, pumping with low bass music. Blue and neon-pink lights flood the walls at random intervals, then drop into complete darkness for a flash of a second. Calla nudges her sword behind herself, keeping the sheath tucked under her coat. She has already spotted the staircase that goes up into the rest of the building, but she doesn't follow it. The moment anyone narcs and Anton Makusa runs, she will lose him. She was a princess once, after all—she knows how to read people, can see that the bar attendants and dancers started eyeing her the moment she walked in. None of them will talk to her if she asks what they know about Makusa and where he is, but if she acts normal, they'll brush her off as merely another strange customer and let her do as she wishes.

Then maybe she can poke her nose around Makusa's apartment to gather more information. She only needs to make sure she's in the clear first.

Calla looks down at her arm. Even if she still had her wristband, it wouldn't indicate another player's presence unless it was triggered by a location ping. Without it, there's no way of knowing which face Anton Makusa wears. It's the fun of King Kasa's games, the reason why civilians are glued so thoroughly to their television screens every night, why some of them will crane their necks and gape at a player in the flesh despite the danger of hovering near an active fight scene. When players can jump at any moment, one cannot easily stalk opponents and cut them down one by one. There's only chance and following the wristbands.

The analogue clock on the wall is creeping near seven in the evening. Calla holds her knuckles to her mouth, pressing hard as she thinks. At this point in the games, the palace isn't trying to rush their progress yet; they'll do one ping daily, two maximum, and always during waking hours while their surveillance room is well staffed. Everyone's wristband must have gone off once already today, but it's not late enough to mark off the possibility of another and not early enough to retire. By all logic, Anton Makusa shouldn't be at home. Either he would be somewhere around San-Er or . . .

Calla's gaze snags on a private table in the corner. A man sits with his scribbling pad, his fingers splayed in front of him as his mouth moves, talking to himself. Where others in the brothel have their eyes pinned to the writhing bodies dancing onstage, the man is concentrated on his work, pausing on occasion only to stare into the distance, like there is something in the smoke that no one else can see.

. . . or Anton Makusa would be *here*, near enough to his residence that he can rest once the time passes for a second ping, yet still occupying a public space in case the ping does come.

Calla reaches inside her coat, tearing at her own shirt while she watches the man. A waitress sets a drink down before him, and he thanks her with an old familiarity. The wad of fabric in Calla's hands rips easily.

"Can I borrow this?"

When the same waitress passes Calla, she has no time to respond before Calla is plucking the serrated steak knife off her dirty tray. The waitress raises her brow, bemused, but does not protest. She continues into the kitchen; Calla quickly wipes the blade clean, then hides it within her wad of fabric.

Her pulse surges to a steady thud, keeping in accompaniment with the bass-heavy thump of Snowfall's music. She strolls toward the private corner table. In her hand, she holds the steak knife carefully, making it appear as if she's clutching nothing but a handkerchief.

Calla climbs into his lap with a smile. When the man's gaze snaps up, a swoop of dark hair falls into his eyes. Black eyes, reflecting back the neon flashing around them. He's quick to return her grin, hands coming around her hips.

Then she leans in, lips against his ear, and presses the tip of the knife into his throat.

"Hello, Makusa," she whispers. She feels the serrated edge pierce skin. "I want my wristband back."

Beneath her, Anton Makusa freezes, his expression turning stricken. Blood begins to trickle into his collarbone, staining his white shirt.

"Okay," he says. She has to strain to hear him over the music. "It's in my pocket. You'll have to ease up an inch."

Calla does not ease up. She only flips her hair over her shoulder, shifting her weight to her left side.

"Slowly."

"I'm going slow," Anton insists, putting his hand in his pocket. He pauses. In that split second, Calla knows instantly he's about to try something.

"Don't you—" She shoves half an inch of the knife into his throat; he tugs a collection of objects out of his pocket and throws it across the room. By the time

Calla hisses a nasty insult, a flash of light has blinded her. She whirls around. The light ends in the body of another man across the room, who swoops for the fallen objects and runs up the stairs.

"Hold this to the wound," Calla says to the man who startles awake beneath her. She tugs the steak knife out and shoves the wad of fabric to his throat. His eyes are jade green now, blinking back shock as Calla launches off him and books it up the stairs, narrowly avoiding collision with a waitress.

On the second floor, Calla pauses, listening for the direction of Anton's footsteps. She has no desire to walk blindly into a trap, so she draws her sword, closing in on the third floor by following sound instead of movement. There's no room for maneuvering here, only the thinnest stairwell with overturned filing cabinets and half-broken shelves shoved into the corners. The paint on the walls has chipped so severely that the floor is dusted with flecks.

One of the apartment doors on the third floor is wide open, its interior dimly lit. Calla adjusts her grip, stepping in warily. She passes a ragged couch, then a miniature adjoined kitchen. There's a bedroom to her left, as small as a closet, crammed with objects.

Anton is hiding in the apartment. She can sense *presence*, feel with certainty that someone else's qi is within jumping distance.

Calla enters the bedroom. And the door slams closed after her, dropping her into darkness.

"Hey!"

"Wait! Hear me out, hear me out," Anton shouts from the other side.

The handle doesn't budge when Calla gives it a push. Locked. What kind of sicko has a door that can be locked from the outside?

"I'll hear you out," Calla says brightly. She shoves her sword through the door, and Anton yelps, startled by her blade piercing clean through. "I'll hear your pleas when I skewer your—"

"Princess. I can help you."

Calla pauses. Being addressed by title does not necessarily take her by surprise, but it's still strange to her ear. "You recognized me? We never met back then."

"How do you know *my* name, Princess Calla? I've done my research too."

Irritation and flattery battle for a hand in her response. He sounds smug for making the discovery; still, if he put the pieces together after their encounter, he paid attention to details that the rest of San-Er has overlooked for five years.

Calla yanks her sword out of the door and examines the steel. "Shouldn't you at least buy me dinner before trapping me in your bedroom?"

"Calla. May I call you Calla?" He ignores her mockery, his voice getting closer to the door. "You and I are the most likely victors of these games. I have a proposal."

"Oh?"

He clears his throat. "We team up. Take everyone else down and get to the end faster."

Anger flares hot in her stomach immediately. She barks out a laugh. "It is so typical of a palace brat to think cheating the games is that easy."

"Who said anything about cheating?" Anton shoots back. "Collaboration isn't against the rules."

Indeed, there are essentially no rules governing the games. Players can do whatever they like, but the thought of collaboration is absurd, because first and foremost, collaboration requires trust, and trust gets you killed in San-Er.

"You're asking for trouble." Calla rests her sword against the wall, where there's already an indent. "Give the palace a reason to disqualify us, and they'll take us both out."

There is a moment of quiet on the other side of the door. Then: "Princess, there's already reason for them to take us both out. We won't be giving them trouble—we'll give them the entertainment they want. It is a worthy exchange for letting us stay at the top."

Calla purses her lips. The outlaw and the exiled, teaming up as allies—it's almost a laughable thought. But he's right on one thing. A collaboration will catch the attention of the reels for sheer entertainment value. If they play nice otherwise and keep their identities concealed, King Kasa may just allow it.

"Why are you trying to get to the end so fast?" Calla asks plainly. "Are you in such a rush?"

"Yes," Anton replies without a hint of hesitation. "I'm impatient and tired of how slowly the games are moving."

It has only been a few days. Some rounds in previous years have gone on for months. Curious, Calla turns and starts to peer around Anton Makusa's bedroom. Her eyes have adjusted enough to catch most of the details: the pictures on the walls and the papers on the desk. He was the one who locked her in here. He only has himself to blame when she goes poking through his things.

"By your logic, we will end up as the final two in the Juedou," she says, walking to his wardrobe and idly browsing through the shirts hanging there. The games open with the Daqun and end with the Juedou, both in the coliseum. Every year, the Juedou is turned into a spectacle, the coliseum lit up as a true arena, lights glaring down on the final two players as they battle to the death. "But only one of us can win."

"Are you afraid you can't win against me, Princess?"

Calla picks up her sword again and returns to the door, shoving it through a second time. Anton shouts a curse.

"Listen," he says, an edge to his voice now. Though he cannot see her, Calla smiles, finally liking where this is going. There's a hardness to his tone, a sense of ferocity that has been whetted into a weapon. *This* sounds more like someone who could be a victor of the games. "You've seen my kill numbers. My ability to jump. You know that I'm an asset to have on your side. We can work together, then break our alliance at the end. Only at the end."

A book on his bedside table catches Calla's attention. When she leans over and flips it open, angling the first page into the light coming through the window, there's a photograph of a boy with black eyes and a girl with the same. She doesn't recognize the boy, but it has to be Anton's birth body, the image captured at the Palace of Earth before he was exiled. The lean shoulders and messy hair suit him. Anton Makusa was born the tousled sort of beautiful, tall but always slouching, perfectly set features obstructed by a heavy frown.

The girl to his side, however, Calla recognizes immediately. Her tiny nose and perfectly brushed hair. Her calculating smile, invariably scheming away at something.

With a quick motion, Calla closes the book.

"What if you put a knife in my back before the final battle?" she asks, recovering before he can note the pause in conversation.

"Why would I?" Anton retorts. "I've seen your numbers too. I've been holding on to your wristband long past the time it was supposed to deactivate. You have some sort of advantage, and I want in. Can I open this door now? Are you going to skewer me?"

"Eventually, yes," Calla mutters. Just as she is adjusting the table so that it looks untouched, the door opens, and Anton Makusa steps in. The light of the living room streams in too, making him appear larger than life when he stands under its glow.

"I wasn't wrong, was I?" Anton says. "You have an advantage in the games. What is it? A revolution plot? A foreign-funded conspiracy?"

Calla does not answer. Instead, she says: "Okay. I'll team up with you." Her gaze darts to the book again. "On my terms."

Anton throws something in her direction. Calla's hand lurches out and snatches her wristband from the air.

"What are your terms?"

He receives only a theatric air-kiss in response. Calla snaps her wristband back on, then sheathes her sword. She knows she should be careful, but he won't attack her now. Not after all that.

"I'll drop by when I know." She skirts by him, heading for the exit. "Stay out of my way in the meantime."

Anton lets her leave. Perhaps he's taken by surprise, perhaps not. Calla could be making a mistake for not taking the chance to kill him. If he changes his tune and so much as breathes a word toward the palace, then the twin cities will know Er's criminal princess is alive, and they will come after her.

Calla bites her nail, hurrying out of the building. Her boot lands in a puddle; she swerves quickly to avoid running into an elderly woman hauling a bucket on her shoulder, filled to the brim with water from one of the public taps. She won't deny that it would be useful to double her kills and speed up the timeline, bring herself closer and closer to the moment she can take King Kasa's head off. But doing so requires trusting Anton Makusa and having faith that he'll keep his mouth shut about her identity. The only thing she's banking on is that he must hate King Kasa as much as she does.

Because the girl in that photograph was Otta Avia, Prince August's half sister.

Anton's former beloved, who is as good as dead now, all because of King Kasa.

◇◇◇◇◇

Pampi clocks out at nine on the dot, leaving the security room with her bag looped over her shoulder and a folder clutched to her chest. Her heels click down the palace tiles, then echo loudly into the night when she exits through a side entrance. Before long, her steps are drowned by the marketplace's roar.

Her route through San is familiar. She does not go home. She straps her wristband back onto her body, winds through the alleys, and reaches the Hollow Temple.

"You are entirely too confident for someone so new, you know that?" a voice greets when she comes through the doors. It's after hours at the temple, the hall empty except for a single figure at the front. She approaches him, her pencil skirt keeping her movements small.

"I gather you've never had someone so new do so much," Pampi replies easily. She throws the file onto the pew. Its papers skid out: maps scribbled with pencil markings, tracing the players across the city. "How are we progressing? Good?"

Woya doesn't answer her immediately. He stares at the papers and makes a noise beneath his breath. The Hollow Temple bristles around them, one of many beating points around the city that make up the network of the Crescent Societies. Each temple functions on its own, led by one cleric. Though Woya holds power within the walls of the Hollow Temple, the Crescents forgo hierarchy any higher than that, choosing to keep their factions working in tandem instead. Different temples manage business and recruit members in different territories of San-Er; if they start doubling up on any streets, members meet to trade information and decide who will take what.

Violence is saved for outsiders. Once a Crescent is sworn in, they regard other Crescents as family.

"Depends on what you mean," Woya finally says. "The killings? They're successful. Passing them off as the efforts of Sican intruders? Eh, could be better. Destabilizing King Kasa's regime and throwing San-Er into anarchy?" He looks up, orange eyes narrowing. "The rest of the temple don't quite see how it will succeed when we're up against the whole guard and then some."

Pampi smiles. Sometimes she feels a thousand years old, like an ancient god who has been sleeping in wait, ready for her moment to come. Her mother called it narcissism, but who's the one still around? The temple responds to her, whispered to her and urged her to become its leader as soon as she stepped in. She brings a knowledge that no one has seen before—at least not here, and it's here that they want it most. The darkest crevasses of San-Er, where the currency most in demand is ownership over yourself. Life is meaningless if you can be shut down at any point, consciousness kicked away because a stronger individual has invaded.

"Someone taught me a most extraordinary thing the other day," Pampi says.

Woya lifts an eyebrow. Half of it has been shaved off, the other half dyed white. "Oh?"

Talin believed in gods once. But San-Er worships technology and productivity in their modern age, so household shrines have become mere aesthetics, and temples alone perform the twin cities' reverence. The Crescent Societies believe that jumping is a gift one cannot take for granted. That the gods gave them this ability and the gods play favorites, listening to the commands of some and ignoring the commands of others. Those who make the right prayers can gain better control, might even perform miracles when it comes to jumping.

Pampi knows how to pray. Under her collar, there are two parallel lines of dried blood, drawn thickly across her chest.

The blood isn't hers. Praying isn't enough. Now she knows how to sacrifice too.

"Would you like to see?"

Pampi throws her hand out. With the motion, Woya goes flying, his back thudding against the temple wall, the impact so hard that it snaps every stick of incense planted nearby. The figurines and the paintings of deities all shudder too, as if they have recognized one of their own among them.

Her qi pounds through her bloodstream. She can feel it: each speck of her inner spirit, merging with her body, merging with the physical world. This is how it is supposed to be. This is the power she always should have had.

"How was that?" Pampi asks.

CHAPTER 10

San's wall is a solid brick formation, traditional and archaic in ways that the twin cities themselves have long surpassed. The buildings inside rise with steel and plastic and machinery, blinking with neon lights that would blind the rest of Talin. In a way, the wall is not protection against the outsiders who flock en masse into the twin cities, but for these outsiders, to spare them just one second longer from laying eyes on the ruin within.

No one *wants* to move to San-Er. No one prefers to be kept awake at night by persistent clanging and neighbors arguing and brothels screaming, especially not after living under the quiet skies in rural Talin. But with peace comes quicker starvation; with open ground comes no money. It is either their children's graves lined up one by one outside the willow trees or a factory job in San-Er, and the choice is easy. Rural civilians make the slow shuffle through the guarded gates of San-Er, clutching their citizenship passes to their chest and blinking in awe at the colossal mess that awaits inside.

People starve in San-Er too, but at least they can say they tried.

From the top of the wall, August looks out into the provinces. Early morning draws its pinkish colors across the sky, and at such a height, the cold breeze finds him quickly, swirling around his arms like it wants to strip him bare. The smoke from Eigi's capital has cleared. Construction has already started on their security base.

"All right." Galipei clambers over the top of the ladder, short of breath. He exhales when he sees August, as if afraid that in the twenty seconds he was gone the crown prince could have somehow been abducted. "I don't think there is anyone running patrol nearby. You'll be undisturbed."

"I told you we weren't staying long," August says.

Galipei comes to where August is standing, to the walkway that runs along the top of the wall. They are both pressed as close to the barrier as they can get, leaning upon the raised metal that serves to prevent patrol guards from accidentally tumbling down the wall if they misstep. There's enough space up here for two people to be running patrol in each corridor, to walk past one another without trouble when they swap places at the watchtowers, which segment the wall into eight sections. The wall does not run in a straight line; it curves in and out at different places, a convex structure that tapers off at each end into the sea. Guards in the other sections cannot see into neighboring corridors, which means no one will mind August and Galipei while they are here, so long as they leave in the next fifteen minutes before shifts change.

And so long as neither of them steps outside the wall.

August takes the ornamental crown off his head with a sigh. Without its weight, he runs a hand through his hair, tugging at the knots that have formed in the wind, easing the tension in his scalp. He doesn't protest when he feels Galipei drop a hand onto the base of his neck. He tips his head down, letting Galipei work his fingers instead.

"Number Thirty-Nine was taken in and put into the palace cells last night," Galipei reports.

"They decided to go after him?" That's a surprise. "The girl survived, didn't she?"

"She's in the hospital recovering. Councilmember Aliha is making a right fuss, though. Kasa's not going to go upsetting him."

The brightening morning illuminates the dirt roads that lead toward the wall, where there will be shipments from Dacia coming in later. With one councilmember designated for each province, their power is limited to their province borders, but that is considerable power nonetheless. If Aliha is grumpy that his daughter was injured in the games, he won't say it outright, but Dacia's imports will suddenly get a little messy, a little delayed. King Kasa must punish the player who was foolish enough to invade the body of a councilmember's daughter to make it right. The official rules make it very clear: jump if you want, but no harm is to come of nonplayers. Though the palace hand-waves its own edicts for the rest of the city, opting to foot the hospital bills instead of filling up the prison cells, it will not hand-wave where the nobility is affected.

"Kasa has bigger problems, if you want my opinion."

Without prelude or context, Galipei seems to read where August's mind has gone.

"There were more?"

"Numbers Eighteen and Forty-One were found dead last night on private properties, burned from the yaisu sickness and positioned in the Sican salute." August speaks in the perfect imitation of an automated machine, no inflection or emotion in his words. "King Kasa insists that nothing is wrong."

"You actually talked to him about it?"

August's grip tightens on his crown. The spires and whorls sting his palm. This is a charlatan's crown. This is a crown that does nothing, that gives him enough jewels to be allowed in and out of the palace but never to say anything of substance. "As soon as Leida brought in the news, I asked for permission to see

San-Er's entry and exit records. His Majesty says that I am making something out of nothing."

The ladder rattles from the wind. Reaching up, August sets his other hand over Galipei's, stilling his bodyguard. The sun has poked itself over the horizon, but San-Er's sun these days doesn't look anything like the images in their history books, nor like the scrolls of art left over from earlier reigns. It is a mere patch of light that moves along the sky according to the hour, too obscured by whatever has gathered up in the atmosphere to see any clear shape or outline.

In other parts of Talin, farther out into the kingdom, the sun shines clearer and the sky stretches with a more proper blue. But San-Er's towering wall marks the limit for residents inside it, and so this dreariness is the most that city occupants are capable of seeing. The council has inquired before whether King Kasa might consider expanding the capital city. Extend the wall outward and add some of Eigi's land to San to redistribute the population. The answer is always a resolute *no*—it would be harder for the palace guard to keep peace; every new street corner would require surveillance and cameras; water, sanitation, electricity would need to be spread outward too, and how are they to afford it?

The palace can afford it just fine. King Kasa chooses not to.

"He doesn't believe you," Galipei states.

"When does he ever? If he can't see it, it's not happening."

"He can't deny that something is happening. These aren't casualties of the games. No player could avoid surveillance like that."

But then, who *is* targeting them? Sican agents in the city is not only a far-fetched idea, but one with no discernible endgame.

August slots his crown back onto his head, and Galipei's hand drops. Immediately, his neck feels much colder.

"Come on," he says, starting for the ladder.

◇◇◇◇◇

After she awakens from a restless sleep, Calla calls a meeting with August. Or rather, she summons him to her, demanding his presence within the hour, or else. She doesn't know what the "or else" is; she just knows that August will come.

She awaits in the Magnolia Diner, already on her third cigarette. From behind the register, Yilas waves her hand to disperse the smoke, wrinkling her nose.

"What are you so nervous for?"

Calla glances at Yilas with a start, stubbing her cigarette out. "Who said I was nervous?"

Yilas picks up a dishrag. Eyes narrowed, she wipes away the ash that has dropped on the counter. "I was your attendant for many years. I do know your tells, believe it or not. You always had those weird habits." She prods Calla's elbow, asking her to move as she wipes. "The others thought you believed in rural superstitions, but I knew you were just strange."

The door to the diner opens, and Calla swivels around fast, her body tensing. Her reaction is an overkill. It's only a little old lady with dark-purple eyes, pausing to type her identity number into the turnstile.

Calla sighs, adjusting on her seat again.

"I'm half-afraid that I'll be hauled in at any second," she admits.

"Didn't you resolve that issue? With the Weisanna who knew your identity?"

Calla resists the urge to light another cigarette. "Someone else knows now."

"You're not very good at this, are you?" Yilas baits, a quirk to her lip.

"It's not my fault," Calla grumbles. "I'm recognizable."

Her former attendant watches her for a long moment, her expression turning very serious. Then: "You could ditch the body."

It's not the first time Yilas has suggested this. In the palace, Calla's apprehension against jumping was the norm, in line with the belief among elites that their bodies were sacred. It was an insult to themselves if they jumped into normal civilians and an insult to their fellow nobility if they were to borrow each other's bodies. After she fled the palace and sought her former attendants' help in San, however, her refusal to jump became a topic of contention. Yilas couldn't understand why Calla wouldn't commit to this new identity when she was putting Chami at risk by using her number. Take over another body—or buy an empty vessel, if she didn't want to invade someone already occupied—and the palace would never find her while she lived as Chami. Her eye color would be the last marker of her identity; given that others in San-Er have similar hues, it would be near-impossible to use that alone to prove she was Calla Tuoleimi.

"I'm not ditching the body," Calla says wryly.

"Cal—"

The door opens again, this time bringing in an unfamiliar man holding an umbrella, which is hardly necessary in San. Most rain gets caught along the sides of the buildings before it drizzles down to the ground, but anyone who walks the streets ends up mildly damp anyway from the leaking pipes.

The man looks up. For a fleeting moment, Calla sees his black eyes and is certain that Anton Makusa has come to hassle her again. Then she remembers that Prince August has an identical color from afar, and walks to meet him just outside the diner's turnstile.

"Come for a walk," August says simply, inclining his head toward the door. He turns and exits without waiting for an answer.

When Calla emerges from the diner, there's someone else waiting with August, an umbrella in his hand too. The rain is so light, Calla hardly feels it.

"Galipei," she crows, throwing an arm over his shoulder. In his birth body, he is taller than she is, so it is a formidable task, but he has always been large, and Calla has always been willing to irritate him. "I haven't seen you in an eternity. Of course, someone with very familiar eyes did try to attack me a while back . . ."

Galipei tries to shrug her off. Calla's grip tightens.

"August," he croaks in complaint.

"No, no, don't look at August," Calla says. "You were so tough when you were running from me—"

"I only sent him to confirm your identity," August cuts in. "He never intended to attack you. Leave him be."

Calla purses her lips, then glances at Galipei. She brings her arm down and threads it around his. "Shall we walk?"

August leads them past the row of shops while Calla makes Galipei increasingly uncomfortable. By the time she's exhausted a list of his family members—rattling off all the Weisanna names she can recall until Galipei has a bead of sweat coming down his face—most of the commercial district has been left behind, and San has settled around them.

Calla lets go of him abruptly and joins August under his umbrella. August doesn't startle at her sudden movements. He is very rarely startled.

"I gather you got your wristband back?"

She lifts her arm, showing him the evidence. "I'll give you one guess as to who took it."

Though August keeps onward in his stride, he turns to look at her.

"Just one guess?"

"Black eyes, left the palace about seven years ago. Any names come to mind?"

No response. But it's clear that he knows exactly who she's talking about.

"He's asked me to team up with him for the games," Calla continues. "I'm going to do it."

August's brows shoot right up. Even in this stranger's body, his dark eyes swallow up his face, widened in disgust.

"I beg your pardon?"

"Unless you have a convincing reason against it," Calla adds promptly. "What do you know about Anton Makusa that I don't?"

"Quite a bit." There's a pause as August looks forward again. Calla would wager that he's calculating how much to tell her, giving just enough information to satiate her curiosity but withholding the rest. August isn't one to play too much of his hand for no reason. All royals are the same. No free niceties.

"But I suppose there is one matter I *should* share. There weren't many other children in our palace, you know. Anton and I ended up very good friends despite our difference in age." A heavy drop of rain strikes his umbrella. It moves down the side like sludge. "Years later, we grew so tired of San-Er that we tried to leave it together."

Calla knows that they were friends, of course, but this part about their mutual escape plot is new. The rain starts to splatter harder, and she sticks her hand out from under the umbrella to catch the droplets. If this drizzle can get past all the awnings and clotheslines looped from window to window, it must really be coming down.

"And that's how Otta fell sick?" she asks. When the news traveled into the city, it only described a conflict with King Kasa.

August shifts his grip on the umbrella, shielding Calla's hand from the rain with an annoyed tut.

"Anton, Leida, and I," he says when Calla begrudgingly returns her arm to her side, "were planning to raid Kasa's vault and flee into the countryside with money and false identities. Leida could bypass security through her mother; I could gain access to the innermost rooms. Had we been successful, it was a scheme that would make us richer than the victors of the games."

"Sounds foolish."

"I know. We backed out." The umbrella teeters to the side as August loses his grip on it. He moves his hand and rights it again. "Anton wanted to bring Otta along. Leida and I thought it was too dangerous. We were going to regroup and draw up a new idea after the school year, but Anton and Otta got impatient. They went forward with it themselves.

"The two of them getting together was a train wreck waiting to happen. Both were obsessive and all-consuming enough on their own—put them in collusion, and at the first sign of danger, it's their lives over everyone else's. You remember Otta, don't you?"

The memories are fuzzy now, but how could Calla forget? Where Calla and August chatted politely by the children's table, Otta was laughing too loud and pretending to knock over a teacup so a servant would sweep it up. Where August once offered to give Calla a tour of the guest wing while the adults were busy talking, Otta got in Calla's face and asked her not to touch anything, lest she leave grubby fingerprints.

"The royal guard caught them in the middle of their scheme. Otta fucked up—I don't know what was going through her head, but she tried jumping into one of the Weisannas, and it didn't work. She tried again and again, a different guard each time, and kept getting shoved back into her own body. I would have been surprised if she *hadn't* caught the yaisu sickness."

"Otta is still alive, is she not?" Calla asks, though she already knows the answer. They saved her in time—or rather, they put her on life support and froze the onset of the sickness, though Otta Avia has not since awoken. "You're keeping her alive."

A sudden laugh from August, which surprises Calla so much that she almost jerks away. She hides her twitch by turning to face Galipei and finds shock in his expression too. Prince August does not laugh. Even made in mockery, the sound is incongruous with his expression. The sound has enough venom to blister.

"We washed our hands of her years ago," August says. "*Anton* is the one keeping her alive."

Calla stops walking. August follows suit, though he has already stridden two steps away, and now Calla is without the cover of his umbrella. She feels the dirty rain hit her neck and slide under her coat into her camisole, growing sticky against her skin.

"So that's his motive for the games," she says. "He cannot possibly afford to keep her at the hospital like that all these years."

"He's been in touch several times, asking for money," August confirms. "He knows his own criminal status, and that he's not supposed to bother the palace. But he does so anyway, because Anton Makusa does not care for the rules."

Calla's mind is still whirring. "What's the point? There's no coming back from the yaisu sickness. Does he think she might wake up?"

"I doubt he thinks much at all," August replies. He tilts his head to summon Galipei. In response, his right-hand man hurries forward, boots splashing into the puddles, slathering mud up his black trousers. "He can't let go of her, and we have to suffer for it."

Calla raises a brow. "How romantic," she says wryly.

"It's the very opposite of romance." August turns away and starts to walk, Galipei close behind. "Collaborate with him if you want. But don't be surprised when he stabs you in the back."

"You can help with that, no?" Calla calls after him. "Hey—"

Before she can negotiate further, however, her wristband is trembling. Calla glances down at the screen, irritated with its poor timing.

August and Galipei are already exiting the alley. They do so casually, uncaring that Calla is no longer following them, the conversation having come to an end.

With a disgruntled mutter, Calla turns and runs the other way, drawing her sword.

◇◇◇◇◇

One would think that the palace surveillance room of all places could afford to fix the broken air conditioner in the corner, yet there it sits with its front half missing, the room growing muggier and hotter around it.

Pampi squints at her monitor, fanning herself with her hand and following the players in her assigned area with keen eyes. Eighty-Six is fast, and two different dots on the screen blip out in rapid succession. Other players don't have the same efficiency, though that's through no fault of their own. San-Er is too dense, and the statistical probability of players naturally congregating in the same area is low. Of course, when location pings push two or three together within the same block, they're already gearing up for a fight, and it's either a fast battle where one ambushes the other, or there's no battle at all because one player has slunk away and run out of range before they could come into contact with the other.

"Whoa, whoa, whoa, what's this?"

Pampi draws away from her desk, glancing three cubicles over. A colleague jumps to her feet, hands held up.

"Hey! Hey, can someone look at this?"

Like everyone else nearby, hungry for some drama, Pampi hastens to the desk. Movement flashes on the screen. Pampi has to bite her lip to keep her smile down.

"What are we looking at?" someone else asks.

"Bottom left corner," the woman answers. She points to the screen too, but as soon as she has directed their eyes down, it's difficult to overlook what is happening.

Number Five, matched to the bright dot on the corresponding screen. But Five isn't moving. Five stands there, surrounded by various garbage bags near the edge of a rooftop, drenched in rain as the downpour continues on. The footage is blurred, affected by the weather conditions, and the woman at the desk types commands into her keyboard in an effort to sharpen and enhance the image. It doesn't do much. San-Er's technology is prototypical to begin with, and sometimes signals do not connect to deliver its demands. Top-of-the-line companies with a councilmember on their board will always offer their products to the palace first and take royal investment, but even then, there is only so much these companies can manage when research moves slowly and advanced resources come in short.

"Did Five jump out?" another voice asks, leaning as close to the screen as he dares. "I didn't see anyone nearby."

"I suppose we can rewind the tape later," the woman answers. "I was switching through cameras quite fast, but then I stopped here a few minutes ago . . . the scene has yet to change."

The surveillance room fades to an eerie quiet. The other desks have noticed the crowd gathered at the back. Though they don't know what so many of their colleagues are enraptured by, a sense of ill ease has creeped in.

"Someone's coming," Pampi says suddenly. She cannot help herself.

A figure has walked onto the screen. Given the camera's high angle, their features are obscured by the deep hood over their head, but surveillance wouldn't have picked out more than two pixels of a face anyway when the rain is pouring down. Pampi clears her throat, glancing at the adjacent smaller screen. She motions for those around her to look as well. No dots near Five. This is not another player.

"Call the palace guard," she says evenly.

The woman hesitates. "I mean, we wouldn't want to bother them for—"

Five crumples to the rooftop floor. A collective inhale travels through the surveillance room, and no one exhales as the hooded figure strides forward, pulling at Five's limp arms. Though the rain pelts down at blurring speed, Five's skin is visibly darkening to a gray shade. The cameras cannot pick up the light of jumping, but the decaying body tells them that it is being performed before their very eyes—again and again, in and out of Five at rapid speed.

"It's another one," someone in the room says breathlessly. Pampi does not know which of her colleagues it was. They blend together, each voice merging with the next.

"Another yaisu sickness kill?"

"But that's not possible. There are only the two of them there. Why isn't the killer burning up too? Where else can they jump to?"

"It must be some sort of foreign attack. We don't know what they're capable of."

"Look! Look what they're doing!"

The figure with the hood hauls Five's arms all the way up. The Sican salute.

"Surely now," Pampi says, "we call the palace guard."

◇◇◇◇◇

Calla dreams of invasion.

She dreams that she is stuck in the ground, buried up to her ankles. Though she struggles and strains, she is stationary while streams of villagers run past her, fleeing their province as it burns, soldiers moving in and taking position outside each stout house.

Help, she wants to scream, but no sound comes. She knows that she is somewhere near the mountains, that she has to leave, that she must move if she is to keep her life. The soldiers are coming, their clothing as black as the night and their swords as bright as the stars. They command her not to resist. They say that the throne of Talin has arrived. That this is salvation; this is the moment they have been waiting for, plucked out from the harsh rule of anarchy at the borderlands and welcomed into civilization—

Calla wakes with a scream in her throat, biting back the sound just before it can escape. She lurches upright, jostling Mao Mao, who was resting peacefully on her lap. Her hands are shaking. As she does each time a nightmare shakes her awake, she reaches out to pet her cat, burying her fingers in his fur. Seconds pass. Her heartbeat starts to stabilize.

Outside, it almost sounds like the screaming from her dream is still going, but the noise is only drunken glee from patrons of the nearby restaurant, as per usual. Calla shifts Mao Mao gently to the bed and shuffles onto her knees, moving her pillows aside so she can see out her window. She pulls a gap in the blinds, then wipes her fingers on the glass to clear the condensation. The blots of neon color immediately crystallize into real shapes, revealing a couple ambling along the alley outside her bedroom. The sight is a far cry from the images still pressed to the inside of her eyelids, to the fields burning and blood running.

Calla releases an exhale. The people inside the twin cities are suffering. But they cannot even imagine how much worse those in the provinces have it. And so long as it is a competition, the blame will only circle around and around instead of going to the top, where it belongs.

The blinds snap back, blocking out the stream of light. Calla pulls the blankets over her head, determined to finish her sleep.

Tonight is for rest. When morning comes, she'll find Anton Makusa, and they'll turn the games into a frenzy.

CHAPTER 11

Y ilas Nuwa has been to the Hollow Temple enough times that she can find her way in without trouble. Its entrance is artfully hidden, tucked inside what might have once been a courtyard, enclosed by four buildings pressed edge to edge. Yilas goes into one of the buildings, climbs up to a market level, then walks through another door and down a hidden set of stairs around the back, turning and turning at the stairwell's landings.

She passes a window on the second floor, where there is no daylight to be seen, despite the morning hour. The temple's green roof tiles are only illuminated by the few sparse rays that seep in through the trash and miscellaneous buildup collected on the metal grille above. The peak-shaped roofing with its stone edges and circular tiling was designed to keep rain and wind away from the temple walls, but urban conditions in San-Er have recast such desires. It is not rain that the temple has to worry about, but debris: broken photo frames, used shampoo bottles, and spoiled baby diapers that fall from windowsills and come tumbling down fourteen stories of apartments on all four sides. When Yilas hugs her bag to her chest and pokes her head through the window—though it is less a window than a rectangular shape cut into the stairwell's outward facing wall—she might be convinced that this solid blot of color is not a metallic mesh grille above the temple but only a poorly installed ceiling.

Yilas hurries down the last set of stairs, exits the building, and walks toward the entrance of the Hollow Temple. She tries not to make eye contact with those outside doing breathing exercises. In her periphery, she catches sight of brass knuckles and chains, curved shapes inked on their necks—some in bloodred, some in regular black.

"I'm only dropping something off," Yilas says to the woman at the door. She doesn't bother with a greeting. The Crescent Societies would mark unnecessary politeness as a sign of weakness and terrorize her before she can scramble out of here.

The woman waves her onward. Yilas enters the temple, gritting her teeth. Matiyu couldn't have chosen a nice job in the financial district. He had to go joining the Crescent Societies.

"Hey," she barks, spotting her little brother at one of the tables. "Here's your stupid lunch."

She thumps the bag in front of Matiyu. He looks up with a start, blinking at her with the same pale-green eyes that she has and pushing his thick-rimmed glasses up his flat nose.

"Oh, good, you're here," Matiyu says. Without waiting for her response, he grabs her wrist and starts to pull her toward the back of the temple. "I need you to come see this."

"Your food—"

"It's okay, no one will take it." Matiyu tugs on her wrist again, hurrying her along. "Quick, quick, come on."

"What's the rush?" Yilas asks, but she quickens her pace anyway. "And since when did you need me for your little scholarly work?"

Yilas was always awful at school. She dropped out early to become a palace attendant, and then she hated attending too, even though Calla was the easiest person in the palace to wait on. After she met Chami, she didn't care for climbing to high places or achieving grand things. She only wanted to water her plants every day in their apartment above the diner, to live quietly and softly.

Matiyu is not the same. He graduated top of his class last year, on a trajectory toward making something of himself. Then, to their parents' horror, he took an accounting position for the Crescent Societies instead of a well-to-do bank.

It's not like I'm actually *buying into their religious cult,* he had said. *But they're where the fast money is. I'll work two years underground, then leave and take up something more comfortable.*

People call them a cult for a reason, Yilas had leveled. *What are you going to do when they start brainwashing you?*

But Matiyu had only waved her off, unworried.

They're coming around to the back of the temple. Matiyu leads them through without a second glance at the people nearby, but Yilas can't help staring a little. One cluster is off in the corner doing qi exercises in synchrony. Another group prays with their foreheads pressed to the ground. When they straighten up again, there's a strangeness seeped into their manner.

Yilas turns away, holding in a grimace. *Magic,* some call it. If that were the case, then jumping would be magic too. But jumping comes from qi, and the gods forged their qi. Everything about San-Er is merely the work of its gods—the true gods in the ether and the false gods ruling from the palace.

"I've been trying to organize the stock numbers coming in," Matiyu explains, opening the door into a storage room. He blows at the thin layer of dust on the boxes stacked near the door, then removes one of them for access to the light switch. The thin bulb doesn't do much for illumination. Yilas struggles to see what her brother is rummaging for when he pulls out a drawer of a filing cabinet and retrieves a thick stack of folders. "But some of these receipts don't look right."

"How am I supposed to help?" Yilas takes the folder offered to her. When she opens it, the papers look to be written logs—an export of heroin here, an import of opium there, some random sales of ephedra from smaller shops instead of the larger underground factories.

"Tell me if anything looks strange to you," Matiyu says. "Run through the incoming numbers, then see what our outgoing prices are . . . it doesn't fit, does it? I can't see—"

The door slams open.

"Why is she in here?" Before Yilas can react, someone has hauled her out by the arm, their grip like iron. She barely has time to look up and see who is dragging her away—by the time she has glimpsed the crescent moon at their neck, she's already been pushed through the temple's doors, Matiyu's footsteps plodding after them.

"Wait, wait, wait, that's my sister—"

Yilas stumbles off the steps of the temple, finally getting a proper look at the Crescent Society member who had pushed her out. They're old and wrinkled, exuding seniority.

"Crescent Society business stays within the Crescent Societies."

Then the temple doors slam, and Yilas is left blinking.

"Well," she says to no one, "at least it wasn't a knife in the gut."

◇◇◇◇◇

Blood is hard to wipe off once it dries, which Anton knows because he's only getting flakes from his neck despite his vigorous rubbing. He thought maybe mixing new blood with the dried blood would help it all come off at once, but alas. It only becomes a smear of red.

Anton gives up. As he walks, he wipes one of his blades clean on his shirt, deciding that he's already a bloodied mess anyway, so what's a few extra stains? He glances over his shoulder at the alley corner, waiting a beat before wiping his second blade. He left a dead body behind on the third floor of a building in the financial district, and although he checked for a pulse and even waved up at the surveillance cameras to make sure they knew the fight had finished, there's a part of him convinced he's still being tailed by an opponent. He cannot let his guard down—not now, not ever.

They're a week into the games. The kills slowed tremendously after the first battle, and they'll only occur further apart the longer the games proceed when there are fewer and fewer players. They crossed the halfway mark for eliminations after the first day of the pings, but they have not moved past ten more deaths since then.

With a grimace, Anton slides his blades back into his sleeve. The whisper of metal echoes in the alley. Then: the ghost of a footstep, from the other end. Before he can be sighted, Anton ducks behind a stack of woven baskets. His breath remains shallow from the last fight. If someone really has been tailing him . . .

"You can come out, Makusa. I know you're here."

The voice is familiar. Anton pokes his head out from the baskets just enough to see Princess Calla Tuoleimi stride into the alley, holding some sort of device in her hands. She looks up, then at the device again, squinting and pivoting around. Typical. August probably gave it to her to track fellow contestants.

Anton stands up. "That doesn't seem to be working very well, does it?"

With dizzying speed, Calla kicks a pebble, launching it in Anton's direction. He barely darts out of the way before the rock strikes the wall, leaving a visible white dent.

"Oops," the princess says, and she doesn't sound the slightest bit apologetic. "You scared me."

"I don't think you've ever been scared in your life," Anton mutters. He rubs his jaw out of phantom pain; that strike could have done some damage if he hadn't moved in time. "I urge you to be careful—the face is pretty, but it is borrowed."

Calla puts the device away. She keeps her hands in the pockets of her long coat. "Like I said, you startled me. Sneak up on me in a new face and it's only fair my sword flies at your neck next time."

Sneak up on her? She's the one who snuck up on *him*.

"Convenient excuse to slaughter an ally," he says.

Calla steps forward and starts to circle him. Though she makes the action appear casual, the hairs at the back of Anton's neck are standing straight up under her scrutiny.

"When did we become allies?"

"Was it not agreed?"

She is silent, continuing to appraise him like he's an object of curiosity at the market.

"Why are you here otherwise?" he asks.

"Why are *you* here?"

"I'm playing the games."

"As am I."

Anton grasps for another retort, but finds none. They're talking in circles while she walks, and he is willing to bet that Calla Tuoleimi could keep going until she's eaten him whole. He switches tactics.

"What will it take to be careful with my life?" Anton eyes her pocketed hands. Who knows what other weapons she keeps hidden in her clothes. "Shall we come up with a code word? Something only I know to say to identify myself?"

Calla stops in front of him. When she lifts her brow, her yellow eyes are so bright that he can hardly believe he did not recognize her instantly on first contact.

"That's unnecessary, given—"

"*What fine daylight we have today*," he interrupts, inspiration striking. "That's what I'll say."

"We never have fine daylight." Calla looks up briefly, her bangs sliding away from her face. "San is a city of darkness."

Anton winks. "Exactly. No one can say it accidentally."

Calla sighs, though she hardly has time to shoot him down before both their wristbands are trembling. She doesn't look bothered, pressing the buttons at the top. Anton, on the other hand, blinks in confusion.

"I just came from a ping. It's too soon."

"It's mine," Calla says. "I haven't had one all day. You've only been triggered by proximity."

Anton slides his knives back out. He should have caught his breath by now, but his throat still feels tight. Calla glances at him, smiling with menace when their eyes meet, and his throat closes up even more.

"So," he says. "Are we allies, then?"

"I suppose we are." Calla pulls her wristband up as she starts to walk, tilting her head for the text sliding across the screen. Anton doesn't bother glancing at his wristband at all. If someone is heading toward Calla, then they are heading toward him too.

"Watch the puddle, Fifty-Seven."

Calla glances back. She skirts the puddle, an ear tipped to the city as she listens. They walk past a pharmacy, where two elderly men sit in the corner playing cards. "Must you call me something as crude as my number?"

"My apologies. Would you prefer Calla? Or perhaps Her Highness, Princess Calla?"

"I," Calla says sweetly, "am going to kill you."

"I was expecting it eventually, but not this soon—*to your left!*"

Calla reacts immediately, hearing the change in Anton's tone as if a switch was flipped. She ducks without looking, narrowly avoiding the arc of a heavy pole-like weapon, which strikes the side of the pharmacy entrance instead.

The player lunges out from the pharmacy, rearing the pole back for another swing. His motions are heavy, powerful. His path through the shop is marked with a trail of fallen bags he's collided with, the back door he surged through still swinging from the vigor of his entrance.

While the pole swings in Anton's direction, Calla twists up and kicks the player in the back, sending him off-balance before the pole can land and crush Anton like a paper doll. One end of his weapon drops onto the alley ground with a clangorous *thud*. Taking the opening, Anton lunges forward, slashing the player's legs and rolling out of the way just as fast. San-Er is too narrow for fights. It is not fit for puzzling, nor for careful navigation and calculated strikes. It is speed and strength in a quick grapple, and when it comes down to it, two people working in close tandem will always overpower one opponent.

Calla shoves her sword through the player's stomach. He freezes, losing grip on the pole entirely while he attempts to claw the blade out of him. If only he would glance inside the pharmacy again, he might be able to jump. He might see the two elderly bodies, ready for the taking. Instead, he panics, tries to move away, and Anton has already taken advantage of the pause to reach over and slash the player's throat.

Anton feels the hot gush of blood on his hand. Feels it creep into every line of his palm, coat his skin as another stain impossible to clean off. He has ended so many lives, put on and washed off layer after layer of red. But these are not his hands, and this is not his body. Maybe there is no need to stop until he is reunited with his birth body, and only then will he start to count the infractions.

The player falls. By the time he hits the ground, he is already taking on the appearance of rot. Anton breathes a long exhale, the alley now quiet. It was a quick battle. He watches Calla shake her sword, getting most of the blood off before leaning down to tap the player's wristband screen.

"This was Thirteen," she reports. She wipes her chin as she straightens up again, cleaning the red smeared there. When she sheathes her sword, she looks away too fast for Anton to determine whether he was imagining her odd expression.

"Who are they going to log for this hit?" he asks curiously. "You or me?"

"Probably you," Calla answers, striding away. "I have too many already."

Anton hurries after her. "Show-off."

◇◇◇◇◇

San-Er is already inventing narratives. The reels play them on repeat: blurry footage of Anton and Calla outside that tiny pharmacy, fighting together like such a well-oiled machine that even August can't believe they didn't know each other prior to the games.

He picks up a teacup, his grip tightening. Any other person might have thrown it against the wall. He almost wants to. But he keeps his composure, taking a sip and setting down the teacup afterward, lest the porcelain shatter in his fingers and bring Galipei inside to investigate.

The television screen fuzzes and glitches, the citywide signal hitting trouble. When the large screen in August's bedroom clears again, the newscaster is relaying the crowd-favorite theory on players Eighty-Six and Fifty-Seven. Through the afternoon and into the evening, they have run down the list of every possibility—from long-lost relatives to foreign agents—but the narrative that has caught the most interest is that of lovers, each of whom registered for the games because of depleting funds, not knowing the other had done the same.

August drops into a satin-lined chair. He props his arm on his knee, then lolls his head onto his fist, thinking. San-Er's viewers are fascinated by the idea of an alliance, wildly entertained over how it might take shape. And first and foremost, that is what the games are. Entertainment. A distraction. Players in the past have never teamed up before, at least not long-term. Anton and Calla are delivering for the masses better than King Kasa ever could.

The reels give Calla ample screen time now that everyone has noticed her lack of jumping too. Enough time has passed since the Daqun for every other player to switch bodies, but Calla's remains the same. Though her face is always covered by a breathing mask, the newscasters are quick to recognize that same long curtain of hair and red leather coat billowing with her movements. They suspect that she doesn't have the jumping gene, which is a fair assumption when rarely anyone risks the games without that fail-safe. Calla likely didn't intend this as a part of her strategy, but the assumption will work in her favor. When King Kasa looks upon the scoreboard and sees that it is headed by someone who can't jump, he'll chuckle to himself about this soon-to-be victor with weak qi, unthreatened by the thought of letting them into the guarded palace.

If there is justice in their world, then that unmerited confidence is exactly what will bring him to his death. And if justice does not come, then August himself will hunt it down.

In a smooth motion, August stands and strides toward his door.

"Where are you going?" Galipei asks, looking up from his seat when August enters the anteroom. He puts his book down.

August waits a beat. His hand hovers over the gilded knob. Though he turns over his shoulder, he does not entirely meet his bodyguard's eyes.

"Otta needs to die."

A beat of silence. Galipei blinks once. He is well trained enough not to let a reaction enter his expression.

"She won't wake up," Galipei replies. "Is that not enough?"

"It's not certain. We cannot take that chance."

The palace seems to quiver under his tread. Every floor and wing, every corridor and lavishly bright room. They perk ears to the conversation, rising to attention. The walls remember the boy who would become their crown prince, who punched a fist into them seven years ago. The heavy, golden-threaded curtains, though they do not shimmer as brightly as they did back then, prickle at the memory of being thrown by Otta Avia, her voice tearing through August's private wing, echoing and echoing, "I'll tell! I'll tell! I swear I will!"

"What do you want, Otta?" August had spat. He lunged forward, but Otta shrank farther behind the curtains, as if they would shield her from him. She was only feigning helplessness. Had he gotten closer, she would have drawn her claws.

"Look at you, pretending to be good," Otta sneered in return. "You're worse for San than Kasa ever could be. You'll put us in cages and call us your loyal subjects."

"People *already* live in cages. You have been brainwashed so thoroughly by the council—"

August made a grab, but Otta simply slipped out of range and strode away, throwing her chin high. In her hands: the smallest slip of paper. The only evidence she needed to prove that, for Leida and August, running from the twin cities was not a matter of safety, but a plan to find a forgotten palace out at the edges of Talin. A plan to mobilize and wage war on San-Er. If they could recruit Anton, who was San-Er's best jumper, they would be unstoppable.

Then Otta threatened to tell Kasa before the roots were secure. Then Anton walked away too. Without him, August and Leida were thrown all the way back to the planning stage. Mobilizing war wasn't realistic anymore. They needed to be smarter to get what they wanted.

"August," Galipei prompts.

August steels himself to deliver his next words. "You weren't assigned to me until after Otta was gone, so I don't expect you to understand. Kill her."

Galipei is the only one in the palace that knows of August's treasonous plans to depose King Kasa, about the regicide that has been put in motion. There is no one whom August trusts more than Galipei, but sometimes he wishes Galipei weren't so smart, that he wouldn't fight so hard to know *everything*, because the mere act of knowing drags him down to the dirtiest corners of palace grappling. August is closer than ever to achieving his plans. He must eliminate any threat, and if there is the infinitesimal chance that Otta wakes . . .

August opens the door. Galipei, however, isn't finished with the conversation and clearly isn't deterred by the threat of someone overhearing.

"I'm your bodyguard, August," he says, "not your servant."

In the hallway, a maid glances over, right in the middle of making a food delivery. She's so taken aback by August's sudden appearance that the tray in her hand teeters to the side.

"Your Highness," she greets, scrambling to right the plates atop the tray before they tip off. "I didn't mean to disturb you—"

August opens his eyes, agilely balancing the tray in his hand, losing only a crumb that falls into the carpet. He bends to pick it up, small fingers closing around a thread, and two paces away, Galipei hurries to catch August's body before he falls, his teeth gritted when he loops his arms around his prince's middle.

Galipei glances over and waits. Under the bright lights, his silver eyes look almost molten, seeking . . . well, August doesn't really know.

"Please," August says simply. His voice sounds different, but that tone— that level tone without a hint of doubt—is always the same.

Those eyes turn dull. Molten silver to plain flatware.

"As you wish, Your Highness."

Something has shifted between them. A hairline fracture, settling upon their fitted pieces. But August sets the tray down and walks off anyway, intent on finding out exactly how long these games must last, how long until San-Er—until Talin—is his.

CHAPTER 12

I t takes another week for the games to reach thirty players remaining, and that achievement is only because Calla and Anton start to hunt their fellow contestants down. Though the two are good at making eliminations, San-Er lives and breathes by the million, and a game of eighty-eight is merely a blip in the hustle and bustle.

"They're on the floor above," Calla reports. August has started to feed her locations through her pager. They are unlike the official game pings, which use approximate distances while she runs like a headless chicken. Instead, he has implemented a code in the surveillance room that, when Calla is in the vicinity, sends her a script of text, reporting exactly where the other player stands.

Anton briefly rests his hand on the wall, leaving a red mark upon the white paint. They're in Er's financial district, and so the floors of this building are more proper than the ones they usually tear through. Both their daily pings have gone off already, but to no success. The players slipped away.

"I didn't think Prince August would make it so easy for us, Fifty-Seven."

Calla shoots him a sidelong glare. "Would you prefer to do this the traditional way?"

"Oh, no, don't misunderstand me." He tosses one of his knives. It swings a perfect full rotation in the air before landing back in his grip, ready for battle. "I'm shocked that the games can be manipulated so thoroughly, is all."

There's a rumble past the wall to their right. A sudden *bang!* in the stairwell they just exited. They only came to the fifth floor because the pager reported this as a player's last location, but it's empty, unless the office workers in their glass cubicles count.

Er's financial district is usually orderly, refusing to mimic the rest of the twin cities in clumping a motley of businesses and factories and shops together. Calla had briefly eyed the directory on the ground floor before they came up. Half of this building is owned by an obscure private academy, the other half divided into offices for one of the major banks.

When Calla holds a hand out to Anton and listens, the stairwell quiets again. Like someone barged in and then right back out.

"Wait," she says suddenly. "Do you think—"

"There's an active fight here," Anton concludes at the same time. "A second player. Do we—"

Calla is already nodding, turning over her shoulder in search for the other exit. There are two main stairwells. One runs down the center of the building cleanly, and the other loops around the exterior.

"I'll go around. Let's block them in."

She's running before Anton can grunt his assent, pulling her sword and shouldering through the door. The groggy day greets her, not bright enough to qualify for sunshine in Er, but sufficient glaring gray to light her way as she passes the classrooms facing this side of the building. The kids inside stand at the sight of her. In eagerness, they flock from their desks to the windows, waving happily, but Calla forges on, taking the upcoming steps three at a time.

When she slips back into the building, there's a player doing her very best to slice a schoolteacher in half, her long ponytail swinging in sync with her cuts.

The students here have scrambled for cover, and it isn't until the schoolteacher strikes back with a quick fist that Calla realizes this is in fact another player, the wristband hidden under the cuff of their pressed white sleeve. The sight is . . . unexpected. The king's games tend to draw in riffraff and troublemakers at the end of their line, those who have no other option except to risk their lives for riches. For someone with a respectable living to throw their name into something as vicious as the games . . . what can the motivation be? Not enough pay? The adrenaline rush? It can't be worth this: a blade in the gut in front of twenty of your own students, splattering the front-most row with blood.

A flash of light blinds the hallway in absolute white. Calla is charging forward despite her stinging eyes.

Anton is doing the same from the other stairwell.

Before the player can pull her sword from the schoolteacher, Anton comes within range and presses his knives to her neck. In one fast motion, he has cut a cross into her, deep enough that she drops without a lost beat. While the player with the ponytail is eliminated, the light has taken the schoolteacher elsewhere, and by the time Anton searches the packed corridor—filled with teenagers dressed in uniform, red ties dangling at their necks—he has already lost track of which body the teacher could have dived into.

But just because he wasn't paying attention does not mean Calla wasn't. And as he heaves, trying to catch his breath, he watches Calla slam one of the boys down, foot on his chest.

"Fifty-Seven," Anton exclaims suddenly, a hand outstretching. He wants to tell her, *We don't need to kill him,* or perhaps, *Let him go.* But he cannot. The games end with only one victor. Collateral damage in every direction is how they have always been played. It is only that a part of him prefers to lie if it will spare him from feeling awful, but a greater part of him knows these lies are useless. He can't bring himself to tell one now.

"Will you take this boy down with you?" Calla asks quietly.

"He's innocent," the schoolteacher says with the boy's tinny voice. "Let us live."

Anton has stopped bracing for a new attack. He is watching Calla instead, her sword pressed to the boy's neck. If she looked angry, maybe it would have made for a more fitting picture. Fury for the kingdom, for the games, clouding her moral compass and obscuring her sight. But there is none of that.

Only the levelheaded princess who killed her parents with that same steady stare.

"How foolish," Calla whispers.

When she feels her next breath burn her throat, she brings the sword down, and the boy's head comes off, his life and his schoolteacher's ended at once. One way or another, there would have been a second life taken along the line.

The other students gasp, hands flying to their mouths. Calla can't help the bitterness roiling in her stomach. Shouldn't they be used to this by now? Or is this part of Er more sheltered than the rest? Do they rise every morning with breakfast laid out for them, no hunger and a big, comfortable bed?

She knows it's unfair to think this way. But it's hard to push back resentment at those in the twin cities who have never feared for their lives, who have no idea how the rest of Talin suffers.

When Calla turns to go, Anton follows her silently. Out of her periphery, she can see that his eyes are pinned on her intently. She wonders what he's looking for. Guilt? Delight? Perhaps she *should* feel guilty, if only to prove that deep inside, she is good and redeemable. But each time she swings her sword, the feeling that sits heavy in her rib cage is not guilt. It is a jarring sensation that tells her this is wicked, but wickedness is tolerable. Good kingdoms don't need good soldiers. A good soldier dies on the battlefield and lets the people cry for him.

Good kingdoms need loyal soldiers, terrible ones. Calla is killing people to save them, and before San-Er put its wall up, when Talin fought its war with Sica, it was the same. Lives thrown into the fire, sacrificed so that millions more at home could carry on safely.

Calla swivels around, stopping on a landing in the stairwell. Anton halts too, blocked from walking any farther. She searches his face. He stares back, waiting.

But Calla says nothing.

"Is something the matter?" he asks eventually.

There's blood on his jaw. Calla reaches out to swipe it away, then pauses, her red fingers inches from his face. She would be no help. She would only make it worse.

"We need to rinse off," Calla decides. "There's a public standpipe directly outside. Come on."

Her voice is gravelly. They both pretend not to make note of it. She inclines her head at the last floor of the stairwell, and down she walks, Anton close on her heels like some long, lingering shadow.

They push out into a thin alley and the ground-level murkiness of Er. As soon as the door slams shut after them, it is like the building has been cordoned off. Calla imagines a line being drawn in her memories, roping it off for a day when San-Er is no longer at war with itself.

Anton reaches out suddenly to snag her elbow, and Calla jumps, her hand darting for her sword. If he has chosen now to attack her—

"Wait," he hisses. His eyes are trained ahead.

A rustle sounds in the alley, from the little nook where the standpipe is. Calla searches the nook, its one small bulb working overtime to illuminate the whole area.

"I don't see anything," Calla whispers.

Nothing stirs. There are dozens of hose pipes hanging down the wall, tangled on the floor like a nest of rubbery snakes. Most likely, the noise was just one of them detaching from the bunch and falling to the ground. The pipes are connected to the food factories nearby, the singular stop for workers to come by when they need their tanks replenished.

When a few seconds pass and the scene remains still, Anton shakes his head. "Looks like we're clear. Maybe I'm being paranoid."

"Not at all." Calla strides forward and pulls at the faucet, letting the water pour out onto her feet. She cups the water into her hands and washes at her arms, getting the blood off her elbows. The red that is stained into her white shirt will remain. "There have been deaths across San-Er targeting players. The newsreels aren't broadcasting it. But if you pay attention to the numbers, you've probably noticed too."

As Calla splashes water onto her neck, Anton draws near, sticking his hand under the running stream.

"Four." There is no hesitation. He has already been counting. "There are four eliminations that aren't attributed to another player. I thought perhaps they had deactivated their wristbands."

Calla steps away from the faucet, shaking her hands dry. "The work of Sican agents, if you believe Prince August."

Anton rolls his eyes. That strikes Calla's interest—the contempt flashing quick as a whip across his expression.

"I was attacked earlier in the games," Calla continues, leaning up against the standpipe. Her gaze is fixed on Anton while he tries to work a clot of blood out of his hair, waiting for another moment of that repulsion to cross his face. Something about it thrills her, to see his usual insolence falter. "Someone came at me from behind, but as soon as I shoved my sword through their body, it dropped as if it were just an empty vessel. No blood, no qi."

Anton smooths the water out of his hair, slicking dark strands back from his forehead.

"So they jumped?" he asks.

"No." Calla folds her arms. "There was no light."

A beat passes. Anton remains quiet, trying to gauge if Calla is being serious.

"And you think it's a Sican skill?" he asks eventually. He turns the faucet off. "Lightless jumping?"

"I'm not sure what I think." When she straightens up again, the sheath of her sword bounces against her knee. Calla unhooks it, letting her body rest without the sword's weight bearing on her hip. "All I know is, I've never seen it before. If August wants to blame it on foreign intruders, I suppose that's a possibility."

Anton, however, seems unconvinced. "I've heard rumors that we might be able to do it too, if you're quick enough."

Perhaps he can train for that one day, but Calla has not jumped in fifteen years. The palace already thought jumping was the behavior of commoners who didn't have valuable bodies to protect; royalty were warned even more significantly against the act. The stakes were too high for their vessels. She has never been as tricky as August is, flitting from body to body so that he isn't recognized leaving the palace. She can hardly remember how it goes, how easy it is for those born strong with the ability. Jumping speed depends on how near the target body is, but no matter how slow or fast it *feels*, the flash of light is always the same from the outside.

"It could be a matter of technique," Anton is still saying. "We have learned to do it in a way that gives off light. A visible sign of our qi moving. Perhaps the Sicans have learned something else."

"Perhaps they don't have qi."

Anton clicks his tongue. "Everyone has qi."

Like the wind of the world and the salt of the sea. Qi is what gives life in the womb, the difference between a vessel and a body. It is what takes life away when it dissipates in old age.

"I think it would explain a lot," Calla says anyway, sticking with her outrageous claim. "Maybe in the years we've been cut off from them, the Sicans have started evolving into something else."

"Do you"—Anton crouches, submerging one of his knives into a puddle and shaking the blood from the blade—"have any basis to be saying this, or are you merely stringing together nonsense?"

Calla steps her foot forward quickly, pinning the blade down before Anton can pick it back up. Instead of fighting her for his weapon, he closes his hand around her ankle, squeezing hard.

"Careful with my feelings, Makusa," she says wryly. "I don't like being accused of nonsense."

She pretends not to notice the increasing pressure on her ankle. Anton pretends not to be gripping so hard he could snap her bones with just one extra twinge.

He smiles languidly. "Are you playing games with me, Princess?"

"Maybe I am." She peers out from the nook. No one is around. No threats. "Would you like that?"

"I like where this is going. Keep talking."

Calla mirrors his smile. With a swift yank, she tugs her leg free from his grasp and loops her sword back onto her belt, the metallic sound grating at her ears.

"I think we're done for the day. Same time tomorrow?"

She's walking off before Anton has the chance to respond.

◇◇◇◇◇

Although the Weisannas are merely a part of the larger palace guard, they often feel like a unit of their own, pushed into major assignments and sent out on patrol at double the frequency. Galipei knows each and every one of them: his distant cousins and second aunts and thrice-removed uncles. So long as they have the Weisanna eyes, their life has been charted from birth. Their kingdom needs them. San-Er needs them. With such a power, one cannot shirk their duties.

Galipei ducks into the pharmacy, pushing at the plastic curtain draped over the doorway. The air-conditioning rushes out, and he drops the curtain into place again before he's yelled at for letting the cold escape.

At the counter, there's a woman in dark glasses, rushing around her cabinets. Jars of herbal medicine from the provinces are organized side by side with boxes bearing complex labels from the factories in San. When Galipei was younger, he was afraid of the yellow roots in the corner, floating in clear liquid. He used to say they looked like brains, reaching with their stems and ready to invade their victims.

Then he would get a solid thump on the head with a rolled-up newspaper, and he would laugh and laugh, asking to be thumped again because it was funny.

The woman at the counter takes off her glasses as Galipei approaches, crinkling the lines around her silver eyes.

"Hello, Aunt," Galipei says softly. "Have you eaten?"

A Weisanna can leave the palace guard if they wish. But it is the most shameful decision to make, an unforgivable crime as far as the rest of San-Er is concerned.

"Ah, an old woman like me doesn't get hungry often anyway." She pulls open a drawer behind the counter. "What will it be today? Muscle pain? Headache? You need more rest, less running around. What would your parents say if they were still around? Can't start a family if you're bone-tired all the time."

Galipei can't hold back his smile. Though it was the palace who raised him—fed him, clothed him, put him through the academy and supplied extra lessons to train him into the guard he would become—it was his aunt who loved him. She was ostracized when she quit, but that doesn't matter to Galipei, no matter how much his other cousins whisper about his visits.

"It's not for me," Galipei says. His smile drops. He looks around, ensuring that there are no other customers browsing the single shelf in the store. There's one surveillance camera propped up near the clock on the wall, but San-Er's security does not have sound. Nevertheless, he lowers his volume as he leans in.

"Do you have cinnabar?"

His aunt's brow furrows. "For what? Are you trying to create an immortality elixir?"

Galipei shakes his head. "Why is that your first thought? Maybe the palace wants to carve lacquerware and needs decorative powder."

Slowly, his aunt starts to rummage through her lower shelves. Her face is still in a grimace, mostly because Galipei didn't actually answer her original question. Cinnabar, a mineral that Talin mines from its borderlands, comes into San-Er in moderate amounts to be used in the factories for its vermillion-red color.

It's also highly toxic.

"I have it in powder form," his aunt says carefully. Every Weisanna goes through the same training units; they possess the same knowledge from the palace. If Galipei has come looking for a toxic substance, there's little else he might be using it for.

"You keep in mind"—his aunt isn't looking at him as she packs it up, screwing the lid tight and placing it carefully into a paper bag, but he feels the sharpness of her words nonetheless—"you can always leave the palace. It's not so bad out here."

"I can't," Galipei replies. The idea is unfathomable to him. "They need me."

"Your crown prince needs you, you mean" is her reply. With a shake of her head, his aunt passes him the bag. The top has been folded over multiple times, as if she still wants to prevent him from accessing the mineral despite being the one to give it to him. "He is more poisonous than all the cinnabar in the world combined."

"He's not—"

The plastic at the door rustles, bringing in another customer. Galipei swallows his words, keeping his face angled away so that he's not recognized. His aunt, too, puts her dark glasses back on and waves him off.

"Use caution, my boy," she warns. "That's all I have to say."

Dismissed, Galipei nods and leaves the pharmacy, the paper bag clutched tightly in his hands.

CHAPTER 13

Calla is already sweating when she finds Anton the next day, inhumanely early so that they can convene before either of their pings goes off. It's piping hot despite the hour, the air sticky and humid. She swapped out her longer coat for a hemmed jacket and she isn't wearing anything except her underclothes underneath the leather, but her skin still sticks to the inside of the material. At least she can put up with a little discomfort if it means her arms are protected from any flying blades.

"August is already up and at it," Calla says when she stops beside Anton, turning her pager around.

Anton squints, trying to read the scrolling text that August has tacked on to his automatic code.

"Why's he telling you to *be careful?*"

Evercent Hotel. Number 79, the pager says. Then: I believe he is checking in at opening hours. Be careful.

"My cousin highly regards my safety," Calla replies. A lie. August would bite off his own hand before he urged caution for the sake of her health and well-being. Anton seems to know it too, because the dark brow of the body he's wearing today quirks up and stays there. He's dressed lighter than she is: a button-down with his sleeves rolled up to his elbows, the deep-green fabric crumpled in a manner only expensive things can manage. It seems Anton is quite fond of jumping into the rich.

Calla waves her hand at him, starting toward the Evercent Hotel. August's code always chooses targets that are either nearby or heading toward obvious landmarks, and the Evercent Hotel is the largest building in Er. Despite being some distance away, Calla and Anton move through San quickly, weaving in and out of the slowly stirring city, then trekking onto a bridge with their weapons hidden from view. If anyone saw them from afar, one might even think they were a couple taking a brisk morning stroll.

Maybe if couples these days went for matching bloodstains instead of wedding rings.

"You take the front, I'll go around back?" Anton suggests as they approach the hotel.

Calla purses her lips. August's warning about Anton flashes through her head again, and she shifts the sheath of her sword so it is easily within reach.

"I don't see anyone at the desk, though. Seventy-Nine might not have arrived yet."

Or he could be one of the people lingering right outside. A large group waits by the door: high-class escorts, ready to be picked up at check-in like an extra towel or a pair of slippers.

"Stay undercover until we know?" Anton suggests.

"Undercover until then," Calla confirms.

Calla enters first, smacked immediately by the chill from the air-conditioning. She breathes out with a sigh of relief, trying to unstick her armpits from her jacket. Anton is close behind, coughing loudly. When Calla glances over her shoulder with a glare, asking wordlessly why he's making such a scene, he waves around his face and shoots a nasty look at one of the courtesans holding a cigarette. Looks like she blew smoke right into Anton's face. Calla gives the courtesan a smile. Anton scowls.

"Checking in?" the desk attendant asks when Calla and Anton finally draw near, tapping her acrylic nails on the stone countertop. Calla takes too long to answer, making note of the lobby details and its fraying carpet. Anton leans forward instead to stall, asking about the hotel amenities and room layouts. For whatever reason—perhaps genuine nicety, perhaps swayed by Anton's borrowed body and good looks—the attendant tolerates the questions, pulling out reference sheet after reference sheet from the drawers behind the desk. Er is touchier about the games than San. While civilians in San are suicidal enough to risk a stab in the gut for the sake of a paid hospital bill, Er will close its shops early and forbid its children from walking on the streets alone while the games are ongoing. If the desk attendant knew they were players, she would not be speaking to Anton at all.

The doors to the hotel open again, and Calla turns around.

Only to see Seventy-Nine walking in with his wristband right in the open, surrounded by an entourage of ten men.

"What the fuck?" Calla mutters, her hand snapping out to grab Anton. He swivels around too, his eyebrows shooting up at the sight. Seventy-Nine flaunts his wristband *atop* the sleeve of his black suit jacket, flashing with light just as the wide metal rings on his fingers do.

"Have we ever seen him in the reels?" Anton whispers quickly.

Calla swallows. Seventy-Nine is walking closer, but his attention is only on the desk attendant. As far as he knows, Calla and Anton are merely other guests, moving aside for him as he checks in. The men surrounding him have knives. She can see the bulges in their pockets. When one of them looks around to take inventory of the lobby, his eyes flash *silver* under the lights. A Weisanna, likely retired from the palace, gauging by his age. Heavens. This isn't only hired help, but the best of it.

"No," Calla answers. She tilts her head toward Anton, like they are merely discussing personal business before deciding on a room. As subtly as possible, they both slide their arms behind themselves to hide their wristbands. They would remember seeing *this* on the reels: a rich man walking around with others doing his bidding. "Never. Either he hasn't killed or he doesn't kill within view of the surveillance cameras."

Which means the reels have had no reason to talk about him, and other players are taken by surprise when they encounter him. Playing in the games with a whole security team—what could he possibly be here for? Surely not the *money*.

"This *must* be against the rules," Anton mutters.

"As long as the palace allows it," Calla returns, barely audible. And it will allow whatever keeps its people entertained. Maybe Seventy-Nine has made some generous donations. Maybe he is a plant of King Kasa's who can make sure the prize money flows back to the palace. Or maybe Seventy-Nine is doing what he wishes just because he can. The palace will still be sitting pretty when the news clamors to cover this surprise player instead of the unrest swelling in the factories.

Anton grimaces. By now, they have lingered long enough that the courtesans are glancing over, some gesturing for them to come closer. There is no way around this. They cannot fight ten highly trained men at once. The very point of their collaboration is that the two of them together are more likely to take out *one* player.

"We should retreat," Calla murmurs under her breath. "It's not worth—"

At that very moment, her wristband starts to tremble, emitting a low sound from underneath her sleeve. There's no warning before Anton's joins in, and then Seventy-Nine's too. Seventy-Nine's head whips in their direction, and recognition sparks in his eyes. He has never been on the reels, but Anton and Calla are its leading stars.

"*Run*," Calla commands.

They dart into one of the corridors, rushing deeper into the hotel. It was too late to head for the front, so another way out it is, passing room after room—

Calla collides with the door at the very end marked EXIT. Anton skids in closely after her, and curses when he, too, realizes this is no exit at all, but a stairwell.

"Why are they marking doors as exits that aren't the damned exits?" he bellows. "Why—"

Calla yanks him by the arm, pulling him up the stairs just as the door bangs open again and Seventy-Nine's security detail bursts through. "Let's *go*, Makusa."

They climb the stairs and burst through the double doors at the end, emerging into another part of the hotel. The corridor here is dimmer, a soft bulb barely casting any light. Before the men can reach the end of the stairs, Calla lunges for a corded telephone by the stairwell and loops the cord around the knobs of the two double doors, holding them shut. It'll last seconds at best, but that is enough. They each pause for a breath, pressing their wristbands to stop the ping.

"We can hide in one of these rooms," Calla instructs.

Anton is already moving, pushing at each of the handles. They're locked by keypad access, accessible only if the front desk has registered the room to an identity number and that same number is typed in. Just as there is a loud thudding on the stairwell door, one of the hotel rooms opens—unregistered and empty, the keypad unlocked—and Anton waves her over. He darts in and Calla hurries after him, slamming the door shut behind them. She tries to lock it from the inside, but there's no mechanism. With no other option, Calla takes an ashtray and sets it down to act as a block. It looks ridiculous.

"We're fucked," Anton says. "We're so fucked."

There's no window in the room. It's also probably not an exterior wall on the far side but another room: most buildings in San-Er carve out their floor plans with maximum efficiency and don't care about having rooms face outward. Which also means most rooms don't have alternate routes out. Even if they smashed a hole in the wall.

"Will you calm down?" Calla says, pivoting on her heel and pacing the floor. The security team is banging with greater force at the stairwell door, certainly close to pushing through. She's almost embarrassed to be hiding like this. She was trained to lead a battalion, and now a measly ten men have her cramped in a musty room.

A creaking comes from the end of the corridor, then: wood breaking and splintering. They have gotten through. Calla listens very carefully, trying to gauge their next move. With some muffled instructions, doors start to slam open and close methodically while the men begin checking along the rooms in the corridor. They must have a way to override the keypad lock. Does Seventy-Nine *own* the Evercent?

"We've cornered ourselves, haven't we?" Anton intones. If their pursuers immediately started checking the rooms, then they must know that Anton and Calla are here hiding, that they could not have escaped.

"This corridor must be a dead end, yes," Calla agrees.

The men will check their way along the floor, barging in on hotel guests one by one.

Anton releases another chain of curses. He plops onto a chair in the corner of the room and opens the newspaper he has picked up, covering his face.

"How's this?"

"Cut it out," Calla says. "They've already caught a glimpse of us. They'll attack the moment they come in. Be prepared."

Anton lowers the newspaper. "We can't fight well here," he argues. "We shouldn't combat first. We should distract."

Calla considers the suggestion. "How?"

"I don't know," Anton answers, unhelpfully. "But if their formation falters, we'll have a better chance of taking them out." He sets his newspaper down, seeming to acknowledge it as a foolish disguise. The moment it settles against another ashtray, however, he pauses. "I guess you could pose as a courtesan."

Calla turns to face him, brightening suddenly. "That's not a bad idea."

Anton's brows shoot up. There's a *thud* a few doors down, then the sound of yelling.

"What, really?"

"Why do you sound so surprised?"

Quick as she can, Calla slides her sword on the floor, out of sight but within reach. She tosses Anton her wristband; he shoves it beneath the cushion of his chair.

"Because I didn't think you were capable of complimenting me, Princess."

"I said it wasn't a bad idea." She unzips the front of her jacket and peels it off, leaving only her underclothes, red silk holding her breasts in place. "I didn't say you were a genius."

"You didn't have to." Anton is trying very hard not to look. His eyes are pointed to the ceiling, even as he continues winding her up. "I could hear it in your voice. *Anton, my hero, I don't know what I would do without you—*"

Another door slams closed, much nearer this time. When Calla puts her hair up and snaps a rubber band on, she looks very different from the player that Seventy-Nine's security team glimpsed in the lobby.

"Anton, my hero," she mimics, slinking in front of him and positioning herself so that she conceals him from the doorway. He's still staring at the ceiling, so she grabs the back of his head. "You're allowed to look at me."

His gaze snaps down in concert with her command. As soon as their eyes meet, Anton leans back into the chair like he's trying to sink inside the cushions. Calla follows, using one leg to part his knees so she can lower herself onto the plush seat, the other leg holding her balance.

"How close do you think they are?" she asks. Her voice turns sultry as she settles into the courtesan role, smoothing a hand across his temple. She would be lying if she said it wasn't for her own amusement too. She's trying her hardest not to laugh. "Three rooms away? Two?"

She watches his pulse at his throat, the soft hollow beating at rapid speed. Though he's forcing a neutral expression, he can't keep his eyes steady or stop the parting of his lips when Calla runs her touch down his chest.

"Calla Tuoleimi." Anton doesn't sound like he's teasing anymore. "This is a dangerous game to be playing while our lives are in imminent danger."

The corridor outside echoes with more shouting, more disgruntled complaints. *What are you people doing, why are you just barging in like this, no we haven't seen a man and a woman, please get* out*!*

Another loud slam. That's the room next door, for certain. Calla leans over him.

"I thought"—her hand sinks farther then, the heel of her palm digging into his hard crotch—"you liked playing games."

The low sound she draws from Anton delights her tremendously. She hopes they hear it out in the hallway.

"So that's how it's going to be," he manages. He looks to the door, listening. "Fine."

And he puts his mouth to one of her breasts, running his tongue across the tip. Calla almost strays from position, arching slightly at the wet, hot sensation despite herself. He does it again through the silk, even slower, and she would snap at him to cut it out before she's not blocking him from view anymore, only the door bursts open at that second, heavy footsteps hurrying in before pausing at this sight before them.

Anton moves on, pretending to kiss her neck. He leans into her ear. "Three of them. Two in range, the third behind."

As soon as he reports, Calla's nerves sing with awareness, pinpointing the three new presences in the room, sensing their distance and their placements, halted by the doorway.

"Understood," Calla whispers in reply. Then, she plucks out the two knives tucked in each of his pockets and whirls around, throwing them both.

One *thunk* after the other, they land in the two men's throats. The third scrambles to raise the weapon in his hands, but by then Calla has already slid across the carpet and retrieved her sword. She pierces the blade through his stomach. A tug, another swing. He falls.

Anton marches across the room and retrieves his knives. He backtracks quickly for her wristband under the chair cushion and shoves it in her jacket pocket before tossing the garment in her direction.

"Don't get cold."

She catches it with her free hand. "When I'm with you?" Calla grins, swinging her jacket on. "Never."

The fight resumes as soon as they reenter the corridor. One of the remaining men spots them and calls out. Before the force in the corridor have fully discerned how quickly their initial three men fell, Calla takes down two more, then kicks a third hard enough to knock him out. They jolt to attention, their attack turning co-ordinated. When Calla lifts her sword and tries to strike the next nearest man, she's not only pushed back with a fast defense, but another to his left—the Weisanna—almost cuts her in half with a long blade that's appeared out of nowhere. Calla manages to swerve; he only gets a shallow slash across her stomach. The sting is immediate, but she really should have zipped up her jacket. Calla spits a curse and swivels around, eyeing the distance back into the stairwell. Three paces away, Anton sprays blood across the wall when he gets a good hit on his own opponent. Still, they're outnumbered, and from behind, Calla catches the blur of a blade—

"Anton, move!" Her sword slams in as interference, blocking the attack. It creates an opening through the fight, and much to her relief, Anton is fast. In the brief second while Anton is ducking away in the direction of the stairwell, Calla kicks the man back. The moment she has her own opening, Calla charges for the stairwell too and thunders down the steps.

"Front entrance," Calla shouts. Her voice rings with an echo.

"They'll still give chase," Anton warns.

"Then we hide again. Any other useless observations?"

"Princess, I really thought we were getting along—"

When they barge into the lobby, Seventy-Nine is waiting there, unprotected. He stares upon sighting them, calm and unexpressive, as if he's not an active player of the games. The desk attendant has ducked under her chair, shielding herself. The courtesans have huddled into the corner, trying to create distance from the chaos. But Seventy-Nine does nothing. He seems to think that wearing fancy clothes is all he needs to protect him from life's woes. He looks like a fucking fool—utterly useless, asking to be slaughtered.

Calla has her sword raised before she knows what she's doing. She lunges, metal flashing in the light, but Anton tugs her back at once.

"There's no time. We have to go."

"He's right *there*—"

"He'll jump as soon as you attack. His men are on their way. Now!"

Calla stops resisting, letting Anton haul her to the front entrance. They return to the streets of Er, ducking into an alley and hurrying away from the hotel. Each thud of Calla's boots reverberates with the sound of failure, mocking her retreat. By the time they're out of range and have evaded the risk of being chased, Calla is deathly winded, resting against the wall with her arms wrapped around her middle. Her stomach stings with its cut. The bleeding has already stopped, though, so it's nothing she needs to worry about. She zips her jacket, covering the damage.

"Well," Anton heaves, equally out of breath, "that certainly could have gone better. But it could have gone worse too. Good effort." He holds his hand out for her to shake. Calla glares at him until he takes it away.

"Of all players to send us after," Calla mutters. "August didn't think to warn us about one with a ten-person tag team?"

Anton pulls a face. "He did it on purpose, most likely."

Calla's first instinct is to say that he needs her and wouldn't send her into danger willingly. But maybe Anton is right, maybe August thought she could handle it. She left behind a whole throne room of dead bodies, after all, so what was ten men?

Calla closes her eyes and shakes her head, clearing her thoughts. She can hear the Rubi Waterway from here. They have neared the bridges that take them back to San. When she looks up, Anton is watching her curiously. He offers a placating smile.

"My apartment is not far."

"Lead the way," Calla says.

They're both too tired to make meaningless conclusions about the fight they abandoned, so they walk in silence, crossing the bridge into Big Well Street and walking until the familiar brothel looms into view. Today, there are more stalls set up outside, wooden pushcarts with women behind them selling cheap shoes. Calla only peers at the products momentarily before she follows Anton into the building, because if she lingers for more than a second, there is no getting away until they have all hawked their prices.

"An unlicensed doctor rents one of the units on the floor above," Anton says when he lets her through the door to his apartment. "If you hear screaming, that's what it is."

"Charming."

Calla unhooks her sword. Tosses it haphazardly onto the couch. Then she empties her pockets too, dumping their contents onto the pillows. Unlike the first time she was here, she's not in a rush, so she makes a slow perusal of his apartment, walking before his bookshelves. There's another picture of Otta here. It's more discreet, cutting off half her laughing face, but Otta always made her presence known in person, so of course the photographs that capture her are easily recognizable too.

Calla circles around the small couch and enters the adjoining kitchen. While Anton busies himself putting a pot of water on the stove, she peers into his cupboards, trying to gauge how long the candles there have gone unlit, a dusty shrine to the painted figurine of an old deity. Perhaps Anton is one of the few who still pray. If he believes that Otta Avia can be saved, Calla wouldn't be surprised if he also believes in the old gods.

Calla touches the dust on the cutlery shelf. Just as the pad of her finger brushes over the rusting utensils, she hears what sounds like metal running lightly against the countertop, and when she feels movement by her shoulder—Anton's arm, reaching over, holding something, holding a knife?—she snatches the first thing in reach and grabs his wrist, slamming him onto the table behind them and pressing what ends up being a fork to the side of his neck.

Anton winces. The whole kitchen echoes with the sound of his head thudding against the hollow table surface.

"Fifty-Seven," he says slowly. The veins in his neck stand out, trying to brace against the prongs. The utensil itself is blunt, but if Calla shoves hard enough . . . "I was reaching for the *bowl* behind your head. Would you please refrain from attacking me in my own home?"

Calla's eyes trace down the length of his arm, now splayed and pinned onto the table. There's the knife. She had not misheard. But it's too small and short to serve as a lethal weapon. The blade looks like it could barely cut tofu.

"Who said I was trying to attack you?" Calla asks. Her gaze flickers back to Anton. He's close enough that she can see the ring of deep purple around his eyes, and in that flash of a second, when Calla reaches for the knife in his hand to take it away, an unspoken agreement is made: *I'll pretend you weren't testing how fast I'd react, and you can pretend I didn't catch your ploy.*

She leans in, maintaining the farce. "You don't want to finish what we started in that hotel?"

"Go on then," Anton says, unfazed. He knows that she's mocking him. But still, his eyes drop to her mouth. "Don't let me stop you."

Calla feels her wrist apply pressure on the fork, almost absently, pressing harder and harder the nearer they draw together. She doesn't stop until her lips are close enough that she can feel the heat of his, and only then—only then does she come to a halt, mouth and weapon alike.

"Water's boiling," she says, and pushes away, tossing the fork back onto the shelf. She's grinning when Anton straightens up, arching an eyebrow at her before retrieving the bowl and resuming his cooking. What's the point in acting like they're not constantly suspicious of each other? Theirs is a short-term alliance, not a permanent one. They can be friendly, as spiders and scorpions are while preying on the same nests. But let them both starve, and one will attack and devour the other.

Calla draws a chair, taking a seat. Anton finds a packet of some unidentifiable instant food and rips it open. He drops it into the water. Stands over the stove, stirring diligently. After a few minutes, he turns to find her resting her elbow on the table and asks:

"Have you dropped your guard so easily? Perhaps it's poison I'm putting in."

"I'm watching you make it." The chair rocks beneath her. One of the legs is shorter than the others. "No poison so far."

Anton shrugs, turning back to stir the pot. "San-Er adores hits made with flourish."

"There aren't any cameras here to catch your hit. A foolish endeavor, if you ask me."

With a loud snap, Anton turns off the stove. The gas cuts off, its blue flame disappearing.

"Your Highness," Anton says, presenting her with the bowl and a pair of chopsticks. He feigns a genuflection when she accepts it. "Do be careful, however. Poisoning *has* happened once before, eleven years ago."

From her periphery, Calla looks at the small shrine again. "Seems you're a fan of the games."

"I do my research."

Calla takes a bite of the noodles. "Because you're intent on winning."

Instead of sitting opposite her at the table, Anton has decided to lean against the sink. He glances over at her, faintly bemused. "Does anyone play with the intent of losing?"

"I'm sure some do." She chews slowly. Despite all her talk, she wouldn't put it past Anton to drop a shard of glass into the food just for the laugh. "If they only want the money gained in the Daqun. Or fame—get their name in the public eye and the reels tracking their every move."

But indeed, most play for the grand prize. Almost every previous victor has taken their money and built a life away from San-Er: some in the nearer provinces, some farther out. They'll take their family or their closest loved ones, fund the resources and manpower to construct a house that rivals the vacation homes of councilmembers. There may not be running water or electricity or internet beyond San-Er's wall, but there is space and sun and quiet. So long as they have the money to acquire food in bulk, to build a well, to hire people that will cook and clean and work—it makes for a gloriously luxurious life, a far cry from the fates of regular villagers out in the provinces.

"What's in it for you?" Anton asks suddenly, turning the question on her. "I'd assume you're playing under a false identity. Why risk San-Er finding out about its lost murderer princess?"

Calla shoots him a cool look, stabbing at the food. She remains quiet for a prolonged moment, letting the apartment draw into silence. Anton hadn't lied; there really is screaming coming from upstairs.

"Would you believe me if I said the greater good?" she finally replies. It's as close to the truth as she can get. Wanting King Kasa dead is personal, yes, but this kingdom begs for him to be removed from the throne. Talin begs for change, the council eradicated and everything set ablaze, and though Calla wants to light the match just to see Kasa burn, it would be the fire that the kingdom needs.

She won't hear of anything else.

"I believe you," Anton answers easily.

Calla pushes the bowl away. She's not hungry anymore. She wonders how many of these instant food packets are distributed across San-Er at alarmingly low prices, and still, people cannot afford them. Still, dead bodies rot in the corner of large buildings, unfound for weeks at a time until the smell draws the rats and the rats draw the dogs and the barking dogs finally draw a palace guard.

"Do you believe in the greater good?" Calla asks. Saving one beloved and saving the living, breathing mass of a city—do these not feel the same?

Anton scoffs. "Definitely not."

Some other victors do. They try to use their money to lift people from debts, pay off bills, build schools. It never lasts long. The twin cities are hectic, dense, fast. People who are out of debt fall back in again. New buildings consume themselves from the inside out, robbed left and right by employees taking relentlessly from the central funds. Calla doesn't remember it, but there was one victor who used the money to hire an army in the provinces, recruiting under-paid soldiers and untrained farmers willing to play pretend as mercenaries. He tried storming San-Er, hoping to take the city under siege and rule by coup, but it failed so spectacularly that the tale was later told at a palace dinner party over champagne.

There are more members of San-Er's palace guard than there are soldiers in every army across Talin's provinces. When the rebel victor stormed San-Er's wall with his mercenaries, they didn't even break through. The palace guard had them down in minutes.

Calla reaches for a fruit bag on the counter. Anton makes no move to tell her off for rummaging around his apartment without permission, so she pulls out a peach and bites down on it.

Even if they had made it past the wall, a coup was impossible. Who can fight a battle in a place like this? These cities are built for quick assassinations, not war. The greatest defense against an attack on San-Er's regime is the cityscape itself.

"You are a pest," Anton remarks lightly.

Calla offers him the peach. He doesn't take it back, letting her have it. Again, her gaze wanders to the dusty shrine.

"May I ask," she begins, taking another bite, "what you liked so much about Otta Avia?"

Anton freezes. It seems she has taken him by surprise, and a small part of her relishes in the shock that stills his face. Each time she sees him, he wears someone new. His eyes change shape and his nose changes length, his hair alters long and short, his height moves up and down. Yet no matter the body, his same set of expressions remains, and Calla wants to make a game of collecting them. She has seen smug. She has seen eerily calm, a feigned indifference. They are not enough. Anton Makusa is hiding a lifetime's worth of deceit under his skin, and she wants to pick him apart, see what lies beneath. She wants to see his fullest contempt. She wants to see rage.

"August told you." His voice is forcibly level.

"I recognized her," she corrects. "We were in acquaintance."

"What did August say?" Anton asks anyway.

She watches the edge of his mouth, watches him hold down the snarl that wants to curl up.

"That she was a sociopath"—his fists have clenched—"and a lying, manipulative bitch of a half sister."

Anton cannot contain his glower. A rush like no other floods Calla's veins.

"He wouldn't dare—"

"No, you're right," Calla cuts in, examining her nails. "Those aren't his words at all. Those are mine."

Anton raises his hand. Calla lifts her chin, daring it to land. He's not close enough to hit her, but maybe he'll lunge in. Maybe he'll snap. The scream upstairs stretches long, one split second sprawling and sprawling.

That's when a siren blares loud, halting Anton before he can move and drawing Calla's attention to the window with a snap. Her eyes widen. There is no mistaking that high-pitched whine. She has heard it only once before—utterly deafening and so piercing that it's painful to the ear.

"What is that?" Anton shouts.

Calla lurches to her feet. "It's the flood siren. San-Er is flooding."

CHAPTER 14

It's not even the right season. The last time Calla heard this siren, she was still living in the Palace of Heavens. The Rubi Waterway had risen past its banks and sent a flash flood rippling five feet high. It wrought havoc for two weeks, her parents unwilling to handle the chaos. Civilians died, businesses closed, fresh food stalls went under because they couldn't move anything from building to building and it was impossible to carry crates up fourteen flights of steps for the rooftop routes.

"I need to go," Calla declares, pivoting fast for the couch in the living room and picking up her sword. It makes no sense, but she won't take the chance. Chami and Yilas's diner is on the ground level, and floods from the waterway come quick. Much as she would like her former attendants to stay safe, she is most concerned about keeping an eye on Chami, because if Chami needs to get to the hospital, then Calla's false identity starts to crumble.

"Fifty-Seven, wait," Anton calls after her. "There's something shifty about this. It's not the right month for tides to be rising. It could be a ruse—"

"I know." Calla secures her sword onto her belt. "I just need to check on something. I'll find you later."

Then she's gone, slipping through his front door and climbing up instead of down. With the siren whining, the ground of San-Er will be crowded with civilians trying to get their business in order, transporting what cannot be transported if the streets are soon to be flooded for days on end. Calla sticks close to the edge of the stairs, trying not to brush shoulders with the masses surging down, grimacing when she passes a man in scrubs reeking with the smell of blood. They're all yelling at one another, drowned out by the wails of the siren, but Calla catches their confusion, snippets of doubt and their hypotheses that it could be the games drawing its players out for slaughter. It would be a nonsensical plan. Every soul in San-Er flocking down to the ground would only make it harder to find the players. And yet, Calla cannot imagine why else the alarm would be going off.

She emerges onto the rooftop, slapping her hands over her ears. The siren noises are coming from speakers installed alongside the television antennas atop each building. They are relentless, echoing off one another, sound waves bouncing back and forth. Calla has to grit her teeth hard when she breaks into a steady jog, finding a rhythm as she crosses the rooftops and jumps the gaps across buildings. She would have expected more movement here, but there are only pigeons and debris keeping her company.

"Hey!" Calla yells when she spots a child, but she cannot hear herself past the sirens. The child only keeps playing. When Calla glances down, squinting at the ground, she sees no water anyway, only a sea of heads pushing in movement. She swallows her warning, shaking her head.

She's nearing the diner. Instead of risking the considerable jump to cross onto the next rooftop, Calla takes the door down. Once she's back in an enclosed stairwell, she finally releases her clamped palms from her ears.

"I'm going to be pissed if this is a ruse," Calla mutters, taking the stairs three at a time. "But I'm going to be pissed if it isn't too."

She winds through the residence floors, then clutches her nose at the factory floors. Even with the sirens blaring on, some people don't care to move. They continue swinging their noodles out of raw dough, distributing such a thick layer of flour that Calla tracks white footsteps down two more levels.

She emerges from the building's side door at last, finally glimpsing the diner up ahead. Chami and Yilas are already standing outside, nervously in conversation.

"Yilas!" Calla bellows. She steps around three men carrying a caged pig among them. On the ground, the sirens are fainter to her ear, muffled by the buildings.

The two turn at her call, relief flashing when they sight her in the crowd. Calla pushes closer, closer.

Then, as soon as she steps into the open space outside the diner, someone pulls her hair and sends her lurching back into the throng of people.

Calla barely finishes her gasp of surprise before she's throwing weight onto her shoulder, rolling to avoid hitting the ground wrong. A knife strikes the gravel, a hairsbreadth from her ear, and her eyes bulge, latching on to the meaty hand around its blade. Calla is fast to recover, launching herself at the attacker—

Only then she's thrown back by some invisible hand, a fist smacking her sternum and pushing all the air out of her. Calla lands hard on her side, gasping. Her whole chest prickles. For a very long second, she cannot move, not because she's hurt to the point of being out of commission, but because her mind is reeling with disbelief. She wasn't even *touched*—how did that happen?

There's a sudden scream that sounds a lot like Chami. Calla scrambles up at the sound, but she's too late. Chami is lunging forward to help, and the attacker has sighted her.

"Hey, wait!"

The attacker pulls the blade up and slashes Chami's throat.

"*Jump!*" Yilas screams.

A flash of light. Chami drops—or her body does, a gaping wound in its throat but no red to be seen. She left before any of her qi leaked, her body becoming an empty vessel. Calla shudders with a breath of relief, still half kneeling on the gravel, her palms cutting into the stones. Everyone else on the street is giving her a wide berth. No one stops to help or stare too long, in case they're caught in the scrimmage.

"Are you okay?" It's her attacker's low voice, but Chami is asking the question. Chami extends her new, thick hand, and Calla takes it, getting to her feet.

"Let's get inside," she says in lieu of a reply. Yilas is visibly shaken, but she says nothing as she hooks her arms around Chami's birth body. Calla grabs the legs. They file into the emptied diner, climbing over the turnstiles, and set Chami's body onto one of the tables.

"Oh dear," Chami says. In the attacker's body, she ducks to avoid hitting her head on one of the dangling overhead lights, then examines the wound. "Let me stitch this up. I have some alcohol in the back."

"Hold on." Calla is frantically trying to think. "Are you wearing a wristband?"

Chami looks at the new body she's occupying. It's masculine, so she pats around the waist gingerly, a grimace on her face.

"I don't see one."

If Chami managed to jump in, then the body wasn't doubled, so there was only one occupant before. But there's no wristband, so this is not a player. Why would a stranger on the streets try to attack Calla? She reaches for the knife that Chami is still clutching, and Chami relinquishes it quickly, letting Calla examine the blade. It looks standard. Could have come from any one of the three weapons shops.

"Chami," Calla says quietly. "Would you . . . mind jumping into Yilas for a second?"

Yilas straightens up, concern immediately marring her expression. "She can't *leave* that body, he'll come back and kill us—"

Calla draws her sword, getting into a battle stance. She doesn't think she needs to, but she'll do it to make Yilas feel better. "Trust me. I have a hunch. Can she, Yilas? Just for a few seconds?"

Chami turns a questioning glance to her girlfriend. When—after a few seconds of holding a tight grimace—Yilas finally nods, there's another flash of light, arcing from the attacker's body to Yilas. Yilas's eyes turn from pale green to pink. And the attacker . . . drops right to the floor, not a fleck of color in his blank eyes as they stare up at the ceiling.

Calla puts her sword away.

"How is that possible?" Chami gasps in Yilas's body. "This—this—did you see another light?"

"There was only yours," Calla reports. Though she doesn't visibly show it, she's equally flabbergasted. She rubs at her nose, trying to ease an itch that won't go away. "There isn't even anyone *around* right now for him to have jumped into."

A short scream pierces the streets outside, close enough in proximity to be heard over the sirens. Though Calla waits to see if it will come again, she doesn't make any move to investigate the sound. For all she knows, it could be San-Er itself, screeching a dying call in response to the blaring sirens. Quick as they came, the sirens suddenly stop, and then the silence almost rings louder.

Chami jumps back into the attacker's empty vessel. She rolls herself upright again with a cumbersome grunt. Meanwhile, Yilas blinks, returning to consciousness, and hastens to kneel down so she can help Chami.

"What happened?" Yilas asks.

"We've got a vessel," Chami explains. "It's vacant." Her sweet voice transfers over even with such low vocal cords. Until the wound on her birth body heals, she cannot jump back in. She'll have to stay as this body—this mysterious, hostless body.

Calla heads for the door, peering out through the glass. There's no water to be seen. It really was a false alarm. Could it have been a trap, just for her? But then, why would the attacker jump away so quickly?

"If you can," she calls to Chami and Yilas, "lock the doors and don't open shop for a few days." She pushes at the door, facing San-Er again. "I need to get to the bottom of this."

◇◇◇◇◇

Pampi plugs her portable desktop into the jack socket, watching the monitor feed. The sirens in San-Er are connected, and it was no trouble to trigger them all by sending a command into a single one. She almost craves more of a challenge, but it is what it is.

She's turned the sirens off now. She only needs to input her last trigger, using a different feed that will erase the evidence of her remote interference. A low mist has started up on these rooftops, clouding her surroundings. Pampi's hands fly over her keyboard, string after string of code that she reads only once before sending through.

A door bangs from the other side of the rooftop. Pampi inhales sharply through her nose, taking in the acrid scent of burning rubber. Her code finishes. With a quick glance at the screen, she lets it load for one second more, in case there are stray signals to be caught, then unplugs her monitor and shoves the wire back into the briefcase. Just before the footsteps come within range, she hauls the computer to her chest and scurries off, ducking behind a mound of rubbish and concealing herself against a broken washing machine.

She waits. The footsteps shuffle toward one of the antennas, and Pampi wonders if it's the building's maintenance, having entirely ridiculous timing. Then she peers out from her hiding space and sights a tall woman with long hair prodding at the siren speakers.

Not palace affiliated. Not a guard. But this woman looks like she knows what she's doing, pulling at the wires and refiguring them into different slots.

Pampi carefully eases her briefcase open again, letting the computer monitor blink on. By some instinct, she swipes her fingers across the pad and remotely logs on to her games surveillance. She zooms in on the map, closer and closer until she is looking at surveillance footage of herself hidden on the rooftop, tucked a few feet away from the woman in the black jacket, who now straightens with a pensive expression on her face.

Yellow eyes, gloved hands. There's an inherent power present in the way she is standing, or else Pampi wouldn't be paying so much attention. If Pampi knows how to identify anything, it is those who hold power, so that she can squeeze them dry.

Pampi switches screens, pulling up the locational view of the players' wristbands, and the number 57 flashes in a little dot right where she stands. Fifty-Seven, star of the scoreboards. Pampi supposes she shouldn't be surprised it is this particular player who has shown up here.

Fifty-Seven turns around suddenly, as if she hears something, eyes flashing in the gray light. There's smoke from the factory nearby turning the mist into a heavy smog, so she reaches up to take off her mask, revealing the rest of her face. For the first time, without the pixelation of the screens and the washed monochrome of San-Er's footage, Pampi gets a proper look at Fifty-Seven, who starkly resembles . . .

"Princess Calla," Pampi whispers under her breath in awe. "How *fascinating*."

◇◇◇◇◇

The palace publicizes a statement. It takes Calla wholly by surprise, unable to believe what she's hearing. She spent an hour trying to reach August's phone line without success, and as soon as she gives up and comes home, she gets her answers on the news instead, where the broadcast is speaking about the sirens. Rather than brushing the matter under the rug and withholding an explanation, as Calla would have thought, the newscaster cleanly reads the lines she has been given.

"San-Er has been infiltrated by rural rebels. They have no identity numbers nor the legal right to be within city limits, but those without morals and rules will always try to disrupt what is flourishing."

Calla peers into the fridge, sniffing at the empty shelves. The broadcast continues in the background while she shuffles around the kitchen, trying to find something to eat. She retrieves a single egg and cracks it into the heated pan.

"A few casualties in the games have been attributed to these rebels, and today was another attempt. Official instructions from the palace bid us to remain calm. There is no need to worry as the palace guard is working day and night to search for the perpetrators."

The sun is setting. The evening outside turns from a sad, dingy gray to a dark, velvety one. When Calla flops the fried egg onto her plate and shuffles to the couch, Mao Mao trots after her, purring. Her living room falls dimmer and dimmer, but she makes no move for the overhead lights. She only pushes at the cushions absently to make space for her cat, then sets her plate down. Her apartment consists of the living space, her tiny bedroom, and the tiny bathroom, but there is an even tinier laundry room behind the cramped shower cubicle, perpetually illuminated in varying red and blue and green. The brothel that operates in the building next door directly faces the laundry room's window, providing enough light for her to see what she is forking into her mouth.

The news broadcast continues. It decides that the troublemakers are only intent on killing players of the games to turn their nose up at the king, that they disrupt the cities' affairs out of spite. Any civilian who sees suspicious activity should report to a palace guard immediately. Calla supposes there is no harm in feeding the civilians this story. If it's solely the players of the games being targeted, then there is no safety threat across San-Er.

There is only King Kasa's dignity at risk.

Mao Mao butts her hand.

"It doesn't make sense, does it?" Calla asks.

Mao Mao makes a noise of agreement. August said the dead bodies were being placed with the Sican salute. There is no reason for rural troublemakers to do that.

Unless the rural rebels are somehow linked to Sica. Could Sica be recruiting out of rural Talin?

Mao Mao's head suddenly lifts. His feline gaze has turned sharply to the bathroom, and Calla reaches for the remote, putting her television on mute. The apartment falls quiet, leaving only faint conversation in the hallways and music from the apartment upstairs. Then: a rustle from the laundry room.

Calla bolts to her feet, scooping up her plate. It's the nearest thing that will serve as a weapon, and she doesn't hesitate to throw when the stranger steps out from her bathroom, putting as much gusto into her arm as she can manage.

"Fine daylight!" the stranger shouts in a rush, swerving away. The plate smacks the doorframe, shattering into a hundred pieces on the bathroom tiles. "What fine daylight we have today!"

Anton. Calla exhales in a huff. Her heart is still clamoring against her ribs when she flops back onto the couch, putting a hand to her chest.

"The whole point of a code phrase is that you say it *first*."

Anton runs a hand through his short hair, a collection of rings glimmering on his fingers. Red light illuminates him from behind, making him look like the type to be working at a brothel rather than just living above one.

"How did you find me?" Calla demands when Anton remains silent. "Did you climb through the window?"

Anton shows her something in his hands. The tracker that August gave her, linked to Anton's wristband.

"You left this at my apartment," Anton replies. "I took it to a shop and reversed it. Tracked your wristband here. And yes, you have a pipe directly outside your window that gave me a boost up. Your place isn't very secure."

Clearly. "I suppose we're even now."

Anton strides closer, tossing the tracker up and down. "We're not even until I get to keep this—*what* is that?"

Calla starts. It takes a prolonged second, searching the living room while it's lit up with silent ads running on the television, before she realizes that he's talking about her cat.

"This is Mao Mao." She scoops up the bundle of fur and holds him out. Anton flinches back. Mao Mao goes limp like a child's rag doll. "Don't tell me you're afraid of cats."

"I'm not afraid," he insists, and Calla leaps to her feet. She adds blatant dishonesty to the list of expressions she has collected from him.

"He won't bite," she says. Anton takes a step away. He collides with the wall, trying to put distance between himself and the cat, but Calla follows him anyway. "Here, hold him."

Calla plops Mao Mao into his arms. She walks off before he can toss the cat back, heading toward the light switch on the other wall.

"They finally admitted to it."

The room flares white-blue, no longer bathed in darkness. When Calla returns to the couch, Anton is still standing where he was before, Mao Mao resting comfortably in his stiff arms. He looks too nervous to move.

"Foreign invaders?" he guesses, eyes swiveling to the muted television.

"Almost. Rural invaders. Still Talinese."

A whine echoes from upstairs, drawing a thump against Calla's ceiling. Mao Mao leaps out of Anton's arms to follow the sound, and Anton sighs in relief, putting his hands in his jacket pockets. The apartment falls into an eerie hush again. Though there is no true silence in San-Er, one learns how to tune out the sounds beyond their four walls, to keep the machines and voices pushed to the back of their mind until it almost, *almost* fades out. This is as close to noise-lessness as San-Er will ever reach. And without anything to fill it, Calla feels the hairs at the back of her neck prickle, watching Anton regard her from the other side of the living room. This is different from their silences on the streets, from when they prowl the alleys for a sign of the games' scuffles. This is silence without a purpose. Something that might settle between a soft shoulder brush, a meeting of hands.

It has no place here.

"I came to check on your safety, like a good ally," Anton says after the long moment. He has provided an explanation without Calla asking, clearly sensing the oddness just as she does. "You ran off in a frenzy."

"*San-Er* was in a frenzy." Calla puts her finger to her mouth and bites on a nail. It's an old habit that she's long kicked, so the moment her teeth make contact, the move feels foreign and she removes her hand, grimacing at herself. She reaches for the plant by her couch instead, pulling off a strip of the flax lily. "Someone came after me again. Same as last time. Lightless jumping. Empty body."

Anton frowns. He walks over. Takes a seat right atop the coffee table, although the couch is directly beside it. "You sure you haven't pissed anyone off recently, Fifty-Seven? This is starting to sound personal."

"Perhaps it is. But that doesn't change the fact that we can't jump without light."

The overhead bulb flickers, as if it wants to weigh in on the subject. It is only the electric lines being overexerted, but Anton glances up in concern, the line of his jaw tightening. Calla doesn't pay the lights any heed. She starts to braid the flax lily into a bracelet, wondering if she needs to get a new plant from the markets. The stalls that sell these don't last long, but there are always new ones popping up. Smaller vendors buy from big companies, and big companies have the permission to funnel them through the wall in bulk from the farmers outside. The plant threads will stiffen in mere days and become impossible to wear without rubbing her wrist raw, but it's soothing to build them, to create something even if it is all to be thrown away in the end. Her body itself has memory: it remembers each flax lily bracelet that has dug in and left a little notch behind. Most others in San-Er refuse to think of their body as their own. They let their selves and their bodies stand separate, so that their mind is the only thing that follows them around as wholly theirs. Calla refuses to do the same. Each scar on her arm is hers. Every inch of puckered skin speaks to the knives she took during palace training, to the sparring matches where she defeated her tutors and rose above them in skill. What are memories if not stories told repeatedly to oneself? Her whole body is the very narrative of her existence.

"I tried jumping without light, when I was invading this one," Anton says, interrupting Calla's thoughts. When she looks up at him, he flicks the inside of his elbow, indicating the body he's wearing. "After you mentioned the idea earlier, I thought it wouldn't hurt to try."

Calla wants to roll her eyes. Of course he thinks that an impossible thing is merely a matter of trying. That rules can be overwritten by belief alone.

"And you failed."

"I failed," Anton confirms. "But it felt like I was a fraction of a second away. If only I could cross that last hurdle more quickly, it would be manageable."

"You're talking nonsense," Calla says plainly. "It's not a matter of speed."

But Anton doesn't seem to hear her. The idea has grown wings in his head and flown right toward the skies. He props his palms on the table, looking contemplative.

"It's always bothered me, you know. There's not a body that I can't intrude on, so long as it's not already hosting another intruder. I could probably occupy the king himself if I got close enough. Prince August too."

Calla says nothing in response, focused on braiding her bracelet.

"But it's just not possible to be discreet about it," he continues. "I can't move fast enough for the light not to flash."

Calla finally completes the bracelet. She holds out her hand, and Anton blinks. A few seconds later, he offers his wrist to her hesitantly. Calla hauls his entire arm closer, ignoring his startled, suspicious wince.

"I jumped for the first time when I was eight."

She doesn't look up when she speaks. She doesn't know why she is speaking at all, except maybe to test whether Anton Makusa will see what no one else does.

"Everyone always describes it like wading through something solid," she goes on. Her concentration is fixed on the miniature knot, maneuvering its ends carefully so they do not slip from her fingers and ruin the whole bracelet. Anton is equally careful in his stillness, though he has no knot to make. If anything, he is watching one unravel before him.

"But I was yanked in. I couldn't control how I was moving, I just *was*, and it felt terrifying. One second I was in my body, and the next I was in another. When I opened my eyes, I could still feel my qi settling. I thought I was dying. I never wanted to move so fast again."

"You were only eight years old," Anton counters, his voice low. Maybe this body of his really was plucked straight from a cabaret stage: one of its singers, crooning into the microphone. "It would be different if you jumped today."

Calla shakes her head. She is finished securing the bracelet and finished with this conversation. Her fingers graze Anton's wrist before she draws back, and his hand twitches, like he's about to reach out and stop her.

"It's not the speed. You'll have to trust me on this one."

He watches her stand, stride across the living room.

"Fifty-Seven."

Calla stops. If he is smart, he will have caught it. If he is smart, he will say—

"When you jump once . . ." Anton pauses, like he is doubting whether he should even ask. A beat passes, then he continues, and Calla almost laughs, because she shouldn't be shocked at all that Anton Makusa was really listening. ". . . you still have to jump back out. Wasn't the second time better?"

She's smiling when she looks over her shoulder. But there is nothing nice about the expression. It is bitter and jagged and everything she is.

"You can show yourself out, I'm sure," she says, before walking into her bedroom and shutting the door behind her.

CHAPTER 15

The palace has begun preparations for a celebratory banquet, readying for the moment the Juedou is called and the final two of the games are summoned to the coliseum. King Kasa oversees these matters personally each year, taking pride in his selection of curtain colors and matching tablecloths. He has more passion for directing where the chopstick holders should be placed than understanding food shortages in San-Er, and August watches with disgust. Each second spent here is oil pumped into his stomach, turning him utterly nauseated. But until King Kasa is gone, he will not throw up. The kingdom of Talin must likewise be patient.

Number Eighty-Eight was found dead last night, hands placed in the Sican salute. It feels like an ill omen.

"Your thoughts, August?"

King Kasa turns around, showing August the two trays in his hands.

"The left one is more fitting for a grand occasion," August replies easily. King Kasa nods his approval and echoes the same sentiment to the advisor waiting with a notepad in his hands. August almost frowns, but he holds it back, as he has done for years upon years. He cannot falter when he is so close. He can almost imagine it: the fear in King Kasa's eyes when he grabs his father's silk collar and hauls him away, the glee in the servants' eyes when they set down their bowls of fruit and step aside, when they push the king toward his execution and let his blood run in rivulets down his body, along the marble floor, out the balcony. Let it color all of San; let it gather so thickly on the streets that it overpowers the stink in the city.

August swallows hard, his throat burning. But it cannot be him. How would that end? The councilmembers calling for answers. A power vacuum in San-Er, both palaces fallen and controlled by incompetent nobility. There are no other heirs left. Royal blood has dried up on both sides of the waterway after Princess Calla disqualified herself by committing parricide. He must not rush. He must not slip up for fleeting gratification. There's no pleasure to be had in stepping on King Kasa's neck and spitting in his eye, in monologues or great big theatrics. King Kasa will not see it as justice finally catching up to him; he does not understand that he is anathema to this land.

He will have no regret for his reign. He will only think it a wrongful coup. And when he dies, despite how good it would feel for August to stand over him and see the terror set into Kasa's eyes, August knows there will be none. Calla can make the cut. He'll stay out of range to avoid the blood spray. That's how he will save this damned kingdom.

"Your Majesty," August says, "would you like me to check on the food deliveries?"

They'll be coming in from the rural provinces today. Quotas to be filled in villages that can barely feed themselves. Rations taken from those who need it more.

"Excellent idea," King Kasa says. "Ask about the fish, would you? We want one for every banquet attendant."

"Of course. I'll be right back."

August turns on his heel, reaching into his pocket for a handkerchief. He wipes at his mouth when he exits, like he can wipe the grime off. When he rules, there'll be no such silly matters. When he rules, he'll do good—spread his resources, spread his education to every corner it is needed.

August finds his way to one of the kitchens. The palace is unlike the rest of the city. Its tables are clean; its floors are always mopped. The machines rumble loudly to pull noodles and scale fish, yet the smell is free of damp flour stink and putrid sea salt. Although the atmosphere is just as busy and August is nearly bowled over when he opens the door, having to quickly assure a cook that it's all right, that there's no need for prostrating on the floor in apology—the people here are different. No one is worried about going as fast as they can to make their next meal.

"Your Highness," Galipei greets when August appears in front of him. He offers a spoonful of the bowl of stew in his hands. "Would you like some?"

August waves it away. "What's the situation at the hospital?"

"It's always work with you, no fun." Galipei tips his head back, eyeing their surroundings. In the time that he takes for observation, three kitchen hands walk by—one with a basket full of vegetables, imported from the provinces; one with a giant fish, brought in from the bays of San-Er; the last with a sack of rice.

Galipei continues speaking without fear of being overheard: "I'm working on it. There are a lot of moving parts if we're trying to make it look natural."

"Don't fret too much about that," August says. "Who's to prosecute us if it looks like foul play? Maybe the hospital itself made the decision out of mercy. Or because she's been there for too long—bed space is precious."

"Hmm." Galipei spoons another dollop of stew, then puts it in his mouth.

He's not dressed for work today, which means he's skirting tasks from Leida. August will pretend not to notice, as long as *his* tasks are fulfilled.

"So, what does she have on you?" Galipei asks.

August narrowly stops himself from balking. Instead, he reaches over and slaps the stew out of Galipei's hands. The plastic bowl is almost empty already anyway. August kicks it beneath one of the tables and hauls Galipei off by the wrist toward the doors.

"Not here," August hisses under his breath. "Have you lost your mind?"

"How am I supposed to protect you from threats when you omit information, Your Highness?" Galipei replies evenly. He doesn't resist being dragged, though he could easily exert his superior strength and halt their progress.

The doors give way, leading them into the quieter corridor. A golden light fixture dangles above them, crystals twinkling when it senses the disturbance in the air.

August continues onward until they come up to a window. They're on a lower floor, so the view is half stone, half gray-hazed light, the roof of the apartment complex beside the palace marking a perfect red line in the middle. He pushes the window open. A warm breeze blows in.

"You might as well tell me," Galipei says when August remains quiet for a long moment. "You have sent me on many strange tasks, but none as insane as killing your half sister who has been in a coma for seven years."

August sets his elbows on the windowsill, his face inclined toward the light. His shoulders are tense, held together by a contradiction of steel bones and brittle tendons. No matter how strong he makes himself, it will not take much to pick him apart entirely.

"Perhaps I am less sane than you know," he says.

Galipei frowns. "Do you doubt whether I know you well enough? You are mine to guard, August. I know you, under any circumstance. Tell me what's going on."

August considers refusing. Stubbornly, he wants to hold on to this secret, but Galipei looks at him now with an expression bordering on defiance, and he cannot allow this. In his mind's eye, he sees the two of them spending their late nights in the palace turrets, going over the cities' problems and peering down at San-Er as if they are the only people who remain awake. Very little sound makes its way up to the turrets when they are so far above San. The cities become a picture of stillness, separate from the work that August and Galipei do, separate from the world they create together.

There's not much that August has all for himself. But he has Galipei, who was made for him, not for the kingdom, and if Galipei is drawing away, then he must be reeled back.

Prince August turns to his bodyguard levelly.

"I fear," he says, "that Anton will find some way to wake her." August pauses, considering his next words very carefully. "I don't know how, or if it is even possible. But if he manages it before we seize power, then we are in trouble."

Galipei leans his shoulder against the wall. He folds his arms. "Otta was on your side before she fell sick."

"Otta was never on one side," August returns. "She did whatever she pleased for whoever pleased her most. She should never have seen—" August breaks off with a frustrated noise. He doesn't speak again until he has found his composure. "It is better if you don't know."

"Why are you making that decision for me?"

August shakes his head. "She can procure evidence that I have always been trying to uproot the king," he says. "What more do you need? If I point you to see what she saw too, then it is one more burden you must bear."

The window shudders, impacted by someone slamming a door inside the neighboring apartment complex. There are always palace guards in droves watching these nearby residences, making sure there aren't any troublemakers climbing the walls and lunging for the palace. They would be whipped for even attempting it.

Galipei pushes away from the wall. He doesn't look pleased, but he won't complain. "Nothing of yours is ever a burden," he says. He turns on his heel, waving over his shoulder. "I'm off. Page me if you need me."

August stares after him, eyes narrowed. When he catches his own reflection in the window glass, he's convinced he sees a stranger, though this is his birth body.

I know you, under any circumstance.

"Do you?" August asks the now-empty corridor.

◇◇◇◇◇

Be careful coming around now people weird I can get my own lunch its okay love you

Yilas leans on her hand, her elbow resting upon the desk. The diner remains closed after yesterday's scare, so she clicks through her pager messages in the back office, filtering through her brother's last few.

"I'm going to check in on Matiyu."

Chami looks up, her nail filing coming to a halt. Her birth body is upstairs, tucked in bed, a bandage over its neck while the skin knits together. Damaged vessels heal on their own, but it is a slow, arduous task. It relies on the presence of its base qi, rather than the swirling, active qi of an occupant, where the stronger they are, the faster they can urge their own wounds to close. Chami could jump into her birth body early and go around wearing a bloody bandage to speed up the process, but since she has a spare body to mooch around in anyway, it's better to let hers heal on its own and avoid unnecessary exertion.

"Hasn't he warned you to do the exact opposite?" she asks.

Yilas is already on her feet, searching for her keys. "Yes, but . . ." She finds them under a stack of papers. "I want to get a few of those pendants the Crescent Societies sell. The ones they say protect against jumping."

"Yilas." Chami reaches out, gingerly stopping Yilas in her path. She doesn't close her fingers all the way down when she catches Yilas's wrist, as if she's afraid of tightening her unfamiliar grip too much. "It's okay, love. We're going to be okay."

"I know," Yilas says, and it is not entirely a lie. But she doesn't just want to be okay; she wants to keep Chami safe. And that is a mighty big ask in San-Er, so she can only try for a smile before shaking Chami's grip loose and heading out the door.

Though the news stations have declared there to be rebels in San-Er, the streets remain raucous with activity. The same crowds flock around the gambling dens, the same elderly pull their chairs out to smoke outside a corner shop.

Aren't you scared? Yilas wants to ask. There have never been infiltrators past the wall before. Perhaps there's something assuring about the numbers game of the twin cities. The odds say that today is not the day you will die, that San-Er has far too many people to make you the target of an attack. Perhaps that's why the crowds of San don't stay indoors even when the games are at their height. Blood doesn't spill only for entertainment; it spills in factory accidents and robberies and random waves of plague. If they live in fear, then they might never emerge.

Yilas lets out a deep breath, but it doesn't ease the twisting pain in her stomach. A drop of dirty water falls from the air conditioners above, and she wipes it off her neck.

The Hollow Temple is busier today, to the point that the front doors are left wide-open. Yilas flicks at a piece of the chipping red paint as she steps in.

She's met immediately with noise.

"You're not finding the right ones! I'm sure of it!"

"And so? How many times do we keep trying?"

Yilas eyes the two arguing men, then turns away. A fight might break out any second, and when they pull the chains attached to their belts, Yilas doesn't want to be nearby.

But she doesn't see Matiyu either. As cautiously as she can, Yilas wanders about the temple, trying to blend in with the rapid activity. There must be some event underway. Or perhaps a new goal for the team in this territory, Crescent Society members preparing to send reinforcements onto the streets.

Eventually, Yilas wanders to the back of the temple after finding his room empty too. He wouldn't be at their parents' cramped apartment during these hours. His job is to stay in the temple, in this Crescent Society sector's home base, and run their inventory. The only place left to check is the storage room Matiyu took her to last time.

Yilas shoulders open the door, already calling out, "Matiyu? You really made me look up and down—"

But this room, too, is empty and dark. From the door, she can see an array of boxes left hazardously in the middle of the room, papers scattered on top. Yilas gropes around for a light switch, and when the room is bathed in an off-putting yellow, she inches in. What was it that Matiyu was so curious about last time? Something about wrong numbers . . .

Yilas picks up the papers. These aren't the same storage logs. These are printed maps—all time-stamped in the corner—looking like second-by-second screenshots from the palace's surveillance.

It's their log of the games and the movement of each player.

"What the fuck?" Yilas says aloud, leafing through the papers. At random, she retrieves one where 57 and 86 are marked with two dots in the corner, circled in red.

But before Yilas can fold it up and take the map with her, something comes over her face from behind, turning her world dark.

CHAPTER 16

King Kasa is always airbrushed when he comes on television. A serene expression, bushy eyebrows low and relaxed, beard smooth and laid flat. The background is hazy with light, as is the foreground, though perhaps that could be blamed on the digital alterations the communication rooms are making as the palace broadcast feeds out. Calla can't guess which room the king stands in as he makes his prerecorded speech. She supposes that is the point.

"Even during prosperous times, there will be enemies at our borders," King Kasa begins.

"Prosperous?" Calla echoes immediately, her tone dripping with derision. She strikes a match and lights the cigarette dangling between her teeth. "In what world?"

"It is why we have a wall, why we make the distinction between the city and the rest of Talin. The city is the center of innovation. The city is where everyone desires to be."

"Cit*ies*," Calla corrects the screen, dropping the blackened match and taking a drag of the lit cigarette between her fingers. "We're twin cities, you son of a—"

"As you have heard, there are rebels in San-Er. This is true. They seek to bring down the regime, but you must rest assured that the palace guard is hunting down the perpetrators of such flimsy nonsense. We have already apprehended one of the rebels responsible."

A lie. It has to be, because the palace hasn't even determined how these alleged rebels got in.

"What we must do is live bravely in the face of their cowardice. We must show strength in the face of hardship."

Calla cannot hold back the exclamation that fills her living room.

"What the *fuck* are you on about?"

She gets no answer. Sensing her rage, Mao Mao pads over and rubs up against her ankle. Her pant cuff is folded up: her poor attempt at hemming away the blood-soaked fabric. The rest of her clothes aren't quite dirty enough to warrant a change, but blood at her ankle isn't exactly pleasant either.

The television screen seems to brighten. Sharpening in preparation for whatever announcement is coming as King Kasa clears his throat and stares directly into the camera.

"The games shall speed up, in celebration of the regime and in defiance of those trying to take us down. It is time to come together and resist disruption. Long live the reign of San-Er."

The broadcast goes dark. Seconds later, it switches back to the anchors in the newsroom.

Calla leans into the couch, dangling her cigarette over the armrest and bringing her left hand up to look at the wristband. A shaft of light cuts along her bare skin like a second bracelet, the afternoon rays barely pushing through the window. Both she and Anton had their wristbands go off twice separately today, so they decided to part early and rest. But now, what exactly did the palace mean by *speeding up the games?*

Her wristband starts to tremble.

Calla scrambles to her feet. "Oooh no no no—" She grabs her sword. Slings a jacket over her shoulder. In the distance, she hears footsteps thundering into the building. The clock on the mantel puts the hour at late afternoon. She's being ambushed, with no way to know what's coming, who's coming, how *many* are currently heading her way. Battle in this apartment or the hallways would be claustrophobic—she has to get out of here.

"Mao Mao," she hisses. "Go hide!" Her cat sprints off, noting her rush. There's plenty of pet food stacked in the corner of her bedroom, and there are holes in the walls where Mao Mao can stay tucked all day. Soon as the fur bundle disappears, Calla shoves her arms into the jacket and runs for her bathroom. Her wristband is still humming against her skin, though the screen displays nothing. She skids into the laundry unit, shoves the window open, and climbs out in one fast swoop.

Fuck King Kasa. Fuck him to all eternity. Calla winces when her ankle lands hard in the alley outside, hardly taking a moment to gather her bearings before she is sprinting, burrowing deep into San. Three streets later, she stops and leans against a shop wall, trying to catch her breath.

The wristband has stopped trembling.

The city carries on: its beeping machines and its sagging wires, its winding streets and its slamming doors.

Calla straightens up, smoothing her hair back. She got away this time, but she can't return to her apartment. The player will stake it out, waiting to add a kill to their list. From here on out, she must move where the games take her.

"*Fuck,*" she says once more, with feeling. Calla starts her trek deeper into the city.

◇◇◇◇◇

By chance or by luck, Anton does not catch the king's announcement. He's boxed into the corner of a hospital room, sweating under his layers. The air-conditioning unit has been kicked right out of the window, the broken latches snagged on the sill. There are five beds, laid side by side, separated by curtains. Two beds over, a family loudly discusses transfer options, no longer willing to pay for the space.

Anton runs the washcloth along Otta's arm. "I don't know why I bother," he says under his breath, so the people on the other side of the curtain won't hear him. "I don't know what you would say if you were around to see yourself reduced to this."

His hand stops, the cloth paused by her wrist. Otta's appearance has changed little in these years. She's aging, as is only natural for a body occupied with qi, but not in the way that others do. It's as if her body is playing catch-up with the rest of the world, always a step behind, continually forgetting that it remains alive and must continue to function. It would have been easier if the body had died. If Otta's qi had been snuffed out entirely, then the gods would have made a decision on Anton's behalf to take her away. Instead, she is locked inside something that was halfway saved, caught between life and death. Day after day, Anton must actively choose to keep her stuck in this in-between, because if he gives up on her now, then her death is on his hands.

"Give me a sign if you can hear me," Anton says, as he does every time he visits, for months, for years. "Just something, Otta. Anything."

There's nothing. There has always been nothing, from the moment she fell sick to this very second as the clock on the wall ticks past six. Anton picks up her hand and holds it, but the action is done out of reflex, not warmth. Seven years have passed, and by this point, he remembers the Otta in front of him more than the Otta who was alive, who pushed him to climb the palace turrets and throw eggs at their classroom windows.

In truth, he hadn't known Otta for long before they were caught trying to run. If asked what their favorite memory together is, he wouldn't know what to point at. Evenings spent hiding in various palace rooms, maybe, trying to keep quiet with the guards patrolling the hallways outside. But even that was always tinged with a franticness, with him wondering if Otta was going to get bored and wander off if he wasn't interesting enough.

"Why do you always do that?" he had asked once.

Otta jolted in that private sitting room, her black eyes snapping to him. It was always a little strange looking at her directly, the Avia eyes so similar to Anton's own. They certainly weren't related. The elite bloodlines were well-documented, every bastard child logged no matter how quietly they slipped in.

"What do you mean?" Otta returned innocently.

"You're always peering around. See—you're doing it right now. It's like you're expecting someone to pop out from behind and scare you."

In truth, that was the generous interpretation. No matter if they were in a room alone or surrounded by the palace crowd, Otta's attention was flitting about eagerly. Anton had chosen his phrasing with care so that Otta wouldn't take it as an attack, but it wasn't only that she would peer around—she wanted to be watched, as if every word she delivered to him was also conducted for a hidden audience just on the other side of the curtain.

Otta leaned forward, her chin propped in her palm.

"I'm only cautious," she whispered, like the two of them were engaged in conspiracy. "How else would we survive a place like this?"

Sometimes Anton got the feeling that palace nobles made themselves out to be more important than they really were. That every conflict was contrived and artificial, only a matter of who upset who and who said the wrong thing to who, and no one living within these gilded walls knew a single thing about what real danger was.

But he couldn't say that to Otta. She made a blood sport out of surviving the palace, and she claimed to do it for their sake. While she reached for him and whispered, *You're the only thing that makes it worth it, promise me we'll stay together, promise me, promise me*— there was nothing he could say except *I promise. I promise.*

Whether he knew the true Otta Avia or not, they belonged to each other. He has spent these years in exile desperately aware that she is all he has left, every waking moment spent chasing the next method of covering a hospital bill from months prior. The end of the line is approaching. The debt piles too high to touch. Anton knows that either he wins the king's games and takes the prize, or he loses himself and Otta at once. He won't accept any other alternative. A promise is a promise, and he won't ever abandon her.

Anton sets Otta's hand down, then stops short. Her fingertips are tinged purple.

"I need a doctor," he demands immediately, surging to his feet and smacking the plastic curtain aside. A nurse stands by the table, pouring from a large metal thermos.

"Did you say something?" the nurse asks absently, his eyes flicking over.

"Yes," Anton replies. Impatience rises in his throat. All the hospitals in San-Er are like this. Overworked and overpacked, underpaid and understaffed. The people who run shifts are either short-tempered or entirely apathetic. He supposes it is self-preservation more than anything. Each day, they must throw out more lives than they save, not by any will of their own, but because there are not enough resources or operation spaces.

But still, in that moment, the only person around to blame is the nurse.

"This patient needs tending to."

The nurse walks close, frowning. "I don't see anything wrong."

"So fetch a doctor—*hey*, where are you going?"

Something in the hallway has started screeching. Without any sympathy, the nurse is already hurrying away, holding a hand up. "Press the call button if there's an emergency," he calls over his shoulder. As soon as he exits the room, it plunges deeper into noise, the conversation two beds over turning heated, and Anton resists the urge to punch through the curtain, hitting whatever he can just to feel better.

When Anton looks at Otta again, there's a thin layer of sweat on her top lip. He takes the washcloth and gingerly pats it off. Something is going on. The doctors say that as long as Otta has her vitals observed, as long as she is cared for, she won't deteriorate. The yaisu can be continually combatted. She cannot improve, but she cannot die either.

So why does she look like she is weakening?

There's a sudden rustle at the curtain, and Anton looks up with a start. The shadow of a child moves across the other unit, but it's gone just as fast. Anton waits another second. Nothing. He sighs.

There are no nurses or doctors around to remind him of his bills when he draws the curtain back and exits the room. He turns into the corridor outside. An itch at his chin irritates him, and when he touches it, he feels grit and dried blood and the prickle of facial hair trying to grow in. He's exhausted; when was the last time he took a shower? There's still so much red stained at his collar, perhaps day old, perhaps even older. Any time not spent in the games is spent around the fringes of the casinos and cybercafes, either moving money around or figuring out his accounts.

"Watch out, watch out!"

A gurney comes rushing down the corridor, pushed by a woman dressed like a regular civilian. Anton steps out of the way, pressing up against the chipping green wall paint. The cool-toned lightbulb flickers overhead. He wonders if a civilian has merely taken matters into her own hands or if she's a doctor who hasn't changed yet. The front desk can hardly keep track of its own patients, never mind its personnel. The only thing they can seem to keep track of is payment.

With a loud clatter of its wheels, the gurney disappears around the corner. Anton continues walking, hands in his pockets, eyeing the people he passes. The time has come for a swap. He can feel a discomfort in his chest—a reaction that always comes when familiarity sets in for a particular body, when a face grows too comfortable and the limbs become too easy to move. He has to stay on his toes. It's the only way San-Er won't bowl him over when he's not watching.

By the corner, there's a young man waiting with a cellular phone pressed to his ear. The device is a peculiar sight, rare around San because such technology is limited to the bankers and accountants in the financial districts. He must be rich. Either the son of a councilmember or someone capable enough to have made it out on his own after graduating from one of the three major academies in San-Er. It usually isn't worth getting people like them caught in the games.

Anton does it anyway. He trips in front of the man, knives and pager and coins clattering out from his jacket, wristband loosening from his arm. And when the young man kindly crouches down to help Anton pick up his belongings, Anton jumps.

"—she expects you at *nine*, don't forget. Your mother is—"

Anton removes the cellphone from his ear, making a guess as to which button cuts off the grouchy voice. The body he just vacated is blinking, red-orange eyes bugged wide in an attempt to recollect how he ended up at the hospital, but Anton feigns ignorance, and merely offers a half smile before scooping up the knives and shaking them into this new body's fancy suit sleeve. He feels refreshed. Alert. At some point, he—his qi, his spirit, his essence—will need sleep, but as long as he keeps jumping, he can push it off, like a wound sealed over with tape instead of new skin.

Anton secures his wristband into place again. With new vigor, he pushes through the hospital's front doors, merging into the rest of the busy building.

◇◇◇◇◇

August flips a coin, then catches it smoothly in his hand. The bar bustles around him, each seat filled with regulars. Snake Station is a hole-in-the-wall—or three holes in three walls, to be precise—that involves picking through a series of obscure passageways before reaching the infamous locale. Palace guards frequent these booths often, coming in when they're on break and even when they aren't.

The bartender puts a drink in front of August. Wearing a stranger's body, August nods, tossing the coin forward. Tonight, he gets to the bottom of this mystery. No more talk of foreign intruders. No more lies about rural invaders. Something about this has always felt off to him, but he cannot put his finger on what it is. Something feels . . . orchestrated. Murky, improbable motives. Logic failing to follow through.

Calla reported in this morning. She was attacked yesterday by someone who likely intended to make her another victim of the yaisu sickness.

There was no light when he jumped. There was nobody nearby when he disappeared from the body. How is that possible, August? Since when could Sicans change the rules like that?

Except that's the problem—he doesn't think impossible things can be explained away by blaming what is foreign. There is more to it.

"You hear anything about this?"

The two palace guards sitting around the bar startle at August's voice, but quickly follow his finger to the small screen propped in the corner. The muted news broadcast is talking about the deaths again, showing a grainy picture of one of the dead players doing the Sican salute. August was allowed to release only the blurriest photograph so the people of San-Er could see this was the work of an amateur, someone who didn't *really* know what the Sican salute looked like. The newscasters on screen hurry to assure that it is false, intended to sow discord in San-Er. That part, at least, he *does* believe: this is not the work of real Sicans. He just cannot fathom it being the rural Talinese either.

"We know about as much as you do," the palace guard replies. He doesn't look suspicious in the slightest, and if he has noticed August's pitch-black eyes, there is no indication. August presents in every other way as a regular concerned civilian.

"I'm surprised it's being blamed on outside intruders."

"Oh?" August says.

The second palace guard nods. "The wall has been infallible this long for a reason. It's an excellent system. We watch every section. If anyone climbed in, we would *know*."

August agrees. Which is why he has been hopping bars all night, talking to every palace guard he can find. Because that leaves one more option.

An inside job.

He hasn't decided yet what that would mean. A security breach? Perhaps a whole watchtower is turning a blind eye, or someone in the ranks is opening the doors to the outside. But that still leaves major gaps, like how one might procure identity numbers and evade surveillance cameras.

August jumps. He slams into a body across the bar, and the flash is swallowed up quickly, merely another strange blip ongoing in San despite being the herald of illegal activity. The palace guards here are mostly off the clock; they have no desire to police jumping. Despite that, they're still easily spotted by their uniforms, swathed in black, so August slides into a booth opposite another guard in his new body.

This guard doesn't look up when he arrives.

"Not interested in the news?"

"Mind your business," the guard retorts.

August tilts his head. "Don't you think it's your civic duty to apologize for rural intruders in San-Er? How can you wear your uniform so proudly? How are you to represent the throne of Talin?"

The guard looks up now. With a delayed beat, August realizes he recognizes him, or at least the greenish blue of his eyes. This is one of Leida's closest men, responsible for filling in when she is outside the palace walls or otherwise off-duty.

"What are you so mouthy for, huh?" the guard—Vaire, that's his name—demands.

August waits a beat. "Why so defensive? Are you the one who let in the intruders?"

Vaire lunges, left hand clenching around August's collar. He hauls him close, spittle frothing at the mouth. His other fist is already coming up, in a trajectory to land upon August's jaw, but then Vaire's arm halts like it has met an invisible barrier. The sight is almost comical.

"Your Highness," Vaire says quickly. Ah, so he has noticed the eyes. "I apologize profusely."

"Oh, no need," August replies. "I *was* being irritating, after all." He shakes off Vaire's grip, and Vaire snatches both hands back at once. August stands, lips pursed in absent thought. "See to it that you report to your shift nice and early tomorrow."

He can feel Vaire staring after him as he walks out of the bar. As soon as the guard identified August, he clammed up, so there's no use trying to ask anything else. Nevertheless—why the adverse reaction when asked about the wall? Vaire is not usually inclined toward violence. He's levelheaded and calm, as all palace guards must be when they are selected for duty.

Outside the building, August pauses, turning over his shoulder. He watches the final door swing. His gaze moves up, going to the second floor where a club pulses, the third where a laundromat rumbles on, the fourth floor where a noodle shop is operating at high capacity.

He hasn't quite figured it out yet. But he's starting to get his suspicions.

CHAPTER 17

Smoke dances from Calla's lips in little gray circles, perfect shapes fading into the air while she dusts the kitchen with ash. There are already three finished cigarette stubs littered on the floor, embers burning the ceramic tiles. Calla, meanwhile, sits upon the table, one muddy boot propped on a chair, the other dangling freely.

The door opens. When Anton walks into his apartment, he doesn't look surprised to see her. Of course, she can only assume that it's Anton, dressed like some councilmember's assistant, hair combed back with gel and fancy cuff links glimmering in the low light.

Calla taps her cigarette. More loose ash joins the mess on the floor, and she wonders if he will notice. If it'll piss him off, or if he hardly cares, just another blot added to the apartment.

"Where were you?" Calla demands.

Anton raises an eyebrow. He walks closer, his steps sluggish, like he doesn't have the energy to remain upright for another second. His eyes, however, give him away. That jet-black stare is wary and calculating, operating at peak alertness.

"Do I report to you now, Fifty-Seven?" Anton replies.

"Do you report to anyone?" If he's wearing a new body since she saw him earlier, he has been somewhere public. Doing what? Seeing who? Is the new face to avoid recognition, or was he simply bored of the old one? The impulsion to know what he has been up to tugs at her hands; if he won't give an answer willingly, she will carve open his chest and pluck it from him.

Anton stops before the table. "I'm not in the mood to fight with you."

"Fight with me?" Calla echoes. A petulant laugh lodges at the entrance of her throat. She holds it in with the barest self-restraint. "Oh, *so* sorry to disrupt your schedule."

Anton slams his hands to either side of her. The sudden motion doesn't startle her. Sullenly, Calla traces her gaze along the line of his suit, its fabric so smooth that she can see exactly where he has hidden his crescent knives.

"What are you doing here?" he asks.

"You didn't see the announcement?" she returns. "The games are being sped up. Pings at random. One might go off at any second, and then your apartment will be as unsafe as mine."

By Anton's expression, he did not know. She watches him blink once, twice . . .

"And you still showed up here?"

"How else was I supposed to find you?"

Anton says nothing in response. Calla thins her lips. They are only firing question after question at each other, with no answer on either side.

Something terrible sparks in her temper.

"You can just say it outright." When she flicks her cigarette ash onto the tablecloth, she can pinpoint the exact moment she has overstepped her bounds. "If we're done and you're breaking our alliance."

Anton plucks the cigarette from her fingers. She expects him to throw it away. Instead, he takes a drag, then blows the smoke right into her face. In a flash, Calla's hand springs to his neck, fingers braced around his throat and ready to squeeze. She doesn't, though—not yet. She waits for him to pick the fight so she can start firing her accusations, but she knows that the person she really wants to tell off is herself. She's become accustomed to having Anton Makusa around. Isn't that why it bothers her when she can't find him at a perilous time? A certain reliance has creeped in. She may not need him nearby, but she *wants* him nearby. It's the first thing she has wanted in years other than King Kasa's demise.

"What are you talking about?" Anton says. His free hand comes up just as quickly, gripping her wrist to control her grasp on his throat. "Are you trying to frighten me, Fifty-Seven?"

"You *should* be frightened," she returns, scowling.

"Should I?" Anton's voice is low and derisive. He slides his hand up over hers, but instead of prying her fingers off, he holds them there. "Why are you looking at me like that, then?"

Calla freezes. The words settle in her stomach as pits, the seeds of something parasitic trying to take root and keep her company. Her grip doesn't seem like a threat anymore: it is only pressed against soft skin and hard tendons, feeling the hollows of his neck move with every word he speaks.

"I beg your pardon?"

"Don't act the fool. It doesn't suit you." Anton takes a step closer and inclines his head down. Before Calla can stop him, his lips brush the curve of her ear. "There's no need to threaten me. If you wanted my attention, you have it now."

A sharp whine comes from Calla's belt. The unexpected sound jars her enough that she releases her grip on Anton's throat and shoves him away. He lurches back without protest, his expression unchanged.

"Don't get it twisted," Calla spits, unclipping her pager. It's from Chami. **Emergency. Call the diner.**

A bolt of panic runs up her spine. She meets Anton's gaze again with a wholly new ferocity.

"Where's your nearest telephone?"

◇◇◇◇◇

Anton follows Calla out, his heart thudding against his ribs. He has long learned how to hide it, to school his features in any body so they show only what he wishes to show. Otta was the master at these lessons. She didn't tolerate sentimentality; she hardened tender things until they were shimmering stones.

Now he hears his pulse in his ear, the breakneck thrum going and going as he watches Calla pick up the telephone receiver. A bartender from the front—Ruen—comes by and squeezes through the brothel's thin walkways, eyeing Calla at the phone and then eyeing Anton, failing to recognize him. As soon as he disappears, Anton walks to the other side of the telephone and leans right onto the box, making sure Calla knows he can hear every word of the conversation, even if he isn't really listening.

Adrenaline, he reasons with himself. This reaction to Calla is a primal response, something that works off association. She reminds him of Otta, and not in a good way. She gets under his skin, even more than Otta did, because Otta squirmed and burrowed just to see if she could, but Calla will set her claws deep and then claim that she didn't mean to. She could have anything in the world if she only tried.

"When did this happen?" she's saying into the phone. Her fingers grip the cord, twisting the line tight enough that the tip of her thumb is turning white. When her eyes flick up, catching Anton's stare, it's almost like she doesn't even see him there.

He should know better than to be drawn to her. The palace has already left him scarred. It let Otta stand mighty and unstoppable, then took her away with a grinning leer. He's turned on his heel and thrown himself as far as he can get from its mockery, and still he cannot escape, sent a new test in the form of Calla Tuoleimi, the last living princess of Er. She stains his mind in vivid color, bright and burning and dangerous.

He's always liked dangerous things.

He hates that he knows better. That dangerous things are bound to leave a demolished path in their wake. And still, he tries to hold them anyway.

"Don't panic, just don't panic," Calla says into the receiver, pinching the bridge of her nose. She mouths a violent expletive, which Anton catches but the phone does not. "When was the last time you saw her?"

Before Anton can guess what comes over the line, there's a tap on his shoulder, and he turns around to find Ruen, a tray balanced in his other hand.

"Are you—"

"It's me," Anton confirms before Ruen can finish. "Any mail come recently?"

Ruen frowns, holding up a warning finger. "Stop swapping so often. I almost kicked you out." The bartender reaches into his back pocket and digs something out. Envelopes. Ratty-looking ones that might have arrived a while ago, but Anton is the worst at checking for them, and everyone downstairs has begun passing them around for safekeeping.

"Pay your bills," Ruen warns. He swerves around Calla at the phone. "You're way too behind."

"Are you opening my mail?" Anton calls after him.

"I don't have to! The sheer volume tells me enough!"

Ruen disappears around the corner. Calla slams the receiver down. As she fumes, Anton shoves the envelopes into his pocket without even looking at them.

"What's wrong?" he asks casually.

Her head jerks up. There's a pause—a prolonged second of hesitation—before she answers. "A friend of mine is missing. She went to the Hollow Temple."

Yearly in San-Er, there are more profiles of people missing than people found. Bodies vanish; souls get wiped out.

"So a Crescent Society abduction," Anton guesses.

Calla is quiet, chewing on her lip and resting against the wall. She looks like she's posing for a royal sculpture, if those artworks were forged in steel instead of gold.

"All right." She straightens up suddenly, dusting her hands off. "Come on, Makusa."

She starts to walk, striding at a brisk pace through the brothel. With a start, Anton rushes to follow, stepping left and right around her as her speed hastens.

"Am I coming with you?"

Calla shoots him a sharp look. "We're allied, are we not?" She ducks out through the door, barely pausing to prevent it from slamming into Anton, but he is fast, so he's soon back alongside her.

"We are," Anton replies. He watches her pause on the street. She lifts her chin, seeming to be deciding which way to go, and in the midst of it, a strand of hair blows into her face, sticking to her mouth. Anton almost reaches out to help, but Calla is already brushing it aside.

"Why'd you ask, then?" she says. A ghost of a smile crinkles her eyes. "Of course you're coming."

◇◇◇◇◇

Ruen picks up the telephone. He dials the number slowly, making sure he does not miss a digit, lest he is punished for the delay.

The line connects. He clears his throat.

"She's on her way."

CHAPTER 18

Calla crouches on the building's third floor, scratching at the inside of her elbow through her coat. The wind blows through the rectangular cutout in the wall, swirling dust and dried paint chips along its sides. The whole level looks like it's crumbling, like someone keeps taking bite-size chunks out of the cement.

"There are going to be a lot of Crescents on patrol," Anton warns.

Calla presses her knuckles against her mouth, hard. Sharp pain blooms inside her lips, her teeth cutting into soft flesh, and only once she is anchored to this raw, human feeling can she find the capacity to think.

"A rescue mission shouldn't be hard," she decides. "This was Yilas's last location, so the most likely scenario is that someone didn't like the look of an outsider and decided to rough her up. She's here somewhere—we just have to grab her and go."

Anton cranes his neck out further, getting a better look at what awaits beneath. A thin metallic grille runs over the temple roof, keeping out everything that might drop from the buildings looming at its sides. Night's darkness hovers close to the ground.

"You do realize," Anton starts slowly, "that this is a central hub for vessel trafficking, right? The whole temple is heavily guarded."

Calla doesn't know much about the Hollow Temple, short of what Yilas has told her. Really, she doesn't know much about the Crescent Societies at all. For most of their factions, the guise of being a religious sect mostly serves as a cover for their underground business endeavors. Secrecy becomes a tool to avoid scrutiny; their fierce devotion scares away prying watchers. Though she is sure some Society members really do believe in the old gods, everything in San-Er revolves around survival, and they wouldn't organize this way unless it kept them safe.

Calla stands, placing a foot on the cutout ledge. "We'll be fine," she says. Then she leaps and lands hard on the metal grille above the temple, wincing when the whole frame dips with her weight. Her knees attempt to lock in protest, but she's moving quickly, wading across half-rotted plastic bags and mounds of who-knows-what that's been festering there for years, sun or storm. It's hard to see, the illumination from the tall buildings only casting a weak glow.

The metal grille shakes again, protesting as Anton makes his landing too.

"The entrance is *below*, Fifty-Seven."

"Do you expect us to march in through the front?" Calla whispers. She keeps wading through the trash, kicking until she's at the northwest corner of the protective mesh grille. As quietly as she can, she moves the junk piles until a segment of the grille has been cleared. "Help me lift."

Anton frowns, but he's quick to hurry over and secure his hands on the other two sides of the panel. The grille pieces are joined together in a gridlocked network, but with some prying, Calla manages to lift a corner. Then a square of the mesh comes unaligned from the frame underneath, its sides scraping against metal.

"Toss," Calla instructs. They toss the grille atop the trash bags with a muffled sound. Someone will certainly notice this square hole in the protective layer when trash starts leaking down to the temple, but by then, Calla can only hope she and Anton won't be lurking around any longer.

Anton peers through the opening they've made. They're greeted by the green tiles of the temple roof.

"Is there a back entrance we're taking instead?" he whispers.

If Calla took a guess, she would say yes. But she can do better than a guess. "Follow me."

Her boots strike against the roof tiles, the noise thankfully subsumed by the general clamor in San, and she slides for a quick second before gaining balance again. When she pauses, hovering at the curved edge between the two wings of the temple, she can hear Crescents walking around the path below, bantering among themselves about rising brothel prices.

It's cold. The temple runs their air-conditioning at freezing temperatures.

"Come on," Calla hisses. With a visible grimace, Anton skids down too. He lands solidly on his feet. They wait a beat to see if the Crescents will have heard, but when the voices move around the turn, Calla finally makes it to the paved ground, her sword already drawn.

"Put that away," Anton warns when he's joined her on the pavement. "If we act nonthreatening, we can pretend to be members."

"We don't have the tattoos," Calla replies, but she puts her sword away obligingly. There is logic to his instruction: at a temple this large, anyone coming across them will not necessarily assume they do not belong. Calla can already see a tall window three feet away, its foggy, mud-streaked glass left slightly ajar.

"Give me a boost."

They're inside quickly, having entered a dusty back hall. Out of her periphery, she can see Anton glancing at her repeatedly, as if to check whether she knows their next steps, but the truth is that Calla hardly plans in advance. She establishes one concrete end goal, then rams through whatever barriers stand between herself and the result.

Right now, that goal is finding Yilas.

"Do you know where you're going?" Anton hisses after her.

"Of course not," Calla replies. She pokes her head into a corridor. It looks empty. She steps through, carefully avoiding a puddle. The lightbulbs above glow red, casting their surroundings in a crimson shroud. "Why would I know how to navigate a Crescent Society temple?"

Anton makes a horrified noise under his breath. When Calla turns over her shoulder to inspect him, though, his fright doesn't seem to sink all the way through; that red glint in his dark eyes reflects amusement, whether at the nonsense of their plan or their present success.

A *thunk* travels along the wall. Calla pauses, listening. She presses her ear to the moldy lines and trails her hands across the surface, moving with the bumps and holes.

"I think," Calla says slowly, "that sound is coming from beneath us."

Anton presses his ear to the wall too. The *thunk* comes again, echoing all through the temple.

"It's—"

A round of voices enters the next hallway, fast approaching.

Calla spits, "Quickly," and they tear through the narrow aisle, going and going until, *wait*—her eyes snag on the outline of a door. She kicks. A staircase leading down. Without pause, she hauls Anton by his sleeve, and they descend three steps at a time, emerging in a basement area.

Calla's vision adjusts. First, it's the *bodies* on the floor that capture her notice. Then, sitting on a folding chair by another door that feeds deeper into the basement level is—

"Eno?" Calla and Anton say at once.

Eno jumps to his feet. Anton swerves, shooting a questioning look at Calla. "How do *you* know him?" he asks. "I didn't think you would be acquainted with Snowfall's clientele."

"Pull up his sleeve," Calla says, marching toward the bodies.

By a quick count, there are near thirty, collapsed in a large pile, some splayed on top of others. The first one she turns over is a stranger. When she tugs up an eyelid, she finds color in the iris still, and she can hear their quiet, smothered breath struggling in and out. Not dead. Merely unconscious.

Anton, as instructed, strides toward Eno and holds up his arm. The wristband comes into view. "You're a player?"

"I saved his sorry ass from being cut in half." Calla turns over a second body. Another stranger. She lifts an eyelid and, when she sees a washed-out bronze, keeps moving.

"What are you *doing*?" Anton hisses at the boy. "And when did you join the Crescent Societies?"

"I'm new!" Eno whines, trying to writhe out of Anton's grip. "You think debt is easy to pay? I need every chance."

Shuffling to the next body in the pile, Calla quickly rummages through her own pockets, fingers locking around a mask that lies at the bottom with her coins and pins. There's no telling what could be floating around the air with so many bodies, so she puts it on, just in case. What *is* this place? The Crescent Societies traffic occupied bodies, sure. They kidnap people and sell them off to bidders, but she always thought they made quick work of the trade-off. They picked a target, rushed into their place of employment with brute force, and brought the body in front of the client for jumping. Rarely did the victim need to be knocked out. If the Crescent Societies latched on to you as a target, you were already dead.

Calla puts her finger under the nose of another body, just to be certain. They're breathing. Certainly breathing. But the one under it . . .

A chill sweeps from her neck to her toes, sweat breaking under her thick jacket. By the wall, Anton continues to lecture Eno, paying no heed to what Calla is doing, so he doesn't see her blanche, fingers reaching out to prod the dead body. This is no trafficking scheme. A trafficking scheme wouldn't go killing its assets.

Anton's and Eno's voices drown out. Calla's fingers feel ice-cold when she turns the body over, exposing the ring of blood staining its chest. Its gray face stares at the ceiling, dulled dark-yellow eyes unblinking and beady. Under this light, Calla could almost mistake the color for her own. She shivers, reaching for the corpse's shirt collar, and peels it back slowly, holding her breath beneath her mask.

The wound, if one could even call it that, is in fact a hole, carved through the chest and bones cut clean, an empty space where a heart ought to be.

A strangled noise escapes before Calla can help it, her throat sour with disgust. Her own heart is thudding hard against her ribs when she shoots to her feet and searches through the rest of the bodies, a prayer starting on her tongue. She has no faith in the old gods, no inclination to believe that any such nonsense would work in a place like San-Er, but still she finds herself muttering and muttering as she pushes through shoulders and legs, some cold and some warm.

She doesn't understand. Even if Society business called for trafficked vessels to be stored at this temple, why tangle them up with dead ones? Why carve the hearts out of those vessels at all?

Calla goes still. She sees a familiar lock of dyed red hair. At once, she surges forward, her pulse racing so fast she could vomit. She turns Yilas over.

Yilas's chest rises and falls with life, qi humming in her veins.

Thank the heavens—

"Yilas." Calla gives her a rough shake. "Yilas, get the fuck up."

Groggily, Yilas starts to stir, struggling to pry her eyes open as if they've been glued together. The same jade green. The same Yilas.

"Calla?" she murmurs.

"Shh," Calla hisses immediately, throwing a glance at Eno. The boy is still arguing with Anton and hasn't heard them. "Can you get up?"

"I—yeah, I think so. Where are we?" Yilas struggles into a sitting position, then teeters immediately, her face visibly paling even in the horrible red light. Calla mutters a curse, her arm shooting out to catch Yilas before her former attendant can smash her temple against the floor. With every iota of strength, Calla hauls Yilas to her feet, holding her weight with a firm grip under her shoulders.

But before Calla can take a step, her wristband is trembling, as are Anton's and Eno's.

"Ah, shit," she mutters.

"I'm sure they're only responding to each other," Anton assures, switching his off. "Maybe the surveillance room thought—"

A heavy rumble of footsteps. Right above. One voice, bellowing over the rest, feminine and sharp, giving commands to scatter and search. Then: so much movement that the ceiling trembles. There's definitely another player in the Hollow Temple, which can only mean trouble. If they're a Crescent, they may be able to call on an entire entourage for the kill, and though Calla doesn't recall seeing anything like that on the reels, if there's anyone who knows how to avoid the surveillance feeds across the city, it's a member of the Crescent Societies.

"Yilas, do you think you can walk on your own?"

"Absolutely not," Yilas replies, her words slurring. At least she's honest. Sometimes Calla really hates honesty.

Calla bites down on the insides of her cheeks. She'd give it thirty seconds before they're found.

"Eno!"

The boy jumps to attention, his eyes wide and terrified as he presses his wristband to stop the ping. He's so damn *young* that Calla cannot comprehend why she keeps seeing him in the most dreadful places, but given the situation, Calla can only push the thought away. She shoves Yilas at him, and Eno scrambles to hold his arms out before Yilas sways right to the floor.

"What—"

"I'll owe you another favor, okay?" Calla snaps. She points down the hallway, deeper into the basement. If Eno is hanging around here guarding the bodies, then he must know how to navigate the place and find another exit. "Help my friend out of here. Makusa and I will keep them distracted until you get away."

Eno casts a desperate glance at the stairwell. "But my status as a novice—"

"What will being a novice offer you?" Anton cuts in. "Likely a place as one of these bodies. *If* we don't eliminate you from the games first."

Eno grimaces. With a small grumble, he hauls Yilas by the arm and surges into the hall, disappearing into the shadows.

Calla silences her wristband and draws her sword. She loosens her grip, throwing the handle up an inch to adjust. When the weapon lands back into her palm securely, she is ready.

"Fifty-Seven." Anton, however, does not pull his knives. His eyes are on the door. "As soon as they come in, we have to jump. Invade our way out."

Calla's glare is immediate. Her hair whips against her mask, curling against the edge of fabric as she scrunches her nose, trying to convey with her eyes how much she disapproves.

"No. We fight. Don't be a coward."

"It's not being a coward," Anton snaps back. "The games are only easy for us when the players are isolated, every man for themselves. Don't you remember how we had to run from Seventy-Nine's security team? Will you be growing extra arms? Extra legs? Summoning more weapons?"

Calla bites down, gritting the back of her teeth so hard she hears something crack.

"I'm not jumping."

Anton whirls to face her. "Don't think I won't fucking leave you here, Calla Tuoleimi—"

The door blows open. Society members pour down the steps, spilling into the basement, surrounding them all sides. Calla loses count after the first ten.

They move with such cohesion that confusion slows her movements. Why are they gathering like this if it's only one player among them who wants to make a kill? How could the games possibly be important enough to the Crescent Societies for this?

"Pampi," someone calls down the stairs. "You can't just move everyone away from—"

A woman at the back of the crowd throws her arm out. Though she is at the bottom of the steps and the other man is at the top, he staggers backward, like an invisible fist has hit his chest, slamming him into the wall.

Calla's sword arm falters, the blade lowering. The man who attacked her during the flood sirens. The empty vessel, who somehow jumped without any light, without sighting a new body nearby. He had been able to fight without contact as well.

The woman—Pampi—steps near, into the red light. Her eyes must be red too, creating an illusion where her gaze is entirely swathed in color.

Suddenly, Anton stumbles, his hand going to his sternum. He inhales like he can barely catch his breath, then he turns to the Crescent nearest to him, fury burning in his eyes. "Did you just try to invade me? Piss *off*."

"Watch your tongue."

Pampi's voice is high-pitched and syrupy. She reaches a finger out, prodding Anton in the chest. Before he can make a move to counter her, she has tied a swath of ribbon around his eyes, some material that sticks tight even as Anton exclaims, hands flying up to move it away. He can't get a good grip on the ribbon; the Crescents around him take ahold of his arms while he tries, holding him prisoner.

Through the whole event, Calla watches quietly. Her mind is moving with the flurry of an electrical storm. She doesn't rush to Anton's defense, lest she waste an edge she has not yet identified. She only shifts the sword in her grip, feeling sweat build up in the lines of her palms. Pampi's sleeves are rolled up.

There's a wristband sitting high up on her arm, alongside a canvas of puckered scars. When the screen turns in her direction, Calla catches a 2 on display.

"You," Pampi says lightly. She's addressing Calla now, ignoring Anton as he rattles off a chain of expletives. "Fifty-Seven. I was hoping you'd show up."

Calla doesn't say anything. How long has it been since Eno took Yilas? Has he left the temple yet?

"What's the matter?" Pampi moves closer, seeing that she is receiving no response. "Can't speak Talinese?"

Calla strikes hard, shoving her sword through Pampi's gut.

In the palace, she had once asked what the point of a brute-force attack was if it achieved nothing in the forward march. The general training her that day had an easy answer. In the enemy, even a single shred of fear is better than nothing. A single cell of infection is how the fever starts.

"How *dare* you—"

Pampi tugs the sword out, letting it clatter to the floor. Without any light, her eyes turn from red to gray. She just *jumped*. Somehow, she jumped, and the body with the stab wound crumples to the floor, its original occupant clutching the wound and gasping with pain. A new red-eyed body steps over the old vessel from behind, looking down with disdain curling her lip.

Calla feels as though she is losing her mind. She is certainly losing her grasp on every rule in Talin she knew to be true.

The Crescents stir. They hurry to hold Calla in place, gripping her shoulders, her elbows, trying to keep her locked at every turn of a limb. But Calla does not struggle. When Pampi hisses a command, they force Calla to her knees too, pulling at her hair so that her chin tips up.

Pampi strides closer in her new body. The Crescents in the room look to her as if she is their leader, waiting for further instruction on what to do. Yet there was still someone who questioned her earlier, a conflict of authority. While each of the Crescent Society temples follows one cleric, the transitions of power are constant and fast, switching without notice depending on who can promise the most at any point in time. Pampi must be new, still shakily established.

The body on the floor has stopped gasping. Their head lolls back, eyes dull, neck craned and exposed. In such a position, the collar of their shirt falls back to show the skin below, and there: two parallel lines of blood, smeared almost artfully.

Calla's eyes flicker away. Pampi must have done that when she was still wearing the vessel. It doesn't seem like an aesthetic choice.

"Let's try that again," Pampi says, her tone unchanged.

One of the Crescents yanks at Calla's hair once more to keep her looking forward. She catches another glimpse of the bodies in the room, the ones with their hearts carved out. Despite the roar in her head, she thinks she might be putting something together.

"Try what?" Calla asks, speaking her first words to Pampi. She adopts her palace voice, glacial and haughty and a thousand feet above everyone else. Two steps away, Anton snorts. Though he is still blindfolded, he has stopped struggling. He is listening, head tilted toward Calla. "Your poor attempt at intimidation? Do you hope to loom over me like some divine conqueror? You will never be one. The desperate never are."

She used to observe her parents very carefully. Mornings in the breakfast hall. Afternoons in the indoor garden. Nights in the recreation lounges. Though they were not the closest family in the world—far from it—Calla spent plenty of time with them, tailing them at their daily tasks and learning how the Tuoleimis ruled their palace. She watched how they treated the servants, the rural women who had abandoned their children to work in the kitchen, the rural men standing guard where numbers were needed. If there was ever the barest hint that something was wrong, palace servants prostrated first, then checked what mistake they made second. It never really mattered what it was, or whether there had been a mistake to begin with. As soon as they heard a rise in volume from the king or queen of Er, submission was the only answer.

Those who hold power in their hands are the same. They want to walk through the world reminded over and over again of their might, and if they do not get that response, then they will force it.

Calla lifts her brow, inviting argument. Suddenly Pampi reaches out and tears Calla's mask off, and Calla can't help but grin, knowing she's hit her mark. Whatever consequence is about to come, at least she has not lost.

"I know who you are." Pampi crumples the fabric in her hands.

"Of course you do," Calla replies. "You've seen me on the reels. I am the future victor of the games."

Pampi lands an enraged slap across Calla's face. When Calla rears back, she almost laughs, but then she sees one of the Crescents pass Pampi a knife. Calla's eyes dart around the room as she runs through her escape options. The man holding her left shoulder has a weak grip. Her gaze drops down to his collared shirt. There's only the barest glimpse under the red light as he jerks in movement, but Calla could swear he has the same two vertical lines of dried blood.

"I want her heart," Pampi says. "It is a very special one."

"Right now?" the man asks. "We have others about to expire—"

"Hold her *still*!"

They're doing something to the qi of the trafficked bodies on the floor. Using it to change the way they jump, altering the very properties of the physical world and how they interact with it.

Calla slams her left elbow out, catching the man in the jaw. She tips hard into that opening, moving so suddenly that her shoulder veers to the floor. She lasts two seconds, freed and winded, gasping for breath. But as soon as she's rolled upright, there's an invisible grip on her throat, and Calla feels the first real hint of panic setting into her bones. She stops, hands flying to grip at nothing, and then they've got her again, nails and claws tearing her jacket off and digging into the softness of her skin.

The knife flashes. Pampi lifts it.

"A waste of power when it's in you."

"Fifty-Seven," Anton shouts, alarm rising in his tone. He still can't see. "Fifty-Seven, *jump*."

Calla jerks to the side. It doesn't do anything. Her jacket is a crumpled shield on the floor, her sword scattered afar.

When Pampi puts the blade against her heart, Calla swipes a hand forward. She's not trying to escape. She's trying to get another look: two parallel lines of blood on this vessel's chest too.

"You think that's going to do anything?" Pampi plunges the blade in, and then Calla can only see white—blinding white. What has it hit? It's too far to the left. They don't intend to damage the heart, but to carve it right out, whole and beating.

Someone's screaming. Someone's screaming, and then Calla's nerve endings jolt to life again and it's her that is screaming, her chest cold and hot and a hundred other sensations at once.

"Jump!" Anton is yelling. "Jump or they will *kill* you—"

Anton stamps his foot hard, then hooks it around the leg of the nearest body beside him. The Crescent stumbles, and when he feels the air move, when he feels them lifting a weapon with intent for harm, Anton leans right in, letting his face take it.

It cuts, and it cuts deep. But it also slices through the blindfold, which tumbles to the floor in one long piece.

Anton shakes his wristband off and jumps. He takes that nearest body first, the one who slashed him, and turns the blade on his own throat. It's a risk, but he leaves fast and breathes a sigh of relief when the next body accepts him. He won't stay that lucky—many Crescent Society members are doubled, resistant to jumping. The element of surprise is on his side, though; with his opponents clustered shoulder to shoulder, they can't see where he keeps going, light darting in and out the closed space, light blinding and blinding each time it flashes, pushing him in and out even when he fails, onto the next within a split second.

Calla is still screaming. Anton takes his cold sweat with him when he moves, and it's hard to determine what exactly is going on, hard to see what they are doing to Calla, until he is right beside Pampi, a chain in his hands and within arm's reach.

He swings the chain over her neck. He tugs, slams her to the ground. Calla drops too, hand clasped to her chest and blood pouring through her fingers.

Hard to tell whether it's fatal. Whether he has just lost his best ally.

Anton bares his teeth.

"You like blindfolding so much?" he hisses. And before Pampi can look elsewhere and jump, he finds a sharp knife in the pocket of this body's jacket and slashes across her eyes. He thinks he blinded only the left, but it's enough to shove her aside when she screeches, counting her incapacitated.

He swivels to Calla. Grabs her by the arm, uncaring whether she can stand or not. She must. If she's stupid enough to stay in this body, then she must be strong enough to carry it through. The other Crescents in the room are all injured and bewildered. There is an easy path—a quick shove and then through, his arm swooping down to retrieve the wristband he'd tossed onto the floor before hurtling up the steps with Calla and barging out from the basement.

Anton looks left, right. The corridor is empty. There's no one here.

"Fifty-Seven?"

Calla teeters sideways. He catches her immediately, his shirt staining with red where she presses close.

"I've got you," he promises. "I've got you, Princess."

And Calla passes out.

CHAPTER 19

The curtains stir with a soft breeze, a humid warmth blowing through the open window where daylight won't. When Calla blinks awake, that is what catches her eye first— the swirling of the curtain's white lace hem, incongruous with the rest of the room, installed over the blinds and pushed to the side. She hadn't noticed it the first time she was in here.

The next sensation that registers is a soft tugging on her hair. A steady, delicate brushing, smoothing the strands away from her face and along her temple.

Calla turns her head. The stranger pauses, his fingers halting as soon as he sees that she's awake.

"Anton," Calla greets, looking at his midnight-black eyes.

"Oh," he says. "I didn't even say our catchphrase yet."

Despite her dry throat, she manages a croak of a laugh. "Go on. I'll let you have your fun."

Anton reaches for a glass of water, already prepared by his bedside table.

"What fine daylight we have today," he says, passing her the glass. "Careful not to—"

Calla lifts onto her elbow to reach for the glass, but then there's a sudden searing pain at her chest, and her hand jerks up, her last memory flashing through her mind. Her wound needs immediate tending. It needs—

Calla peers down, her hand halting. It has already been tended to. Someone—Anton?—has sliced her shirt along its middle, stopping just before she is indecent, the exposed skin slathered with herbal leaves that cover her wound. All the blood on her chest has been wiped clean. Only her torn shirt shows the remnants of her torment, though it has long dried, the fabric dyed into a deep red brown.

A sense of weightlessness stirs in her stomach. The same suspended vertigo as peering over the edge of the tallest building in San-Er, except she's looking at her own mended body.

"You should have let me die," Calla says.

Anton rolls his eyes, pushing the glass into her hands. "And lose your help? That would be incredibly foolish." He rises from his chair, stretching upright. There's little space for him to move around, but still he pivots and starts to pace the length of his bedroom, rolling his neck left and right. "You've been out for almost a day. We're down to fifteen players, maybe less since the last reels played when I was watching from a barbershop window. I took your wristband and ran around with it each time it went off."

Anton digs into his pocket and, finding her wristband, tosses it back to her, the silver buckle landing with a heavy plop beside her hand. Calla peers at the screen. Nothing looks different. Anton could have smashed it up, pulled the chip out. He could have done anything in those hours she was gone to the world.

He could have let her die.

Calla struggles upright, swinging her legs over the side of the bed and setting the glass back down. Meanwhile, Anton returns to his chair, his lips thinning.

"I hope you recognize," he says when she remains silent, "that you were being really fucking stupid at the temple."

Her eyes snap up. She blinks once, her fingers twisting into the sheets. She can't say anything to defend herself. She knows this. She watches him, and every little detail she has ever let slip unfurls between them, one after the other, culminating to here, to now, to her with a gouge in her chest because she refused to jump when she easily could have.

Anton draws closer. His hand lifts, brushing along her face, fingers burying into her hair. It's not the same soft gesture as when she was asleep. He is not trying to soothe her; he is holding her in place to get a good look, like an investor putting his prize up to the light.

"You're a wild, terrifying thing, do you know that?" he asks, a tremor in his voice.

"Have you worked it out?" Calla asks in return.

It is unbelievable enough to be beyond comprehension. Something that no one could have guessed before the Er massacre and no one considered after, though they speculated about every other possibility.

All except this one.

Anton lets out a long breath.

"This is Calla Tuoleimi's body," he whispers, "but you're not Calla, are you?"

<><><>

The girl hasn't eaten in days.

The village has depleted its resources, and the crops have withered for the season. She hears the grown-ups whispering about how there's something wrong with the soil, but she doesn't know what that means. She only knows that there's a gnawing in her body. That she is so *tired* all the time, and no amount of playing with the sticks and twigs under the browning trees can solve the problem.

When the invaders come, she's one of the first to sight them. The riders on their horses, swords strapped to their belts. A battalion carrying torches, setting fire to the houses, letting the flames engulf every shop front, eat up each wooden pulley cart before anyone can think to escape.

The girl screams. She screams and screams, but no one hears her. Not until the flames have consumed everything, not until the village is surrounded by those declaring themselves agents of the palace, acting on behalf of the kingdom of Talin. *Worry no longer*, they declare, *because everyone here is now a citizen of Talin, and they will be under the protection of two mighty kings.*

The ash doesn't settle for days. The ash clogs up the girl's lungs, until she can't even feel hunger anymore, because she has only burning pain crawling up her esophagus. If anyone asks, she can't say whether she's lost her parents, siblings, friends. Whether it was the palace invasion that took them or if they were already gone. Her memory is too hazy, her mind too young. All she remembers is before and after.

The girl is sleeping outside a small shop the night she hears of the royal family visiting soon. Her legs are scabbed over with bug bites, clothes fraying so terribly that the hems have turned into loose string. The shop's owners come out to empty their buckets of water, dumping on the step without checking to see if there are vagrants first. The girl scrambles away in time to avoid being splattered, but the owners are engrossed in conversation anyway.

"Er's royal family," they say. "They want to bring us offerings, accept us into their rule."

They scoff, but they will not look a gift horse in the mouth. When the shop doors slam closed after them, the girl doesn't think much of it either, because when would an offering ever arrive for her; when has anything ever been for her?

The next time she hears about the royal family, they have arrived in the village. They have traveled for weeks by carriage to get here, the very outer boundaries of what is now the edge of Talin. The villagers still think of themselves as another part of the borderlands, as the nearest center one can stop in before the land blends with the rough mountains in the distance. If they voice it aloud, though, the soldiers will draw their swords, so they keep their mouths shut. They stay silent and discreetly turn their heads to the mountains any time they are asked about their allegiance.

Gifts flow through the crowd. Food and shoes and jewels. The people cheer, and it's hard to say how much of it is pretend and how many are genuinely won over by so little when they had nothing to begin with.

The girl doesn't join the crowds. She stands by a field one street away, prodding at a muddy puddle with a stick. That's how she hears the rustle nearby. That's how she is alone, with no other eyes to bear witness, when another girl joins her, well-dressed and prim in her steps, squinting at the puddle.

A princess, she thinks immediately.

"What are you looking for?" the princess asks. She's wearing such beautiful items. Pink silk for her sleeves, trailing almost to the ground. A golden bodice, bright under the sun. The circular headpiece wrapped around her hair is studded with so many gems that it twinkles with every minute movement. "That's a deep puddle. Be careful you don't fall in."

The girl doesn't know how to reply. Even the princess's speech is something different: each word enunciated in a way that this village has never heard before. The burning in her stomach has returned. Frantic and angry and inflamed. Bread is not enough. Small offerings once in a lifetime when they can bother making the trip out into the borderlands is not enough.

She wants more. She needs more.

The girl looks up.

She wants to be *her.*

Wind swirls in from the mountains. The girl drops her stick into the puddle, but she doesn't notice it sink to the very bottom. In that moment, she can only feel her fists clenching tight, her spine tingling, a desperate tremble moving along every inch of her skin.

Her eyes snap open. Somehow, she is standing three paces away. A horrendous pain overwhelms every other function in her body—churning, roiling, tearing apart her very cells.

Then, slowly, the pain fades. Sensation returns: the silk under her fingers, the pinch of her shoes.

She blinks. Once, twice. Beside her lies a body, arms flopped onto the grass and legs splayed crooked.

When she kicks her own birth body into the puddle, the vessel sinks right down into the mud, buried perfectly under the water and out of sight.

⬦⬦⬦⬦⬦

Calla opens her eyes. She hadn't realized she'd closed them. Sometimes, in her dreams, she still remembers the other language that was spoken in what is now Rincun Province. They switched between two—one for the people who came from all over Talin and another only for themselves. But just like her other memories, it moves and disfigures the moment she tries to grasp for it, and the knowledge slips away like water through a sieve.

"I was eight years old," she rasps. She pulls back, lurches her body away until she has torn out of Anton's grasp. "Now I am twenty-three. You must understand: I have had her longer than *she* had her. But if I leave this body . . ."

"She cannot possibly still be in there after fifteen years," Anton says.

"She might. No one has been able to invade me in these fifteen years. Maybe it's because I'm still doubled."

Anton shakes his head, as if the very thought is preposterous. "It's because you're strong. No one could invade me in my birth body either."

"You don't know that."

"Yes, I *do*," Anton insists. "If you don't lose your mind after invading a strong body, then you have won it as a vessel. Most dormant occupants fade off after five years. Forget ten. Forget *fifteen*."

"*Most*," Calla emphasizes. "But when we're talking royal blood, anything goes." If the real princess has remained after all this time, if the real princess takes her body back the moment that she leaves, then this Calla has nothing left. Because who is she, if not Calla? She doesn't even remember what her name used to be. She remembers nothing of the life she was born into. She remembers only the princess that she stole.

"This body is all I have." Calla rockets to her feet. Her wound throbs, but she swallows her wince, pulling her shirt higher to keep the leaves out of sight. "I was so young that I wasn't even expected to remember my—*Calla*'s identity number yet. The tutor recited it back to me when I said I had forgotten, because never could they have thought a child managed to jump at eight years old, much less take over their equally young princess."

Anton catches her arm; she looks at him dully.

"Stop," he instructs. "Sit down."

"I have to go."

"Go where? You're injured."

Anywhere but here, she thinks. No weapon in her hands, only her bare skin, needing to brave harsh elements like the sweltering heat outside and Anton's sympathy inside.

"Release my arm," she commands.

Anton frowns. "You're being stubborn."

Stubborn. As if this is only a trifling disagreement, debating whether they should change the television channel, instead of her whole life undone.

"And what about it?" Calla snaps. "Why do you care?"

For several seconds, Anton is silent. Then:

"Have you lost your mind?" he fires back. "I am only mortal, Calla. Clearly I care about *you*."

A terrifying whine begins in Calla's ears. Maybe it's her injury, shutting her down. Or maybe it's the existing fault line in her heart, triggering every alarm bell whenever the risk of harm arrives.

"Release me immediately," she says again. "I need to report to August. You won't stop me from that, will you?"

"August can't help you." There's a plea in Anton's eyes. "He is as powerless as the rest of us."

Another breeze swirls into the room. The curtain dances up and down.

"He can help me more than you can," Calla says.

Finally, Anton releases his hold on her arm, his whole face going blank. As soon as she's free to move, Calla is walking out of his apartment and securing her wristband. She doesn't spare a glance back or a single moment of pause as she hurries down the stairs and through Snowfall. If she stops, it will set in. The vulnerability will scrape at her insides; his unguarded eyes will return to the forefront of her mind. August was right. She never should have agreed to this alliance. She signed on to play a game and kill a king, nothing else.

"Get it together," Calla tells herself. It's good that she's not really going directly to August, because he would immediately read the oddness in her face and scold her—rightfully so, because Prince August is perfect and has never made a mistake, unlike everyone else in San-Er.

Calla ducks her head as she moves through the city's evening bustle, weaving by shop fronts and climbing shortcuts as they appear before her. She barges into the Magnolia Diner promptly, leaping over the turnstile, and though she has no attachment to her former attendants and oversees their safety for selfish, self-protecting reasons, a rush of warm relief floods her the moment she sights Chami in her restored body, fussing over Yilas at the counter.

Calla's knees go weak. She barely manages to catch herself on the corner of one of the tables. The motion draws half the diner's attention, and when Chami spins around, she yelps at the sight. Yilas, too, makes a loud noise, lunging forward and sweeping in front of Calla.

"*Oh*, you're okay. You're okay, you're okay, thank goodness—"

For someone who rarely expresses an iota of emotion, those few exclamations from Yilas are the equivalent of a heartfelt speech.

"Was there ever any doubt?" Calla asks. She grins, but her head is spinning. She starts to see Yilas and Chami in doubles, then triples.

"Yes!" Yilas snaps. "Last I saw, you were surrounded. I couldn't get back inside."

"A boy brought her back here," Chami adds. "I asked him to stick around until you arrived, but then it got too late into the night, and I had to send him on his way with some food. What *happened*?"

Bright white is edging into Calla's vision. It starts to hurt, a sharp sting spreading from the base of her head to the front, and when she lifts her other hand to her forehead, she can feel herself burning up.

"Yilas didn't tell you?" she asks, tightening her grip on the table. If she pushes through, it should go away. If she holds still, this feeling must surely fade. "The Crescents at the Hollow Temple are experimenting with qi. Funny business. Don't go anywhere near them."

"My brother came to find me just then—" Yilas grabs Calla's shoulder. "*Shit*. You're bleeding."

Her ears are ringing even louder than before, drowning out the noise of the diner. Calla takes a deep inhale, trying to clear her senses, but nothing feels like it is going in. She grips the table so fiercely that she might snap the edge right off, trying to seek sensation across her body. It's not working. Her body is shutting down.

"Get a piece of paper," Calla slurs, "paper . . . and pen. Get a pen."

Rustling. It could be Chami rushing off to fetch the materials, or it could be her own imagination, her senses finally detaching from the world.

"Hey—hey—are you—"

Nothing is coming in through her ears; nothing is visible in her eyes. Calla lets go of the table, and she gives it one, two, three seconds, swaying on her feet. She feels her mouth move. She feels her tongue curl to recite a string of numbers, to croak: "Call August. Ask him . . . ask him . . . shut down my location pings—"

She finally collapses to her knees, and her instructions fall short. Before Chami and Yilas can loom over her in concern, before they can so much as confirm they received her instructions, Calla pitches onto her side and closes her eyes to rest.

CHAPTER 20

August gives her ten days. Though Calla was unsure whether he would help, he shuts down her wristband—or at least puts it into stasis mode so that she is kept in the games without pings every few hours, sent on a chase across San-Er like the other players. The reels have noted her absence. The newscasters have remarked on Fifty-Seven's idle number, unmoving while the rest of the players catch up and overtake her, with Eighty-Six now in the lead, running his own battles across the city, always in direct line of the surveillance cameras. They gather that she must be hiding out of view. If someone knew their way around San-Er well enough, the newscasters muse, perhaps they could stay free of the pings, keeping away from the other players. They hypothesize. A sick mother. A mental break. A fight with Eighty-Six—who's swinging harder and faster day by day, which doesn't help dispel the rumors that the two had a lovers' spat. It doesn't matter. So long as Calla's wristband is still active, there's no reason to eliminate her from the games.

They just can't comprehend why she would hide.

She stays in Chami and Yilas's living quarters above the diner, sheets drawn up to her neck and sweating out her fever. The clacking of plates, the snippets of elderly gossip, the hiss of cigarette butts stubbed out in the teacups—they all drift up, harmonizing with her delirious dreams. By the fourth day, her fever has broken, and she can move without pulling at her wound. By the sixth day, it's scabbed over, no more blood seeping down her side. Her qi is strong—it helps her heal more quickly than the ordinary civilian. Still, she stays hidden under the blankets, legs pulled up to her chest and her chin pressed to her knees. Yilas comes up every few hours to talk, and though Calla is too exhausted to reply, she knows that Calla is listening. She talks about the games, about how they're progressing. She talks about what she was looking at just before she was kidnapped in the Hollow Temple, how she had stumbled onto screen printouts that indicated someone in the Crescent Societies was tracking the locations of the players. Yilas says that Matiyu has since left the Hollow Temple. It's certain that there's something peculiar going on there, and he's smart enough not to mess around with that, no matter how much money he earned working for them.

On the eighth night, after Chami and Yilas have already retired into their bedroom, the reels are playing on the television box in the kitchen. Calla wanders over, a blanket pulled around her head and a cup of tea in her hands that she's been nursing for so long it's gone cold. When Yilas isn't giving a straight-forward report into Calla's ear, Chami tries to care for Calla like the attendant she used to be. For as long as Calla is willing to sit still, Chami brushes her stick-straight hair—falling back to their old routines in the palace—but Calla usually shakes her hair loose and messy again in minutes, waving Chami off to go tend to the diner. Chami brings up plates decorated with food and piping-hot teacups perfect for drinking too, except each time, Calla doesn't pick them up until hours have passed. She needs to make her food and drink more suited for the body she's putting them into: icy and miserable.

The reels are moving through the day's footage. Her feet bare and the night dark around her, Calla walks closer and closer until she is directly in front of the clunky box. She kneels before the counter. Her nose is a hairsbreadth away from the thick screen. The television is muted, but she can hear every image, pair up the clang of metal and the high-pitched shouts outside the window with the screen as it flashes and glows, white and blue light casting shadows inside the silent apartment, white and blue light caressing down her face.

Her hand lifts for the screen. Before she can touch it, the reels change to show an alley fight between two players, and her fingers move to her chest instead, circling around the wound, now freed of bandages and allowed to air past her thin cotton shirt.

"Anton," she whispers, recognizing his movements. His knife slashes a straight line down, throat to stomach. It's so quick that the other player doesn't seem to feel a thing before falling in pieces to the ground.

It's possible that she is still delirious from the remnants of her fever. That her brain is rotting from the inside out as a result of this idle behavior, waiting for her body to stitch back into commission. While her head burned and her heart bled, she could think of nothing save the pain. Somehow, it was worst when the injury started to get better, because then her mind *could* wander, and wander it did, to that basement in the temple, to the knife in her chest, to Pampi standing over her. That shouldn't have happened. No one should *ever* stand over her. What lesson slipped from the palace? What practice did she forget in those years hiding out? For the first time since she became Calla Tuoleimi, she felt *powerless*, and that isn't allowed.

The reels change to a display screen of the kill numbers. Nine players remain in the games. Calla's numbers have sunk down to be ranked fourth. It doesn't matter, she supposes. First or fourth, it is still the final survivor who is crowned victor, who gets to shake hands with the king. The numbers are a different part of the games, mere entertainment for the masses who tune in every year and watch the blood run.

Forget the renown and the rankings. She's playing to win. What matters except making sure every person in her way dies?

Her fists curl; her lungs grow tight. Anton comes back on-screen, and this time he looks directly at the surveillance camera, tugging his mask off and flashing a grin. Now that they're nearing the final players, San-Er will have started making bets. Life savings and personal assets drawn up at the casinos, because why should the victor of the games get all the fun when it comes to monetary reward? Those who can identify the final victor with as much confidence as they're willing to wager shall have their reaping too. Anton will be leading the bets. He radiates with promise, with . . . power.

That is what this pull to Anton Makusa is, Calla tells herself. The kitchen rustles around her—water pipes settling and rats darting between the dry walls—and she can't stop watching him on these reels, tearing through the darkness of San-Er with his coat billowing behind him. Sheer power. An uncompromising, unwavering power that she is drawn to, that she has been drawn to since the beginning, when he convinced her it would be beneficial to work together. And now she feels like there are thorns growing under her skin because she's losing grasp on her own power while Anton whirls about like a rival prince, someone who could sweep into the throne room and do exactly what Calla has been preparing to do for five years.

I hate you, she thinks without hesitation. Seconds later, her mind catches up, stutters, provides: *Wait, I don't mean it*, and then the hatred only grows. She hates him for his strength, which doesn't make sense, not when she agreed to team up because she wanted to make use of it, but that's the only way to justify the heat burning up her throat, to explain why watching him fight prickles at her neck and flushes her face.

"I hate you," Calla says aloud.

These games allow only one victor. His death is fated by her hands, or her death in his. Calla doesn't want to die. So this hatred will make her killing blow come easier.

"Calla?"

The kitchen floods with sudden light, and Calla flinches, throwing a hand over her eyes. It takes her a few seconds of rapid blinking, adjusting to the overhead bulbs, and only then does she lower her arm, rising from the cold kitchen tiles. Yilas is standing at the doorway, one hand on her hip and the other on the light switch.

"What are you doing, kneeling in the dark?"

"Praying," Calla answers easily. Half a lie, half a jest. Half a truth, wholly out of character.

Yilas raises an eyebrow. Her eyes swivel toward what sits before Calla: the screen running into commercial. "To the television?"

Calla is looking at the television, but she does not see it. She stands in the kitchen, but she does not feel it, the ceramic floor under her bare feet and the grimy counter beneath her fingers fading into the abstract.

"To the television," Calla confirms lightly, "and the gods inside."

CHAPTER 21

I t was player number two, Calla had reported over the telephone. *They called her Pampi, and she was Crescent Society. The leader of the Hollow Temple now, in fact.*

A small drizzle of evening rain leaks onto the street level, adding to the puddles that collect on uneven ground. August picks his way through, pulling a hat low over his hair. There was no time to find a new body today. He's out and about in his own face, fingers flexing every minute to adjust his rings. San whispers for his attention—a toy seller hawking from the corner, a prostitute trailing her fingers across his chest when he passes by—but he ignores it in favor of the temple ahead, observing the Crescent Society members bustling outward.

She did something unbelievable, Calla had continued. *Used her qi to strike people without touching them.* A pause. *Another man did the same the day of the flood sirens. The one who jumped without light.*

August could hardly believe it. This was so much information at once that he needed to backtrack. *Are you sure it was qi?*

I could feel it. Don't ask me how, because I don't know. But there are piles of dead bodies below their temple that have something to do with it.

There had been another pause over the telephone. *One more thing. Yilas—you remember Yilas? Before she was knocked out, she found a set of printouts at the back of the Hollow Temple. She said that they looked like screen captures of surveillance from the games. From inside the palace.*

Calla's voice had faded out then, too tired to keep going, and August had released the line, letting her rest. It didn't sound like she thought much of the Crescent Societies and their use of qi past these anomalies, but the gears in August's head were turning. His first move was to check the records kept of the games, searching for a list of every player who had been drawn. Right at the top, under number two, was Pampi Magnes, followed by a series of numbers that made up her identification serial.

But when August plugged that number into San-Er's system, it gave nothing. A ghost. The only matching record was an *employee* in the palace surveillance room, which explained Calla's warning about the Hollow Temple having access to the players' locations. August had pulled up security footage and employee data to confirm that it was the same woman, except she didn't *exist*, so how had she enrolled in the games *and* found work inside the palace?

An inside job.

August walks into the Hollow Temple. His head is still whirring. This temple is experimenting with qi, letting them move people without being touched. It lets them jump without light. Without seeing a new body first. It gives them the ability they need to be flitting about the twin cities, killing players of the games and summoning the yaisu sickness without being caught on the surveillance cameras.

He has always suspected that this was not foreign intrusion, but internal anarchy, coming right from the group that has always wanted the palace to fall. Now he has only one question.

August comes to a stop in the main hall. No one stopped him from entering, and no one asks now what he's doing here. Someone, though, is watching. When he looks around, he spots a woman with red eyes, seated by one of the shrines and smiling at him.

If the Crescent Societies are attempting to sow anarchy in San-Er, how did they get the proper access—into the games, into the palace—to do so?

August doesn't walk up to Pampi Magnes. He turns on his heel and chooses a random path deeper into the temple. From his periphery, he sees the woman frown, as if she expected August to confront her. She's dressed nicely and doesn't appear to be carrying any visible injuries, which means she's probably changed bodies since she encountered Calla. No one who goes up against Calla walks away without some sort of bleeding or bruising.

August ventures along the temple's corridors, pressing deeper and deeper, until he comes across a small nook where a shrine of a single deity is propped in the corner, illuminated by a semicircle of candles. There is no other light here, only the glow of false worship.

"Your Highness."

Pampi has followed him, of course.

August glances over his shoulder. "Hello," he says. "I've heard a lot about you these past few days."

"Oh?" This gets her attention. She gravitates forward slowly, practically floating on her shined shoes. "Tell me more."

"I've heard mention of heart tearing and rapid jumping. Qi being used in ways the gods never intended for us." The shrine remains steady when August crouches in front of it. The candles, however, all flicker, like they have sensed a disturbance. "Tell me, did the gods themselves come down and show you how?" He pinches a candle, snuffing out the flame. "Or was it someone mortal, offering you a false identity number while they were at it?"

A light, discordant laugh rings from Pampi. It sounds cold to the ear—practiced, rehearsed.

"You won't find what you want here," she answers. A thud echoes through the temple.

August is running out of patience. "Someone put you in that surveillance room. Someone gave you a false identity. *Who?*"

"The gods let us jump so that we could be free," Pampi goes on. "And instead, this kingdom decides to root us down, trap us in its hold. We will stand for it no longer. The wall will fall, the throne will crumble—"

"I will not ask again." His hand flexes. This is foolishness. There is no peace in anarchy. There is peace only in good rule, which August can provide. "Who put you in the palace?"

A soft sigh. Although August doesn't crane his neck to look, he knows that Pampi is standing right behind him now. The candles flicker with her exhale.

"You must know, Prince August, that your reign will soon be over."

She will not offer a name. But that alone is enough for August. The refusal means that a name exists: there is a traitor in the palace. His job here is done.

"You are mistaken," August says. "My reign hasn't even arrived yet."

He pushes on one of his rings. When the blade flicks out, the quiet *schick* sound is the only warning before August shoots to his feet and runs his knuckles across Pampi's throat, cutting a clean red line.

Her mouth gapes open. There's no time to jump, no time to summon whatever unnatural abilities she has been cultivating within the walls of this temple. She pitches sideways, blood flowing from her throat like a faucet has been let loose. In seconds, she is still, pallor gray and expression frozen, her red eyes unblinking.

At the end of this desperate scramble for power, Pampi remained human, and humans can always die.

The gods let us jump so that we could be free.

August shakes his head. "There are no gods in this world." He reaches out to close her eyes. "Only kings and tyrants."

◇◇◇◇◇

On that tenth morning, Calla rises early. She can barely see what's in front of her when she tiptoes to the door of the apartment. Day has not broken yet, and the world is shrouded with a hazy pall. Grimacing, she pulls Yilas's borrowed coat over her shoulders, then pats around her pockets to check whether her dagger is secured. Her sword is lost now. There's little chance she can get it back from the Hollow Temple without coming into conflict with the Crescents again. She won't be allowed to go back to the weapon stores and acquire another, so she has to make do with the rusty dagger that Chami has kept around since her palace days, smuggled out from whatever strange ladies' network traded in blunt daggers.

It's better than nothing.

The air outside is colder than Calla expected. The doors of the Magnolia Diner close behind her, the cool pane of glass thudding against the side of her arm and giving her that last nudge she needs to step forward. She has been indoors for so long that the season has tangibly shifted, a wintry chill seeping into the usual mugginess. It will fade in a few hours—as soon as San-Er starts rumbling again and the last of the night turns into the early morning—but it's the first hint of coming change.

"All right," Calla says quietly. "I guess we're back."

She adjusts her wristband, starting to walk. Her wound is healed enough that she can move without too much caution. Her shirt is skintight, thick and stiff just as her pants are. A pipe drips water onto her neck, the wetness collecting against her collar. A shop raises its security gate, the rapid *clunk-clunk-clunk* of its panels rolling into itself as Calla passes by. She barely lifts her head to peer into the shop. *Dangerous,* she realizes with delay—anyone could have dived at her from inside. Still, she continues walking.

Maybe it's only that she is too rusty after more than a week of sitting idle. Try as she might to summon some energy, Calla cannot feel anything: not the curiosity she had as a princess in Er's palace allowed out for a few hours, not the smallness she had as a wanted fugitive sniffing around the markets for food. She slinks through the streets and floats to the edge of San where the sea smashes against the rocks, and there, she pinches the inside of her elbow, telling herself, *Wake up.*

A rustle.

A beat later, Calla's wristband starts to tremble.

She ducks, only she's already taken the chain across her shoulder, hissing as it burns a line down her arm. Calla knows then that she has let her guard down too much. At this stage of the games, she may not need to top the rankings, but that doesn't mean she can let herself get *killed*.

"Where the hell have you been hiding?" the other player spits. His body is lanky and tall, hair dyed a stringy yellow. As if he had attempted to go blond like August, but the bleach didn't mix quite right because he used cheaper chemicals. He lunges forward, and Calla catches sight of his wristband in the rising light. The screen reads 19.

She avoids the next whip of his chains, an inch away from her cheek. If it had landed, it might have blinded her. He's quick. This isn't looking like a fight she can skirt easily.

"I was on a comfortable couch, thank you for asking."

The chain strikes down again. This time, Calla catches it, wraps it around her wrist twice over and yanks as hard as she can. Nineteen anticipates the move, and releases fast before the momentum can reach him. Instead, Calla is the one who is rendered unsteady, stumbling back two steps. There's a new weapon in her hands, but she is off-balance, which is just enough of an opening for Nineteen to lunge at her, throwing them to the very edge of the rocks, half of Calla's body dangling off.

Shit.

She's *really* out of practice.

"How were you the one leading the games for so long?" Nineteen sneers. "Pathetic." He punches; Calla jerks her head aside. If this fight had happened before her injury, she would have long found her advantage. Right now, she can barely summon the energy to reach for the dagger in her pocket. She's so tired already. Her body has healed, but her qi has not.

Move, she urges herself. *Move, or he's going to—*

Nineteen's fist rears back: one last hit to knock her out and throw her into the sea. Perhaps she can take it. Perhaps she can swim back up.

Then he's tumbling off her and down onto the rocks, landing with a hard splash in the water.

Calla hadn't even moved. She blinks, letting her senses return. A familiar little face with violet eyes pops into her field of vision.

"Did he get ya?"

Calla rises onto her elbows, wiping sweat from her forehead. "Why are you everywhere I go, Eno?"

Eno shrugs, shoving his hands into his pockets as Calla clambers to her feet. She picks up Nineteen's discarded chain, testing the weight on her arm, and slugs it over her shoulder, adopting the weapon. When Eno reaches for it, trying to inspect the little blades embedded at its end, Calla slaps his fingers away.

He draws back, scowling.

"Where did you disappear to?" Eno asks. "Where's Anton?"

Calla doesn't answer. She hurries away from the rocks, reentering San through a gap between two buildings. Though the space is so thin she must turn sideways, Eno darts right in behind her, galloping at her heels.

"The other players were trying out your technique," Eno continues when

Calla remains unspeaking. "They saw how effective it was to team up, except it isn't working out as well for everyone else. Nineteen had a partner last week before he killed him in front of the coliseum. There was a disagreement over his walking speed, I hear."

Calla emerges from the thin walkway, entering a main thoroughfare that is wide enough for a morning food cart to be pushed through. She swipes a small bag as she passes. Eno darts to her side, keeping pace.

"Eno," she says, untwisting the bag and tossing pieces of a bao into her mouth. "Thank you for your help, but you can leave now."

Eno ignores her. "No, really. Where's Eighty-Six? Don't tell me you really did have a fight."

The bag crumples in her hand. When she reaches for another bit of the bao, its round, soft shape is disfigured under her grip.

"Something like that."

Calla takes a sharp right turn into a thinner alley, toward the south of the city. She passes a grimy window that looks into someone's bedroom, then another with a set of shades poking through the broken glass, revealing a damp bathroom inside. She hopes Mao Mao is all right, but she knows her cat is probably having the time of his life hiding in her bedroom walls.

Eno continues to follow her. He thuds at one of the control boxes they bypass, triggering a spark of blue in the dark passageway before he yelps, hurrying away from the wires.

"You're not going to go looking for him?" he presses.

"Why"—Calla heaves a breath—"would I do that?"

Eno frowns, his legs working twice as fast to keep up with her stride. A distant clanging has started in another alley, which means the city is waking properly.

"Because you were allies," he says, "and allies rescue each other."

"Oh, he's not in *trouble*." Calla scoffs at the thought. She hasn't seen Anton in trouble once. Even at the temple, he had had a way out. It was *her* refusal to jump that had kept them tethered in that room, surrounded by Crescents. And still, he hadn't left. Kept committed to their alliance.

Foolish. How can they claim to be allies while competing in a contest only one person can win? It's his head or hers, and no sentimentality is enough to let them both achieve their goal. She hasn't returned to his side despite being newly healed and back in the games. He must be expecting to hear from her soon, for her to maintain the bargain they made to conquer these games in tandem until they are the final two.

She has to stay away from him. She can't keep playing nice, nor can she continue acting the part of his ally to the end. This was only supposed to be a temporary collaboration so that they could face each other in the arena sooner.

But after the way Anton Makusa looked at her, his hand scrunched in her hair and his eyes betraying a whisper of devotion, she can't bear the thought of killing him.

Calla glances toward the approaching intersection, the coliseum looming in her periphery before it disappears from view, blocked again by the buildings. That's where they will end up, and the dreaded day is fast approaching, given the number of players left. She can convince herself that maybe another player will take Anton's life before the games whittle down to two, but he has shown himself too sharp to be defeated by anyone else. If he is to die, then Calla trusts only her own hand.

For Talin, she'll win the games, and King Kasa's head will roll.

Eno yelps suddenly, tripping on a protruding underground pipe. Calla's arm shoots out fast. She grabs his elbow and hauls him upright before he can fall.

"Thanks," he breathes. He makes a show out of brushing his clothes when Calla lets go, saving face by pretending nothing had happened. Perhaps it is only a trick of the light, but his lip seems to quiver— a quick flash of fear, and then gone.

"Eno." Calla gives him a rough thump on the shoulder, if only to lessen the rebuke in her tone. "You should pull the chip from your wristband. Leave the games. Your life is worth more than this."

She expects him to argue or stomp his feet. Instead, Eno's expression screws up, and then Calla is certain she hadn't mistaken the fear she thought she saw. He's not wearing the stubbornness of someone refusing the raft tossed his way. He's entirely awash in relief, spotting the red flag of rescue waving in the distance.

All this time, was he only awaiting a command from someone else? Had he never been told that his life was something he was allowed to hold on to?

"Yeah," Eno says quietly. "Maybe I will."

Calla purses her lips. There's a deep rumble overhead, like thunder approaching. Nothing of the skies is visible from here, so it's impossible to tell if a storms is rolling in until the downpour begins. Still, something about the air is starting to smell violent.

A beep sounds from her belt. Calla unclips her pager and watches a string of text from August scroll across the screen.

Welcome back. Number 6 by the wall near Gold Stone Street.

"All right." She tilts her head at Eno, toward the direction of the city wall. "Until then, wanna help me out?"

CHAPTER 22

Maybe it's because the air builds with an electric charge the closer they get to the wall, but Calla's energy starts to return, gathering in her chest and flowing out to her limbs.

She raises a finger, pressing it to her lips to hush Eno. There's a very clear distinction where the city ends and the wall begins. The buildings at the edge of San halt in a line. Beyond that, there is a wide swath of yellowed grass, the clearing used to hold piles of discarded computers and every loose unwanted item that gets pushed out of San-Er if there's no way to repurpose it.

The wall only climbs to the sixth floor of its nearest buildings. From outside, any onlooker with good eyes could peer up at the higher windows and observe San-Er's civilians going about their daily routine.

Eno hovers over Calla's shoulder, the both of them waiting at the end of Gold Stone Street.

"You'd think we would get some better sunlight here," he says, blinking at the clouds. "Maybe blue skies are just a myth."

"Blue skies are real," Calla mutters in reply. They are what she remembers most about rural Talin: the endless blue, stretching into the horizon until it joins with the green ground. "There are just too many factories causing pollution in San-Er."

But Eno only frowns. "Why are we here?"

"There's supposed to be another player nearby. I don't see anyone, though."

They did walk relatively slowly, so it's possible that the player has since wandered away. Nevertheless, they can't have gone far, especially if they aren't aware they're being hunted.

"Stay put and be my eyes," Calla says. Her eyes trace up the wall. "I'm going to have a look around."

"Stay put?" Eno calls after her, though Calla is already striding across the ugly grass. "Didn't you want my *heeelp*?" That last part turns into a whine, loud enough for Eno's voice to echo across the whole clearing.

Calla whirls around, pointing a warning finger. "Keep watch. Be good."

She approaches the rusty ladder and shakes it vigorously to make sure it is securely fixed. When she's satisfied that the ladder won't detach from the wall anytime soon and throw her to her death, she props a leg up and starts to climb, taking the rungs two at a time.

Her ascent is fast. Halfway, three-quarters, then the top. She pauses there, hands clutched around the end of the ladder. Though she climbed up to get a better look at her surroundings inside the wall, she's suddenly mesmerized by the view outside instead—the grass that stretches on as far as the eye can see, the peaks and valleys that glisten off in the horizon.

Her wristband sits heavy on her skin, dull in the gray light. The clouds are getting darker and darker, and when another roll of thunder comes in the distance, Calla almost lets go of the ladder, taken by surprise. Her skin prickles. The first drop of rain falls, landing a fat drop on her cheek.

When she became Calla, she gained insurmountable power, the unbelievable capacity to mold the world as she saw fit. She's never really thought about everything she lost.

"Hey!"

With a start, Calla whirls around, facing San again. Eno. She can't see him anymore, though his panicked shout echoes up the wall.

"Eno?" Calla calls. She slings herself onto the left pole of the ladder, opting to slide down its side rather than sparing the time to go rung by rung. Her hand is reaching into her coat, where she shoved the chains she stole, but the moment her feet land on solid ground, she feels a whistle of air. Calla slings the chain forward, narrowly blocking a knife hurtling for her head.

Two people, running toward her. Their sleeves are pushed to their elbows. No wristbands.

What?

By a narrow margin, she swerves to the left and avoids the blow of a sword from one of the attackers. A man with a stud in his lip. Calla straightens up. Is this the work of the Hollow Temple? Are they after her or Eno?

No time to consider it. Calla lunges for the knife that was thrown at her, stepping hard on the handle so the weapon whirls into the air and lands in her palm.

"Eno?" she shouts again. There's no response. Where *is* he? She whirls up fast and throws the blade, embedding it dead in the man's eye. She doesn't wait for him to hit the ground; before he has scarcely stumbled from the attack, she hauls her chain up and whips the second man hard, metal links colliding with the blunt new weapon he draws. The end wraps fast around the pseudoblade. A hard tug, and the weapon slips. Just as the second man ducks, scrambling for retrieval, Calla whips the chain again. It wraps around his neck. She pulls him in with one fast yank.

"Who are you?" Calla seethes. As soon as the man is close enough, she seizes her catch, squeezing his jaw hard. "Who *are* you?"

"No one, I'm no one!" the man answers fast, tears rising to his eyes as he struggles against her grip. "Please, let me go, let me go——"

"You're not a player." Calla hauls the man up, and his legs kick out, trying to find his bearings. There's no use——the chain is still tangled around his neck. It only takes another tug to hold him tighter. "So why did you attack me? Are you Crescent Society?"

"No," the man gasps. "No, we were recruited by an outside source. I have no grudge against you, I swear. Spare me my life."

"Who?" Calla demands. Her nails dig in deeply, gouging five weeping wounds into his face. "Who sent you?"

"I don't know!"

A slight twist, an attempt to move away. Calla releases his face, only so she can pull Chami's dagger from her pocket.

"Please," he tries to wheeze past the chain. His struggling legs leave tracks in the grass, overturning the yellowing plots with brown sludge instead. "Please, I was only taking on the paid tasks. They gave us instructions to hunt you down. That's it, that's it!"

"Useless," Calla spits. "Damn useless——"

"They had black eyes! That's all I saw!"

For a second, Calla stops. She feels her hands go cold, loosening on the chain just enough that the man tries to twist up.

Black eyes.

A flare of rage rushes through her chest, and before she knows what she's doing, she's slashed his throat, the blunt dagger catching on skin and crudely tearing through. The jagged rip opens his thickest arteries and veins, spurting blood with a vengeance. In seconds, the man is unmoving, surrounded by a puddle of crimson. His eyes turn dull.

Calla rocks back on her heels. Her breathing comes hard.

Every royal is bound to lose their mind sooner or later, drunk on the power in their hands. For Calla, especially, who remembers what it was like to be helpless, power has an unimaginably tantalizing pull. When she's not careful, she feels the poison seeping into her thoughts. She entertains what it would be like to kill for the throne rather than for liberation. She imagines taking the divine crown for herself and never having to be weak again, imagines the whole kingdom—the whole *empire*—kneeling before her.

"Eno?" Calla yells, snapping back into the present. "Eno, where are you?"

She gathers up the chain in her hands, shaking blood off the slick metal. The clearing near the city wall has turned eerily quiet. A twinge of panic twists her throat, then numbness—a terrible, aching numbness.

Calla doesn't break into a run and scramble to search the vicinity. She doesn't call out again. If there was no response the first time, then it isn't a mystery. She can wish otherwise as much as she wants, but she understands San-Er well, better than she understands herself sometimes, and when she walks over to the alleyway, she isn't surprised to find Eno's body.

His eyes stare glassily at the sky. There's a wound at his side, impaling right into his heart.

Calla crouches down.

"You little shit," she mutters, and her voice breaks.

It was going to happen sooner or later. There can be only one victor.

But he could have pulled his chip. He could have chosen life instead . . . a miserable, dirty life, hungry and sick and cramped, persistently in fear of debt collectors.

Calla knows that most who take part in the games have no other options. The kid wasn't stupid; no one would be throwing their name into the king's lottery if it were that easy to walk away. Still, there was a part of her that had hoped otherwise, that there was some third path for Eno with a bag of coins and a comfortable nook in Er to settle in. San-Er offers the chance at a middling life, and for some, that is plenty. Out in the provinces, that wouldn't even be an option. The provinces are split between two extremes: either utter destitution or palatial opulence reserved for councilmembers and former victors of the games.

Yet somehow, out of all the people in the kingdom, from San-Er to the borderlands, it was Calla who had invaded her way into becoming a princess. Wouldn't she have ended up exactly like Eno if she hadn't?

"I hope you are among the last," she says, smoothing Eno's eyelids down until they are closed. "I hope . . ." She trails off, daring a glance up at the wall. She hopes they count this death as hers in the games. Add it to her tally. The guilt can smear her hands. This death is on her conscience to avenge.

Everyone who is responsible for this misery will fall, one by one.

There's movement atop the wall. Border guards. Calmly, Calla rises to her feet, waving at them for a brief moment before slipping back between the buildings. By the time they clamber down the wall, she will be gone. Eno's body will be the palace's responsibility.

Calla clutches her fists tight and makes a sharp turn. She steps over a crate, then enters a building at random and treks up the stairs, heading for the rooftop to navigate San-Er from above instead. She is soaked to the wrists in blood. Her sleeves are stained, as is the hem of her shirt.

Black eyes, the man said.

She knows only two people in this city with black eyes. August and Anton. And Prince August needs her alive to do his dirty work.

Calla shoves the door open, almost blowing it off its hinges as she barges onto the rooftop. Her boots strike heavy against cement, her coat billowing to either side of her. She is not merely a contestant of the games moving on to her next kill. She is initiating a battle march.

They gave us instructions to hunt you down.

So the time has come.

Anton Makusa has turned on their alliance.

CHAPTER 23

Thunder rolls across the twin cities. When Calla arrives on Big Well Street, the rain has just started, and she barely misses the downpour, ducking into Snowfall before the pavement is splattered. She stomps up the stairs and around the stairwell corner. Outside Anton's apartment, she doesn't bother knocking to be let in. Just like the other times, the handle turns easily under her hand, and she shoulders through the door.

She pauses at the threshold. Waits. Her blood is simmering beneath her skin.

"You're here."

Calla swivels, turning to face the kitchen. There in the doorway, Anton stands with a bowl in his hand, which he sets down upon sighting her. He wears a new body, this one tall and lean: a fighter's build. He's dressed in black, like she caught him just as he was about to head out and increase his kills for the day. Red-hot intensity rushes from her throat to her stomach as she takes him in.

She's unsteady. If she didn't know better, she would have thought she downed ten shots in a row right before she barged through.

"Why?" Calla asks. "Why did you do it? You couldn't come and make the strike yourself?"

Anton frowns. "What are you talking about?"

Calla yanks her sleeves up and shows him the blood on her hands. She doesn't intend to yell, but when she speaks, it comes tearing out at earsplitting volume. "The hitmen, Anton! The fucking killers you sent to attack me. Eno's *dead*. Dead!"

"What are—" A clap of lightning flashes across the kitchen window. A rare burst of illumination in an otherwise dark city. Every corner of the apartment seems to come aglow, cast in blue and lined with white. When the light fades, Anton is squinting, like he is still bracing against the brightness. "Eno's dead?"

Calla cannot stand this performance. Is he intent on feigning ignorance? Was Eno not his friend too?

"Stop it," she hisses. "Stop lying to me." Another clap of lightning; an accompanying roll of thunder. Now the rain is coming down hard enough that it can be heard colliding with the side of the building, water pelting the rattling windows.

"I don't know what I'm lying about!" Anton exclaims. The confusion in his brow holds fast, but when he lifts his arms, Calla catches a glimpse of ink under his wristband. A single crescent moon.

Calla hisses in through her teeth. This body was taken from the Crescent Societies, which means Anton was just there. Doing what? Arranging her murder? Even if the hitman claimed not to be a Crescent, she knows there are dots to connect here, and she makes the quickest link.

"You *traitor*," she spits. Then she pulls the cleaned dagger from her pocket and lunges at him.

Anton reacts fast, sidestepping as his eyes grow wide. With the next swipe that Calla makes at him, he seems to figure quickly that this is not a fight she is holding back from. She throws her elbow hard, landing a hit to his face; he kicks out, striking her middle and putting distance between them when Calla slams into the wall, her head colliding with a picture frame. The frame pitches to the floor, glass shattering in tandem with another strike of thunder outside. Though Calla recovers fast, her grip tightening on the dagger, every inch of her hands prickles with discomfort. Her fingers feel stiff and her joints ache. They tell her to stop, but she cannot. There is already a charge that runs like static through her system, responding to the betrayal that she knew was coming. An overwhelming grief buzzes in her bones, strikes liquid rage into the lines between her ribs.

"I don't know what idea you're stuck on," Anton heaves. He wipes at the corner of his mouth. There's a spot of blood, the skin swelling slightly from her hit. "But you've got it wrong."

Calla draws a breath. She flips the dagger, adjusts her grip on the handle.

"Regardless," she says, "I think we've reached the end of our alliance."

She closes the distance and swings. Just before the blade can make contact with the side of his neck, Anton catches her wrist, his eyes snapping a quick motion from the blade to Calla. He still looks taken aback, surprise marring the wide shape of his eyes.

"So easily?" he asks. He twists her wrist; against Calla's will, the pain triggers a nerve that forces her to release. The dagger clatters to the floor. Just as she raises her other fist to get a hit in, Anton ducks, and the hit is deflected. The metal zip of his jacket scratches Calla's arm as her fist rushes past, but before she can gear up again, Anton twists his hold on her other wrist until her arm is arched behind her own back. In a blink, he's slammed her up against the wall, pressed against her to keep her still. The plaster trembles. There's a nail jutting out from it, probably where the picture frame had been hanging, and as Calla's head spins, she wonders if she hit her head too hard before and that's why she can't get a single thought in order.

"Calla," he tries, his breath warm against her neck. "Stop this."

"Why?" she hisses. "It's only postponing the inevitable." She kicks out from behind, her boot making enough contact with his leg to buckle him away. The moment there is the slightest give, she whirls around with a backhanded hit, striking his jaw. Before he can recover, she kicks at him again and follows him down—making *sure* he goes down—braced atop him when he lands flat on his back. The floor beneath them is cold. The linoleum tiles of his living room are cluttered with papers and boxes, all of which have skittered in every direction during the fight. As the two of them grow still, the disturbed objects settle to a stop too.

Anton Makusa is vulnerable. Throat exposed, heart facing out.

Now he is hers to take.

Calla heaves for breath. One of her hands is braced on his chest, the other reacquainting with the blade that has landed on the floor. As soon as she has secured the handle, she raises the dagger high, imagining how its arc will come down. She can feel his heart thudding beneath her touch: fear and something else.

"Calla," Anton says again, desperation creeping into his voice, and Calla wants to tear him apart. Because she has him completely under her mercy, pinned like prey, but all he can do is look up at her like that.

"Don't even try it," Calla spits.

"What?" Anton asks. His eyes trace along her face. His pupils have blown so large that Calla can't see the usual purple that rings his black irises. In an effort to keep him down, she presses upon his hips harshly, and then she can *feel* him, can gauge exactly why his pulse throbs at his throat. "What am I trying?"

Hesitation creeps in, her breath caught in her throat, her pulse hammering an equally overwhelming war song. Then, she swipes everything away with a vicious thought. If she gets rid of him, then she can get rid of her own troubling desire too.

Her hand comes down fast, the blade slicing through the air. The dagger plunges in an inch, threatening toward his heart, before Anton catches her arm, stopping the blade from doing any real damage. With a muttered curse, Anton tears her hand away. She barely has time to wince with pain; he sits up with startling speed, knocking his head against hers and tugging the dagger out from his chest in the same motion. Her world spins, her skull rattling from the hit. That pause is enough for Anton to turn the tables, her blade now in his hand and his knee pinning her down. He's heaving for breath when he braces his arm beside her. She's struggling to fill her lungs when he presses the dagger to her throat.

"Is this really what you want, Calla?" he whispers. There's a hot, steady trickle of blood coming from the wound on his chest. It lands, drop by drop, onto Calla while he hovers over her, marking her skin and staining a pattern onto her clothes. He's not looking in her eyes anymore. As the window shakes and the whole building shudders from the increasing roar of wind, he's looking at her mouth. "Do you *want* to fight me?"

She doesn't. Of course she doesn't. But when has that ever mattered?

Anton leans closer, the blade digging in. He's drawing this out, letting the threat whisper against her neck, letting fate decide when her skin will split open. Is he waiting for a plea? For her to beg for her life? She won't. If she dies here, she dies proud.

Yet he's still not making the kill. The room flashes with another strike of lightning. Perhaps the blood loss has stalled his attack. He looks drunk. His hand, solid before, suddenly turns unsteady.

Calla shifts toward the blade, just to test how firm his grip is. It stays pressed to her neck, but *Anton* flinches.

It's not the blood loss swaying his hand. It's her.

"Yes," she breathes. "I want you dead."

And she moves again—not to the side, not away from the dagger. She lifts her chin, bringing her head nearer, and kisses him.

The walls around them are roaring with sound, with the staccato of rain. At first, Anton tastes of blood. Then his lips part, and the hint of something sweet hits Calla's tongue, passing between them in that second that he relaxes. The blade slips away from her throat.

As soon as the blade is gone, Calla pushes him hard. They part abruptly, the dagger clattering to the floor. Anton darts back with a sudden inhale; Calla is fast to rise. In her jacket pocket, she still has a set of chains.

She's got it around his neck in a flash. The metal crisscrosses in front of him, both her hands gripping each end of the chain, ready to pull. All it will take is one fast motion. Then Anton is no longer her problem, eliminated from the games. There's nowhere to jump from here. No one around for him to occupy.

Calla steadies her hands. Anton watches her. He merely watches, even while his life is under threat, even when he has the opportunity to find some way out.

"Go on," he says evenly. "Kill me. Be the murderous princess they say you are."

"Do you think you're insulting me?" Calla tightens the chain. Though his throat must be closing, breathing made intolerable, Anton makes no move to claw at the chain. "You sent people to murder me. At least I have the guts to come after you *myself.*"

"If you don't believe me, then I have nothing to say." His hand shoots up and grips her wrist. She doesn't know if it is his hands that are covered in blood, smearing the red between them, or if her arms were already this bloody to begin with. "But you *do*, Calla. I can tell that you believe me. Why are you doing this?"

Because this is how it must end. Again and again, she tells herself there will be only one victor in the games. It would be foolish to think otherwise.

Her grip loosens the barest fraction.

She is a fool.

"Did you kiss me just to distract me?" he goes on. "Or because you wanted to?"

Her heart is close to tearing through her rib cage, beating a path outward and spilling blood everywhere it goes. She hates that he keeps asking such questions. Calla has never had the luxury to consider what she *wants*. It has always been about what needs to be done. Want is dangerous. Want is . . .

She lets go of the chain. It falls around him, the weight of one end dragging heavier than the other, coiling around the ground like a serpent. Anton moves immediately—not to seize the chance to get the upper hand once again, only to clasp both his hands around her face. His lips find hers again with a vicious energy, and Calla responds with the same franticness, abandoning caution and reason. She pulls at his shirt collar and feels the stickiness of blood beneath her palm. The stench spills the more they move, metallic and violent. It is on their clothes, their skin, the floor, but Anton pays no heed to the wound. The red only spreads when Calla tears his shirt off entirely, the gash evident even in the low light.

"Anton," she warns.

"Leave it," he commands immediately, pulling her coat off and pushing her to the floor. Her back collides with the tiles, cold when she slips her own bloody shirt off her shoulders, but there is only the barest pause before his lips are on her throat, her hands in his hair, his hands gripping her waist. It's as if he is trying to pin her into place, afraid that she might change her mind and run off at any second. But then one of his hands is sinking lower, trailing a path along her hip, fingers brushing the waistband of her pants. His mouth hovers close to hers again, and Calla captures his bottom lip, pulling with her teeth and resisting the urge to *bite* when her skin prickles with goose bumps. She's never once felt out of control since becoming Calla Tuoleimi, but this comes close. It comes closer than anything else as her stomach flexes under his touch, his fingers skimming at her navel, and then lower, moving beneath her waistband, sliding between her legs. On instinct, Calla pulls at his hair, her eyes flying open, her head tipping back.

"Fuck," she whispers, because she has nothing else to say, all thought fleeing.

Anton, unbothered, nudges his mouth along her jaw to the space behind her ear. His fingers press down harder, finding a rhythm against her, and it's everything at once, barreling at her senses. A clap of thunder comes outside, almost startling her from the trance she is sinking into. She cannot bear it, cannot handle all the sensation at once while she tries to push into him. By some primal urge, she puts her hands on Anton's chest, and then presses down on the very wound she's made, her heart thrumming at breakneck speed.

"Does it hurt?" she asks, barely able to catch her breath or keep from writhing.

Anton winces. His hand slows, but he does not stop. His gaze is heavy, mouth brushing against hers again, only to whisper above the rain, "Everything you do hurts, Princess."

The floors seem to tremble, the very structure of the building shaking under the thunder that approaches closer and closer. Calla draws an inhale, trying to control her racketing pulse.

"So hurt me back," she offers.

Anton withdraws, rising on his arms and bracing to either side of her. His wound has stopped bleeding. He blinks at her, a smear of red on his cheek, another along his neck. When he rocks back onto his knees, Calla lifts off the floor too, propping herself up by her forearms to watch him.

Anton shakes his head. It's a subtle movement, barely visible if lightning had not briefly illuminated the room. Without looking, he reaches for her ankle, unzips her boot, and tugs it off. The other follows. Calla's gaze tracks him intently when he reaches for her waistband next, and without hesitation, she lifts her hips.

The barest smile twitches on Anton's lips. "Thank you for being so cooperative."

"Don't get used to it," Calla warns.

"I would never."

There's the sound of leather striking the floor. Calla takes a short inhale, releases it in a short exhale. When Anton sets himself between her raised knees, she lets him. When he leans forward and presses a kiss to her thigh, to her hip, to the curve of her breasts, working his way up until they are eye to eye again, she lets him, awaiting his endgame. Perhaps there is none. Perhaps there is only this.

"I didn't send them," he says. He speaks so quietly, drowned out by the rumble of the storm outside, that she can hear him only because he is this near. When Calla brushes a lock of hair out of his eyes, his gaze is swallowed entirely by the shadows of the room, and Calla cannot read anything except what he shows her, cannot know that he means not to hurt her when his hand comes around her throat. She's almost sick from delirium, sick by the ache from her stomach to her toes, willing to throw preservation out the window if it means relief. But Anton does not tighten his grip on her throat. What should be a deathly squeeze becomes merely a caress, and he leans in to kiss her, more softly than any of the times previous.

"I know," Calla replies, matching his volume. She closes her eyes, her hands tracing down his back, nails running along the muscle. There's some feral feeling humming in her chest, and she has to resist the urge not to attack him when her hands sink low, feeling how hard he is. She's going to lose her mind.

His hand runs another caress at her jaw. She can hear the teasing in his voice. "Is something the matter?"

"You are wicked," she breathes. "Take your pants off and *fuck me.*"

He complies. There's a pause as he drops his clothes and draws nearer, like he's waiting it out, gauging her response. This is someone else's body, but in San-Er, that detail is as normal as jumping. When it comes to this sort of use, bodies are only accessories, discardable and utilized based on need.

Calla yanks him close with a hiss. She must seem impatient, because Anton laughs before pushing inside her in one fast thrust, his hand sweeping up her waist and his mouth on hers, pressing a groan onto her tongue. A gasp, from her—probably, possibly. There's sensation building along her thighs, a humming spreading through her every limb. She shifts her hips with each motion, her legs lifting to hook around him. Anton doesn't rush, and still a frantic pressure emanates from her very core, scrambling her mind with each movement. She knows she's leaving marks on him, her nails digging deep, and by the intensity of his fingers on her hips, he will have left a canvas of damage too. Let it bruise. Let him mark her skin permanently as a memory of what divine agony is.

"Calla," Anton murmurs when their mouths separate for a moment, "I won't hurt you. I refuse."

A mighty large promise in this city. After everything else has come off, they both still wear their wristbands.

Calla kisses him again so he will stop talking. Anton seems to know what she's doing, because he clasps her throat to hold her down and stops thrusting, and Calla almost kills him then and there.

"Anton."

"Was that a whimper?" he asks, grinning. "That's the first time a princess has ever whimpered for me."

But despite his taunt, his hand snakes down as he pushes into her once more, then again and again. He moves against her hips, and she matches each push until Calla is arching back on the cold floor, her body freezing with pleasure. Dimly, she is aware of the storm outside, of the windows shuddering from the onslaught of rain, wooden frames trembling. But those raging elements are nothing in comparison to what is building and building to a crescendo inside her, hitting a peak just as Anton tenses too, the lines of his arms flexing as he holds his weight over her.

For a moment, there is no outside world. The rest of the city ceases to matter. All of San-Er could blink out of existence, and Calla would not care.

Anton is whispering her name. Relaxing against her, then rolling to his side, an arm still locked on her hip. With a sigh, Calla presses a kiss to his jaw, almost chaste given what they had just done, and he smiles, his eyes fluttering closed.

◇◇◇◇◇

Calla stirs awake later that night, a corner of the bedsheet tangled around her naked waist. They had moved to the bed at some point, which was just as well when they went at it again, because she could have tolerated only so much of the cold floor.

The storm has stopped. It's quiet outside the apartment, a momentary lull after the rain cleared the streets and chased people into their homes. Paired with the hour, the food carts have been pushed in and shop gates have been pulled down for the owners to rest, casting San-Er in a hush. Calla lifts her head, staring at the light beams streaming through the blinds: red from the nearby nightclub that keeps its sign bright even after its dance floor has dimmed, blue from Big Well Street's emergency siren that is perpetually activated, spinning on silent alarm. When she props herself onto her elbow, her vision sharpens, focusing on an object by the closet. She hadn't noticed it before when they kicked into the bedroom in a tangle. Now, she recognizes her sword—the sword she had dropped back at the Hollow Temple. It rests upon the wall, casual in its stance, the sheath polished and gleaming under weak neon.

"Oh," Calla whispers into the night. She turns, facing Anton. He has his back to her, his breath rising and falling with the heaviness of deep sleep.

He had gone back for the sword. That's why he's in the body of a Crescent Society member. Not because he was plotting against her, but because he wanted to find her weapon.

Calla settles onto the pillow again slowly, her hair splaying on the soft fabric. The red light has changed to a bright gold. The nightclub responsible for this light show must be running its electric bills high. When Anton shifts in his sleep, Calla draws a finger along his bare spine and marvels at how he doesn't startle, like he has let his guard down, even knowing that she could take a sword to his chest.

She could kill him right here if she wanted. The apartment hosts only the two of them. The rest of San-Er sleeps within its own walls. He would have nowhere to jump.

But she won't. She trusts her life in his hands, and for that she wants to deserve his trust too, offer him safety in her embrace.

Suddenly, Anton turns, nudging his shoulder closer toward her. Calla snatches her hand back with a start, but he's not stirring against her touch. He has not awakened at all: he only adjusts until he is facing her, eyes still closed. Before Calla can react, Anton draws her near, seeking her body amid the sheets. He reaches for her, an arm curling around her waist, solid and steady.

Even asleep, he reaches for her.

Gently, Calla puts her arms around him too, returning the gesture. There's a surge of emotion in her chest—a foreign feeling, twisting at her insides like a rapid-setting infection. She brushes at his hair, and when his arm tightens at her waist, a tear slides down her cheek, landing silently onto the pillow. It would be easier if he had betrayed her. That's familiar territory, something she knows how to navigate.

Calla can handle pain. She can handle blood. But this—this is somehow all and none of that at once, a wrenching in her very soul.

This is tenderness. And she is more afraid of it than anything else in their forsaken kingdom.

CHAPTER 24

The first hints of morning seep into the room with sluggishness, streaming effortfully through the blinds. Anton rubs at his eyes, turning over in his bed. When he reaches his arm out, it comes down on nothing, and he blinks awake, finding only sheets where Calla had been.

He jolts up. It wasn't a dream, was it? She really was here.

His hand goes to his heart, and he exhales, finding a puckering, clotted wound. Never did he think he would be so relieved to confirm an injury on himself. The last of his confusion eddies away from his sleep-addled mind, and he runs his gaze along the wall. Her sword is gone too: the one he was caught retrieving yesterday, though fortunately, he had invaded the body of the Crescent who saw him before anyone else took notice.

Anton squints at his wristband. He presses his identity number in, running the timer back on the next twenty-four hours. He wonders when it's going to ping today. He wonders if he ought to scramble up before it happens while he's in his apartment, then wonders if that's why Calla wandered off.

Why didn't she wake him?

The clock on the mantel turns to half past five in the morning. It's early. Most of the establishments downstairs have not opened yet, hovering in that the brief quiet segment after night has fully shuttered but day has not quite arrived. Anton finds a clean shirt from his wardrobe. He shrugs into pants fit for combat and the same shoes that came with this body. When he walks into the living room, his clothes from the previous night are still discarded on the floor, but Calla's are gone.

He opens the front door. A rush of cold morning air swirls through as he stands on the threshold, thinking.

It's strange that he has not been in Calla Tuoleimi's acquaintance for very long, and yet he knows exactly where to go to find her. He doesn't take the stairs down onto the streets. He walks up instead, then pushes through the door to the rooftop. And indeed, there she sits at the very edge with her back to him, one leg swinging along the side of the building and the other propped up beside her. There's a cigarette dangling from her fingers, the heel of her hand resting on her knee. Even like that, slouching in the most casual fashion, she looks every inch a princess.

"Those are bad for you, you know."

Calla turns slowly, her expression level while she takes him in. The morning light is brighter here than it is from the streets, but the clouds are as gray and heavy as the plastic bags that litter the gutters. Another storm floats on the horizon.

"Are they?" Calla asks. "I hadn't heard."

Her sword has been reacquainted with her hip, hanging where it belongs. When she moves her leg to make room for him, Anton joins her without further prompting.

"Terrible." He watches her take a deep drag. "Rots the qi and ruins your health. Practically guarantees an early death—"

Calla removes the cigarette from her lips and, with the puff of smoke still in her lungs, leans forward and kisses him. Despite his words, he lets her release right into him, taking the toxin down his throat like it is the sweetest liquor he has ever tasted.

As soon as the smoke settles, Calla pulls away slowly, her lashes heavy and dark, fanning down with her indolent gaze. Her fingers remain around his jaw, and Anton watches her as she turns his face this way and that, surveying him under the groggy daylight.

"Are you afraid this body has somehow changed since last night?"

Calla frowns, unamused by his question. "It is not beyond imagination. Perhaps Anton Makusa has fled and this is someone else."

He rolls his eyes, nudging her hand away from his face and lacing his fingers through hers before she can protest. An afflicted expression stirs in her eyes, one that was not there the previous night. Anton thinks he recognizes it—a laceration, a torment. Like approaching a fork in the road, alternating between each option at breakneck speed even as the split approaches, unable to turn back.

"You're not that paranoid," Anton says. He presses his lips to the inside of her wrist. "What's really on your mind, Calla?"

Calla extricates her arm without niceties, and Anton blinks, taken aback. One of the factories nearby must be rumbling to a start, because there's smoke rising through the gaps between the buildings, low-hanging mist gathering around them. The dip in his stomach comes without warning. Seven years without Otta, and he would have thought he had gotten better at this. Would have thought that leaving his youth behind meant outgrowing his need to hold on too tightly to people once he has them. Yet Calla pulling away makes his skin prickle, as if he's been given a slap on the wrist without knowing what he did wrong.

"You never look the same, Anton," Calla says quietly. Her fingers play at the hem of her sleeve, her face turned away. Her cigarette has burned to its end, but she still holds it in her other hand, angling the ash onto the ledge.

He wants to pinch it out. Pluck it from her grasp and press it to his skin if that means she'll look at him. "Why does that matter?"

Calla finally drops the butt of the cigarette. "I don't know who you are." Her eyes shift in his direction at last, glinting with a cascade of color. The yellow of hardened gold; the burning end of an overwrought electric wire. "How can I trust you?"

A high-pitched call comes from the street below, but neither of them reacts. They are mirrors of each other, one head tilted to the left and the other to the right, one with a leg propped on the ledge and the other with a leg stretched inside, effigies hung for display on the edge of this rooftop.

Anton doesn't understand. Or he does, he supposes. He understands that she's searching for an excuse, and he doesn't want her to find one. Calla, despite her grandiosity and confidence, is just as trapped as anyone without the jumping gene. She is stuck on the idea of her body giving her power, so much so that she has forgotten who the one moving that body is.

"You know who I am," he says. He dares to reach out again. Skims his finger along her temple, brushing her long hair back. "I am Anton Makusa. It doesn't matter what body I'm in."

The rooftop stutters, its gurgling pipes coming to a pause.

"You must understand," Calla says evenly, "that by the same logic, I am nothing. No one. I don't even have a name."

Anton snorts. At the sound, Calla shoots him a sharp glance, indignation ready in her expression, but he shakes his head before clarifying.

"You are Calla Tuoleimi. If you choose to be."

"Don't you—" Calla cuts off, huffing. "I *stole* her."

"You have *been* her for fifteen years. She is more you than anyone else." His hand runs along her face now, along her soft skin and the sharp angles of her cheek. She lets him, and he knows she catches the exact moment his jaw clenches tight and his voice hardens. "Who cares if you stole her? You deserve this power more than the girl who was born into it. Forget your name and adopt the title instead. *Calla*. Soon, people will be saying it just as they whisper *God*."

Calla shifts toward him slowly. He almost wonders if he should be afraid, if her hands are coming around his shoulders to throw him off the side of the building. Thankfully, she's only twining her arms around him, drawing near until she can rest her chin on his shoulder.

"Calla," she echoes, putting on a tone of reverence. She makes a thoughtful noise. "Would you know me in another body?"

"In any body," Anton promises, "you would still be the same terrifying princess."

That draws a laugh from her, and the sound sends a thrill shooting along his body. When she lifts her chin to grin at the look on his face, he can't help but feel that he is giving away more than he should, yet he can't stop himself.

Calla touches the ridge of his ear. "I have to tell you something."

"It is more or less shocking than your identity?"

"Less." The building jolts beneath them. The restaurant on the fifth floor has activated its industrial-size exhaust fan. "I entered the games to kill King Kasa."

Anton doesn't know if he is supposed to act surprised. He figured it had to be something like this. Why else would she emerge again in San-Er? She single-handedly enacted the most audacious massacre in its history and got away with it. She could have easily lived the rest of her days in quiet hiding.

"And that requires victory in the games," he guesses. No one outside the palace has access to King Kasa any other way. He pauses. "Would you like me to offer my heart in sacrifice?"

Her eyes narrow into a glare. "Don't be ridiculous."

"Good," Anton replies. "I would have thought that a mighty ask."

He wouldn't have enrolled in the games either if he didn't need to win. He wouldn't have done any of this unless it was the last possible option.

Calla has traced her finger from his ear down to his neck. The smoke from the nearby factory lessens as the machines find their rhythm, dispersing into the air more evenly. It feels easier to breathe.

"I don't suppose you'll pull your wristband out of commission?"

San is starting to wake up. The rooftop doors are opening and closing as wayfarers move in and out, but there's no reason to be concerned; few will recognize them as players, and other combatants cannot creep up on them in such an open space.

Anton exhales. "Calla. I cannot."

She pulls a fistful of his shirt collar. Not in threat, if her blank expression is any indication.

"Do you love her?"

There's little doubt who she means. Otta Avia—the one he's doing this for. Does he? He loves her the way everyone loves keepsakes from their childhood. He loves her the way no one can let go of the first person they ever wholly adored.

"Will it change how these games end?" he counters. An image of Otta flashes in his head. Not her cunning smile in the palace, but her comatose form lying in that hospital bed. How can he walk away from the only money that will keep her alive?

Calla lets go of his shirt collar. Her hands turn idle in her lap while her chin rests back down onto his shoulder. He can no longer see her expression.

"I suppose not," she says. "But I have an idea, nevertheless."

"An idea?"

"For us to survive and claim a victory on both fronts."

"You want the king dead, and I want the victor's prize," Anton states. Of course he wants them both to survive, but he hardly dares hope. "To have the king dead, you need the victor's prize. Am I missing something here?"

"Yes. Kasa watches the Juedou from the throne room every year. His location is set."

"And we'll barge in, weapons raised?"

Calla pulls away with exaggerated exasperation. "May I finish, Makusa? Or would you like to draw the plan instead?"

Anton isn't sure if he still loves Otta, but he thinks he loves Calla. He loves her quick temper, her sharp words, even when they're directed at him. He loves the rush every time he turns her scowl into a grin, or her grin darkens into a glare. Is that love? It's not as if he ever really learned what love is supposed to feel like.

"No, please," he says. He tugs her back. "Continue."

Calla grumbles something under her breath, crossing her arms. Anton doesn't catch it, but since she settles into him again, he figures it cannot be anything too worrying.

"We're not both barging in," Calla continues. "*I* am. Soon as we filter down to the final three, I'll pull my chip. They'll call the Juedou, summon you to the arena battle. You must play it as if everything is normal, as if these games are proceeding like any other year."

"And are they not?" Anton asks, only to annoy her.

"And *then*," Calla says, ignoring him, "I make my way to King Kasa. The Juedou is always one of the busiest days of the year, practically a citywide holiday. The palace guard will be widely dispersed and surrounding the arena instead of the palace proper. I know the layout and the grounds. I don't need a victory to kill him, I just need access."

He loves that too. The pure confidence. The resolve in her voice as soon as she has set her mind to a task.

"Even on such days," he says, "the palace is highly guarded."

"I have a secret weapon."

Anton raises his eyebrows. There's a new shroud of smoke wafting up, bringing the scent of factory ash and burning plastic. He nudges his nose into Calla's hair, so that all he can smell instead is something sweet and metallic.

"Don't tell me your weapon is yourself."

"Do you think I'm that conceited?" Before Anton can give his answer and risk being pushed off the building, Calla says, "It's August. I have his cooperation, so surely he can get me in."

August. Anton goes rigid. Calla must feel it, because she straightens, throwing a concerned glance over at him.

"I'm not sure you can trust him," Anton says. He has chosen his words carefully, trying not to betray his total doubt. With a curious noise, Calla draws her leg up from the side of the building and rests it across his lap.

"Trustworthy or not, he is a necessary tool. He won't help *you*, which is why you need to win the prize fairly. Me, however . . . if he stabs me in the back, he'll be receiving a sword through the heart too."

Anton grimaces. "That doesn't assure me very much."

"Well"—Calla leans in, her mouth an inch from his, and he draws a very low breath to control the hitch in his throat—"it's either we try this, or we fight each other in the coliseum. Which do you prefer?"

Anton tries to close the distance instead of answering the question; Calla swerves back, her lip twitching in amusement.

"Anton."

Ugh. "You've made your point," he replies. That doesn't mean he has to like it.

The corners of Calla's red lips curve up properly, rewarding him with a full smile. Despite Calla's conviction, the sinking feeling in Anton's gut only grows stronger, each worry weighed down by waves of memory. He has always been afraid of August Avia holding power over Talin. Prince August sees the kingdom as made up of playthings, people to move around and make choices for without first asking what they need. Prince August will step on his friends if he needs a rung up and squeeze his closest loved ones for use until there is nothing more they can offer. It would be within his very nature to stab Calla in the back if the occasion calls for it, because August Avia has worked tirelessly to become August Shenzhi, to become the heir to these seething cities, and no one good can want power that badly.

"What's going to happen when this succeeds?" Anton asks after a moment. "Will you take the throne?"

Calla casts him an incredulous look. "Of course not. The throne is August's."

"I hoped you wouldn't say that." He shakes his head. "Why give it to him so easily? The Palace of Union has joined San-Er into one now. You're as much the heir as he is."

The line of questioning seems to surprise Calla. She raises her shoulders, keeping her neck warm in the collar of her coat, her brow furrowed while she chews over an answer. Then:

"Because I'm not doing this to rule," she says quietly. "I just want to stop King Kasa."

"Stop him?"

Calla gestures over the rooftop, at the streets below them, into the twin cities and beyond. "From all this. Only caring about himself and his throne. Expanding ever outward so that his kingdom can claim more land to take taxes on but refuse to feed. What good is a ruler without a sense of responsibility? I'm wiping him away."

"You don't think August would be the same?" Anton asks.

"He wouldn't," Calla retorts confidently. She tugs at the fraying shoelace on her boot. "I know him."

As does Anton. In fact, he might argue that he knows Prince August even better than Calla does. Only it's not worth arguing about this, because if Calla won't seize the crown, then short of August taking over upon Kasa's death, there is no other contender except mass anarchy.

"This is Kasa's rot," Calla continues steadily. "And when he's gone, no child will go hungry again."

Anton examines her. She must know that this is unrealistic. Calla Tuoleimi is too clever to be fooled into such elementary thinking, too sensible to believe that a kingdom could change so wholly by merely swapping one mortal man for another.

Though perhaps . . . perhaps she is simply weary enough to be fooled. She looks at the cities with such duty, the weight of the kingdom hefted upon her shoulders by her own appointment. Allowing August's heroics to swoop in means reprieve from the never-ending, immeasurable task of keeping watch; a savior to replace a tyrant, justice restored so long as one cruel king bears the burden of his whole lineage's wrongs.

"Do you want to stop Kasa from letting another child go hungry again?" Anton broaches slowly. "Or do you want to punish him for letting *you* go hungry?"

A spark of ire flashes in Calla's eyes. Then, that glint fades just as fast as it came, because Calla must know that it isn't an unreasonable accusation, and Anton does not ask to be scornful.

"Can't it be both?" Calla replies. She tucks her loose shoelace deep into her boot, tidying the knot before it can trip her up. "The kingdom is starving. My purpose is to save Talin." Her lips thin. "But the king of San and the king of Er also let me grow up in misery, forced my village into their kingdom without seeing us as people. For that, they must answer with their lives. One down, another to go."

The rooftop door bangs shut. A child cries from below. And inside Anton's body, his heart takes on a clamor, fearing for the unflinching drive that has hardened Calla Tuoleimi's voice.

"Okay," Calla says suddenly, breaking the gravity of their conversation.

Her tone returns to normal, humor creeping back into her manner. "I need to go find August." She starts to rise onto her feet. "Don't get into too much trouble while I'm—"

Anton snags her by the wrist, stopping her before she can stand. Though it's a basic impulse that launches him into action, if he searches deeper, he knows it is fear: the very real possibility that she could wander away from him and he might never see her again.

"Not yet," he breathes. "Wait until the day begins proper, at least. Stay with me."

Calla complies. He wonders if he is the first to beg before her like this—not for a lack of people who want to, but because Princess Calla Tuoleimi will not let them get close enough to try. Slowly she eases back onto the ledge with her legs inside the rooftop this time, set on the solid, cluttered ground.

"Until the day begins proper, and only until then," she warns. Her eyes crinkle. She has been with him since the previous night, he has not seen her adjust her cosmetics, yet the dark liner on her eyes remains intact, pulling the corners until they look feline. "How do you suggest I make use of such time milling around?"

By all counts, the day proper has already begun. The sounds, the calls, the cries—everything that makes up San-Er, rising to a fever pitch by the minute. But still, Anton closes his eyes and elects to block them out, entreating Calla to ignore them too.

"Kiss me," he says. "Kiss me and make every dreadful second here worth it."

Calla only needs to be asked once. She presses her lips to his, and the rest of San-Er drowns out, fades to nothing, shrunken into oblivion by sheer will. All Anton can hope is that this is enough—that this time around, outsmarting the cities with a plan pinned on love will finally succeed.

CHAPTER 25

For the first time in five years, Calla steps into San's coliseum marketplace, and she hasn't missed it at all. The stench of fish hits her first: salt-soaked, laid out in rows by the entrance with their guts scooped out. She adjusts her mask over her nose when she enters, both to hide her face from the coliseum's surveillance cameras and to protect her nostrils from the pungent scent.

High noon. Though the clouds are thick, the marketplace is awash with light, and Calla almost has trouble opening her eyes fully. She's not used to unobstructed daytime actually reaching the ground, each of her steps made cleanly and not in guesswork. It's strange to be seeing where her feet should go instead of listening to the beating pulse of the city, stepping where it tells her, trusting its growths and dips.

Calla pauses. She checks her wristband. No pings yet, but she doesn't know whether that's by chance or if August decided to pause them when she asked to meet.

"A treat?"

The voice is startlingly close, and Calla twitches, looking over her shoulder. There's an old woman standing far too close for Calla's liking, but before she can reach for a weapon, her eyes flicker to the woman's arms. Visibly bare—no wristband, no weapon, no tattoo. Calla relaxes. The woman, with her sleeves rolled to her elbows and fingers covered in flour, reaches out and grasps Calla's wrist, likely taking the lack of resistance to be a good sign.

"We have a dozen good treats back here, anything to your liking," the woman goes on, hauling her in front of the stall. It's not enough to set Calla there: the woman takes her by the shoulders and leans her close to the offerings too. "Plenty of flat cakes, glutinous rice cakes—"

"Yes, yes, I'll take some," Calla cuts in, nodding at the rectangular jelly cake in front of the woman. She can't remember the last time she had one. It was far too low-class for the Palace of Heavens. The provinces are filled with these cheap treats, rolled out on a cart in the middle of the village square, an elderly shopkeeper dicing the cake into neat rectangular helpings with a piece of string. They can't be cut with a knife. The blade would move in every which direction, gliding through the gelatinous blob until some pieces are as large as rock and others are mere speckles. They require something a little rough.

The woman hurries behind the stall and pulls the string taut. Her hands are steady as she cuts a perfect four-by-four, sliding each piece away from the others as they wobble and glimmer under the lightbulb hanging from the top of the stall. While she's wrapping one in tissue paper, Calla digs into her pocket for a handful of coins and passes them over just as the woman is offering the cake.

Calla takes the cake. The woman, meanwhile, has frozen.

"Are . . ." Calla looks at the coins in her fingers. "Are you all right? Is this not a sufficient amount? I have more, hold on—"

She drops her coins in the hand the woman already has outstretched and digs back into her pocket. The woman finally breaks from her daze, shaking a lock of white hair out of her face before gasping, "No, no, this is sufficient. This is more than sufficient."

Oh. Is it? Prices at the market have really nose-dived. Calla is hardly carrying around much cash in her pocket to begin with.

And yet, as the woman stares at the coins in her hand, she begins to tear up.

"Well, don't *cry*," Calla chides, shifting on her feet. "If you cry, I'll have to empty my whole pocket on you, and what good will you be for the next customer, sobbing all over their cake?"

The woman's next inhale is a sudden guffaw, and she wipes at her eyes. Behind her, a boy hurries by wearing a pair of thick gloves, handling some squirming animal, but he pays them no mind and carries on, cutting a path through the other stalls. Another child walks through seconds later, wires and screens tangled in their arms, but like the first boy, as long as the market's affairs have nothing to do with them, even when there's a sobbing shopkeeper, they keep moving without another glance.

"Forgive me," the woman sniffs. "This stall is closing tomorrow, so we'll be without means soon."

Calla blinks. "Closing?" she echoes. Her eyes trace the row of stalls, the iron carvers and gadget builders and dumpling makers. "Why?"

Another sniff. At the very least, the woman is no longer crying. "It's— I won't bother you with the details, but the council has brought in new rules. Higher fees and different regulations. They're trying to drive us out, I've no doubt. They want to clean up the market, get the odd businesses out and bring in the people they know. But who will accuse them of doing so?"

I will, Calla thinks immediately. *Don't worry. I will.*

A sudden *bang* sounds from the next stall over, and Calla turns sharply. It's only a rack that has collapsed, but her gaze catches on a figure standing nearby. An unfamiliar face, but a familiar set of black eyes with a cold, even stare. Prince August, causing a commotion and waiting for Calla to take note of him. Without confirming that she has indeed recognized who he is, August turns on his heel and begins to walk away.

Calla curses under her breath and takes a big bite of the jelly cake she has purchased. Then, wiping her hand clean, she scoops out the rest of the coins from her pocket and sets them on the stall table.

"Take them, you need this more than I do." Then: "Don't you dare cry. Suck those tears back in right now."

The woman can only nod, making a valiant effort to follow instructions. Calla offers a salute, merging back into the crowd to follow August. She has to shake her head at the other stall hawkers waving their hands for her attention, though she falters every few steps, wondering if they all have the same story. Hundreds and hundreds set up shop here at the rise of dawn, then pack away only when it seems the crowds have filtered thin. It will never be entirely empty in the marketplace, only empty enough when sleep deprivation isn't worth a sale. Hundreds here, at the mercy of whatever decision the palace feels like making. Thousands more, scattered in the buildings of San-Er.

Calla lifts her head. The palace's turrets rise higher than anything else in San, looming over the stalls like some foreboding watchtower. Gold-plated tiles and polished wooden whorls interrupt the walls of the coliseum, making the Palace of Union look like some miracle growing out of the ugliest crevasses. There's movement, on the nearest balcony. Someone—Galipei, most likely—lurks in the throne room, keeping an eye on August.

Calla comes to a stop beside her cousin, who is examining a display of newspapers. The selection is sparse. Paper has been trickling out of fashion ever since televisions grew more affordable, and even those who can't afford a television would rather stand outside a barbershop to catch the reels.

"So," August begins. His eyes dart to her rapidly, then back to the papers. Slowly, he retrieves one and feigns reading. "This better be good."

A cloud clears in the sky, letting down a brighter sunray. Calla visibly winces, buying time by glancing up and holding a hand over her face.

"I need your help," she says. There's no use beating around the bush when August knows she wants something. "I think there might be another way to go through with our plan."

August spins on his heel. In one sharp and precise turn, he is facing her, the newspaper rustling in his hands.

"I beg your pardon?"

"I—" Calla pauses. In that second, every variation of her idea sounds ludicrous to her ear, each suggestion halting and curdling on her tongue. Sweat gathers at the small of her back, and it only presses more slickly against her shirt with the jostling of the crowd behind her.

Let me keep him, she wants to say. *Let me have this one thing.*

She can still feel the press of Anton's lips kissing her goodbye before she left the rooftop. She can feel the twist in her heart, that persistent prodding at the back of her mind when she looked at him, knowing there were only so many ways this could play out. He gazed at her with such abandon, like anything she said would come to fruition by her mere utterance of the words. She isn't sure she deserves it. If it comes down to it, if their end goal requires sacrificing everything, will she do it?

"I have an alternate proposal to get Kasa off the throne," Calla settles on saying, swallowing hard. "If I pull out from the games, I can make my hit during the Juedou. He'll be in the throne room. I just need you to get me in."

August's expression furrows.

"That's entirely unnecessary," he says. "In fact, it's seeking trouble where there needs none. Stay with the original plan. Await being crowned victor and make the hit inside the palace."

While Calla grasps for a suitable reply, a shopper suddenly bumps her arm, distracting her attention. She turns a glare over her shoulder, making eye contact with two girls walking together, both of whom stop dead in their tracks when they sight her. Though Calla thinks little of the encounter and turns back, she's listening just well enough to hear one whisper, "Isn't that Fifty-Seven? The one who doesn't jump?"

Calla whirls around again. The two continue strolling, but it doesn't stop their conversation, voices wafting over as if the subject of their gossip doesn't stand a few feet away.

"Who is that with her? Eighty-Six?"

"Maybe. It's sad they'll probably end up fighting each other, though."

The two girls are swallowed by the crowd, disappearing deeper into the market. Calla takes in a shallow breath. Sometimes she forgets that these games are televised—that she lives, even in blurred, pixelated form, on every television set across San-Er for entertainment. While she bleeds and fights and risks her life to get into that palace, the rest of the twin cities see only a game. Either she is good enough to claim victory, or she will die to the sound of their cheering.

"You're not hearing me," Calla manages carefully, pushing the words through her teeth when she finally collects her thoughts. "I . . . I don't want to kill every player."

Doesn't she deserve *something* selfish? Something as Calla—not as a princess, or as player Fifty-Seven. She wants to pose the question aloud, but she already knows August's answer. Golden, noble Prince August.

He casts her a steady look. With that alone, she knows he has heard exactly what she refuses to say.

"Anton," he guesses. "You've gone soft for Anton." August folds the newspaper in his hands and sets it down. Mutters, "I thought you were smarter than that, but I suppose I should have pushed you away from him earlier."

Calla blinks. "Pushed me—" Her outraged echo fades off. Eno's face flashes in her mind. "It was *you*. You sent people after me."

Prince August doesn't bother denying it, nor does he appear to have any shame in admitting to it.

"You were sitting idle for too long. I needed you back on track."

Eno, ambling after Calla with a shine in his eyes, convinced that she could keep him safe. He could have pulled the chip from his wristband at any moment and walked away from the games. Calla should have yanked off the damn thing and demanded he go find a safe place to sleep, and even if he hated her in that moment, it would have saved his life.

"What logic was going through your tiny brain?" Calla hisses. "Slit my throat and let my floating qi do your dirty work?"

"They wouldn't have killed you, Calla. You're too well trained for them. They were mere threats in your path."

Calla lunges forward and seizes him furiously by the collar, uncaring if she makes a scene. The rest of the market hardly casts a glance over. August, meanwhile, narrows his gaze, tipping his chin toward the palace balcony. It is both a warning and a threat. He might not push her off, but there's someone waiting in the shadows who will.

"I thought we were in cooperation." Calla's fist tightens. "Instead you're *testing* me."

"I'm *reminding* you. This isn't just another year of the games. This is high treason for the throne, and you're gallivanting around like it's no life-or-death matter. Remember what we are working for. Your resolve cannot falter."

How dare he speak of her resolve. She wants to strike his cheek, feel her knuckles make sickening contact with bone. If she doesn't release her cousin in the next second, Galipei will come charging down, and then there will really be trouble. Calla almost welcomes it. Let a fight begin, and she can explode outward, draw the attention of the entire fucking twin cities. Set destruction upon everything in her path, level San-Er's buildings until she is surrounded by rubble, and maybe then the kingdom will finally build anew without the misery that their every selfish ruler has given them.

But Calla releases August's collar slowly, lowering her arms back to her sides and tamping down her rage. Not now. Not yet. August smooths his shirt, looking nonchalant.

"I will see King Kasa dead if it's the last thing I do," she manages evenly. If it weren't for the twitch in her jaw, it would be impossible to know what seethes inside her at that moment. She knows August sees it; he pretends not to.

"Good. Then you'll also accept my reminder, I hope, that we are to depose Kasa by whatever means necessary. And that includes following the plan with the highest chance of success. Wouldn't you agree?"

Calla turns toward the palace. She traces her sight along the top of the coliseum walls and wonders how quickly someone could climb them.

"Do not mistake my tolerance for weakness, August," she says quietly. "Do not forget who you're talking to. You've gotten used to ordering people around, I know. Day in and day out, they must heed what you say, because you are the crown prince, and they cannot offend such a man." Her eyes flicker back to him. "But I am Calla Tuoleimi." The lie no longer feels like a lie. "I am a princess who sacrificed my own throne for this kingdom. You do not order me around."

A beat passes. August shakes his head.

"I'm not ordering you around," he counters. "I am telling you quite vehemently that it's a mistake to try to find an alternative when this is a very simple task."

There is no winning this argument. August will not allow her plan; Calla does not wish to carry through anything else. All they can do is stare one another down, neither willing to relinquish. August may issue threats, but they will be empty. Before they collaborated on treason, perhaps he could have hauled her in. Now, too much blood has spilled between them. All this messy, traceable evidence—the reek of the kills he made on her behalf staining his hands. August has everything to lose, and Calla has her righteousness.

"We can resume this discussion another day," Calla finally says. "There is still some time before the Juedou."

August is silent for a long moment, surrounded by the sour aura of his displeasure. Instead of agreeing or disagreeing, he squints at a digital clock inside the stall and says, "Meet me at the wall tomorrow near sunset. I require your help with something."

The change in topic makes Calla blink. She scrambles to make sense of the instructions. Funny . . . the stall has been empty for some time now. She doesn't know when its keeper wandered off, leaving his newspapers for anyone to take.

"What sort of help?"

"Something strange is going on. I don't want to use the royal guard."

"Something strange?"

"Yes," August says coolly. "Regarding San-Er's alleged intruders, who may not be intruders at all."

Calla makes a thoughtful noise, then glances at her wristband. "Very well, I suppose." She flicks her finger at the newspaper rack and takes a step away. "I won't keep you for long. Tomorrow, it is—"

"One more thing," August cuts in. He remains facing the stall, speaking quietly. Calla watches the back of his head and the clasp of his hands behind him. No one else in the coliseum can hear him save Calla, and still he lowers his volume. "Mark my words, Calla Tuoleimi. When it involves Anton Makusa, what you have is not love. It is obsession."

A hot flush spreads down her neck and across her chest. She keeps her expression neutral against such brazen words, though her skin dances again with the urge to lash out, to use violence where she knows her words would fail. August might win every argument he picks with her. But she can still tear him apart in retribution: she can tear apart anyone who tells her what she doesn't want to hear.

"What," she spits, "would you know of love?"

Calla turns and leaves, her throat scalding. She has spoken with such vehemence, leaving no doubt that she thought August was full of shit. All the same, as she pushes through the coliseum, emerging from its walls and into the darkness of San's streets, his words echo after her, trailing her all the way back to Anton.

CHAPTER 26

Galipei brings his collar to his nose, breathing in deep. He can't tell if he's imagining it, or if the sterile hospital smell has really followed him back to the palace. He followed August's instructions: enough poison has been dropped into Otta Avia's intravenous lines day by day that her heart should stop soon, for no apparent cause save that San-Er stops hearts on the regular.

"It's done," he says when August finally comes to stand beside him. The palace is a flurry of activity, the final details of the banquet being put into place. All they need to fill are the vases and the seats. The palace doesn't send a mission out for flowers until the very minute the final two players are called: an effort to make sure the petals don't wilt and the leaves remain plump and green. It's always a variety of bright-red blooms from Gaiyu Province, where the trees grow them in abundance, trailing down the branches like wind chimes. If Galipei were an angry rural dweller, he would cut down every tree just to put a thorn in the palace's side.

August's gaze is piercing when it snaps over to him, like he heard more than those two simple words, like he can hear Galipei's treacherous thoughts. What's the matter? He was the one who put them in there to begin with.

"Dead?"

A pair of guards pass by. The foyer sees a stream of movement coming in from the left, exiting from the right. Only August and Galipei stand by the wooden table in the middle, where a statue of a creature sits atop a beige cloth.

"Not yet. But soon. It'll be a full-body shutdown by tomorrow night at the earliest."

August thins his lips, a flicker of impatience crossing his face. Still, there's nothing more that Galipei could have done. Death is easy to summon in San-Er, though one cannot go offending it either.

Galipei touches August's wrist. It is a small brush, nothing more than the pad of his finger making contact with his prince's exposed skin just below the cuff of his sleeve.

"Relax," he urges. "The crown will soon be yours."

◇◇◇◇◇

There are six players left.

Calla twirls the dagger in her hands, watching the metal glint and flash under the artificial light. On the television screen in the corner of the diner, one network's reels begin their rerun for the morning crowd, and Calla's jaw tightens, her dagger stilling. Before she can slam the blade into the table, Anton's hand snakes out, catching her wrist. His other hand is braced around her ankle, where she's got her legs thrown over his lap.

"Princess, perhaps refrain from doing that."

"Yes, don't make us get a new table," Yilas remarks. She approaches from behind, carrying a pot of steaming tea in one hand and a plate of egg tarts in the other. When she sets the glistening tarts down, the yellow custard filling wobbles in movement, pushing against the firm pastry sides. "Here's your food, Anton Makusa."

Anton lifts a brow. "Thank you. You don't have to call me by my full name."

"You're welcome, Anton Makusa. Enjoy, Anton Makusa."

Yilas walks off, taking the pen out from behind her ear. The diner is empty, having just opened for the day, so Yilas doesn't bother being careful about the name she is flinging around. In fact, she looks quite entertained.

"Ignore her." Calla sets the dagger down. "She likes being a pest."

"She reminds me of a palace attendant."

"That's because she was my attendant." Calla pours herself a cup of tea, sparing a glance up when the diner doors open and bring in a group of people. They look engrossed in their conversation, making no cursory glances around while they punch their numbers into the turnstile, so they are unlikely to be threats. Just ordinary civilians, excited that the king's games are nearing the final battle. "I wonder who took Seventy-Nine out."

His image had flashed on the screen as part of the death count from the previous night, but without attribution to another player. Perhaps his own security team, sick of being bossed around. Perhaps someone in the palace, at last catching on to his funny business.

"As long as he's not our problem anymore," Anton says, putting an egg tart in his mouth.

But Calla only voices a small *hmm* under her breath, staring at the leaves swirling around in her tea. There's a foul taste in her mouth, and it's not because Yilas lost her touch at brewing. Six players. This could end tomorrow if they are fast about it. Yet August has not agreed to her plan. She's running out of time.

"We may have to begin avoiding the pings," Calla says.

Anton's brows shoot up. "*Avoiding?* Don't we want to end this?"

"Yes." She pushes the answer out sharply. "But on our terms. Or else we will both land in the arena."

There's a sudden chime from Anton's belt, and his attention pivots, whatever reply he had on his tongue lost. He glances at his pager. Calla watches him swallow hard.

"I have to go. I'll meet you later."

Now it is Calla's turn to be surprised. "I beg your pardon?"

He unclips his pager and presses a button to clear the screen. "The hospital is summoning me. It won't take long. I need to see Otta."

Otta. The one he's risking his life for. The one that has him refusing to withdraw, even though it would be so *easy* if he would just eliminate himself and let Calla enter the arena with another player. Despite Calla's best effort, she can't quite block August's warning from ringing incessantly in her head.

Mark my words, Calla Tuoleimi. When it involves Anton Makusa, what you have is not love. It is obsession.

Anton slides out from the booth. She turns and snags him by the sleeve as he is standing, halting him in front of her. Some dark shadow presses into her throat, turns her warm blood into acidic bile. He is hers now, no one else's.

"I love you," Calla says, the declaration snaking off her tongue and dropping into the space between them—as red as her mouth and as sharp as her sword. Like everything else she has wielded, her words are a weapon.

A smile presses to Anton's lips, though he appears confused. "What a strange time you have chosen to say so," he replies, "but I love you too."

Relief washes through her coolly, tamping down the flames that burn within her ribs. But it is not enough. Calla tilts her head, letting a strand of hair untuck from behind her ear.

"How much?"

"How *much?*" Anton smooths her hair back. "There's beggary in a love that can be counted and calculated."

She catches his hand, grips it hard. From the diner counter, Yilas is watching her with mild concern. "Can't I be curious about how far your love stretches?"

Anton laughs then, shaking her grip off gently. "You would have to find new skies and new earth, or else it would never stop stretching." This time, when he takes a step away, she knows she cannot grab him again. "I'll find you later, Princess."

He walks out of the diner, clipping the pager back onto his belt. Calla watches him go, her jaw tight.

At the first sign of danger, it's their lives over everyone else's. You remember Otta, don't you?

"Why won't you let go of her?" she whispers aloud.

Of course, there is no answer. The diner only offers another clatter of its turnstile, bringing in more patrons.

CHAPTER 27

By early evening, the skies have turned dark to bring in squally weather again, which means Calla navigates the alleys with more difficulty than usual, feeling around with her hands to make sure she isn't tripping on a trash bag.

She glances at her pager, arriving at the section of the wall where she is needed. Just before she can emerge fully from the alley, she only pokes her head out, cautiously perusing the scene. Ahead, August and Galipei are waiting with a considerable number of palace guards.

"I thought you didn't want to use the royal guard," Calla mutters beneath her breath. She cannot fathom what he needs her here for. There hasn't been a single location ping from her wristband today, even though night is crawling in. Maybe the games room is distracted.

A hand closes over her shoulder. Calla jumps, her sword already half-drawn, before the stranger whisper-shouts: "What fine daylight we have today!"

Calla's hand drops from her sword. "For the final time, Makusa, quit sneaking up on me."

"That's my only mode. You wanted me to come *stomping* around while we're trying to avoid getting killed by other players?"

Anton puts the tracker back into his pocket. Calla forgot that he was still holding on to it, following her wristband wherever it went.

"Well"—she tilts her head—"I suppose not." The new body he's wearing looks like another plucked from the financial district: a young banker or an accountant or some newly graduated strategic consultant for the few companies that have survived long enough in Er to build a legacy. His clothes are so unworn that there's still a gleam to the cotton fabric.

"How is Otta?"

She watches for Anton's reaction. A slight frown. The curve of his lips hold a troubled stiffness.

"She's fine. The hospital doesn't know what's wrong, only that her vitals are all over the place. I was summoned as her emergency contact."

Calla doesn't have much of a reply. She casts a look out to the wall again and sees that the royal group is still in discussion among themselves. Heated discussion. A denser rain cloud rolls in above them, and Galipei Weisanna doesn't seem to notice because he's more caught up making frantic gesticulations in August's direction.

A cool touch brushes her forehead. When Calla ignores him, Anton grasps her chin, snapping her gaze in his direction by mild force. "Why do you look so glum?"

Calla's brow quirks. His light tone is a mask, overcompensating for another emotion he doesn't want her to see. She knows him now, for better or worse.

"We are players in a set of games that demand slaughter," she says. "I bid you to look more glum."

"Ah, there's no use," Anton replies easily. "The games go on whether you approach them glumly or not." He leans in, and when Calla arches her neck for him, he trails his lips along her jaw. "In the face of danger, we might as well have fun."

Calla casts a glance out the alley again. They're still arguing. The storm clouds are growing heavier and heavier as the sun begins to set, but it doesn't appear that the rain is going to come down yet. Instead, the skies heave with motion, like a balloon filling toward capacity.

"Terrible scruples," she whispers. She slides her hands around his torso, burying them under his jacket and smoothing down the fabric of his white shirt. "I hope you realize that your crown prince awaits a hundred feet away."

"He can get fucked," Anton says, and Calla doesn't think he is joking.

"Sounds treasonous."

Anton presses his lips harder into the hollow of her throat. His hands settle on her hips. "Getting fucked is certainly not treasonous. In fact, one would encourage it."

Little shivers dart down her spine. Calla's eyes flutter shut. "Oh?"

"Especially for royals. It prevents them from becoming sticks-in-the-mud." His whole body is pressed into her now. "Maybe up against a wall, with—"

"*Ahem.*"

Anton freezes. Calla sighs, recognizing the sound and the person it came from. She gives Anton a small push, and he draws away from her slowly, a frown already setting into his expression.

"Hello, August," Calla says pleasantly, like he didn't just catch her committing unruly business in an alleyway. She straightens her jacket. "Did you need something?"

"Yes," August replies. He does not look amused. "If you go to Galipei, he can direct you. Anton Makusa, could I have a minute?"

August is already walking off, pushing between them and heading for the end of the alley. Calla blinks. Anton's displeased frown twitches, the plainest confusion crossing his face before he swallows it away.

"I suppose so," Anton says evenly. He squeezes Calla's shoulder once, then follows after August.

With a small grumble under her breath, Calla pivots the other way to go to Galipei.

◇◇◇◇◇

Anton folds his arms, waiting for August to say whatever it is he needs his minute to say. The crown prince of San looks ill-fitting here amid the rotting trash. Even in a fancy stolen body, Anton has grown right at home with the grub and the grime, but August stands like he might get infected by ten illnesses if he so much as touches a bare surface with his hand.

Prince August doesn't speak for a long while.

Then: "How have you been?"

Anton almost starts laughing. "Don't tell me you pulled me aside just to ask *that*."

When August swivels to face Anton head-on, the flash in his eyes is dangerous. "Fine. No. I pulled you aside to ask how often you've been seeing Otta."

Otta? Anton sobers quickly, taking a step away and nudging one of the alley trash bags. "What does it matter? She's lying comatose in a hospital bed."

"Answer the question, Anton."

Something has happened. Or else August wouldn't be acting the dutiful younger brother seven years after the fact. Anton reaches up. Grabs a handful of his own hair and scrunches it. He might change bodies at every corner, but he cannot seem to shake his old habits, and August brings out all of his old habits, starting with his nervous tics.

"Once a fortnight." He forces himself to stop messing with his hair. "Why?"

"Before she fell ill with the yaisu sickness"—a shout comes from the top

324

of the wall, but both August and Anton ignore it—"what was the last thing she told you?"

Anton doesn't like this one bit. He had thought he was being pulled aside about the games, about Calla, about anything that August might have a problem with at this precise point in time, but now it feels like an interrogation of the past, and because Anton cannot fathom *why* he is being interrogated, he worries that he must have been left out of something. *Should* Otta have told him something important? Did she keep it from him instead, and will August believe him if he says so?

"To wait for her by the Rubi Waterway if we got separated fleeing the palace," Anton answers truthfully. "We were set on leaving even if *you* bailed."

August doesn't rise to the bait. His brow furrows in thought, silent until there is an even louder shout from the wall that startles them both. At once, the two of them lurch forward. Someone is fighting. The clang of metal echoes into the clearing.

"Calla?" Anton bellows.

August's hand snaps out quickly, holding Anton back. "Don't interfere."

"*What?* Let go of me, you—"

"It's a ruse. Number Six is one of mine. I put him in the games as a fail-safe, and he's being attacked now by hired help. Calla is fighting off the attackers. All I need to do now . . ."

August pushes him aside and walks forward. Utterly bewildered, Anton follows, watching August pick up the pace steadily before breaking into a run, rushing onto the scene. He looks odd to be running too. One would think a prince should never break a sweat.

Anton draws his knives, in case he needs them on hand. It is an empty gesture: August lunges in front of Number Six, giving an instruction that is drowned out in the clanging of swords. Calla, meanwhile, is locked in combat with a mysterious figure swathed in black, but the moment she sees August, she withdraws her blade. Her mouth opens, perhaps to shout an instruction for August to step back. She does not get the chance. Her opponent turns away from her and starts for August instead.

What is August playing at?

Calla doesn't intrude. When Anton turns to search for Galipei, wondering how August's *bodyguard* is taking this turn of events, Galipei is unmoving too. The rest of August's guard team is a different manner. They surge forward, expressions under their masks terrified, and when the figure raises his sword high, right above August's head—

Leida Miliu's voice booms across the clearing, echoing under the heavy storm clouds despite the muffle of fabric.

"Vaire, *stop!*"

The figure clothed in black halts. A long second passes, where nothing can be heard or felt but the slowly rising wind. When the figure tugs the covering off his face, pulls the whole square until it is a ball scrunched in his fist, it is not Leida whom he is looking at for further instruction, but August.

Leida staggers back. Whoever this is, it's clearly not the face she was expecting. The man who stands before them—sword lowered placatingly like he hadn't been slashing mere seconds ago—has dark-pink eyes.

"Why did you think that was Vaire?" August asks lightly, taking on the tone of small talk.

"I—" Leida looks to him, then back to the man. Her gaze, finally, settles on Calla, whose grip tightens on her sword.

Silence descends across the clearing. Then Galipei pulls a blindfold over Leida's eyes without warning, announcing, "Leida Miliu, you are under arrest."

◇◇◇◇

There's something dangerous about this moment. Calla doesn't know what it is, but as she watches the palace guards descend on Leida and force her to her knees, her senses are screaming for her to leave, lest she risk becoming entangled in business that isn't hers. Her sword feels heavy in her hand. The weight doesn't lessen even once she's sheathed the weapon.

She spots Anton hovering near the alleyway, eyes wide. He hadn't caught the beginning of the fight, hadn't caught Galipei's quick, whispered instructions to Calla before pushing her off to combat the other player. He definitely hadn't caught the whirl of confusion when another figure burst out of the shadows and started attacking them both, or else he might have wondered why Calla was holding back from the fight.

Galipei's instructions had been simple: *Don't kill anyone. None of us are in danger. It's someone pretending to be one of those "rural intruders" targeting players of the games—just stall and make it look convincing until August gets back on scene.*

Calla pulls her mask tighter, securing it around her nose and mouth. She doesn't wait for August to dismiss her, nor does she make eye contact with Galipei as she passes.

"Hey!" August calls anyway. The first syllable of her name almost slips from his lips, but then he casts a look at the guards and visibly holds back. "Where are you going?"

Calla waves a salute. When she reaches Anton, she snags him by the elbow. It's not her safety she is worried about. It's Anton's. Every moment they linger here in view of August is a moment their prince might pull one of a thousand plans from his sleeve without consulting the people involved in them first, manufacturing a false fight just so he can catch his culprit.

"You're on your own for this one, Your Highness. You know how to reach me for other business."

She slips her hand into Anton's and pulls them both out of view, away from San-Er's wall.

CHAPTER 28

"You set me up."

August doesn't bother denying it. He leans on the cell bars, arms folded across his chest. Beside him, Galipei hovers at the ready. No other guard has been allowed into the cells, not even another Weisanna, in case Leida tries jumping. They occupy unknown terrain with Leida Miliu now, watching her in the corner of the cell with her blindfold taken off, her legs propped up and her arms resting on her knees. After all that Leida has taught the Crescent Society members, who knows what else she's learned to do? Perhaps she really can invade a Weisanna.

"You're a fool," August says. Since all the other cells are cleared out, he's not afraid to continue: "I already had a plan to depose Kasa. I was already *on it*. Why would you feel the need to intervene?"

Leida flexes her hands. Most of the glitter around her eyes has smeared off. The few specks that remain are light on her skin, making her face look mottled and bruised.

"You're not endeavoring to depose him," she replies quietly. "You're endeavoring to replace him. You will take the throne, and nothing will change."

August scoffs, backing away from the bars. "You think *I* would let the people starve? You think *I* would throw banquets while the provinces suffer drought after drought?"

"I think you would fix it for a year or two." Leida's voice remains faint. "I think you would smooth over the holes you saw appear while King Kasa was on the throne: feed the people, dissolve the councilmembers who were not governing their provinces well. Then other holes would appear. The outer provinces will want independence. San-Er will want the wall to come down. And you will not want it, you will think it useless."

"Stop," August says.

Leida does not stop. "The years will catch up. You'll start to resent those who are loud about their demands. You punish them by withholding resources and food. Poverty will strike. Balance will shift again. Before you know it—"

"Shut *up*," August demands. "I mean it."

"—you'll be a tyrant, just as King Kasa is. It might not even take years. It could be mere hours after he's deposed, when you feel the power at your fingertips and realize your armies will do whatever you say as long as you wear the crown."

Leida finally stops when Galipei slams an arm against the cell bars, shaking the whole wall with a metallic clang. She doesn't look frightened, only tired: her eyes narrow, her gaze downcast.

"Of all people close to August, *you* should know better," Galipei snaps.

"I do, Galipei. I *do* know August." She straightens one of her legs out, rolling her ankle in her boot. "I could have incited an open coup, but I didn't. Why do you think I bothered with this facade, training an entire temple of Crescents to use qi tactics that have long been forgotten in the royal books? Why invent a storyline about Sican intruders? This was never supposed to end with your head under a sword. I wanted this reign to topple quietly. I wanted to start with the monarchy's power diminishing."

"That's not separate from me," August counters tightly. "I *am* the monarchy."

"And you could let go of that. But you won't. Do you think you can fix this by taking power?" Leida shakes her head. She is smiling, though the expression has no humor. "Either you're fooling yourself, or you're trying to fool everybody else. No king is selfless. No throne is built on bloodless ground. There can be no freedom until the crown is broken."

August turns to leave. He has no interest arguing about this. Somewhere along the path, he has lost Leida, and he won't waste time trying to bring her back. He smooths the cuff of his jacket, fingers fixing the metal that holds his sleeve down.

"When my mother died, she had me promise to serve the people, not the kingdom." Leida raises her voice now, choosing to increase her volume only when August begins to walk. The echo bounces on the stone walls, trailing him like a wild animal. "The *people*, August. The guard was not formed to conquer land and territory. The Weisannas were not born to protect one pitiful royal from the consequences of his greed."

August keeps walking. Galipei is close on his heels.

"Half of the provinces in Talin have their own language. Did you know that? *Did you know?* They don't want your benevolent rule, they want *freedom*! We are not a kingdom anymore—we have long been an empire, and you are to blame if you won't acknowledge it!"

Her voice cuts off abruptly as August and Galipei emerge from the cells, slamming the security door shut after them. A glance is exchanged between the two, no words spoken before they proceed down the hall. August nods at the guards standing afar, signaling that they may resume watch.

He stays quiet even when the guards are out of earshot. All down the palace halls and corridors, the hard soles of his shoes make a thunderous sound, beating a rhythm through the floors. To his own ears, each step is in careful harmony with his steady, even heartbeat.

Leida is never going to walk out of that cell. Ever.

◇◇◇◇◇

"You've been staring at that wall for an hour now."

August barely stirs at Galipei's voice, not acknowledging that he's heard him. His eyes stay pinned on the glistening golden wallpaper in his study, face turned toward the open window where the warm evening air floats in. He's thinking about Leida's capture, about how easily she let them take her down. But that's not the detail that has snagged him: it's Calla.

"I deactivated Six from the games," August says in lieu of a reply. "We are down to five players."

"Oh, so we're just bringing up random matters now?" Galipei jibes. "Very well. My second cousin reassigned the palace guard into new units, in case there was further collaboration with Leida inside the ranks."

August's attention snaps to him. "Is there a power vacuum opening up?"

"No, don't worry." Galipei leans back onto the desk, his legs crossing at the ankles. "The heads of each unit will simply report to you now, I suppose. Unless you are opposed."

"No," August says. "I'm not."

A loud ruckus floats in from the window. They're clearing out the market below, getting the coliseum ready to be used for the approaching Juedou. The stalls nearest the center can remain functioning until the last minute, but the ones on the outer circle must move so the palace can set up the audience ropes. A final battle needs its spectators. What fun are the king's games if not witnessed by all, plucked straight from the reels and pushed into reality?

"You're still looking rather pensive."

332

August clasps his hands together over his stomach. Tightness thrums there—this unsettled feeling is not new, but it is more prominent today. Five players left. There is only so much time before the games wind down, before Calla takes her victorious title, before she is brought into the palace and fulfills August's plan.

She *needs* to fulfill his plan.

"I'm concerned," August admits.

Galipei uncrosses his ankles, pushing off from the desk. He walks over to where August sits and crouches beside him so they are eye to eye.

"About Calla," he guesses.

August nods. "She's too attached to Anton. She thinks she can avoid killing him." He tips his head up, lolling his neck onto the plush chair. "He may kill her instead, and then where will we be?"

The question is rhetorical, but Galipei thinks it over nevertheless.

"You said Calla proposed a different plan."

"It won't work. Especially now, with the palace guard so on edge. She cannot possibly bypass them to get to Kasa."

"She could jump. She's royal blood. She's strong."

August sighs. For whatever reason, Calla Tuoleimi has always refused to jump. He used to think she was brainwashed by the palace's teachings, yet from what August had witnessed, Calla never regarded the palace's other rules that highly anyway. She would smuggle food to her attendants when she thought no one was watching; she would be handed the responsibility of sorting through petty theft charges in Er and shrug indifferently when whole piles of claims went missing. Her refusal to jump is a mystery, but August supposes it doesn't matter much. If one could get away with killing King Kasa by jumping into the throne room, he would have done it a long time ago. The king has Weisannas surrounding him at all times. The only solution would be jumping into Kasa himself and using Kasa's own hands to take a knife to his throat, but August doubts even he has that ability.

"It won't work," August says again. "Nothing will, except the plan we started with: Calla winning the games and brought in to greet a willing king."

They won't be expecting her. With her face obscured by a mask, she presents as just another one of the masses. And as far as the rest of San-Er is concerned, Princess Calla Tuoleimi is dead. Number Fifty-Seven is only an extremely rule-abiding civilian who has played heartily for the kingdom's greatest monetary prize.

The marketplace outside hushes in volume, more of its groups ushered away to make space. Galipei taps his fingers on the armrest, mulling over the matter. August, on the other hand, has already considered it thoroughly. He has pondered every angle and come to one conclusion.

"She's going to disobey me. I know my cousin."

Galipei looks up sharply. His jaw tightens. "Do you want me to put a stop to it?"

After a pause, August nods.

⬦⬦⬦⬦

In synchrony, Calla's and Anton's wristbands begin to tremble.

They jump up from the shop stoop they were resting on, weapons raised in seconds, looking around wildly. But there is nothing on their screens. No directions, no display of how far away the approaching player is. Both wristbands shake against their skin, first at a light scale, then so vigorously that Calla wants to tear the thing off.

"Finally," Anton says. "I was starting to think these things were broken—"

"Anton, to the right!"

Calla rushes forward to block the hammer from swinging down on him. The player appeared out of nowhere, leaping off the second-floor balcony that juts out above the shop. With a vehement push, she deflects the hit, the blade of her sword whistling through the air when she brings the weapon close to her chest again. A breath in; Anton is getting into stance again. She throws a glance back, and with a single nod, he darts left, knives going up as Calla ducks low, rushing for the other player's legs. She cannot remember the other numbers that are left. Number Thirty-Three? Number Fifteen?

The hammer comes down, and Calla allows the hit to land, catching her hard in the shoulder so that Anton has an opening to push a knife into the player's back. The player grunts, folding down where the wound was made. Calla's entire right arm has gone numb, but it's easy to transfer her sword into her left hand, easy to make a cut—albeit clumsier than usual—and fold the player at the knee by opening a gash in his thigh.

"Throat," Calla wheezes. "The throat."

Anton cuts the man's throat. Blood spurts wide, dotting his face and decorating Calla's neck like abstract art. The player gives his last exhale, pitching onto his side. Calla releases her breath too.

"That was close," Anton remarks. "They're getting too fast."

"We're almost at the end," Calla replies tiredly, closing her eyes to rest. They sting terribly, as if they had dried out completely in the span of that fight. "It makes sense that the best players have made it to this point."

"How did he last so long with a hammer? How do you kill with—*augh!*"

Calla's eyes fly open at Anton's sudden muffled shout. She blinks to clear her eyes, right in time to catch someone hauling Anton off, a cloth clamped over his mouth and an arm around his middle.

"Anton!"

A hard thud lands at the back of her own head. And without any chance to fight, Calla crashes to the ground, her forehead smacking concrete.

◇◇◇◇

Her eyelids flutter open slowly. They're as heavy as steel, heavier than if something had sealed them shut.

Calla coughs. She manages to turn onto her side, one of her hands snapping forward and splashing into a dirty puddle. The other stays splayed underneath her, gripping the concrete. She is exactly where she fell, or perhaps two feet to the left. Some passerby probably kicked her out of the way when she was blocking the path.

Her head is ringing.

Anton. Where is Anton?

Calla scrambles upright, her lungs burning with effort. She releases another cough, and then she cannot stop, as if all the weight in her chest is trying to make its way out. She tries to recall what she saw in that flash of a second before Anton was grabbed. Someone tall, clothed well. A thick jacket, purchased with good coin.

A palace hire. It has to be.

She turns out of the alley and onto a minutely wider street. A man with a flour sack over his shoulder shuffles aside when she pushes by, then almost misses his next step when he turns to look at her. It takes Calla a second to attribute his reaction to the blood she has dripping off her body. Her collar is soaked. As are her fingers, stained in red up to her wrists. How long was she knocked out for? Surely no more than half an hour, since the metallic stickiness has not yet dried. Surely not long enough for Anton to be in serious trouble.

Her fear, in honesty, is not that he's in trouble. Her fear is that they did not take him to kill him, but to save him. To keep him alive until the other players are eliminated, so that Calla has no option but to fight him in the arena, so that Calla cannot yank him by the sleeve and hide him, store him somewhere safe while she rips King Kasa apart.

"I know this is your doing, August," Calla mutters under her breath. She draws her sword despite the crowded streets, making her way toward the palace. "This is your doing, and you will answer for it."

The civilians of San-Er notice her and start to scramble away. She is a sight: she looks exactly as she does on the reels. Now that the games are winding down and so few players are left, there's no purpose to being subtle anymore, no purpose slinking around the cities in fear of an encounter. Everyone should see her. Everyone should shrink out of her way and out of her path.

Calla's eyes lock on the dental shop to her left. She pauses quickly, then tries to play off the moment as if she's eyeing the dentures in the window display. It isn't the dentures that caught her attention. It is the flash that came off the reflection.

Calla ducks fast. The throwing star embeds into the window instead of her head, fracturing the glass. In seconds, another joins it, and Calla whirls around, her heart thudding at her throat. Her sword is already drawn. She merely needs to lift it while she searches the startled crowd.

Where is the attack coming from? Calla's grip tightens on her sword. She isn't sure if there are three players left or four. If it's three, then they're closing in on the very end of the games.

Instead of searching for the combatant player in the crowd and taking the risk, she turns on her heel and starts to run in the other direction.

The throwing stars follow her immediately, one skimming her arm, one slicing along her boot, and another barely missing her square in the back as she swings around a corner and flattens against the wall. For a perilous moment, she can't see anything, dropped into darkness under a drove of drying laundry. Then her eyes adjust to the alley light, and Calla inches her head slowly around the corner again.

This time, she doesn't have to search for her combatant. A woman steps into view in the middle of the road, waiting to be sighted. She smiles and gives a small wave.

"What the fuck?" Calla mutters beneath her breath.

The woman doesn't move.

Slowly, Calla inches out from the alley. "What do you want?" she calls over.

The woman doesn't say anything. She waves again, but this time with her other arm, revealing her wristband, which shines with 12 on the digital screen. Streams of people flow around her on the street because of her inertness, but she doesn't notice. They grumble and shuffle; they exclaim, *Hey, can you not block the path?* but the woman only stares at Calla, and when Calla takes another step forward, she sees the woman's eyes.

Weisanna silver.

With a gasp, she pivots fast and tries to run again, but the woman is too close. No more throwing stars—the woman simply pounces on Calla's back and slams her down, knocking into a little wooden stool that some street seller has left behind.

"Kill me," the woman hisses. "Kill me, and play the games right."

Calla kicks away, flipping off her stomach. Just as fast, the woman has her pinned again, knees on her legs and knuckles gripping her shoulders ferociously. The pain is agonizing, pressing bruises into her body. When Calla cranes her neck, trying to lift her head away from the sharp gravel, she spots a surveillance camera above them, and another not three paces away. The people want their show. The reels want to capture every final hit.

"I don't know if it's you, Galipei," Calla spits, "but this is fucked."

"Kill me," the woman wails, as if she didn't hear Calla at all. Her hands come around Calla's throat in one fast motion, fingers pressed around her windpipe. Though this is a scheme, though Calla *knows* that August has decided to interfere, panic slams into her bones, her tongue restricting and her lungs begging for air.

Pinpricks of purple dance in her vision. No one comes to her aid, not a single one among the hundreds in the vicinity. They watch her like there is a screen between them. They watch her like this is already a program on replay, stored in the video companies' data systems and ready to be spun around again when a new customer makes the purchase.

Calla stretches for her sword. Her fingers make contact with the grip. And on her last snatch of consciousness, she makes the plunge, shoving the blade into the woman's side.

The woman stiffens. Her head jerks up, her iron grip around Calla's throat loosening. There is only satisfaction in the woman's expression. This was exactly what she wanted.

Calla pushes the woman off, the tail end of a cry caught in her bruised throat. She's not surprised when a blinding light pierces the space before her, darting into the crowd. She's not surprised when the woman sprawls onto the gravel, head lolling up to the sky, and in death, shows eyes that are dark brown instead of silver.

"Please," Calla whispers. "Please, don't be—"

Her wristband begins to whine. The moment the sound echoes into the night, she knows the plea is for naught. It is the same sharp, dissonant tone played in unison every year, broadcast directly from the palace, interrupting the television programs and news anchors to bring its important message.

The announcement of the last two finalists. The games have reached the Juedou, the grand finale.

She looks at her wristband screen. The text runs slowly, as if to emphasize every word. Across every screen in San-Er, stills of Anton and Calla appear side by side, along with their numbers.

Congratulations, 57! Your competitor is number 86. Please proceed to the coliseum immediately.

"No!" Calla drops her head into her hands. *"Fuck."*

CHAPTER 29

The coliseum looms ahead of her. The longer she stares at it, the more it blurs into some abstract shape, losing all meaning. Its lights are on their highest setting; its crowds are already gathered thickly, the rumble of conversation audible even at a distance.

One foot in front of the other. One cut after the other. That is all that needs to be done. It is all that can be done.

Calla takes a shaky breath. She presses into the crowd, stepping through the coliseum gates and merging into the audience. They don't pay attention to her, not looking closely enough to realize she's one of the very players they are waiting for. She pushes forward. Keeps pushing until she has approached the ropes delineating the boundary between spectator and player.

Calla's hands touch the velvet. It feels as clammy as death.

In one swift movement, she ducks underneath and is on the other side, the sheath of her sword clattering against her leg. Without the stalls, the coliseum looks absolutely vast in size, her footprints in the rough dirt appearing like specks in the gargantuan battleground. She is a lone figure, half her face masked and the other half squinting furiously up at the palace, circled on all sides by spectators.

Calla is at an impasse with herself.

King Kasa must die, and she will not gain access to him unless she is the victor of this battle.

There can be only one victor, but she doesn't want to kill Anton.

With every cell of this forsaken, stolen body, she doesn't want to kill Anton.

The palace balcony stirs with movement. Calla strides forward. It feels as though the whole coliseum is leaning in her direction, as if the structure itself shifts with her every step. She knows it is the people, that their attention and movement make it seem like the walls are bearing down on her, but nevertheless, she fantasizes about the coliseum growing legs and running off, taking its arena and its vicious games along with it.

Calla comes to a stop below the balcony. Seconds later, August steps out and leans over.

"Hello," he calls down.

"What have you done?" Calla asks furiously.

August splays his hands flat on the balcony rail. He looks so much like a diplomat prince, his hair shining under the light, his white robes with nary a stain upon them. Beneath him, Calla might as well be a peasant again, slammed right back into the body of the girl the rest of the kingdom—including herself—has forgotten about. Her hands are bloody; her forehead is bruised. Her hair is a mess, as is her clothing, ripped and torn and disheveled.

"What is more important to you, Calla?" he asks. "Your lover or the kingdom?"

Calla doesn't say anything.

"You cannot answer me," August continues. "So I chose for you."

He points forward. Calla whirls around. From the farthest end of the coliseum, a figure ducks under the velvet ropes, looking dazed. Calla almost doesn't recognize Anton, but then he stumbles closer, and she identifies him by the jacket he was wearing earlier in the day.

Anton throws a hand up over his eyes, adjusting to the lights of the arena. Bruises mar the skin along his cheek and down his jaw. Though he continues forward, looking like he can barely comprehend where he is and how he got there, he does draw his knives, pulling them from his jacket.

"Ask yourself, cousin." August's voice floats down more softly now, each word delivered like gentle poison. "If you refuse to kill him, will he refuse to kill you? Was winning for Otta important enough to risk both your lives?"

He steps back, receding into the balcony's shadows. Though he doesn't say it aloud, his unspoken question reaches her all the same.

All this time, has Otta been more important to him than you?

Calla clenches her fists. She starts to stride forward, toward the center of the arena.

"WELCOME," a voice booms across the coliseum. She doesn't know where it's coming from. She doesn't know whose voice it is, only that it must be accompanying the reels, broadcast out to every viewer who cannot bear witness in person. "WELCOME TO THE FINAL ARENA BATTLE. NUMBER FIFTY-SEVEN. NUMBER EIGHTY-SIX. PREPARE YOURSELVES."

From the other end of the arena, Anton begins to move at a quicker pace. His expression is stricken, brows knitted together in bewilderment. He waits until he and Calla are close. Then, he halts where he stands, raising his arms as if to indicate surrender.

"Princess," he calls, and Calla curses him: curses him in the name of every old god, because even looking at him makes her flesh and blood and guts hurt like they are being strewn apart. It doesn't take a blade to carve open a heart. It only takes a soft glance.

"They took you," Calla says. Her voice cracks. She has to shout to be heard, voice muffled through her mask, but her volume doesn't matter. The rest of the coliseum can't hear her, words drowned by the vast space and stamped into the red dirt before it reverberates outward. "They took you, and I couldn't stop them."

Anton shakes his head. There's a faint purple imprint across his neck, like the burn of rope, marking him alongside the rough scratches on his cheek. They must have tied a bag around his head to prevent him from jumping until they brought him to the Juedou. They must have planned this with every intention of forcing her hand.

"It doesn't matter." Anton surges forward. "Calla, we can leave. We can cut a line right through the crowd, run for the wall, and leave."

Bitter anger crawls up her throat. He should have pulled the chip from his wristband and exited the games before they ended up here, head-to-head in the arena. Because he knows that she can't leave. She will not leave before her task is complete.

"BEGIN THE FINAL BATTLE."

"It's too late, Anton," Calla says, and she draws her sword. "It's too late for us."

Something is breaking in her chest. By every known rule, qi is as incorporeal as light, too sacrosanct to be felt by the ordinary human, known only in concept and never in perception. But at that moment, Calla thinks she can feel hers. Her qi splitting into two, becoming two separate beings with two separate souls. One half is an inferno, a deep, visceral rage that has been burning since Talin rode into her village. The flames fuel her bones, breathe life into the first inhale she takes every morning. The other half is a lonely breeze. It searches for a distraction, an oasis, an escape. It doesn't want to save the world; it wants more moments in the dark of night, staring at the neon that streams through the gaps of the blinds, held in someone's arms.

Calla swings. Anton shouts out, like he hadn't expected she would actually do it. Like he can't comprehend that they are fighting—truly fighting, witnessed by thousands upon thousands who scream for blood to be spilled, who scream to satiate a different hunger in their stomachs.

"This isn't the only way," Anton says. His words come short, his breath winded as he blocks Calla's next swing. She had been aiming for his ribs, but with his quick block, she only cuts a shallow surface wound. Nevertheless, the draw of first blood is enough to send a roar through the crowd. "We don't have to play by their rules."

"We *do*." Calla grits her jaw tight, her teeth ringing when metal clangs against metal, her sword colliding with the bend where Anton's two curved knives meet.

She pulls back and kicks out, but Anton only meets her with defense, grasping her ankle and throwing her off-balance. Calla falls, elbows colliding with the brittle dirt for the barest second before she rolls up again, both hands around the grip of her sword. One inhale. Forward. Exhale. Lunge to the left. Anton stops when she stops, attacks when she attacks, but with every clang of metal, Calla hears August's voice curling in and out of her ear, tainting her thoughts. She can't stop fighting now.

Anton blocks her hit, angling her sword down. In the process, his knives slash the back of her arms, and Calla cries out, almost dropping her weapon when a deep cut tears through her jacket and blood appears.

"Calla, there will be no end to this," he heaves. "Look at us. We've fought before. We are evenly matched. We will both be dead by the day's end."

I know, Calla thinks. *You will die. But once King Kasa is dealt with, I'll follow you.*

"I love you," Calla says aloud. She swings her sword even harder. She breaks through the block that Anton makes with his knives and cuts at his thigh. The gash opens deep. "I love you, so this is a favor to you. I will spare you from having to land the blow on me. I will take the burden."

Anton's lips thin. Though the arena is uproarious and overspilling with havoc, Calla catches the exact moment that his eyes darken.

345

"That's ridiculous," he spits. "You take no burden. Kill me, Calla, but tell the truth. Kill me because you love your kingdom more."

Calla stills. Anton moves, and she almost crumples to her knees, taking the cut right across her chest. He controlled his attack. It wasn't meant to be a killing blow; it was only meant to hurt.

"You don't know what you're talking about," she says.

Anton makes another cut. He asks, "What has Talin ever done for you?" This attempt, at least, Calla swivels from, letting her jacket take most of the blade. The omnipresent voice of the coliseum has risen in volume as it narrates the fight. "Why does it deserve your love?"

"It doesn't have to do anything for me." Calla's breath is turning shallow. She is tiring. But she can find an opening. She knows she can. Every opponent has a weak point, the palace used to tell her. They'll show their hand at one point or another, peeling apart their shields to welcome a killing blow. "Love isn't deserved. It is given freely."

Anton's eyes flicker up. He looks at the palace, at the glorious structure that looms above them in the darkness, backlit by the glow of the coliseum.

"My dear princess," he says. "You fight to change who sits on the throne. But I'm afraid that will not achieve what you think it might."

Perhaps it will not be so easy once King Kasa is gone. Nevertheless, it is a start. It is more than anyone else in San-Er has ever managed to do.

Calla leans back, putting weight onto her heels. This time, she doesn't lunge immediately. She follows Anton's gaze, sighting August at the edge of the balcony again. He rests his elbows on the railing, shoulders braced in tension, hands clasped together. He is waiting. Waiting for Calla to finish what she said she would. What she promised she would.

Calla turns around. She blocks August from her sight.

She drops her sword.

"I can't do this," she rasps. Tears flood her eyes, more tears than she has let herself cry in years. They drop down her face in abundance, flowing with all the sorrow that has been tamped down.

The audience is stirring in commotion. Spectators push against the velvet rope, leaning as close as they dare to get, trying to catch whatever words are being exchanged. From above, Calla thinks she sights motion: cameras, flown overhead for the reels. She blocks it out. She blocks all of it out and sinks to her knees, too exhausted to hold herself upright.

Anton's knives fall from his hands. He comes forward—slowly, gingerly— until he is directly before her. Both of them are stained with blood, old and fresh.

"Calla," he says, kneeling as well. His arms come forward to wrap around her. Calla leans in, and the arena, the broadcast, the constant hum of the twin cities—everything fades away. She clutches at him and lets herself have that second, that moment of reprieve, her cheek resting on the warmth of his shoulder.

"It's okay." He presses his lips to her ear. "I believe in us. I believe there's another way out."

Calla exhales shakily, her hand tracing down his spine. All these years, hiding in the dark corners of San-Er, she has never been looking for a way out: she has been looking for a way back in.

"Anton," she whispers. Every opponent has a weak point, the palace used to tell her. "I'm sorry."

Here was what they taught her next. How to reach the heart from behind, so long as the blade is long enough.

She lets her dagger fall from her sleeve. She plunges the blade in.

The dagger sinks to the hilt, and Calla draws away.

Anton does not move. His expression is shocked, frozen, but he does not look surprised. He must have known that this is who he chose to love. He must have known when he first watched her play in the games, unsympathetic toward those who fell to her sword. He must have known when he learned of her true identity, because a past like that requires vengeance, carves a hole too deep to fill with anything less than rivers of blood.

"Calla," he says again. This time, the pain in his voice cuts Calla deeper than any dagger through the back could, but she bears it, she bears it as his breathing shortens, as his eyes lift and desperately seek some sort of help.

None is coming.

"I'm sorry," she whispers. Her hands clutch at his sides, at the red stain that spreads and spreads and spreads. "I'm sorry, I'm so sorry."

Anton's eyes close. For a second, he seems to have stilled, rendered into a statue. Then he sways, and when Calla catches him, holding his head toward her, his breathing has already stopped.

"Anton."

Calla sets him down. She acts in a daze. For several long seconds, she puts her hand on his chest, believing that he must be feigning the act. But the gray pallor is already setting in, the stiffness of a body with its qi extinguished.

Anton Makusa is dead. She's truly killed him.

All around her, the coliseum starts to cheer, first at a humble magnitude, then growing to a fever pitch. They clutch one another and scream at the top of their lungs, delirious with the finality of the games. The Juedou has been won. The king's games have a victor.

Number Fifty-Seven, the star of the scoreboards.

Calla cannot catch her breath. She can only close her eyes, feeling the weight of the world crushing down on her shoulders.

They cheer for Fifty-Seven, the final survivor among a crowd of eighty-eight, all of whom have given their lives for this very moment. They scream praises for the spectacle that helps them forget everything else in San-Er, the player covered in blood who kneels before them in penance.

The crowds do not know. They cheer and they cheer, thinking this is simply another year of the games come to a close. A coldness sinks into Calla's bones.

A sheet of invisible steel, plating over her heart, over her chest, building her up for one final strike. The crowds do not lose their exuberance; the noise only grows when Calla staggers upright, somehow managing to stand steady on feet she cannot feel.

They don't know that they are cheering for their lost princess, the cause of Er's worst bloodbath, returned to finish her violence.

Calla's eyes snap open, glowing royal yellow.

CHAPTER 30

Everything happens as if she's in a dream.

And she has dreamed about this, again and again. It proceeds just as she imagined it. The guards come into the arena, making a path for her up to the Palace of Union. They stretch their arms out, directing her forward, then through the doors, up the stairs of the main wing. The inside of the palace unfolds for her. Golden walls, gilded banisters. Whole rooms that are larger than some school buildings, turrets that climb up to the skies. Her shoes come down on the plush carpet. Her blood-matted hair curls around her shoulders. They always let the victors meet the king in their slovenly state immediately after the final match, as if to emphasize the brutality of the games. King Kasa wants to see how his people have bled for him in appreciation for his patronage.

They open the doors to a hall. A long table has been set out: a full banquet with people already milling about in the corners, some seated in their chairs.

Calla doesn't see August anywhere. She does see Galipei, standing by the corner, eyeing her as she comes in. Her mask remains clasped around her nose and mouth, though the fabric is unsavory now, stained and dirtied. If she removes it, King Kasa might recognize her face, so she does not risk it. She stands in the room and waits.

Waits for the moment the other doors open and King Kasa sweeps in, his crown fixed atop his head.

Calla's next breath stops in her nose, burning when she refuses to exhale it back out. He looks older than she remembers—sickly, unwell. She cannot believe that one person can represent so much: one man who looks like he could keel over at any moment stands as the source of this kingdom's suffering.

"This year's victor," King Kasa declares, his voice echoing through the banquet hall and sending his other guests into a hush. "I looked at your file just now. Number Fifty-Seven, Chami Xikai. How does it feel to have made it so far?"

Calla needs a moment before she can think up a worthy response. "Like everything I've ever desired."

King Kasa chuckles. He waves at the guards by the wall, and it is Galipei who comes forward, Galipei who is holding a clipboard, handing it to the king.

"Your prize," King Kasa says. "Once you accept, the banquet may begin. All in celebration of you."

"Thank you," Calla says blankly.

King Kasa extends the clipboard. With his other hand, he reaches out to shake. Calla reaches forward to meet his hand, her grip firm and unyielding.

When King Kasa begins to pull away, she does not let go. When he tries again, her free hand reaches across her body and draws her sword from its sheath.

"Uncle," she says. "You don't recognize me?"

King Kasa's eyes widen, but by then she has slashed: one solid arc, a hearty knock of metal meeting bone. His head falls, landing some distance away from his body, then rolling toward the banquet table, sending the elites screaming in absolute terror as they shoot to their feet.

His body slumps down. The neck continues to spurt blood like some decorative scarlet fountain.

Calla knows that she should feel more in this moment. Some sense of victory; everything that she has been working toward for years, fulfilled.

But she only feels empty.

Calla looks up. Galipei is still staring at her with no particular expression on his face, making no move to wipe at the blood splattered down his front. What is there to do now? She can only wait for his move, wait for him to put a stop to the screaming that echoes and echoes through the banquet hall.

"Seize her," Galipei finally commands to the other guards in the room. There's not a single note of conviction in the instruction, but the guards don't particularly care. They are only relieved to have something to do while the banquet hall is in pandemonium, and the guards rush to flock her, to push her arms behind her back.

She doesn't struggle as they take her away. She turns over her shoulder, watching the puddle of blood spread larger and larger. This is the last outward conquest King Kasa will ever make: the spirit of his life, soaking into the threads of his delicate carpeting.

If Calla had the capacity for it, she might laugh. One swing of her sword. One measly little swing.

She can hardly believe that regicide was the easiest part of all this.

◇◇◇◇◇

Somewhere in San, there is a disturbance in the hospital morgue.

They put a flatlined patient in here earlier, shoved her with the rest of the dead until the bodies could be processed and incinerated. They thought nothing of it, didn't assign a nurse to check why the body looked like it was still burning from the inside out, though it had been going through the yaisu sickness for seven years now—shouldn't it have long finished? What had life support been doing?

With a shudder and a wave of qi, Otta Avia opens her eyes to the world again. All the glass in the morgue shatters; all the nearby bodies implode and splatter blackened guts on the wall. At the very center of the gory scene, Otta bolts upright on her gurney, heaving a desperate breath.

The nurses who run in almost drop into a faint. They look at Otta in shock. They hardly believe it when she opens her mouth to speak.

"The palace," Otta croaks, trembling in her thin gown. "Take me to the Palace of Earth. *Now.*"

CHAPTER 31

The cell door rattles loudly, stirring Calla from her sleep. Blearily, she turns toward the bars, rubbing her eyes until the world clears. Reality comes barreling back. The arena. Anton. King Kasa, his head rolling away so easily.

Calla closes her eyes again, trying to grasp the last remnants of the sleep she has emerged from. The world was brighter there. If she falls back into the dream now, maybe she won't feel this agony clawing at her chest. Maybe she would feel less cold, could stop shivering from her very soul.

Shoes click into the cell, then the rustle of clothing. Fingertips, padding lightly at her shoulder, giving her a firm shake.

"Princess Calla, would you kindly awaken?"

"No," Calla murmurs. Her voice scratches at her throat.

"You are needed," Galipei continues. "I don't want to have to drag you."

Slowly, reluctantly, Calla lets the cell take shape around her again, eyeing the gray walls and the single lightbulb on the low ceiling. "I was dreaming."

"Dreaming?" Galipei looks around too. His uniform is crisp, the collar ironed and pressed cleanly to his neck. No one could have known it was slathered in blood the previous day. "About what?"

Calla swallows hard. Afar, some other cell is being drawn open, the metallic clank of its bars echoing loudly in the underground space.

"I dreamt there was an emperor Anton," she whispers, almost incoherently. The wisps of the dream come back to her in a haze of colors, in jewels and thrones and golden-wrought crowns. "Let me slumber once more, to see him."

"All right. Up we get."

Galipei yanks her arm and tugs her out of the prison bed. She stumbles after him without much resistance, one foot after the other as they pass the other cells, the other prisoners in their shabby rags and chained ankles. They don't bother shouting after her when she walks by. They have been exhausted into submission, nothing but piles of bones collapsed at the foot of a bed or atop the dirty sheets, staring with empty eyes. Will August let them out? Will August start liberation from within the palace first, or will he stretch out into the provinces, starting at the edges before sweeping back into San-Er?

Calla stumbles on the steps leading up to the exit.

"Hey, hey," Galipei exclaims immediately. "Don't try any funny business."

"Why would I?" Calla replies warily, straightening and finding her footing again. She dusts her hands off. "I thought August only needed me in here until he took power."

"Well, yes," Galipei mutters. He shoots a look over his shoulder, then continues hurrying her along. "I've just never seen you stumble before. Forgive me if my suspicions were raised."

They emerge from the passage, walking through a set of doors that the palace guards hold open, eyes trained on Calla as she's pulled along. Aboveground now, she winces against the light. Brightness shines through a palace window, leaving a four-panel design on the red carpet. Under Calla's heavy shoes, the flooring feels like it might give way. Like she could stomp a little too hard, and the soft padding might split in two, breaking a hole through the palace so she falls all the way down.

"There's a first time for everything," Calla says quietly, and she wishes the palace *would* crumble beneath her feet. The ground ought to do her a favor, open a hole and swallow her up, crush her lungs until she stops breathing, plug up her nose and mouth with rubble and dust. King Kasa is dead. Her role in this is fulfilled. The exit light of her world is flashing, blinking neon like the ones that light every hospital corridor. She's ready to join the lover she put in the grave.

Calla's hand twitches as she continues to follow Galipei. *Not here,* she decides, easing her fingers away from her body. She swallows and moves her tongue to rest at the bottom of her mouth too, away from her sharp teeth, the veins there throbbing as if they know how easily she could bite them open.

When August is crowned, he will free her. She'll leave the twin cities, keep walking to the edges of Talin until she sees the true sea. She doesn't want the rocky shores in San-Er. Elsewhere, they have talked of sand and smooth, polished stone. There, she can have her choice. She could spill her own blood, run a blade down her arm and let the beaches run with red until a gradient spreads along the golden sand. She could sweep out with the water, wash away into the wide, open world. It doesn't matter how. As long as it takes her. As long as it brings her to Anton.

Galipei stops before a wide set of doors, knocking once. Before Calla can search her memory for which part of the palace this is and who he's taking her to see, the doors have already opened. A dozen palace servants stand inside, towels and clothes clutched and readied in their hands. They pull her into the room, their grips firm, muttering amid themselves.

Calla lets them examine her without protest. August must have seized power by now, must have sent instructions through the palace to prepare for the crowning ceremony, inviting San-Er's civilians to come witness a new divine choosing when the crown is set on his head. The people inside the palace have always been loyal to him anyway. There couldn't possibly have been any dissent. She wonders if he has also confirmed her return.

"So this is Princess Calla," one of the servants says. There's her answer. Of course he would have jumped to the announcement, to assure the people that this violence could only be expected of someone who was already an outlaw. "She looks half-dead."

A brave soul, to say so in Calla's presence. Or perhaps the elderly woman who spoke has no hesitation because it is the truth: Calla barely has the strength to stand upright, never mind take offense.

"That's her own fault. We didn't do anything to her down there," Galipei replies. His hand lifts, then pauses in hesitation. A beat later, he sets it down on Calla's shoulder. "His Highness wants her ready in an hour. Can you get it done?"

The servant huffs a breath. "Yes. That's not a concern."

Galipei removes his hand. He clears his throat, as if to confirm with Calla that he shall step back now, but Calla doesn't turn nor look at him at all. Soon his footsteps thud away, and Calla only eyes the woman standing before her. She is short and stout, white hair pulled in a tight knot. When she grabs Calla by the wrist, her hold is surprisingly sturdy.

The other servants part to make way as Calla is pushed into the wide bathing hall. They fan out to run the faucets, powder the clothes, activate the steam. They sidestep and charge ahead, quiet when they need to be and yelling instructions back and forth on matters that need deliberation. Calla is passed around: one station to the other, clothes peeled off and skin scrubbed until she's red. She tries to take in their faces without letting them blur together, but there's something about the palace uniform that muddles the servants together. If they cannot stand apart from each other, they cannot lose their life with one mistake. When August moves onto the throne, will he tear down the palace? Dismiss the palace servants, give them new jobs, tell the councilmembers that no one will wait on them any longer inside these walls, that they must learn to wipe their own dirty behinds?

Maybe she's giving August too much credit. She can't imagine what his next move is. Perhaps she should have asked, but the two of them were so intent on their one mutual goal—King Kasa dead and gone—that it hardly seemed to matter what would come next.

Maybe that *was* a mistake.

Calla winces suddenly, one of the cleaning rags digging hard into her shoulder blade. The servant doesn't pause, even when Calla glares up at her. They don't fear her. They see the dried blood in the lines of her hands and dotting the edges of her collarbone and wipe it away without blinking.

"This way, Princess."

The old servant has returned, directing the others. Wrapped in robes, Calla is pushed out of the bathing hall and into the room, shoved in front of a long, glimmering mirror. The glass is clear enough that every mote of dust in the room is visible in the reflection, haloing around her head as she disturbs the chair cushion. She hardly recognizes herself—if this body has ever been recognizable. These sharp cheeks and deep-yellow eyes. Surrounded by an overabundance of red curtains and golden statues along the walls. Calla glides her hands along the smooth wood of the vanity table and marvels at the heaviness of the furniture, like she is eight years old again and newly in the palace, wanting to keep up the pretense of being a princess but unable to push back the astonishment that gnaws like a sickness in her throat. She runs her bare foot along the plush rectangular rug that hems the room, burying her toes into the threads while they tear her wet hair into shape, untangling the knots and dried blood clots by simply ripping them out.

The elderly servant clears her throat.

"In the palace here," she says, speaking to Calla properly now, "we had given you an alias. That way, the king would not know we were discussing you, discussing Er's downfall and how it would take so little to bring San into the same fate." She takes ahold of Calla's hair and begins to braid, wrapping a loose chain through the dark strands as she goes. The metal glimmers in the mirror, shining with hidden gems.

"*Glory of Her Father,*" she continues. "As far as King Kasa knew, it was some village girl from the folktales whom the poor servants loved dearly. A country girl who had performed filial deeds and would be remembered forever. Remember Glory of Her Father. Remember her sacrifice. Remember that we must keep going and going until she returns. The elites in the palace thought you were some god, some minor deity we prayed to on our shrines. But you were out there, real and pumping with blood, lurking within the city."

Calla tries to nudge the braid when the servant pins it atop her head, but the woman tuts and flicks her hand away, then secures the circular loop from the base of her skull to the top of her forehead.

"I took a sword to my father," Calla replies quietly. "It was no glory to him when I forcibly removed his life and his power."

"It was not your father you brought glory to. It was your fatherland. Your kingdom. Talin. You did what we needed."

The servant takes a step back. The others bustling around her pause too, admiring the crown of hair that has been pulled up, not a single strand out of place. Calla closes her fist in the folds of the robes, scrunching the fabric into her fingers. What would happen if they knew? That her father was not her father at all, that their king in Er was no one to her, that the fire burning in her chest had first been set ablaze in a starving, rotting village out in the farthest reaches of Talin?

They would find her less brave, certainly. If they knew that she was no royal who went against her blood, only a country girl who had found power and seized it without mercy. They would think it was her duty, that any person in her position should have done the very same.

The servant brings a small brush near Calla's face, dabbing at her pale cheek. "Do you have any suggestions?"

It takes Calla a moment to realize that the woman is referring to the cosmetics. Brushes and powders have been brought near and within her reach.

"What's the point?" Calla asks dully. Her voice still scratches at her throat. "I gather no one is looking at me."

"On the contrary, everyone will be looking at you."

They spritz something into her face. She shuts her eyes. She can't let the tears start running again, or they might never stop.

"There is no need to use an alias anymore," the servant says softly. Her voice is almost drowned out by the chatter behind her, by the heavy swishing of curtains as they are drawn back. "Every wing of this palace is filled with talk about the princess. Or rather, no one is calling you a princess anymore."

The brush presses in hard. Calla welcomes it. The sting goes right down to bone, tingling with a chill.

"And what do they call me?"

Her cheek smarts from the pressure. There has been a decorative design drawn in, a whorl moving from the line of her jaw to the side of her brow. When she opens her eyes, she's staring at someone else in the mirror, at a Calla who was never exiled from Er, at a Calla who spent the last five years within these walls, surrounded by opulence and molded into the image of power.

The servant's hands close in on her shoulders. She presses down, gripping at skin that has already been rubbed raw.

"*King-Killer*," she hisses. "Live up to it."

Quicker than a blink, they have Calla up again, shoved into a shirt made of white silk and pants made of something that looks like the unpolluted night sky. Three corridors, four, five—one corner bend, two small staircases, and then a door, arched with a golden frame that ends a hairsbreadth away from the ceiling. They push in, and the throne room unveils before her, clustered with knickknacks and swirling with a breeze from the open balcony doors.

It was foolish of Calla to think that she might have been able to gain access to this room if the palace was distracted by the arena. It would have been an impossibility. As August said, there was never any alternative to the plan they had started with, the plan they have executed.

Calla walks in. They gave her new boots, smaller than the ones she wore before. Her steps are more delicate. Outside the balcony, the masses have already gathered. She can hear them calling for August, shouting their blessings.

"August?"

She searches the room once over. She misses him at first. He stands at the far side, almost in the corner, staring at an oil painting hanging from the shimmering wallpaper. It's not until Calla does a second scan that she catches sight of his golden-robed back, blending in with the rest of the room.

There's no doubt that he is royalty. There's no doubt that he belongs here, no matter where his birth put him.

"Princess," someone whispers over her shoulder, and Calla turns around. The servant nods at her and indicates his hands, where a headdress awaits on a pillow—the king's crown. The divine right of kings: nothing but two twined prongs of metal. If there's supposed to be an exorbitant amount of qi inside this crown to choose its ruler, Calla cannot feel it at all.

"August," Calla prompts again. She wants this done. She wants him crowned and declared, so he can pardon her and she can be freed from these games, freed from San-Er, freed from Talin. They call her King-Killer and ask her to live up to it, but she already has. August is the most fit to rule. Calla has done her part. She will give him the power he needs to fix this kingdom.

August steps away from the painting. He clasps his hands behind his back, then turns in a quick pivot, eyes snapping to meet hers across the throne room. She expected glee. She expected pride. Instead, when their gazes collide, she finds barely concealed fury, and it is potent enough that Calla jolts from the fog in her head to wonder if she has done something wrong.

Before she can ask, August has already walked up to her, his expression smoothed over. His forehead is dusted in gold, his black eyes appearing as two colorless voids. Maybe Calla is imagining it. She's hardly in the right state of mind.

"Are you ready?" she asks.

"Ready."

Calla bites down hard on her teeth. Releases her breath. "Very well."

She steps onto the balcony first, and the crowd stirs with vigor. Calla tries not to flinch at the attention. It is sundown, the skies colored with an orange glow—rare these days, with the clouds so thick. Each civilian below is cast in a strange tinge, like their skin is on fire, the entire crowd one match strike away from combustion.

August steps onto the balcony too, and then the crowd properly erupts. *August, August, August,* they chant, but amid it all, there is another name to be heard too. *Calla.*

Forget your name and adopt a title instead, Anton had said. Calla. Calla. Calla. *Soon people will be saying it as they whisper* God.

Calla shakes the thought away before it can haunt her.

I will beg your forgiveness in whatever afterlife awaits us, she thinks into the fading twilight. *Wait for me. I'll show myself the same violence if it puts us on even ground once more.*

Calla turns to the servant behind her and takes the crown off the pillow. It feels painfully cold to her fingers. Still, her grip is steady when she holds the crown high, when she sets it atop August's head.

The both of them pause in anticipation. They wait. For divine intervention, for lightning to strike down.

Nothing comes.

He's been accepted.

The crown has accepted Talin's newest ruler. Calla's breath comes out in one long exhale.

"The king is dead," she bellows to the crowd. Her voice doesn't waver. When she holds her hand out for August to take, he is prompt, putting his palm atop hers for her to raise high, high, high. "Long live the king!"

Long live the king, the crowd echoes back, and Calla thinks she hears it from behind too, from the servants awaiting in the throne room, from the guards stationed in the hallway outside. Again and again, they continue to repeat themselves: *Long live the king, long live the king, long live the king ten thousand years.*

"They will write this day into our history for a long time to come," Calla says quietly, speaking only to August as the crowd keeps chanting. "The day the palace finished flooding with blood and the adopted son rose from its guts."

The wind blows hard into her face. It curls against her neck, disturbing the hair that had been so painstakingly arranged.

"Yes," August says. Calla shoots a sharp look at him. This time, she knows she's not imagining things. She's not imagining the anger that accompanies the grip she feels closing on her palm.

"August." She winces, trying to move her hand.

"It will be remembered," he goes on, like he doesn't hear her. "And what fine daylight we have today to ensure its longevity in their memory."

Calla freezes. Her breath leaves her in a rush. Every muscle in her body locks, her mind stuttering to a complete and utter halt as the crowds shout their chorus below them. San-Er fades away, the calls and summons shrinking smaller and smaller until they are naught but a tinny whine. All she can feel is an immense pressure on her hand, tightening to a vise under her new king's grip.

Night is falling. Across the palace, the electric lights activate, each bulb blinking on one after the other. The crown glimmers. Its metal entwines with blond hair, making for a familiar sight. But then its wearer turns his head toward her, letting her catch his eyes at last—fully, properly.

It is not August Shenzhi, the rightful crown prince of San, that Calla has put on the throne.

It is Anton Makusa.

ACKNOWLEDGMENTS

I mmortal Longings is my first adult book, and it's also the first book I wrote as an adult—in my eyes, at least, because growing up is complicated and the line is somewhere ambiguously around turning twenty-one or graduating college or, I don't know, starting to talk about taxes for fun. So I want to begin by thanking the passage of time, which I am aware is an incredibly weird way to open my acknowledgments, but as much as I always bemoan being an adult because being an adult is hard, I needed this new life stage to write this book in particular.

Thank you to my agent, Laura Crockett, to whom this book is dedicated. For your belief in me when I was a teenager cold-querying into your inbox with a *Romeo & Juliet* retelling to your continued excitement down the line when I burst into your inbox with, "I think I have an *Antony & Cleopatra*–inspired trilogy . . ." It feels like so much has changed in these years between my young adult debut and my adult debut—in life and in publishing—but your support as my champion has never wavered.

Thank you, always, to Uwe Stender, Brent Taylor, and everyone at TriadaUS. Thank you to my editor, Amara Hoshijo, particularly for your incredible ability to read an incoherent sentence I've put down and somehow still understand what I'm saying to help me fix it. Thank you to the entire team at Saga and Gallery, especially Joe Monti, Lauren Carr, Bianca Ducasse, Tyrinne Lewis, Alexandre Su, Caroline Pallotta, Lisa Litwack, John Vairo, and Kathryn Kenney-Peterson. Thank you to the entire team at Hodder & Stoughton, especially Molly Powell, Natasha Qureshi, Kate Keehan, and Callie Robertson. Thank you to the entire team at Hachette Aotearoa New Zealand, especially Tania Mackenzie-Cooke and Sacha Beguely. Thank you too to every team in every country working on getting *Immortal Longings* onto the shelves. Also a big, big thank you to everyone who has left a fingerprint on this book in some way, because I just know that the curse of inevitably forgetting someone in your acknowledgments will get to me.

Thank you to my family and my friends, who are the joy that keep me going when my manuscripts are trying to go one-to-one with me in the fighting pit. (Which is a frequent occurrence.) And my cat, for inspiring Mao Mao. Thank you to booksellers and librarians and bookish advocates everywhere. Thank you to bloggers and bookstagrammers and BookTokers. Thank you to Halsey for writing "I am not a woman, I'm a god," and giving me a theme song that played on repeat while I was writing this book. Finally, thank you to my readers, whether you followed over from my young adult books or whether this is the first thing you've read from me. As always, I couldn't do it without you.

A CONVERSATION
WITH CHLOE GONG

The twin cities of San-Er, which serve as the backdrop to *Immortal Longings*, are inspired by 1990s Hong Kong's Kowloon Walled City. Can you tell us more about this place, which no longer exists, and how you came to learn of it?

I love working with historical eras that have a very specific feel to them, which probably comes as no surprise to readers familiar with my previous work. It was during one of my rabbit-hole-research dives in high school—probably me getting distracted from a class project, which happened often—that I first read about the Kowloon Walled City and learned that it had remained Chinese-governed territory even while Hong Kong at large was occupied by the British in the 20th century. The city was essentially lawless, because Chinese police couldn't enter and British police didn't care to, which led to the context for its infamously hazardous living conditions. (It also wasn't really a walled city for much of its existence since there was no wall, but the name stuck because the territory started as a Chinese military fort.) Without regulations, the slums grew denser and denser as buildings were haphazardly tacked on to support the growing population of the enclave. The Kowloon Walled City's boundaries were small, though, confining the whole territory to 2.7 hectares—meaning there was only so much it could expand before sunlight no longer penetrated to the ground and every street became a tiny alley. At one point, it was the densest city in the world, yet despite the criminal activity and squalor, accounts say there was a real sense of community among the people there who were living their day-to-day lives. That is, until the city was torn down in the '90s. As I researched further, I felt that the Kowloon Walled City was a place unlike anywhere else in the world during any historical period. I wanted to work with this unique atmosphere to create a similar world, where a failed institution causes chaotic conditions (my San-Er is much, much larger, but still just as dense), then investigate the effect of a place like this on its individual inhabitants.

Anton and Calla's relationship can be called many things: love, obsession, weakness, or even danger. What was it like, forging and navigating such a tumultuous relationship on the page? Were there specific tropes that you were drawn to or wanted subvert?

Though I pitch *Immortal Longings* as inspired by Shakespeare's *Antony and Cleopatra* (the play), what I really mean is that it was inspired by Shakespeare's Antony and Cleopatra (the characters). I was much nearer and dearer to the Shakespearean source material when I wrote *These Violent Delights*, a *Romeo and Juliet* retelling, but with *Immortal Longings*, I mostly wanted the codependent, obsessive relationship between Calla and Anton to be the beating heart behind the story. Putting their relationship on page was the most fun part of writing this book. I remember reading *Antony and Cleopatra* in my sophomore year of college for a Shakespeare class and being utterly delighted by how quickly these characters switched from declaring their undying love to each other in one act to seething with anger in the next, assuming they had been betrayed. The drama! The angst! The spectacle! When the two are figureheads of opposing sides in a fierce war for power, it makes sense that each move they make toward the other person is felt tenfold, and that the consequences of this are so much vaster than an ordinary character's. In my adaptation, Anton and Calla are competitors in a game that only one can win—and how can you trust someone under those circumstances, no matter how much you want to?

Immortal Longings has the air of a classic "enemies to hesitant allies to lovers" trope, which usually shows up for characters in an opposing-sides dynamic, but since I had already done that with *These Violent Delights*, I wanted to take this dynamic even further (i.e. nastier) when writing for adults. In the spirit of Shakespeare's volatile Antony and Cleopatra, why settle for just enemies to lovers when you can have enemies to lovers to enemies to lovers to enemies to . . .

The ability to take over someone else's body using qi provides ample opportunity for deception and cunning power plays. Pampi's experiments hint at an expansion of this ability—without too many big reveals, can you tell us how qi might evolve and be used the next two books of the trilogy?
There will absolutely be an expansion of this power, and it's one of the aspects I'm looking forward to most as the trilogy continues. My favorite thing about reading a series is the ballooning-outward effect that kicks in after the first book, whether it's with magic systems or worldbuilding. I want *Immortal Longings* to introduce the reader to Calla's single-minded mission in the dense, hectic world of San-Er while everything else exists in the periphery, and when she loses the tunnel vision for her mission, suddenly the world starts to grow, too. The next two books are going to explore *what* exactly body-jumping is, and how people might have used it in the years before San-Er put up its wall to separate the capital from the provinces. In chapter eleven, Yilas says jumping isn't magic, it's just qi—whether that's true or not remains to be seen, because what is magic, after all? As the series goes on, certain characters are going to start learning to use their qi in ways they might only be able to call magic, and the repercussions will be high.

The choice between one's own desires and duty to one's country and people haunts Calla as she realizes her feelings for Anton. She also must make the heavy sacrifices she deems necessary (e.g., other players, those whose bodies they occupy) to fix a broken system. How does this affect her as a character? Does she see herself as a monster, or perhaps a necessary tool for justice?

There's a quote in Shakespeare's *Antony and Cleopatra* that fascinates me. Cleopatra says, "The quick comedians/ Extemporally will stage us, and present/ Our Alexandrian revels; Antony/ Shall be brought drunken forth, and I shall see/ Some squeaking Cleopatra boy my greatness/ I' th' posture of a whore" (5.2). During Shakespeare's time, Cleopatra was indeed played by a boy because women weren't allowed to act, so she's describing what the audience member sees onstage—but not completely. I keep coming back to this quote because it creates so many layers in an instant: Cleopatra is spiteful of the actor who will portray her as a laughable whore, and yet the actors who were in this production probably did a very serious job of depicting its dramatic elements. She's a squeaking boy; she's not a squeaking boy. Before I go full English major—because I could probably fill ten more pages with analysis—I think this line captures what makes Cleopatra one of Shakespeare's most complex characters in a very meta way. She knows how Roman history will portray her, and she somehow exists in this space between playing to their portrayal and defying that caricature. I was certainly influenced by this nebulous space when creating Calla Tuoleimi. I wanted the complexity of someone incredibly self-aware, yet being tugged toward becoming exactly who you would expect a royal to be. On one hand, there's her duty to tear down the monarchy. On the other, there's Anton, selfishness, and power. Calla is only mortal at the end of the day—how much temptation can one bear before they can no longer resist the allure? While she sees herself as a righteous tool in *Immortal Longings*, I really love the ending of this book, because it sets *everything* up to be questioned, and I get the chance to build more layers to Calla's character throughout the series.

For Laura Crockett,
If book publishing were an arena battle,
you would be my most trusted ally.